DEFIANT HEART

"You do strange things to me, Mariah Marie Morgan." Jamie tipped her chin up with his fingers. "I've wished you out of my life almost since the first moment you entered it. At times you exasperate me to the point where I'd like to turn you over my knee. You're stubborn and opinionated, beautiful and courageous."

With every word he could feel the carefully built barrier deep inside him cracking, weakening. If he walked away now, he'd be safe. *Do it,* he ordered himself. *Do it before her lips whisper your name again.*

"Jamie . . ."

His arms pulled her hard against him. He kissed her suddenly, roughly, and felt her tremble. "Don't be afraid Mariah," he whispered against her soft mouth. "Listen to your heart. Hear what it's saying to you. I want you. What is your answer?"

"Kiss me, Jamie, and you shall have your answer . . ."

Other Books in
THE AVON ROMANCE Series

Coming Soon

DEFIANT HEART

NANCY MOULTON

AVON BOOKS ◆ NEW YORK

AVON BOOKS
A division of
The Hearst Corporation
105 Madison Avenue
New York, New York 10016

Copyright © 1989 by Nancy Moulton
Published by arrangement with the author
Library of Congress Catalog Card Number: 88-92947
ISBN: 0-380-75730-3

First Avon Books Printing: June 1989

AVON TRADEMARK REG. U.S. PAT. OFF. AND IN OTHER COUNTRIES, MARCA REGISTRADA, HECHO EN U.S.A.

Printed in the U.S.A.

K-R 10 9 8 7 6 5 4 3 2 1

To Barbara Brooks, my cherished friend,
for so many reasons
and
To all my wonderful friends

If true friends could be measured by gold, I'd have wealth uncountable. All of you know who you are, but I wanted to set down your names within these pages just the same. You're the greatest!

Chapter 1

"Samuel!" Mariah Morgan cried, forgetting to use her employer's proper title in her haste to reach him. He lay slumped over the oak desk in the middle of the stifling hot, cramped room. Her heart pounded hard as she grasped his shoulder. When he stirred, relief flooded over her.

"Don't fret, Mariah," he mumbled tiredly, sitting back in the chair and running a hand through his graying, sandy-blond hair. "I was only resting my eyes a few minutes. I've been going over this list of names to find someone from whom I haven't yet solicited funds to pay our exorbitant expenses. But I fear we've exhausted all of our sources. The rumors of yet another war with the French have made people very tight-fisted. I have a terrible foreboding that we're going to lose the hospital."

Defeat showed in the droop of his shoulders and his bloodshot brown eyes. Dr. Samuel Hastings was an unprepossessing man, of average height and weight, but Mariah thought of him as a giant, with a pure, unselfish heart. She longed to reach out to

1

soothe his burdened shoulders and free them of their crushing weight. But she hung back, restrained by a sense of propriety and a timidity unusual for her.

"Oh, Dr. Hastings, don't give up. We can't be finished yet. There must be someone left who will support us. We must have faith that we'll find a solution. You're working much too hard. If you continue at this exhausting pace, you'll become ill yourself and be of no help to our patients. Let me relieve you of some of the work."

He rose from his chair and flashed the indulgent smile she knew so well.

"Dear Mariah. What would I do without you? Your hard work and constant encouragement mean a great deal to me. But you already have duties enough."

"But you've taught me well these five years since I started as the hospital laundress. You've said yourself I'm capable of more responsibility than midwifery and the other duties you give me. Please let me help with the patients tonight so you can retire early."

"No, I've told you before, the patients expect me to make the last rounds of the day. They want to see the physician. And I have several reports to fill out after that."

"Your pardon, Doctor," a younger man called from the doorway. He was tall and thin to the point of gauntness, with scraggly brown hair and pale, unhealthy-looking skin.

"Ah, Geoffery, I was just about to come and find you to do rounds with me. Mariah, see to the leeches and putting away the medicines."

Samuel Hastings led the way out of the cluttered, back-room office. Mariah gritted her teeth and forced her expression to remain inscrutable as Geoffery Henderson cast her a smile which could only be read as gloating triumph before following in the older man's wake.

"You pompous baboon!" she grumbled vehemently under her breath. He always got to do rounds. Where was the fairness in that? He was a conceited fool with very limited medical abilities and a condescending attitude toward the patients. She was far more compassionate, and quicker in diagnosing diseases and grasping medical techniques. Geoffery knew this and resented her for it. He insulted and belittled her, seeking to put her in a bad light with Dr. Hastings at every opportunity. But in the end, what frustrated Mariah most about the whole situation was the fact that she'd probably never be named Samuel Hastings' apprentice, simply because she was a woman.

Mariah had known she wanted to be a doctor ever since she was a little girl. As she'd grown she'd discovered that society placed limitations on the opportunities a female could pursue. She'd been told again and again that medicine was a profession for men only, but Mariah Morgan had refused to listen. She knew some American women stalwartly challenged tradition to become respected medical practitioners, and she determined to grasp every chance she could with all her might. Then she'd met Samuel Hastings. She admired him more than anyone she'd ever known. He was a fine doctor, with extraordinary healing skills, a man who devoted himself to all who came to him for aid, re-

gardless of their station in life. Over the years,
when his destitute finances had prevented him from
hiring more doctors to staff the charity hospital he'd
founded, he'd been forced to let Mariah help. She'd
been an eager student, and an able assistant.

So many times, though, she'd tried to persuade
Dr. Hastings to let her do more. She was determined to increase her knowledge of doctoring
practices and try to gain a place in the medical
field. She wouldn't give up. She'd achieve her goal
by perseverance. And she wouldn't let the likes of
Geoffery Henderson stand in her way.

Now she stood over a tray of supplies on a table
in the corner, carefully returning medicine bottles
to a small wooden cabinet hanging on the whitewashed wall.

She revered Samuel Hastings as a teacher, and
though she was twenty-five and he twenty years her
senior, her feelings for him had gone even beyond
friendship and mutual professional interests. But
she hesitated to examine those disturbing emotions
too deeply, for fear they might somehow jeopard-
ize her close relationship with him.

Next, she attended to the unpleasant but necessary task of making sure the hospital's supply of
leeches was well maintained. Venesection, or
bloodletting, was an important medical practice;
thus leeches had to be available whenever needed.

She carried a pottery pitcher half-filled with
water to the wooden shelf case lined with wide-
mouthed crocks of the slithery creatures. Removing each heavy lid in turn, she poured in a small
quantity of the fresh water, quickly replacing the
top before the worms could wriggle out. She held

an aversion to leeches, especially when she was required to help attach and detach them from patients' bodies during treatment. But what was necessary, must be done.

"Oh, Doc Hastings ain't here," a plump older woman noted from the doorway. "I was lookin' for him and you. There's a man in the examinin' room askin' after you, Mariah," Esta O'Flinn explained. "A troublemaker, I'd say, by the look of him, despite his fancy clothes. He's busted up some. Been in a tavern brawl, he says. Has a little feller with him, a dwarf I guess you'd call him. The doctor must be in the ward. I'll look for him there. He'll fix up the injured feller. Don't know why he asked for you."

Mariah frowned as Esta bustled away. Even the hospital cook, who'd known her these five years, still doubted her abilities. Well, she could attend to this man's injuries as competently as the doctor.

With an emphatic nod, she wiped the back of her hand over her damp brow and pushed up the fitted long sleeves of her homespun cotton dress. She grimaced with discomfort when she felt perspiration trickle down between her breasts.

Hurrying from the office, she threaded her way purposefully through the crowded open ward. The injured and sickly patients occupied all of the twenty available beds and much of the floor space as well. Not a breath of fresh air penetrated the six open windows she passed in crossing the high-ceilinged room. Only the noises of passersby and horse-drawn vehicles from the busy street outside filtered in. The hot July night air hung oppressively over the ward, as did the stench of sickness, form-aldehyde, and medicines.

Mariah approached the curtained cubicle at the end of the ward, then paused at the entryway, taking in the scene. Before her she saw the broad back of a man who was sitting on the narrow examining table. His glossy black hair was gathered up in a leather band and his loosened shirt revealed the strong, sun-tanned muscles of his shoulders and neck. Mariah found herself staring, though she didn't know why.

Only after she'd forcibly turned her eyes from the man did she notice another person in the room, an individual no taller than Mariah's waist, apparently a dwarf. He was probing at the other man's side.

"Damn!" growled the black-haired giant on the table. "That's the place, all right. But don't jab so hard, Dimetrius." As he spoke, he turned his head so that it appeared to Mariah in profile. His features were boldly chiseled and, she had to admit, incredibly handsome.

"You know," the tall one went on, "you weren't much help back there at the tavern."

"I figured it was your battle, Jamie. You're the one so all fired up over politics." The dwarf chuckled and pushed an animal-skin hat to the back of his head, then stroked his bushy beard. " 'Sides, I thought you could handle 'em. You took 'em two on b'fore without gettin' trounced."

"What seems to be the problem?" Mariah interrupted at last as she walked around in front of them. "Broken ribs?"

The injured man was clutching his left arm

against his side. His white, ruffled shirtfront was unbuttoned, revealing a V-shaped expanse of muscular chest lightly covered with black hair. Mariah met his gaze and suddenly froze, startled by the intense ice-blue of his eyes.

"No, I've had broken ribs before. I think they're just bruised," he answered.

His compelling eyes swept boldly over her, pausing at the curves of her full breasts. One dark eyebrow cocked with interest. Apparently, he wasn't deterred by her austere demeanor.

For a moment, she felt overwhelmed by her patient's direct scrutiny and by the man himself. He was ruggedly handsome, his physique emanating power. His disheveled, straight black hair matched the condition of his clothing, attesting to the brawl Esta O'Flinn had mentioned. Mariah found herself wondering what his politics were that had brought about such damage to his person.

"I'll judge the extent of your injuries," she informed him briskly. "Remove your coat and shirt, please."

"*You're* doing the doctoring? A woman? I'm not birthing a babe. I don't need a midwife."

Mariah bristled at his reaction. "Delivering an infant would challenge my skills far more than merely wrapping ribs cracked in a tavern altercation! Now, remove your coat and shirt."

Impatiently waiting for him to comply, she reached for a bound book of lined paper and a quill pen lying on the small pine desk next to her. Glancing up, she saw the two men exchange looks. The dwarf grinned widely as he leaned against the only solid wall of the examining room. The tall man appeared to be near thirty. His age was easier to discern than that of his smaller companion.

"What is your name, sir?" she asked curtly, readying the pen to enter his answer in the admissions log book.

"Lancaster, James Lancaster. Jamie to my friends. And this is Dimetrius Cobb." He gestured toward the dwarf, then carefully proceeded to remove his crimson velvet coat, cream-colored waistcoat, and white silk shirt.

Mariah left the log volume open on the desk to allow the ink to dry, then obtained two rolls of wide cotton bandaging from a side drawer, all the while trying not to notice the rippling cords of muscle bulging in her patient's arms and chest. She began prodding his rib cage.

"You're not poking a tree, woman!" he snapped, one dark brow lowering when she found the tender spot. "I've no wish to leave here more damaged than when I arrived!"

"I don't believe your ribs are broken," she informed him, ignoring his complaint. "Here, hold this." She thrust the end of the bandage into his hand and began to wrap the three-inch-wide strip of cloth around his midsection. She saw him grit his teeth as she pulled the strips tight.

"If you don't care for the cure, Mr. Lancaster, then I emphatically suggest you avoid brawling in taverns." However, inwardly she felt much less confident than she sounded. She'd often helped Dr. Hastings treat male patients in various states of undress, but in the past, they'd always been unconscious and thus unaware that a woman was tending them. Dr. Hastings set those rules, and she gladly adhered to them. While she'd defied her traditional female role to pursue medicine, she was often torn by the pull of her strict upbringing, with its dictates of modesty and propriety between men and women.

She knew Dr. Hastings wouldn't approve of her treatment of James Lancaster now, because this patient was very much alert, his body vibrant with strength. If he hadn't insulted her abilities, she probably would have followed procedure and left him to Dr. Hastings or Geoffery Henderson. But she had a point to prove to him here—that she knew what she was doing. And while she was proving it, she'd try to ignore how handsome he was and how his wide shoulders tapered down to a tight, narrow waist.

Her eyes inadvertently followed the line of thin dark hair covering his belly to where it disappeared in the top of his snug crimson breeches. She blinked in surprise and felt flushed. Taking the end of the bandaging from him, her hand brushed his. A bolt of energy suddenly surged through her fingers. She wished he *were* unconscious and not watching her so intently. His steady, steel-blue gaze unnerved her, jumbled her thoughts. She paused, confused.

"By all means, don't stop inflicting your torture, Madam Physician. You seem intent on leaving me no means of breathing at all."

"Tight wrapping is necessary," she snapped back, angered by her momentary lapse and his sarcastic tone. She gave the cloth strip another vigorous tug.

Frowning fiercely, he roughly grabbed her wrist, yanking it away from his rib cage.

For several tense seconds his icy stare locked with hers. Neither of them spoke a word, yet a battle took place in the space of those brief, lightning-charged moments.

The fingers of Mariah's captured hand clenched into a fist. His grip hurt her, but she refused to flinch.

"Unhand me, sir!" Her arched brows dipped together into a deep frown, equal in wrath to his.

Then a slow smile curled at one corner of his mouth. His grip lessened a fraction, allowing her to yank her arm free.

"What's going on here, Mariah?" Geoffery Henderson demanded, suddenly appearing around the end of the cubicle. His glance swept to the examining table, and he immediately glared scornfully at the scene. "How dare you take it upon yourself to treat this patient!"

"I'm quite capable of attending to bruised ribs and you know it, Geoffery." She frowned, shifting her anger from Lancaster to her nemesis.

"Well, we'll just see what Dr. Hastings has to say about this!" With that he whisked the curtain aside and strode from the cubicle.

"*You're* Mariah Morgan?" Lancaster asked, showing surprise as she finished tying the bandage around his torso. Next she touched his swelling right cheek, causing him to wince slightly.

She suddenly recalled that Esta had said this man had asked for her specifically. "Why do you wish to know?" she demanded, instantly on the defensive.

He didn't answer her immediately, only scrutinized her brazenly. "I'd say she's Dunny's daughter all right, wouldn't you, Dimetrius? Aqua eyes like the Caribbean Sea," he noted. "And without a doubt, she has her father's acerbic tongue."

"Aye, that she does," the small man chimed in, grinning.

"And I'd wager she could be a pretty wench if she'd free her flame-tinged hair from that bun and wear a decently fitting dress instead of that drab, baggy excuse for a garment."

Mariah frowned and her mouth dropped open at his bold assessment, and then she recovered to lash back. "Keep your insulting observations to yourself, sir! They're of no interest to me. What do you know about my father? Explain yourself."

He appeared amused by her reaction. "I'm a friend of Dunny's. We were shipmates for several years and had many an adventure together. He sent me to find you. I regret that I must be the bearer of distressing news. He has several serious ailments which have weakened him to a state of almost complete disability. He's back in Framingham now, in the house where you grew up. His physician has given him little time to live. He wishes to see you."

Mariah reached out to grasp the examining table. She felt the blood drain from her face. Old hurt and anger over her father's past neglect rushed up from a place deep inside her.

"After all this time he summons me, when we haven't seen or communicated with each other in over nine years. How did he even know where to find me?"

"Dunny knew you still lived in Boston with your aunt and uncle. Your Aunt Josephine told me that you were here at the hospital. Unfortunately, on the way, I was drawn into a disagreement at the Royal Crown Pub," he said, smiling wryly. "But my bruised ribs won't hinder me from accompanying you on the day's journey to your father's house in Framingham."

"You assume much in thinking I might wish to rush to his bedside. We had a difficult parting many years ago."

"Perhaps I didn't stress enough that this may be your father's *deathbed.*" The seriousness in Lancaster's tone intensified. "That fact alone should bring you to him. But perhaps this will persuade you as well." He reached for his coat beside him on the table and foraged inside the breast pocket, withdrawing a parchment envelope and a brown leather pouch. "Dunny sent these."

She sensed his disapproval, but chose to ignore it. He might think her cold and selfish, but he knew nothing of the years of terrible rejection and loneliness her father's desertion had caused her. Long ago, she'd closed her heart to him to lessen the pain.

"Open the letter first."

His authoritative tone drew her back from the painful memories. She wanted to resist his order, but her curiosity about her father's correspondence caused her to comply. Slowly, she reached for the letter and broke the wax seal, drawing out a single sheet of matching parchment stationery. The missive was written in what appeared to be a shaky hand, but she recognized her father's writing and his blunt, succinct style.

Daughter,

This is to apprise you of the fact that I'm dying. I know this information will be welcome news to you. However, before you are overcome with joy, I demand that you accompany my friend, James Lancaster, to your former home in Framingham to see me. Your future depends on this action. Don't delay!

The letter was signed simply, "Dunsley Morgan." No endearments, and certainly no love, showed in the penned words.

Mariah bristled at his command. Seemingly, she had no choice but to obey him; she'd been taught all her life that she should respect her elders and comply with their wishes. But her father didn't deserve that respect, not after the death of Mariah's mother, when he'd shirked his parental responsibilities and happily run off to sea, abandoning her to her strict Puritanical aunt and uncle.

Forcing herself to let no emotion show on her face, she carefully refolded the parchment and slipped it back into the envelope. But before she could give it back to James Lancaster with a terse refusal, he thrust the leather pouch at her.

"Now open this!"

He wasn't giving her a choice either, and that fact made her clench her teeth and glare. She almost refused, except her curiosity edged around her anger again. It couldn't hurt to see what was inside the small bag. Then, if she wanted, she could toss it and the letter in Lancaster's face!

Frowning, she loosened the cord drawstring and tilted the pouch so the contents—three exquisite gold coins—spilled into her hand.

"Those are uncirculated Spanish doubloons," Lancaster informed her. "Your father says there are many more of them connected with your inheritance."

"Inheritance?" Mariah's thoughts whirled. Spanish gold? How could her father have such coins? For years, her Aunt Josephine had recounted to her tales of her father's shiftless ways and his life of irresponsible adventuring, during which he'd squandered away the Morgan fortune. Her aunt had married a Puritan, and devoutly espoused that faith. Mariah knew that her father's sister, who had raised her since the age of ten, never told falsehoods.

"How did my father obtain these coins?" she demanded.

"That's something you must ask Dunny. I'm only his messenger and your escort to Framingham."

Mariah felt confused. She didn't like being ordered about, and she didn't want to go to her old home to see her father. Yet this possible inheritance captured her interest. Gold could help save the hospital, and enable her to continue assisting Dr. Hastings. Had James Lancaster brought her the solution to those difficult dilemmas?

She lowered her eyes to focus on the coins. Could she bear to see her father again, just on the outlandish chance of gaining an inheritance? Pain jerked her heart in two directions—on the one side, she remembered her father's desertion and neglect, but on the other, she felt a sudden little-girl yearning to see him, perhaps for the last time. Uneasy about the latter thought, she pushed it to the back of her mind and, instead, made herself concentrate on the opportunities the doubloons offered.

"Very well, Mr. Lancaster, if Dr. Hastings can manage without me here at the hospital, I'll accompany you to see my father."

She slipped the coins back into the pouch and placed it and the letter in the side pocket of her dress. When Lancaster remained silent, she looked up to see him gazing steadily at her. A jolting force seemed to emanate from his penetrating stare as it locked with hers.

His speech and clothing seemed to be those of an educated gentleman, yet he was an admitted adventurer and tavern fighter—to Mariah's mind, too much like his friend, Dunny Morgan. Her attitude toward him chilled even more with that comparison, and she tried to overlook the fact that even bruised and cut, his handsomeness stood out boldly.

"I'll see to this patient, Mariah." Samuel Hastings' tone sounded stern and he frowned as he entered the small enclosure, followed by a smirking Geoffery Henderson.

"Yes, Doctor, but this involved a simple procedure, one which even Geoffery might have been able to accomplish. I had no difficulty administering the bandaging." She turned a challenging look toward Lancaster. "Wouldn't you agree I did an adequate job, sir?"

For a long moment his steady look clashed with hers, with no indication of his answer showing on his face. Then he lazily swung his light-blue eyes toward Samuel Hastings.

"I can attest the wrappings are most secure. She did a fair job."

Mariah frowned at his judgment. A fair job, indeed! But she bit her tongue to keep from saying anything more, knowing it was more prudent to drop the subject. She was already in enough trouble with her employer as it was. At least Lancaster had given her a measure of a compliment rather than another complaint.

"Well, I'm glad to hear that assessment, ah, Mr. Lancaster," Hastings replied, glancing in the log for his patient's name.

"Mr. Lancaster has brought a summons from my father, who is gravely ill," Mariah said. "If you can spare me, I would like to visit him." She decided not to mention anything about the possible inheritance yet, in case it proved to be a false hope.

"I'm sorry to hear that news." Hastings looked genuinely regretful. "Of course, family obligation must assume priority under such circumstances. But it will be difficult to manage here without you. When must you leave?"

Mariah was warmed by his comment, glad to know she was appreciated. She hated to leave Samuel, but the separation would be worthwhile if the gold could be obtained.

"Our departure time, Mr. Lancaster?" she asked, glancing at him. She felt a twinge in her stomach when their eyes made direct contact.

"Tomorrow morning, on the early public coach."

"Yes, that will be fine," Mariah concurred, nodding and looking away from him. "I'll meet you at the coach office."

As she left the crowded examining room, she began to question her impulsive decision. She sighed, then her thoughts flashed to James Lancaster. Even though she was away from him now, his overpoweringly virile presence and compelling blue eyes haunted her. Could she trust him to help her return to her father? Should she trust him in anything? She didn't even know the handsome stranger who was her father's messenger. But for that matter, she didn't know much about her father either.

Chapter 2

Shaking his head to discourage the huckster trying to sell him a squawking chicken, Jamie pulled
his gold watch from his tan leather vest pocket.
Thirty minutes until departure. He wondered when
Mariah Morgan would arrive.

Across the street in front of the transportation
office, two men readied the public coach harnesses
and began to hitch up three pairs of stout-haunched
horses. Shouts and laughter drew Jamie's attention
to nearby Faneuil Hall. Argumentative voices filled
the air as merchants, farmers' slaves, and customers haggled over the prices of goods, including piles
of fresh farm produce, rows of plucked turkeys and
chickens, and stacks of casks filled with butter and
cheeses. Housewives bustled about buying the food
needed for the day, hailing and gossiping with
friends as they tended to the task.

Thriving, prosperous Boston. Jamie knew it
well. He loved the city. To a seafaring man, it was
a mecca for ships and trade and people from every
walk of life. He loved the sights, the sounds, the
opportunities.

Above the skyline created by wood and brick

houses, shops, meeting halls, and churches, he glimpsed the open sky over the busy harbor. Countless soaring timber masts of colonial and foreign sailing ships lying at anchor etched dark silhouettes into the low-hanging pewter-gray clouds. Some five thousand vessels—merchantmen, whalers, sloops, schooners, ferries, and fishing ketches—cleared the port of Boston during a year's time. And he'd sailed on his share of them in the last decade. He'd be shipping out again, just as soon as he completed this business of daughter-delivering for Dunny.

The day would remain overcast, perhaps even plagued by more rain, he noted with a scowl. The highways they'd be traveling were bad enough—rutted and rock-strewn—without the added hazard of mud that rain would bring. And he didn't want anything to hamper their progress to Framingham.

Another time, he might have indulged himself in becoming closely acquainted with the lovely and saucy Mariah Morgan. But this woman was different. She was dedicated to doctoring. For a woman to pursue such a vocation was extraordinary in the colonies, but it wasn't unheard of either. Dunny had told him she wasn't married. She should be keeping a home, husband, and children, occupying her conventional place. He himself balked at society's rules, but a woman had no business doing the same. Surely she'd had a wide choice of potential husbands. Her beauty would have guaranteed the attention of many suitors.

He considered himself an excellent judge of women; after all, he'd had years of experience with them. He'd immediately noted Mariah's delicately arched brows, elegantly contoured cheeks, full lips, small chin, and voluptuous figure. Not even her austere hairstyle and drab clothing could conceal her loveliness. And those tropical sea-blue eyes of hers—how they flashed with intelligence and quick wit, revealing a fiery spirit within! Some men might be put off by a female who could match them in wits, words, and knowledge. Perhaps Mariah Morgan's prospective suitors had all been of that unadventurous type. Therefore, she'd chosen spinsterhood rather than wedlock, he surmised. He found her challenging, though.

At the hospital, she hadn't shown any intimidation or coyness when treating him. And while she seemed to respect the older doctor and acquiesce to his wishes, she'd certainly held her ground against his whining assistant.

He found himself admiring her spark and wanting to learn more about her. But there was the old business of Toby Jones and Lem Hollister to rectify.

A month ago, Jamie had returned from a trip up north, where he'd been trapping for the two of them. He'd known Hollister and Jones for years, never liked them much, but had managed to do business with them when he wasn't at sea. This time, though, they'd betrayed him, stealing his pelts and leaving him to die in the wilderness.

But Jamie Lancaster had as many lives as a cat, and on this occasion had dragged himself into Framingham, where he'd recuperated in the home of Dunny Morgan, his old seafaring friend. After he was back on his feet, he'd intended to head straight for Boston to find Dimetrius and track down his enemies. But then Dunny had called him on a long-standing debt, sending him on this errand to Samuel Hastings' charity hospital.

Jamie was anxious to hand Mariah over to Dunny as soon as possible, so he and Dimetrius could settle the score with Jones and Hollister. Then he'd ship off to sea again. He wasn't one to be tied to the land, to anyone or anything for very long. There remained so many places to see, so much of the world yet to experience.

"Looks like the coach'll be leavin' on time fer once," a voice observed behind him.

"Good morning, Dimetrius," Jamie greeted the small man who'd been his closest friend since his earliest days at sea.

"You reckon the Morgan woman'll be on time?"

"I've yet to meet a woman who could prepare herself enough in advance to meet a departure. I'll be surprised if Miss Morgan breaks that pattern. Perhaps a few coins might persuade the driver to delay leaving a bit if she's late. Do you have any money?"

"Sorry, Jamie. You know I'd give you anythin' I had, but my purse's just plain flat. You?"

"Slim of funds as well, only two shillings. I'll just have to hope she's punctual. What did you find out about Lem and Toby?"

"Rumor has it they sold off the pelts and headed Framingham-way, jus' like you suspected."

Jamie smiled. "Good. Then there's a chance yet to catch up with them. And when I do, I'll take the worth of my skins out of their no-good hides!"

"That I'll sure like to be seein'," chuckled Dimetrius. "Lem an' me've had a run-in or two in our time."

"I hope I'm not late, Mr. Lancaster."

At the sound of a lyrical female voice behind him, Jamie turned around to see Mariah Morgan standing there.

"Not at all, Miss Morgan. In fact, I'm surprised that you're quite on time. You're prepared to travel?" With a sweeping glance, he took in her somber, high-necked gray dress and unbecoming, tightly drawn-back hairstyle.

Her blue-green eyes sparked like flint on steel when she noticed his disapproving appraisal.

"I believe that was the arrangement. Mr. Cobb." She nodded curtly in the smaller man's direction, then addressed her escort again. "I have only this one valise." She held up a faded luggage piece fashioned of tapestry-designed carpeting material.

"The coach is due to leave at seven-thirty," he explained. "We should arrive in Framingham late this afternoon."

"The jostling of the ride may distress your bruised ribs. It really isn't necessary for you to accompany me on this journey. I can accomplish it alone."

"Possibly you can. But your father's instructions specifically stated that I escort you, and so I shall."

She started to protest, but thought better of it. She read a definite finality in his tone. Arguing with him would likely be fruitless and might create an improper scene on this public street corner. She didn't want to be in the middle of such a commotion.

"Very well, sir, if you insist, then I, too, must comply with my father's wishes. Let's hope the journey passes quickly," she acquiesced, her manner aloof.

The coach driver called for boarding, and all six passengers settled inside for the long ride ahead. Mariah found herself wedged between Lancaster and a very rotund man named Mr. Bodeen, who made an annoying hissing sound through his nose every time he exhaled. The faded brown leather seat across from them was occupied by a grim-faced matron and a young woman with a boy of about five. Since Dimetrius Cobb purchased his ticket late and no more room remained inside the coach, he rode outside with the driver.

Once the coach's hard lurching settled into a steady side-to-side heaving, Mariah braced her feet to sway with the motion while she fidgeted around on the lumpy seat to find a smoother spot.

With an awkward stiffness, the passengers attempted to get acquainted. The older gray-haired woman, who introduced herself as the Widow Horton, behaved haughtily, as though she considered it beneath her dignity to travel in a public conveyance. She was well dressed in a corded blue traveling suit, complete with a hat decorated with a tall white ostrich plume that bent against the coach's low ceiling. A large, square-cut diamond sparkled from a gold chain around her neck.

Mariah noticed that the younger woman, Nora Fortrell, stole furtive glances in James Lancaster's direction from time to time, as she pretended to tuck her blonde curls neatly around the edges of her pink silk bonnet. Once, Mariah saw him smile with interest at her in return, and she felt annoyed at their flirtation. The attractive young woman must have noticed the way his tight buff breeches, tan shirt, and long brown leather vest fit his manly frame so precisely. She'd observed that fact, unwittingly, herself.

Mariah sighed. Despite herself, she couldn't help envying the other women's becoming apparel. She'd never owned anything so grand as the colorful ensembles they wore. Her aunt's view of clothing had always been completely utilitarian. Lace, pink silk, and feathers were strictly forbidden. She'd heard so all the while she was growing up, especially each time she'd gazed longingly into a store window. And Samuel Hastings' charity hospital was no place for such finery, even if she'd had the financial means to purchase it, which she didn't.

Mariah forced herself to shift her gaze out the rectangular opening which served as a window. She wished she were sitting on the other side with the women. She felt uncomfortable between the two men. The coach's lurching over the rough road rendered it impossible for her not to bump into them. When she did, she couldn't help but notice the difference between their thighs. Mr. Bodeen's upper leg was soft and flabby, while Lancaster's felt steel-hard with muscle.

"Oh!" she cried, flushing with embarrassment when a particularly hard bump nearly bounced her onto her escort's lap. She was thrown against his arm and felt taut muscle bulging in his shirtsleeve, too. The contact with him had a strangely disturbing, quickening effect on the rate of her heartbeat.

"Easy now. I have damaged ribs, remember?" he cautioned with an amused smile as he steadied her and let his eyes slip over her. He half-wished the jostling might loosen the tightly secured bun at the back of her head so he could see her shiny hair cascade about her shoulders. The rich russet hue of it would shimmer like flame if sunlight touched it, he was certain. He could envision her laughing and tossing her head, making the waves of hair swish about her face. And how would the tresses feel slipping through his fingers . . . like cornsilk or satin?

"We should all write to the governor protesting the poor condition of these roadways," the Widow Horton exclaimed with a huff.

"There are a few advantages to ruts and rocks," Jamie noted, glancing sideways at Mariah.

"None that I can see, sir," Mariah observed, haughtily lifting her chin. Frowning, she realized he seemed to be enjoying her awkward contact with his powerful limbs. Well, she didn't like his closeness at all! His grip on her arms hadn't bruised her, but she'd felt the strength in his hands. The heat of them easily penetrated the fabric of her dress sleeves and, even now, seemed to linger on her flesh. Determined not to fall against him again, she planted her feet more solidly against the floor and took up the book she'd brought with her in her corduroy drawstring purse.

"*Human Anatomy,*" he read aloud over her shoulder. "A most informative text. I recommend the chapter on spleens and livers. You'll find it particularly absorbing, I'm certain. Those organs are definitely topics to titillate the imagination."

Mariah tried to frown at him again, but his mock-serious expression tested her control.

"You've studied medicine, Mr. Lancaster?" she asked coolly, looking back at her book to try to avoid contact with his direct pale-blue eyes.

"I'm curious about many things, Miss Morgan, including medicine, though I must admit my learning has been limited to what I've discovered while patching up my shipmates."

"I see. I take it, then, that you believe the school of experience provides the best lessons in life."

"I regard it as the only school of any worth."

"Requiring neither discipline nor concentrated study," Mariah noted tartly.

"But providing enough knowledge to enable me to dig out a musket ball whenever necessary. I'd wager my skill at that operation against yours any day, Miss Morgan."

"The very idea of a woman becoming a physician is most unusual!" the Widow Horton announced, glaring at Mariah. "I certainly would never allow a woman to tend to my ailments. Why, it's entirely inappropriate."

"I quite agree," Jamie spoke up. "However, there are those women who have no regard for propriety, who do not seem chagrined when viewing a patient of the opposite gender in any manner of nakedness." He cocked a dark eyebrow and looked pointedly at Mariah.

"Are you actually suggesting that I enjoyed seeing you naked?" she retorted indignantly, frowning at him. Then her hand flew to her mouth when she heard the Widow Horton gasp, and she realized what she'd said. "I—I mean, you weren't unclothed—not completely. That is, only your chest and back were bare so I could wrap your bruised ribs. I couldn't do that while you wore your shirt. Every other part of you was covered!''

Her face was scarlet, she knew. She could feel the telltale heat of embarrassment moving down her neck. Her eyes darted around the inside of the coach, seeing Mr. Bodeen and Jamie's obvious amusement and the Widow Horton's stern disapproval.

''Disgraceful!'' the older woman declared.

Mrs. Fortrell grabbed her son and pulled him as far away from Mariah as possible, as if trying to protect him.

Mariah sank back into the cushioned seat, wishing the floor would fall out of the coach and deposit her in a gaping hole in the road. Seething with anger and mortification, she thrust her book up in front of her face.

''Well, if the discussion is ended,'' Jamie commented matter-of-factly, ''I'm going to try to shorten this tiresome trip by taking a nap.'' He crossed his arms over his chest and closed his eyes, leaning away from her against the side of the coach.

Mariah was left to try to recover her composure. She'd *never* forgive James Lancaster for purposely baiting her for his sport. Damn him!

The highway dust had been doused by rain the day before, so the leather window coverings could be kept rolled up for air circulation. Mariah glanced past Lancaster to watch the countryside slide past. She'd been a child of only ten the last time she'd traveled this route between Boston and Framingham, when her father had deposited her with her aunt and uncle. She didn't remember the sights which met her eyes now. She hadn't traveled anywhere except within the city of Boston since then. At times, she longed to see more of the world, but her work at the hospital and a lack of financial means prevented any such activity. So now she contented herself with watching the forests, dense with wildlife and lush, green-leafed trees, pass by.

Her gaze slipped to her handsome seatmate, who was still asleep. He didn't appear to be too bothered by the bucking coach. She must have done a good job of wrapping his ribs; she congratulated herself.

She noticed the dark bruise on his left cheek, and felt the strange twinge strike at the pit of her stomach again as she studied the sharply cut contours of his tanned face. Even relaxed in sleep, his straight nose and square jaw presented a strong, uncompromising profile. She had to force herself to look away from him and concentrate on her book.

Mr. Bodeen, the heavyset man next to her, tried to strike up a conversation several times, but she gave him only short answers to his questions. She didn't wish to talk to him or anyone else, for the closer the coach traveled to Framingham, the more uneasy she became about seeing her father again.

Fifteen years had passed since he'd left her with his sister-in-law. Then he'd disappeared from her life almost completely, barging into it on only four occasions for short visits. After those brief stays, he'd gallivanted off again on some new adventure. Nine years ago, they'd had a bitter quarrel, and Mariah, then aged sixteen, had ordered her father out of her life completely, saying she wanted none of his halfhearted fatherly attention. They hadn't seen or spoken to each other since, although he still sent some money to her through her aunt at regular intervals.

"When will we get to Grandpa's?" Nora Fortrell's little boy suddenly asked, throwing down a small wooden horse he'd been playing with. He squirmed in his seat, kicking the Widow Horton with his leg.

"Be careful, dear," his mother cautioned wearily. "Please play with your toys. We have quite a distance to travel yet." But the little boy only continued to whine and fuss.

"Have you seen what's behind your mother's ear, boy?"

Mariah jumped at hearing Lancaster's strange statement, for she didn't know he'd awakened. Glancing in his direction, she saw him stretch his muscular right arm.

"What do you mean, sir?" the child asked, his brown eyes bright with interest.

"Don't you see that shiny coin?" Jamie continued. "Look closer. It's meant to be yours."

The boy leaned toward his mother, anxious to discover the money.

"Where, sir? Show me."

"Why, it's right here, lad." He reached across the narrow aisle to the young woman's left ear and produced a sixpence coin in his fingertips. The child's eyes widened in wonder as Jamie handed it to him.

"Is there more, sir? Some behind her other ear?" The boy turned back to his smiling mother.

"I think there may be. Let's have a look, shall we?" He conjured up a like coin from the mother's right ear. "But before I give it to you, let's see what it can do."

He proceeded to maneuver the coin over and under his fingers, making it disappear and reappear as if by magic. The boy watched the sleight of hand and then listened to Lancaster's adventure stories for the next hour.

Mariah noticed the other passengers were enjoying the entertainment as well. Simple jester's tricks, she thought. Expertly performed by Lancaster, to be sure, but illusions nonetheless. He was no doubt nothing more than a clever charlatan who survived on his wits rather than by good, honest labor. He had a presence about him, she had to admit, an air of almost arrogant self-assurance; yet a touch of devil-may-care recklessness showed through, too. More than ever, she understood why he got along well with her father. The two men, though far apart in age, seemed cut of the same cloth.

Suddenly, the sounds of shots reached the inside of the coach. The driver cracked the whip, rousing the horses to a faster gallop, and the cumbersome vehicle plunged forward with a lurch.

"Highwaymen!" Jamie shouted, throwing a look out the window. "Everyone stay calm. We'll let the driver handle the situation. But I suggest, madam, that you find a safe place to hide this!"

He reached over to the Widow Horton and pulled the scooped neck of her dress out. Then he yanked the expensive necklace from around her throat and let it slip down into the cleavage of her ample breasts. The matron's mouth dropped open and her eyes widened with shock. Mariah was stunned, too. Under any other circumstances, Lancaster's actions would be outrageous. But now it seemed an expeditious thing to do.

Mariah tried to stay calm, but the coach was tossing from side to side so violently, she greatly feared it might overturn. Several more shots rang out, sounding much closer this time. They heard a cry from the driver, then watched in horror as he fell past the window off the coach.

"Damn!" Jamie cursed, jumping from his seat and kicking open the door beside him. While he climbed outside and up to the top, the coach swerved wildly as the uncontrolled horses panicked and sped on in fright.

"Put your weight into the brake!" he yelled to Dimetrius, who gratefully tossed him the leather reins. Jamie yanked on the straps with all his might to direct the galloping horses around a tight curve. The coach leaned precariously to one side, negotiating the turn on only two wheels.

A flat, open section of road loomed into view. He gave the horses their heads, shouting and slackening his hold on the reins. But the winded team couldn't outrun the highwaymen. One of the attackers urged his mount alongside the lead coach horse, and with expert agility leaned down and grabbed the mare's bridle, pulling it back until the animal began to slow its pace. The other horses followed. Jamie had no choice but to pull the team to a complete stop.

"All right, *out*, all of you!" commanded one of the six thieves who quickly surrounded the coach with pistols drawn.

Slowly, the passengers emerged, shaken by their frightening ride and the danger in which they found themselves. The stockily built leader who'd spoken waved his pistol toward Jamie and Dimetrius, gesturing for them to climb down from the driver's box.

"Well now, looky what we got here, boys." The leader dismounted and strode to the half-circle of passengers. The little boy cried hysterically and clung to his mother's skirt.

"Shut that whelp up!" The pock-scarred robber struck the child with the back of his hand and leveled his pistol at the mother.

"No!" Mariah shouted, stepping in front of Nora and the boy without thinking. The outlaw roughly pushed her aside.

"Git outta the way. I'll be gittin' to you in a minute!"

Jamie caught Mariah around the waist to keep her from falling. "Stay back," he ordered fiercely under his breath. His sharp frown of warning frightened her almost as much as the outlaws did. Was he in league with the robbers? He *did* stop the coach . . .

Mariah straightened and pulled away a little from him.

"Git them valuables," the leader ordered one of his men, who quickly dismounted and walked down the line of passengers, holding out his tricorn hat for their money and jewelry. Mariah noticed that the sober-faced Widow Horton clutched her hand to her throat, but the expensive diamond necklace was nowhere in sight.

Mr. Bodeen reluctantly produced a bulging leather wallet from the breast pocket of his coat.

"We hit it good on this'n, Bench," the man declared to his superior with a wide grin, showing blackened teeth. Then he turned to the Widow Horton and yanked on her hand. "Gimme that ring, you old crone."

"No, please spare this. It was the last gift my husband gave me before he died." She nearly wept as she tried to wrench her hand away to keep him from removing the sapphire ring.

"Who cares about that tripe?" Bench sneered as he stepped forward and thrust his cocked pistol into her side. "Give it to him—*now!*"

The woman's face turned ashen with fear. She trembled as she pulled off the ring and tearfully handed it to the thief.

Mariah was still standing next to her escort. Out of the corner of her eye, she saw him exchange glances and a slight nod with Dimetrius Cobb.

"There's no need to mishandle the ladies and the child, gentlemen," Jamie spoke up suddenly, drawing the thieves' attention. "We'll give you what you want."

"Is that so?" Bench asked sarcastically, swinging his pistol toward him. "Tellin' us how to run our business, are ye?"

Mariah saw that the burly outlaw was as tall as Lancaster, but outweighed him by at least fifty pounds.

"No, I'd never presume to do that. It's obvious you're quite experienced in bullying women and children. It's a lesson in manners I'd like to teach you."

Mariah couldn't believe how calmly Lancaster confronted the threatening thief. His tone was almost conversational! Was he insane? Did he wish to be shot?

"Why, you puff-chested rooster! I'll teach *you* a thing or two!"

Mariah watched in horror as Bench lunged at Lancaster. At that instant, Dimetrius Cobb threw himself across the big man's path. The leader fell over the dwarf like a lead weight. As he crashed to the ground, a glint of steel flashed in the sunlight, and before anyone knew what was happening, Lancaster was on one knee in the dirt beside Bench, holding a nasty-looking knife at the outlaw's throat.

"Now, my inept and exceedingly clumsy friend, unless you want your gullet sliced open, I suggest you order this gang of dullards to throw down their weapons and surrender!"

Bench stared dumbfounded. Tension crackled in the air like a fiercely gathering storm.

Mariah realized James Lancaster was gambling with all their lives, and she hated him for risking so much. They could all be killed, shot to death by the outlaws in the next instant. Yet she knew his gamble might just save all of their lives, too, for she had a feeling these cutthroats were not the types who would leave their victims alive to testify against them later.

"So you choose death over surrender?" Jamie demanded, pressing the sharp point of the blade deeper into the outlaw's throat until it drew blood.

"*No!* Don't kill me! Throw down yer weapons,

you fools, before he cuts my throat!'' Bench cast
a ferocious look at his men. That seemed to be all
they needed to make them comply. Pistols were
quickly uncocked and dropped to the ground. Cobb
gathered them up, tossing one to Jamie.

"Well done, as usual, Dimetrius.'' Jamie rose
to his feet, dragging Bench up with him. He jabbed
the pistol in the outlaw's ample belly while he addressed the rest of the gang. "Don't make any sudden moves, gentlemen. My friend here is going to
tie you securely to your horses so you won't wander off before we can get you to the proper authori-
ities in Framingham.'' He turned to the passengers.
"Is everyone all right?'' His glance swung to Mariah specifically.

The rest of the passengers murmured affirmative
answers, but she was too amazed by the exciting
turn of events to do anything but nod. She felt a
surprising twinge of pleasure that Lancaster had
taken the time to see to her well-being.

Like the other passengers, she watched the small
man as he moved from outlaw to outlaw, tying their
hands and feet to their saddles, then secured the
bodies of the dead driver and coachman. The
thieves themselves looked as stunned by what had
happened as the passengers did.

Her glance kept returning to their rescuer, who
calmly stood guard over Bench, and finally bound
him to a saddle, too. The knife he'd used before
was no longer in sight, making her wonder what
had happened to it. Where had it come from? The
poniard hadn't been visible while they were riding
in the coach.

With an eyebrow cocked in contemplation, she studied his handsome features, wondering about more than just a knife now. At the hospital, he'd said his friends called him Jamie. The more informal name seemed to fit him. Though he was still virtually a stranger to her, and an exasperating one at that, there was one thing she did know about Jamie Lancaster—he certainly wasn't like any other man she'd ever met!

Chapter 3

Jamie drove the coach into the bustling settlement of Framingham early in the evening, with the murderous outlaw band bound and in tow. Their arrival generated considerable commotion among the townspeople, who quickly gathered around to gawk at the captured men and the body of the driver.

"I was certain we were all going to be murdered!" the Widow Horton declared to the middle-aged constable. "Mr. Lancaster acted most heroically. He and Mr. Cobb saved us all. They should be highly commended for their bravery."

"Please, no thanks are needed," Jamie said. "We were glad to be of service in capturing that band of dangerous brigands. Murder and thievery must be put to an end so decent people needn't fear for their lives every time they leave their homes."

His valiant words were cheered by the many citizens standing at the open doorway of the constable's office. Mariah agreed with the people, but she was too occupied watching their rescuer to join in.

She usually avoided crowds, preferring to remain in the background, pursuing her goals with quiet determination. But she was drawn to be a part of this one now, and James Lancaster seemed perfectly at ease at the center of attention. He stood straight and proud, looking devilishly handsome as he delivered his short speech. Yet she heard conviction in his words, and sensed no idle boasting. She felt privileged to be acquainted—if only slightly—with the man who'd saved them from the gang of ruthless outlaws.

She experienced something else now, too, she realized as she let her gaze sweep over his straight black hair hanging rakishly down over his forehead, loosened from the queue in back during the frantic ride he'd undertaken with the coach and his tussle with the bandit leader. He'd rolled up his shirtsleeves to the elbows, revealing his muscular forearms. Studying him, she comprehended that she suddenly felt a surprising attraction to him. Her pulse rate quickened, her stomach fluttered, and her eyes seemed riveted on his handsome face.

"Mr. Lancaster and Mr. Cobb 'ere deserve a pint o' stout after what they done," a man shouted from the crowd. "Let's take 'em to the alehouse an' see they gits it." More cheers of agreement erupted.

"I can't join you, lads. I must finish here with the authorities and see to some other business," Jamie explained, glancing toward Mariah. "My thanks anyway, friends."

"Well, I could use a pint 'r two," Dimetrius Cobb piped up.

The townsmen seemed appeased as they gathered around the small man and led him away toward the tavern.

Soon the other passengers left, too. Only Mariah remained. She was feeling much more kindly disposed toward Jamie Lancaster now. Her heart had jumped when he'd looked at her just now. Perhaps he wasn't the ne'er-do-well she'd first judged him to be. She was about to offer her own thanks to him for his bravery when she heard his next words to the constable.

"By the way, good sir, Mr. Cobb and I were only too glad to risk our lives today to do our civic duty in capturing those dangerous criminals. And believe me, the safety of this community is reward enough. However, if you should find that there is a monetary remuneration due for the apprehending of that gang, we wouldn't be opposed to receiving it or even sharing it with a loyal civil servant such as yourself. Because of some business setbacks of late, we find ourselves a bit shy of funds at the moment."

"I understand, Lancaster," the constable replied, his expression telling of his interest. "I'll be glad to find out what I can an' let you know."

Yes, the constable understood Lancaster, and Mariah did, too. His selfishness caused her to regret her momentary softening toward him and bite back the words of gratitude she'd been about to express.

"Concerning a possible reward, gentlemen, I'm certain such compensation would be greatly appreciated by the family of the driver who sacrificed his life today. Don't you agree, Mr. Lancaster?" She cast her cool blue-green eyes on him with the sternness of a reprimanding schoolmistress.

"Miss Morgan is correct, of course," Jamie replied, meeting her challenge with an unwavering gaze. "By all means, see that any reward is dispersed to the families."

She didn't miss the chill in his voice. It made her think better of allowing a triumphant smile to spread over her lips as she turned to leave the office.

Mariah stared at the single-story, white clapboard house she hadn't visited in fifteen years, wondering if it was all that remained of the Morgan family estate. This house had once belonged to a distant cousin of her father's, passed on to her parent by bequest. The main family estate, called Windhaven, was located just outside of Boston. When Mariah was ten years old and being packed off to live with her aunt, she'd heard her father speak of his financial need to liquidate Windhaven. Likely, it had been sold off long ago.

The front porch of the small house before her now showed the old crisscrossed trellises on each end that she remembered. Morning-glory vines interlaced in intricate patterns on the framework, almost hiding the wood from view. The chipped and peeling paint on the house testified to the lack of maintenance over the years.

Mariah wasn't aware that her steps on the weed-strewn stone walkway had slowed the closer she came to the house. She gazed around the tiny front yard, noticing how much larger the two maple trees she'd climbed as a little girl had grown.

Her heart pounded rapidly in her chest. Again and again over the years, she'd rehearsed what she'd say to her father if they ever met again, the bitter, vicious words she'd practiced so often. But could she speak them when she actually came face to face with him?

And other sensations curled inside her now as she stood so close to the house she'd lived in happily as a child—all the bewilderment she'd felt when her dear mother had died, followed by the fear, the loneliness, the terrible homesickness she'd known when she'd suddenly found herself living with her strict aunt and uncle in Boston. Suddenly, she wanted to turn and run away, but a hand on her elbow stopped her.

"Are you all right, Miss Morgan? What is it? Are you ill?" He'd seen her lovely face grow pale, and sensed her reluctance to continue up the walk. He couldn't help wondering how difficult returning here might be for her. He was paying a debt to Dunny by bringing his daughter home, but did the daughter consider it a favor? Had she really swayed a little when he'd taken hold of her elbow? Or was that only the excuse he gave himself for touching her? Her arm was bare because of the short-sleeved dress she wore, so his hand made direct contact with her soft, warm flesh. Too well, he remembered the feel of her body against his when they'd been jostled together in the coach.

Slowly, she raised her large blue-green eyes to look at him, but it was a moment before she consciously registered who he was.

"What? No, I mean, yes, I'm all right, Mr. Lancaster. Forgive my momentary lapse. Please, let's proceed." She straightened her shoulders and walked briskly forward to the four steps leading up to the porch.

"Lord have mercy, you've come back, Jamie!" exclaimed the small, plump woman with gray hair who answered their knock at the front door. Her plain brown dress strained tightly over her stout figure as she wiped her hands on her white apron and reached up to give him a hug of welcome.

"That I have, Minnie." He squeezed her in return. "And as you can see, my trip was a success." He turned to the side a little so the older woman could have a clear view of Mariah.

"Saints be praised, is it really you, Miss Mariah?" Wilhelmina Hooper hesitated a moment as if she weren't quite sure what to do, then she seemed to throw caution to the wind as she reached out to gather Mariah to her in a hug. "Welcome home, child. I'm sure you remember your old nanny."

"Y-yes, of course," Mariah stammered, shaken at seeing Minnie again. She hadn't expected her to still be a part of her father's household. But soon the aging Minnie was explaining how she'd served as caretaker at the house, keeping it ready for those occasions when the erratic Dunsley Morgan arrived home. To Mariah, Minnie didn't seem much changed at all. Her gray hair was braided and twisted into a coil on top of her head, just as it always had been. And her rounded, plump figure still offered the comforting haven she'd often run to with her hurts as a child. The pain of recollection she felt from the older woman's warm welcome hurt deeply.

Minnie slipped her arm around Mariah's waist and drew her into the house. Jamie followed.

The inside of the house had a similar effect on her. Little looked changed. Even the dark-blue carpet of the front entryway was the same one she'd known as a child, except now it showed many faded and frayed places.

Mariah clenched her jaws together tighter and mustered all of her considerable willpower to control the jumble of emotions she felt. She must keep calm, not allow herself to be ruled by the pain being in this house resurrected. She'd come here for a purpose—to find out about the Spanish doubloons.

The sound of a slight commotion along with a murmur of voices filtered through the partly opened door of a room down the dimly lit hall.

"Your father has no doubt heard our arrival," Jamie noted. "Do you feel up to seeing him now? You must be fatigued after the long journey."

Mariah looked at the shadowy door, feeling apprehension steal over her again. Once, that room had belonged to her parents. Her own old bedchamber had been a little farther down the corridor. A kitchen, small front parlor, and a dining room made up the remaining sections of the small house, she knew.

She took a deep breath and cleared her throat. "In view of what you've told me about my father's failing health, perhaps I should see him now for a short time, if he's up to it."

"Mariah Marie . . ." Dunsley Morgan greeted his daughter for the first time in nearly a decade.

His brown eyes stared fixedly into her face as he raised himself up in the big canopy bed, then fell back against the pillows, his stark white nightshirt billowing around his gaunt frame. A fit of coughing overcame him.

"Don't exert yourself, Dunny," a balding man in his sixties cautioned, stepping closer to the bed. "This isn't one of your good days."

Mariah recognized Dr. Owen Osborn, their old family physician. Memories of him bent over the same bed with another patient rushed over her. Her mother had spent the last days of her life in this spacious, rose-colored room with its long mauve draperies, walnut desk, and Chippendale camelback sofa. She'd died here too, a memory that caused tears to burn in the corners of Mariah's eyes.

"Oh, stop fussing over me like a blustering old woman, Owen," Dunny complained. "I get enough of that nagging from Wilhelmina there." He sat upright again and directed his next remarks to Mariah.

"Well, come here, girl, so I can have a look at you. 'Tis a long time since we've been eye-to-eye. I see your mother's self-righteous sister has put her mark on you. That gray dress you're wearing is ugly, and so is your hair. It's bad for your brain, pulling your hair back so tightly. Inhibits the flow of blood so you can't think straight." He started to chuckle, but then a hacking cough rose from his throat. When it at last subsided, he went on. "No wonder you never married! Who'd have you, as homely as you dress? Your Aunt Josephine wrote me a time or two. She said you were too particular about husband prospects, too haughty for your own good, with ridiculous ideas about becoming a physician! Thought I'd see for myself before it's too late. That's why I had Jamie bring you here. Well, speak up, girl. You have a voice, don't you? You *are* my daughter, aren't you?''

Jamie studied Mariah, noting how her finely arched dark brows dipped to a slight vee at the bridge of her small nose, but she otherwise showed no outward sign that Dunny's cutting words had affected her.

''Yes, I'm your daughter, Father. Don't you recognize me?'' The sharp retort spilled out before she realized it.

''Do I detect a note of bitterness in your words?'' Dunny seemed amused by her taunt. Another coughing spell kept him from speaking for a few moments.

Mariah shot a look at Dr. Osborn, who only raised his bushy eyebrows to indicate his lack of influence with his patient.

''Perhaps you should rest,'' she suggested coolly, turning back toward the bed. ''We can talk later.''

''We'll talk *now! I* decide what happens around this house. I don't know if I'll be breathing later, so there's no time to waste. Let's get to the point. I sent for you, but why did you come, girl? Tell me the real reason.''

Startled, Mariah wasn't certain how to answer his blunt question. Everything about her father astonished her. Unlike Wilhelmina and Dr. Osborn, who looked very much as she remembered them, her father had changed greatly. Where was the robust man she'd known as a child—big and barrel-chested, hearty in his laughter. Then his bright red hair had always looked as if he'd just come in from a windstorm. But no longer. Only freckled scalp showed atop his head, where once there had been a wild red mane. What little hair remained on the sides was dull red in color, shadowed by gray.

Her father looked incredibly small and fragile now, as well. His hands, which had seemed so huge to her when, as a child, she'd slipped her much smaller one into his, were purple-veined and bony. Wrinkles and dark circles lined his brown eyes. His face was gaunt, his skin yellowish.

"Well, quit gawking at me, girl, and answer!" Dunny ranted. "No doubt you felt glad to learn I was close to a meeting with the Grim Reaper." He reached out and grabbed Mariah's arm when she started to protest. "No, don't deny it. I know you must be hating me for what I did to you, shipping you off to Josephine and seeing you for only those few short visits over the years. So don't be making any dutiful remarks that we both know are falsehoods."

"Very well, Father," Mariah agreed curtly, pulling her arm from his grasp and stepping away from the bed. "I'll tell you the truth. If you must know, I feel nothing for you—the same nothing you exhibited toward me all these years. I came because Mr. Lancaster informed me of the possibility of an inheritance. I want nothing from you for myself, but a man I admire very much is in dire need of financial assistance to continue his medical work with the poor. I'd give any legacy to him."

Jamie heard the softening of the sharp inflection in her voice when she spoke about the unnamed man. He was almost certain she was referring to Samuel Hastings, making him wonder about their relationship at the hospital.

"She's my daughter, all right," Dunny snapped, a thin smile curling his ashen lips as he exchanged a quick glance with Owen Osborn, then looked back at Mariah. "When you were a small lass, you'd stand up to me like this and speak your mind even if it meant a whipping. You'd set your chin and stiffen your shoulders just like you're doing now. I knew your heart then and I know it now. You wouldn't come to me out of a sense of duty as my daughter, even to watch me die. That's why I sent the doubloons. I wanted to make sure you'd come."

His words made her sound calculating, even mercenary, but she didn't care. When it came to her father, her heart felt like a dry creek bed—cracked and empty of its life force.

"There'll be an inheritance for you, girl. What you do with it will be your choice. And you'll be having it soon enough." He coughed raspily, as if to emphasize his morbid point. "Leave me now. I'm tired and feel like resting. I've decided to live a day longer. Tomorrow will be time enough to tell you of your inheritance and what you're going to have to do to acquire it. Now go, get out, all of you." Dunny waved a hand of dismissal at them, took a deep, jagged breath, and turned toward the wall.

Mariah was certain her father's illness must be affecting his mind. Without speaking another word to him, she left the bedchamber, followed by Dr. Osborn, Jamie, and Wilhelmina Hooper.

"From what malady does my father suffer, Doctor?" she asked after the door was closed behind them. She allowed no emotion to tell in her tone.

"I regret to say, he has a number of ailments, all of them severe, and most resulting from his neglectful way of life. His heart is weak, causing shortness of breath, and I fear his liver is rapidly deteriorating."

"Yes, I suspected a liver condition when I saw the yellowish tinge to his skin."

Dr. Osborn looked at Mariah with apparent surprise. "You are versed in medical practices?"

"I've had a good deal of experience assisting Dr. Samuel Hastings at the charity hospital he operates in Boston. Perhaps you've heard of him?"

The doctor frowned as he twisted an end of his thick moustache. "Indeed I have. His unorthodox methods are highly—questionable."

Working to keep her anger from showing, she asked, "What is your prognosis for my father, Doctor?"

"With a heart as weak as his, there is really no way of telling. He could be gone in a day, a week, or six months from now. Last year, he was seriously wounded in a sea battle. Then he became plagued by an acute case of dysentery. These difficulties caused great stress on his bodily systems and further damaged his heart."

Mariah was familiar with the bowel disease Osborn mentioned. She'd seen dysentery ravage many patients at the hospital and often cause death.

"Well, Dunny's not dead yet!" Wilhelmina

Hooper piped up suddenly. "And I, for one, hope he won't be passing on for a good while yet. I'm going to fetch everybody something to eat. Miss, I'll show you to your room now, so you can rest before supper." The woman's manner toward Mariah seemed cooler now, since the scene in Dunny's bedroom.

"Thank you, Wilhelmina," Mariah replied. "I'd appreciate a rest. And I'd like to take supper in my room, if it wouldn't be too much bother."

"No bother at all, Miss."

Mariah turned to Jamie, determined to make her tone formal when she spoke. But looking into his eyes caused her heart to beat like a frantic butterfly's wings.

"Mr. Lancaster, you have my gratitude for accompanying me here. I hope you and Dr. Osborn will accept the hospitality of my father's table before you depart. I regret that fatigue prevents me from joining you both. Good evening, gentlemen."

Chapter 4

Mariah lay awake in the dark. She felt tremendously weary, but her churning mind would allow her no rest. A great turmoil of emotions whirled inside her. After so long, she was back in the bedroom of her childhood, though it was nothing like the special place she remembered from youth. This room was clearly for guests now, no longer the haven of a little girl whose mother had just died. Gone were the white lace curtains, the rocking chair in the corner, cherished playthings. Even the bed in which she now lay was different—wide, with no canopy or velvet hangings to pull cozily closed. The walls and scallop-edged cornices were changed, too. Before, they had been painted a cheery white, but now they were a plain dull green.

She hated green. She hated this room. She hated all the painful memories bombarding her. She shouldn't have come back to see her father.

Father. He required her to be here now, for what bizarre purpose, only he knew. Dying, he wanted her. But where had he been when she had needed him as a child? Sailing the seven seas, fighting wars, adventuring.

Her heart chilled again, and she told herself she

didn't care that he'd looked weak and sickly. She despised him. He deserved to suffer. Perhaps fate was exacting restitution from him for his treatment of her.

Finally, she fell into a restless half-slumber, only to awaken during the night from a haunting dream in which she was a child again and her mother was rocking her in the old chair in the corner.

She sat up, breathing hard, tears stinging her eyes. Feeling hot, she threw back the sheet and climbed out of bed, hurrying across the spacious room to the window. The July night breeze wafted through the opening, touching her perspiring face. She shivered, troubled by the vivid dream of her loving mother—it had seemed so real.

She sank to the cushioned window seat and rested her head back against the wall, envisioning every detail of her mother's face—her warm smile, the lovely features, soft chestnut hair flecked with russet. Gazing out the window into the moonlight, she wished she could see her mother's gentle smile again, see the light of love come into her blue eyes.

Blue eyes. Her brow dipped slightly as she tried to think. Were her mother's eyes blue? She didn't remember. How could the years dim that precious detail when other recollections were so clear?

It was foolish, she knew, but suddenly she felt she must learn the color of her mother's eyes. She'd ask Wilhelmina.

She rose from the window seat and started across the room to the door. Then she stopped, realizing how late it must be. The house was quiet. No sound of passersby came from the street outside the window. She shouldn't awaken the old servant woman.

Then she remembered the oil portrait of her mother and herself done when she was a child. Was the painting still in the parlor? She must know. She must see her mother again.

Her bare feet made no sound on the braided rug of the hall, but when she was outside the parlor door, a loose board creaked loudly underfoot. She stopped, listening. When quiet prevailed, she relaxed again and proceeded into the room, closing the door softly behind her.

Moonlight flooded through the long window on the other side of the parlor, helping her make her way to an unlit opalescent glass lamp on a round pedestal table. But as she approached it, for a split second she sensed danger just before she was roughly grabbed from behind and thrown to the hardwood floor. The attack forced the breath from her lungs, rendering her helpless to scream. She gasped for air and instinctively tried to fight off her assailant.

"Stop struggling or this knife will still you permanently!" a gruff voice ordered.

She froze when she felt the deadly point of a blade press into her side.

"That's better. Now stay still. Who the bloody hell are you?" her attacker demanded.

Mariah's fear quickly changed to fury when she recognized the man's voice and caught a glimpse of his strong face in the moonlight.

"*Mr. Lancaster!* Are you crazed! It's Mariah Morgan. Unhand me at once!"

The tight grip on her wrist slackened immediately.

"What in the name of heaven are you doing

prowling around where you don't belong?'' Jamie hauled her to her feet. ''You shouldn't steal up on a man. That's a good way to get yourself killed!''

''I didn't know you were here! And I didn't expect to have my life threatened when I entered my father's parlor. What are *you* doing hiding here, ready to pounce like some vicious brigand? You nearly murdered me!'' She frowned, rubbing her wrist. She couldn't see him clearly in the dim light from the window, but his powerful bearing seemed to dominate the room. How easily his assault had rendered her defenseless!

''I assure you, if I'd wanted to murder you, Miss Morgan, you'd be quite dead right now.''

His voice sounded tiredly impatient. She watched him cross the room to light the lamp. The glow from the wick silhouetted his angular profile in gigantic proportion over the wood-paneled wall behind him.

''I happen to be sleeping here,'' he continued, waving toward a tangle of blankets and a pillow. ''The sofa proved too short for me, so I made my bed on the floor. Your father requested I stay the night. Usually when I visit, I sleep in the guest room you're occupying now. Somehow I doubted you'd be interested in sharing that large, comfortable bed with me.''

''You were very correct in that assumption. You should put on a shirt, sir!'' she blurted, still shaken by his attack and her sudden awareness of their attire. He was bare-chested. The muscles in his shoulders were still well rounded, but no longer bulging from exertion as they had been only moments ago when he'd straddled her on the floor.

His pantherlike quickness and ready strength lay close to the surface, she knew. She swallowed hard, glad that her white linen nightgown was buttoned to the neck and long-sleeved. But she still felt suddenly flushed.

"I don't usually wear anything when I sleep, so you're fortunate I at least left on my breeches. Wilhelmina sleepwalks at times, though she makes such a noise of it that I'm usually forewarned. Had that board not creaked when you stepped on it, you would have taken me by surprise, and that could have been very dangerous."

"So I discovered."

An awkward silence fell between them. Jamie found himself staring at Mariah Morgan. How different she appeared now than she had all day. She looked almost frail in her clinging nightgown. Finally he could see her fireglow hair released from the restricting bun, falling loosely past her shoulders in shining thick tangles. The flickering lamplight accentuated the delicate contours of her face, the gentle curve of her lips, setting something astir within him—a tiny spark of feeling, impossible to define.

He saw she still held her wrist. "Did I injure you?"

"Except for my dignity, no!" she exclaimed hotly. She felt confused by his question for, though he'd asked it in a clipped manner, she'd heard just a fraction of sincere concern in the words.

"Well, I hope you learned a lesson in caution."

"*I* learn!" Stunned by his reprimand, she glared at him, hands on hips. "I might have known your concern was only perfunctory!"

He let a smile pull up one corner of his mouth. Her eyes flashed again, animating her face, pleasing him. By the heavens, but she was beautiful! The lamplight softened everything about her body within its shadowy glow, but that feisty spirit of hers couldn't be dimmed. It lay ever ready to burst forth in flame, the way a dry tree branch thrown into a blaze instantly catches fire. For a moment, he sobered, remembering how close he'd come to really hurting her when she'd come in. He didn't want to do that.

"Why did you come in here, Miss Morgan?"

"My reasons are not your concern, sir." She sensed his close scrutiny and uncomfortably shifted her gaze to concentrate on the oil lamp. But her eyes were drawn to the shadows cavorting over the ripple-grained cherry paneling of the parlor walls. When a breath of breeze whispering through the open window disturbed the lamp's flame, she unwittingly followed the dark spectral shapes it cast over his naked chest, and her heart's normal rhythm suddenly accelerated.

"Very well, you're correct. No more questions. By the way, my friends call me Jamie. 'Mr. Lancaster' sounds like you're addressing my father."

"Who is your father?"

"Now you're asking a question that is none of your concern. So we seem to have reached an impasse. End of discussion. I'm going back to sleep. If you wish to keep meandering around in the middle of the night, I strongly suggest you do so in another part of the house. Good night." He stretched out on the blankets on the floor.

"Are you dismissing me from my own family

parlor?'' She frowned at his arrogance, irritated by his curt dismissal.

"Not at all. Stay if you wish. I don't snore, so I shouldn't bother you while I'm sleeping.'' He turned on his side with his back to her.

Mariah almost left the parlor. She didn't like being in the same house with James Lancaster, let alone the same room! Yet because he suggested that she go, she didn't want to do it! She had every right to be here. She'd come to the parlor for a reason, and she'd see it accomplished. It didn't matter that she had to think hard for a few seconds now to remember just what that reason was. Her mother's portrait. Yes, she'd come to see it and she wasn't going to leave until she had.

Ignoring his prone form on the floor, she picked up the glass-globed lamp and crossed the oblong room to the unlit gray stone fireplace. Once she'd put the lamp on the mantel its glow spread to the large, gilt-framed painting hanging on the wall.

All these years and the portrait hadn't been moved. There, suspended in time on the canvas, her mother appeared young and smiling, poised at a harp with Mariah, as a child, sitting at her knee. Yes, her eyes were blue. The artist had captured their pure sapphire shade and the light of life in them perfectly. Mariah's heart constricted with the old pain of missing her mother.

"How old were you when the painting was done?'' Jamie's deep voice broke the stillness.

She whirled around, surprised to see him sitting up. "I—I was eight.'' Turning back to the portrait, she continued in hushed words. "My mother always smiled, except when she became so sick. I was ten years old at the time. The terrible cough racked her body night after night. I'd lie awake in my bedchamber down the hall, listening to her gasping for breath in her room, and I'd feel so afraid. Dr. Osborn and two other physicians couldn't do anything to save her. I remember how helpless I felt. I wanted to do something for her, anything to ease her affliction. But in less than a week she was gone, and my life changed forever. My mother's death made me decide to study medicine so I could help other people as I hadn't been able to help her.''

Jamie was struck silent by her last statement. The words slashed into him like a jagged-edged knife and gored open afresh the old wound in his badly scarred heart. They weren't quite the same words he'd heard so long ago, but the inflection and the conviction in her voice matched Evangelene's exactly. She would have said the words in the same unselfish way, never thinking of herself, only of others. With lightning swiftness, a vision of the only woman he'd ever loved leaped into his mind's eye.

Lovely Evangelene. Her flowing long blonde hair, pale features, and soft brown eyes had made her quite different in appearance from Mariah Morgan. But the women both had the same inner strength. God, how he'd loved her. So many times over the past ten years he'd wondered what his life would have been like if she hadn't traveled with her clergyman father to that French outpost, where they'd been massacred by Indians. He would have married her, settled into banking, had a home, children, just as she'd wanted. Losing her so brutally had dramatically changed the direction of his life. He'd tried to forget his love for her and the pain of her loss, but now Mariah's words caused those memories to well up in him again.

Mariah continued to stare up at the painting for a few moments longer, blinking back tears. She was startled that she'd said so much to him. He likely wouldn't understand the all-pervading sadness she felt for a mother long dead. He wouldn't agree with her determination to be a physician. Women weren't expected to pursue such ambitions.

A small gasp of surprise escaped her lips when he suddenly came up behind her and placed his hands on her shoulders.

"There's no greater pain than losing someone you love . . ."

He spoke barely above a whisper. A poignant tremor touched his words, making her realize he knew the anguish she felt in her heart now. She sank back against him, lowering her head and allowing the tears to come.

Jamie turned her around and held her in his arms, stroking her hair as he would if he were comforting a small child. The strands felt soft against his hand. Her tears were hot and wet on his bare shoulder. He had only meant to console her, but he couldn't ignore the sensuousness of her body in contact with his, its easy molding to him.

And Mariah, too, was acutely aware of the heat of his body radiating toward her. She knew she should have been repelled by this intimacy with a virtual stranger, but instead, she felt drawn in, melded by his strength. And for just these moments, she needed his protective embrace, welcomed his steadying arms around her.

Finally, her tears slowed and she became calm again. Quickly stepping back from Jamie, she brushed at the wetness on her cheeks and nervously cleared her throat.

"I—I'm sorry, Mr. Lancaster. I don't know what made me act so foolishly."

"You weren't foolish. You haven't been in this house since you were a child, have you?" He forced himself to ignore her disturbing nearness.

Mariah shook her head. "My aunt warned me against coming here, but, as usual, I refused to listen to her. I didn't consider that returning might revive so many difficult memories. But I'm quite all right now." She averted her eyes from his searching gaze and turned to reach for the lamp on the mantel. "Please go back to your bed. I'm sorry I interrupted your sleep."

"You've had quite a trying day. Are you certain you're all right?"

"Yes. Don't trouble yourself further about me. Good night, Mr. Lancaster."

"Jamie."

"I beg your pardon?"

"Call me Jamie."

"No, Mr. Lancaster is better, I think."

Their eyes met and held. And in that moment, he sensed that she'd raised an impenetrable barrier between them. The coolness of her liquid blue-green gaze told him so. She appeared controlled, serene, invulnerable. He was glad to see that demeanor. Her weeping had touched a part of him that he'd hidden deeply inside long ago, when he'd closed his heart off and determined that he'd never allow it to open to anyone after Evangelene.

The look he exchanged now with Mariah was one of mutual understanding. The intimate sharing that had flowered between them would not happen again. In silent agreement, he nodded, receiving a slight nod from her in return. Then she walked to the door and left the parlor.

Chapter 5

"Dimetrius sends his best and plans to come by the house later to see you, Dunny," Jamie explained when he entered the older man's room the next morning. "He's making inquiries for me concerning Lem Hollister and Toby Jones."

"Trying to catch up with those two, are you?" Dunny snorted in apparent amusement. "Well, I wouldn't want to be in their boots when you do. You're not the type to let anyone get the best of you. I was just like that in my younger days. You could get a score of men to help you hunt down those two jackals. They've made enough enemies from their cheating schemes."

"I see to my own affairs."

"I know you do, lad. I've always been glad to call you friend, but I know you're a loner, with strong ideas about what you want out of life. I just wish I could be around when you make that sailing to the distant shores of China. What an adventure that will be." His brown eyes glistened with a look of longing.

"Aye, that it will, Dunny. I've dreamed of that journey to the Far East for many a year." He strode to a colorful, wall-sized map of the world hanging

next to a hickory chest of drawers, and caressingly
grazed his fingertips over the land mass represent-
ing China. "You've listened to me expound on the
trip often enough. I'd like nothing better than to
have you as first mate on my ship when I acquire
it someday."

"Well, lad, we never know which way the sea
winds will blow us. I think, though, my sailing
days are over." He sighed heavily, sinking deeper
into the propped pillows of the bed and pulling his
white nightshirt collar together at his throat. "I'm
tired, Jamie. A sailor who prefers his rocking chair
more than the roll of the deck beneath his boots
wouldn't be much good to you."

"Dunny—" Jamie started to argue, but the older
man cut him off with a wave of his hand.

"No, you know I'm right, lad. You're young.
You've many an adventure ahead of you yet. I've
had mine. Damn the years for passing so swiftly!
But I wouldn't trade one of my journeys for anything else I've ever done. Great times, they were.
You know. You've shared a goodly number of them
with me over the last five years." He closed his
eyes for a moment before going on. "Do you think
my girl's glad to be back with her papa, Jamie
boy?"

"After the greeting you gave her, you'll be lucky
if she's still here this morning, you cantankerous
old buzzard. I like you sharp-tongued and ornery.
I've gotten used to you that way. But you might
have tempered your nasty disposition just a little in
front of the daughter you haven't seen in over nine
years."

"Bah! If we're going to get along, she'll have to

accept me the way I am. I refuse to change at my age. And I won't have a simpering Puritanical Bible-quoter calling me to task for everything I do in my last days!'' A fit of coughing forced him to stop his tirade.

"Calm down, Dunny," Jamie warned, concern showing on his face as he went to the hickory bedstand and poured a glass of water from a cream-colored porcelain pitcher. "Here, drink this. Is it time for this medicine?" He picked up an amber bottle from the stand.

"No, and I don't know why I bother with that foul-tasting concoction anyway. Doesn't do any good. Wipe that worried look off your face, boy. I'm not going to pass on yet, at least not till I've said what I have to say to my daughter. Go and fetch her for me now before I nod off for my morning nap."

Jamie shook his head but said nothing more as he skirted the big bed to go toward the door. He didn't like the pale, yellow-tinged look Dunny had about him, and his friend's morbid words troubled him.

Jamie startled Mariah when he opened the door just as she raised her hand to knock on it.

"Your father's asking to see you," he explained, stepping aside to let her come into the room. He noticed she was again dressed in a drab dress, the same brown garment he'd first seen her in at Hastings' hospital in Boston. It was a pity to disguise a sensual figure in such unbecoming apparel. She should wear elegant satins, clinging silks, delicate lace to match her fragile features.

"How is he this morning?" she asked.

"Talk to me if you want to know the answer to that question!" Dunny declared impatiently as he straightened the lightweight bed quilt and turned in her direction. "As you can see, I didn't sink with the anchor last night. I hope that fact doesn't disappoint you overmuch."

Mariah's arched brow dipped slightly at his brusqueness. She'd hoped the rude temperament he'd shown yesterday was just the result of being fatigued or pained by his illness. But now she had the unhappy feeling that he was simply exhibiting his normal disposition. He'd soured with age, not mellowed.

Taking a deep breath to fortify herself, she vowed to keep her composure, no matter what. She didn't want to give him the satisfaction of upsetting her.

"How are you feeling this morning, Father?" she asked with formal politeness.

"I feel so terrible, I'm certain I won't be delaying this dying business much longer," Dunny replied with a drawn-out sigh. "So we'd best be about fixing things between us, girl."

Mariah noticed that her father appeared to be even more frail-looking and jaundiced than he had the day before. He didn't try to sit up straight when she came to the side of the four-poster.

"I'll leave you both alone," Jamie said, starting to go out the door.

"No, you won't," Dunny stopped him. "Shut the door and come back over here."

Puzzled, Jamie complied with his friend's demand, joining Mariah by the bedstand.

The silence weighed heavily in the room. Mariah shifted her feet, uneasy under her father's close scrutiny, then tensed, trying to anticipate what he might say next. She felt very wary of him.

"How did you find sleeping in this house again after all these years, girl?" Dunny asked suddenly.

Mariah shot a glance at Jamie, then lowered her eyes when his steady gaze revealed nothing to her. She didn't see that her father noticed the exchange of looks.

"I find it most difficult to be here," she finally answered honestly.

"Well, this business is no easy task for me either, I can tell you, but it must be done." He expelled a labored breath and coughed deeply at the end of it. Jamie started to reach for the glass of water for him again, but Dunny frowned and shook his head.

"I made a promise to your dear departed mother that I'd always see to your care, Mariah. Even if I haven't been the sort of father you'd have liked, I did help your aunt and uncle with your keep all these years. I still don't approve of her leaving good King George's true religion to join those self-righteous Puritans and then converting you into one, but Josephine and Obediah received the money, didn't they? I never missed a payment, and that obligation was a real burden to me often enough." He said the words accusingly, as if daring her to deny them.

Mariah forced herself to bite back the bitter words tingling on the edge of her lips. She must keep control of herself. With difficulty, she spoke calmly, revealing no feelings. "Yes, you helped— with money. If gratitude is what you want from me for that financial help, then I must give it. If you feel that's all a father need do to raise a child and that was all Mother asked of you, then you've fulfilled your obligations. Consider yourself freed from all burdens. Now you can have peace of mind.''

"*I* will decide what's been fulfilled and what hasn't!'' Dunny declared, frowning as he lifted a bony fist into the air and dropped it to the spiral-patterned blue quilt in a feeble show of temper. ''I don't have peace of mind. I've decided you'll have an inheritance from me and that's that! Now, be quiet and listen.'' He paused to take a deep breath.

''Your inheritance is an unusual one, daughter, and the way you must attain it will test your mettle. My death is not required. You may begin pursuing the gold today.'' Dunny smiled when he saw Mariah's confused expression. ''There's a carved box in the bottom left drawer of my desk over there. Fetch it at once.'' He impatiently waved a hand at her when she hesitated. ''Do as I say, girl!''

Reluctantly, she crossed the frayed red braided rug to the massive walnut desk and found the wooden box in the drawer.

''Open it,'' he instructed when she returned to his bedside.

The black-lacquered box measured the width of a ledger volume, its beautifully decorated top exhibiting a detailed forest scene painted in vibrant colors. Mariah tilted the lid back on its hinges, revealing the contents of the box—a small leather pouch, two thin, odd-shaped pieces of wood, and a folded sheet of parchment.

''Give me the box.'' Dunny snatched it out of

her hands and placed it next to him on the bed. Then he handed her one of the pieces of wood. The other he gave to Jamie. "These two puzzle sections will lead you to your inheritance, daughter." He paused to watch her turn the pieces over in her hand. "They're part of a map showing the location of a cache of gold."

Mariah raised her eyes slowly, until they met her father's gaze. He saw the skeptical look in them.

"No, girl, my illness hasn't made me daft. I know exactly what I'm doing. I used ink to etch the map on a quarter-inch thick piece of wood. Then I cut the map into five pieces. You each hold one of the sections. The other three you must find." He picked up the parchment and unfolded it. "This paper will tell you the location of the third piece. You must follow these instructions exactly as they're written and in the order listed. When you do, you'll gain all the pieces to the map and be able to find the gold. It's a treasure well worth the seeking."

"Treasure hunting?" Mariah stated the words disdainfully. "I've never given credence to such undertakings."

"Considering the narrow-minded, pious upbringing you had, I thought such would be the case," Dunny noted, a smirk wrinkling one corner of his mouth. "And that's precisely why I devised this scheme. I want to see for myself if you have the wits and gumption to be worthy of the wealth I'm offering you, because when you obtain it, there'll be many a blackguard who'll try to wrestle it away from you. This undertaking will be a chal-

lenge. Are you up to it? The reward will be great
if you are.''

He picked up the tan leather pouch. Pulling open
the drawstring holding it together, he let the contents of the small bag spill out over the quilt. At
least a score of shiny gold coins dotted the sky-
blue blanket.

''Doubloons, Mariah Marie, just like the ones I
sent to you by Jamie.'' He picked up several of the
coins and let them slip through his fingers. ''Spanish gold of tremendous value. This rich inheritance
can be yours. Think of the unselfish good you could
do with it, all the miserable wretches you could
help.''

Mariah stared at her father. Could she believe
him? Or was this preposterous scheme some ridiculous, cruel joke, a mean game he was playing
with her? Yet here were the doubloons to testify to
his story. The value of these coins alone was considerable, she was certain. The whole idea began
to intrigue her.

''How did you come by this gold?'' she asked
suddenly. ''Why haven't you claimed it for yourself?''

''Good questions, both. A friend by the name
of Bartholomew Post bestowed it on me quite un-
expectedly. He was a miserly fellow. Saved everything. But he was a good shipmate. He left no heirs
or family when he died, so he bequeathed the map
to me. I don't know how he got it to begin with,
but I do know it leads to gold. I decided this treasure would be your legacy from me, so I haven't
touched it, except for these coins I've shown you.

By this inheritance, I keep my promise to your mother.''

Bluntly enough spoken and, therefore, perhaps the truth, Mariah surmised. His words brought the gripping pain back to her heart. Her father clearly felt a pressing obligation to his dead wife. But to his living daughter, he bequeathed only the promise of cold gold coins. No love, not even a modicum of repentance for his years of neglect. How she longed to hear just one tender, caring word issue from his lips.

Realizing none of those sentiments would be forthcoming, Mariah overcame her hurt by closing her heart once more. Didn't she deserve some compensation for the loneliness, the fears she'd endured during all those childhood years? Gold of any amount would help Samuel and the hospital. With wealth such as her father was promising, she could eliminate his financial burdens. He could enlarge the facility, build a better laboratory, purchase the newest equipment for operations and research. She and Samuel Hastings could help so many more people.

She and Samuel together. Her mentor, her friend, and . . . her husband someday? The two of them, side by side, helping the needy—it was a dream she kept hidden deep in her heart.

''There is an important stipulation in this plan,'' Dunny stated, breaking into her thoughts.

''What is it?'' Mariah watched him warily.

''Jamie here must go with you.''

''What?'' Jamie and Mariah said the word at the same time, staring at each other.

''You heard me. You're a defenseless woman

alone. You can't be riding about the countryside unescorted. Savages and bandits menace people everywhere, not to mention the bloody Frenchies who are always stirring up trouble. We're on the brink of another war with them and their blood-thirsty, red-skinned allies. Won't do you any good to find the gold, girl, if you lose your scalp. So Jamie goes along.''

"Now, wait a minute, Dunny—'' Jamie protested.

"My mind's made up, so don't bother trying to change it, either one of you!'' Dunny stubbornly set his jaw. "You owe me, Jamie boy. Three years ago, I saved your life, you'll recall. Pushed you out of the line of fire and took a musket ball in the chest for you. That's likely the reason my heart's acting so poorly now. So, I'm demanding a return on that favor. You'll be rewarded for your trouble. The piece of the puzzle you have in your hand is yours. It'll earn you one-fifth share of the gold. The doubloons are worth at least half a million pounds, maybe more. You could purchase the ship you've always wanted, captain her to China, just like you've dreamed. Help Mariah acquire the other three pieces of the puzzle, follow the map to where the doubloons are hidden, then see her safely back home here with the gold. I trust you and no one else with this task.''

"But, Father, I hardly know this man,'' Mariah argued. How could she even have considered abandoning the hospital and going along with this absurd plan? Having James Lancaster included made it even more ludicrous. She wanted nothing more to do with him. He was arrogant and dangerous.

Why, he'd nearly murdered her in the parlor last night! And then comforted her most gently and kindly. His actions were so confusing! Her father must be deranged to try to force her to cooperate with such a man.

"I don't care if you're acquainted with him or not. *I* know him! He's crafty as a fox and honors his word. There's no one I can think of who's better with a knife. You don't even have to speak to each other as far as I'm concerned. But you'll need a man to take care of you while you're carrying out my orders, and I know Jamie's courage. He'll protect you."

"You are wrong, Father." Throwing her piece of the puzzle on the bed, Mariah said her next words slowly and precisely, so neither man could misunderstand her. "I won't take orders from you or anyone else." She looked pointedly at Jamie. "I have no intention of being a part of this outrageous scheme. Maps and treasures, indeed. I won't be a pawn in whatever cruel game it is you're playing, Father. I'm going back to Boston where I'm needed, where there is worthwhile work to be done. I intend to leave as soon as I can arrange transportation."

Clutching the skirt of her dress, she whirled around and made straight for the door.

worth of these golden doubloons. Just waiting to be claimed. Where are they going to spend their well gotten gains? ...

Chapter 6

"Stubborn wench, just like her mother," Dunny observed, staring at the empty doorway after Mariah's departure. "Go after her, Jamie boy, and make her see things our way."

"*Our way?* Hardly, my friend. What's this wild plan of yours all about, Dunny?" Jamie fingered his piece of the puzzle.

"A gamble for a big prize. An adventure with a pot of gold waiting at the end. You're interested, aren't you, lad?"

Jamie smiled, glad to hear a little life return to his friend's voice. "You know I'm as game as the next man, especially when my money coffers are as empty as they are right now. But treasure hunting can be risky business. If I had only myself to think of, I'd have no misgivings. But you want a woman involved—your daughter, no less. She's used to city dwelling, ordinary living arrangements. Think what a drastic change this undertaking would be for her. She'd be a burden to me on the search. Can she even sit a horse?"

"How should I know? Ask her!" Dunny picked up a handful of doubloons and waved them in front of Jamie. "Think of it. A half-million pounds' worth of these golden lovelies, just waiting to be claimed. Your own ship, that's what your share will get for you. Finding the other pieces of the puzzle and then the gold will only take a fortnight or a month at most to accomplish. Then you're set for the rest of your life. China, Jamie—think of your dream of exploring the trade routes for the King.''

''Why do I get the distinct feeling that carrying out this scheme of yours won't be quite that easy?'' Jamie cocked a dark eyebrow toward his sickly friend. ''Tell the truth, Dunny. Why haven't you ever spoken of this treasure trove before?''

''The gold was Bartholomew Post's secret. I just inherited it from him a few months ago. The plain truth of the matter is just as I told Mariah—I must leave this legacy for her. I made a vow to Faith, my wife, on her deathbed, and I'm a man of my word.''

''That you are, Dunny. But, if you're so set on this plan, why not let me pursue it for your daughter? If I find the doubloons, they'll be hers, less my one-fifth share.''

''You'll find the gold, all right. And I know you'd return with it. But Mariah must be a part of the seeking and the finding. I hold firm in that stipulation, for reasons I cannot reveal to you now. Will you indulge me, Jamie boy, and do as I ask? You'll be required to follow my instructions to the letter.''

Jamie knew that once Dunsley Morgan set his mind in a certain direction, there was no changing it. His terms or none—there was the choice.

The gold pieces sparkled in a shaft of sunlight streaking across the wide bed from the long, many-paned window. Jamie could almost feel the familiar sway of a ship's deck beneath his feet, glimpse the wind-gorged canvases straining majestically against the rigging. His ship . . .

He picked up one of the doubloons from the quilt. "All right, you sly old weasel. I'll assist your daughter in gaining her legacy, and on your terms, though it's against my better judgment."

A wry smile spread over Dunny's yellow-tinged lips. "You won't regret it, lad. You won't regret it."

"Yes, Mr. Lancaster, what is it?" Mariah asked when she answered the knock at her bedroom door and saw him standing in the hall.

"I'd like to speak with you if I may."

She hesitated, not wanting him in her room—or in her life. Her future was well planned out, and she knew without a single doubt that James Lancaster wasn't included in it. She resisted getting close to him. He caused strange reactions in her when he looked at her with those piercing pale-blue eyes, as he was doing now. Too well, she remembered last night and his consoling touch.

"I shall only take a few minutes of your time," Jamie persisted.

"Very well. You may come in if you don't mind that I continue my packing. Kindly leave the door open," she instructed as she walked to the bed and went on placing her few belongings into the worn valise.

"Do you have an imagination, Miss Morgan?"

"What?" She looked up at him with surprise.

"An imagination. It's something we human beings possess which raises us slightly above the animals.''

"What are you talking about, sir?''

"I'm simply asking you if you have an imagination, because if you do, I'd like you to use it to envision what your decision about the gold will mean to your father.'' Jamie paused to let his words sink in. "In your work at the hospital, you must have had occasion to witness people close to death. Last requests place a great burden of responsibility on people. I know your father well. His soul couldn't rest if he died with his promise to your mother unfulfilled. Since you're the only one who can determine whether or not your father will have peace when he passes on, I'd like to ask you to reconsider very carefully complying with his plans for your inheritance.''

"Perhaps I don't mind if my father's soul is tormented throughout eternity. Perhaps it's the punishment he deserves.'' Her gaze didn't waver as she stared directly at him.

" 'Judgment is mine,' says the Lord.''

"Don't quote scripture to me, sir. My opinions about my father and his absurd treasure scheme remain unchanged.''

"I see.'' He stroked his square, clean-shaven jaw thoughtfully.

"I believe in speaking forthrightly, Mr. Lancaster. Tell me, is your heartfelt concern so much for my father's soul, or are you more than a little motivated by your possible share in his so-called treasure?''

Jamie cleared his throat, cocking a dark brow at her astuteness. "All right, I'll admit that the prospect of a wealthy find appeals to me. Gold can make dreams come true, and I'm a man with many dreams."

"Do you honestly think you can find the gold, that it actually exists?"

"*We* must locate it together. That arrangement doesn't appeal to me either, but your father insists. As to the existence of the gold, I'd say we won't know the answer to that question until we go and look, will we? Which brings us back to whether or not you're willing to sacrifice two or three weeks out of your life to take a chance and participate in this venture."

"This folly, you mean."

She stared at him for a long moment. This whole conversation was preposterous. Treasure, indeed. And yet he seemed serious about pursuing it. Why did she feel a measure of confidence in that? She hardly knew anything about him, except that he was an opportunist who happened to exhibit courage and daring on one occasion she knew of—the coach robbery. But could she trust Lancaster? If she went on this escapade, she'd be required to spend a great deal of time with him . . . What would that be like? Even now, his strength, his confident bearing filled the bedchamber. She was all too aware of his overwhelming presence, and she bristled against that mysterious force. She hated the weakness she'd revealed to him last night in the parlor. She wouldn't let him or anyone else see that part of herself again.

Jamie watched the emotions play over Mariah's lovely face, realizing his whole future might rest in the answer she gave him now. He didn't relish giving her that control over his life. He was also wary of the heated tension that rippled through his veins whenever his eyes met hers.

"I'm not so spiritless as to shun adventure, Mr. Lancaster, but I do hesitate to participate in a plan that might prove to be a waste of time and effort. Dr. Hastings needs me at the hospital."

Jamie felt his anger rising. "How can you be so unimaginative? Perhaps, the good doctor *does* need your help. But think of how much more you'll be able to do for him when you have the gold in your hands. We may both be wasting our time and come out of this looking like fools. But it's my opinion that there's something to be gained from every experience, even if it's only a lesson in what one shouldn't do." He paused, letting his eyes play over her features, then began again. "Oh, there'll be dangers involved, all right. Finding the other puzzle pieces will require traveling far afield, facing situations I can't even guess at now. But don't you ever take chances, try new schemes, Miss Morgan? Good Lord, if you don't, and that hospital is all you've ever experienced, then your life is truly pathetic. You have spirit. I've seen it. Use it now to search for the gold with me!"

She glared at him. He was challenging her, testing her common sense and courage. She felt her temper flare. And at the same time a mysterious tremor of excitement swept through her.

"How dare you call my life pathetic! I know how to take risks. I've experienced insults, ridicule, and harassment because I've pursued a vocation considered unseemly for a woman." Fully incensed now, she heaved a hairbrush she'd intended to pack onto the bed and swung around to face him squarely. "Challenge me, do you? Well, I can meet any test you, my father, or anyone else sets for me! I still think this venture will be fruitless, but, like you, I have reasons for wanting to acquire the doubloons. But let me make several points clear. I don't relish being forced into your company."

At that he opened his mouth as if to interrupt, but Mariah hurried on. "I vehemently dislike you, James Lancaster. I don't trust your arrogance, your wanderlust, or your prowess with a knife. I suspect that, like my father, you go wherever the wind chances to blow you, offering no commitments, making no sacrifices. However," she said, folding her arms at the waist, "for the sake of Samuel Hastings, his hospital, and my work with him, I can endure even you and any hardships and disagreeable conditions I must face. I'll even risk my reputation by traveling with you unchaperoned, for I want as few people to know about this folly as possible." She lifted her chin and held out her hand to him. "So, let us strike a bargain. I'll have your solemn word of honor, sir, that you'll conduct yourself as a proper gentleman at all times. Are you in agreement?"

Jamie's mouth curled into an amused smirk. He took her hand, then suddenly yanked her forward, pinning her hard against the front of his body. His fierce steel-blue gaze drilled into her.

"You've made your views very clear, Miss Morgan. Now hear mine. I don't give a tinker's damn about what you think of me. You're a stubborn, opinionated, and bloody bothersome female who wishes she could wear a man's pants instead of the woman's skirt she was born to. I gladly give you my word of honor concerning gentlemanly conduct, for I assure you, you aren't a woman who would *ever* tempt me to act otherwise. I only hope *my* reputation isn't jeopardized by traveling with you!" He abruptly released her and strode away, turning in the open doorway. "Do we understand each other, Miss Morgan?"

Rubbing her bruised arms, Mariah frowned furiously, trying to control the confusing sensations pulsing through her, trying to fathom how this man had made her change her mind about Dunny's ridiculous treasure hunt so abruptly and so completely.

"Yes, Mr. Lancaster. Indeed, we understand each other perfectly!" But once he'd withdrawn from the room, Mariah was left to wonder whether she'd ever understand James Lancaster at all.

Chapter 7

The next morning Mariah stood somberly before her father in the master bedchamber, administering a vial of medicine to him. As she did, she tried to keep her eyes from drifting toward Jamie Lancaster, who was in the room as well, dressed and ready for traveling. He seemed almost sinister in a thigh-length tan leather vest—the same one he'd worn on the coach—over a black, full-sleeved shirt and tight riding breeches. She couldn't help noticing how his handsome features stood out boldly. She felt his pale-blue eyes upon her, appraising her in return even after she looked away. The room suddenly seemed uncomfortably warm.

Her father still looked frail and sickly, propped in the middle of the big four-poster bed, but his brown eyes seemed to hold a sparkle they hadn't before. He's likely glad to be getting rid of me, she thought derisively as she fidgeted with a wayward crease in her navy-blue cotton riding skirt. Her black leather boots felt stiff with newness, pinching her toes a little.

"You charged everything to my account at Waterford's Store, as I directed?" Dunny demanded.

"Yes, Father. And I instructed Mr. Lancaster to see to the supplies we'll need on our journey."

"*You* instructed?" Dunny sat forward in the big bed. "Who put you in charge? And for heaven's sake, call him Jamie."

"Isn't the purpose of this journey to find the gold that is *my* inheritance?" she asked crisply, ignoring her father's last statement.

"It is. But Jamie's in charge of keeping you alive and in one piece with that ugly hair arrangement of yours still attached to your head. That won't be an easy task, because the Frenchies' paid savages might try to lift both your scalps. So he has leadership of this enterprise. There will be no argument about that issue!"

Mariah bristled at her father's reprimand. To calm herself and indicate her intention to depart, she buttoned the short tight-fitting jacket that matched her skirt. Straightening her shoulders, she looked her father squarely in the eye.

"This wild goose chase was not of my choosing, Father, but I've consented to take part in it. I represent a four-fifths' share in this enterprise, as you call it, and therefore have the greater stake in its success. *I* shall be the person in charge. Since I'm forfeiting one-fifth of my share to Mr. Lancaster for his protective escort, I am, in effect, his employer. He'll take orders from me. I want that understood at the outset, or this venture ends now."

She crossed her arms in front of her and raised her chin, as if ready to meet any argument.

"Now, you listen to me, you stubborn—" Dunny started to exclaim, vigorously wagging a finger at his daughter. Then a spasm of coughing choked him, forcing him to fall back against the pillows.

"Don't upset yourself, my friend," Jamie admonished, stepping closer to the bed and putting out a hand to stay Dunny's protests. Then he turned toward Mariah, frowning. "Your daughter may lead our expedition—*if* she proves she's a better man than I am on the trail."

Mariah shot him a scathing look. "I assure you, sir, I'm well able to take care of myself. And now, since neither you nor the stipulation that you accompany me is to my liking, I suggest that we get this escapade going. I've sent a letter to Dr. Hastings telling him that I'll be away for approximately two to three weeks. I don't wish to exceed that estimation, so the sooner we get started, the sooner the journey will end, and you and I can part company. Your friend, Mr. Cobb, has the horses ready?" She pulled on her dark-blue kid gloves and adjusted her matching felt hat down a little tighter on her head. The blue headpiece with the upturned brim and three pheasant feathers decorating it had been her only extravagance yesterday when she'd gone shopping.

"Yes, the horses are ready," Jamie replied coolly.

"Good, you can get out of my sight, the sooner the better. Come here, girl," Dunny ordered his daughter.

As Mariah reluctantly stepped forward, he pulled back the bed quilt to reveal the ornate wooden box he'd shown them the day before. Lifting its lid, he withdrew the puzzle pieces, handing one to her and one to Jamie.

"Guard these carefully. They're important parts of both your futures." He removed the sheet of parchment from the box. "As this parchment says, your first destination is Worcester. Find a man named Ezra Flannery. He owns a dry-goods shop. Present him with this letter. He'll give you the third puzzle piece and direct you to the next one."

With a sudden quick movement, he grabbed Mariah's wrist in a grip so strong it belied his sickliness. Her eyes darted to his in surprise.

"No matter what happens, Mariah girl, never lose sight of the goal you seek—the gold. I may still be alive when you return. I'll relish hearing you stammer your feeble regrets for doubting the treasure's existence and my commitment to my offspring. But if I'm dead, at least I'll have expired knowing I gave you the means to a secure future. Your mother can rest in her grave now, and so can I. Now go, both of you. All this arguing saps my strength. You've a hard ride ahead of you. Get to it!" He abruptly released Mariah's hand and turned his attention to closing the box, coughing violently.

For a few moments, Mariah didn't move. Confusion tore at her. She was very aware of the fact that this might be the last time she'd ever speak to her father. Some unfathomable longing caused her to hesitate now in leaving him. A little-girl part of her wanted to cling to the father she knew so little about. Yet, at the same time, she wanted nothing more than to escape from his presence. His cold sharpness with her cut deeply into her heart. He'd spurned her so many times before, left her heart in shattered pieces. But she refused to let him see the pain he caused.

Blinking back hot tears, she clutched the wooden puzzle piece in one hand and snatched the parchment letter from the bed with the other. Without saying another word to her father, she turned and strode from the room, slamming the door behind her.

"I don't know what you've gotten me into here, Dunny Morgan," Jamie noted, shaking his head. "When I return, I'll either treat you to a keg of rum at the Shield and Bow Tavern or lay you out with a good trouncing, depending on the outcome of this scheme of yours. Take care of yourself so we can settle the score later." He smiled as he grasped his friend's frail hand in farewell.

"I'll wager for the rum, lad." Dunny gave him a wan smile. "Godspeed."

"Thanks. I have a feeling I'm going to need it." Jamie cocked an eyebrow and sent a curt nod toward Owen Osborn, who was on his way in to see Dunny. Then he left the bedchamber.

The gray-haired doctor walked to the open window overlooking the stable. "Do you think they suspected anything?"

Dunny climbed out of bed and crossed the bedroom in nightshirt and bare feet to stand beside his old friend. Carefully he peered from behind the mauve draperies to watch Mariah and Jamie join Dimetrius Cobb in the stableyard. His laugh had a self-satisfied ring.

"No, we planned too carefully. We've both lived long enough to understand human nature. I know Mariah, even if I've seen little of her since she was a girl. And I know Jamie well enough, too. They'll both play their roles in my little drama just as I've scripted them. Have no doubt, my friend.''

"I can't help but wonder if I've done the right thing in helping you to manipulate Mariah's and Jamie's fates,'' Owen Osborn said speculatively. "For from this day forward, those two young people's lives will never be the same again.''

"So, you're having reservations about playing God, are you, Owen?'' Dunny glanced sideways toward his trusted cohort, a glint in his brown eyes. "Well, I'm not! No one held a pistol to their heads to make them accept the challenge I offered. They complied of their own free wills. I merely held out the apple of temptation and offered a map to the destiny that will be best for both of them, if they follow it to its culmination.''

"Ah yes, its culmination . . .'' The wrinkles creasing Owen Osborn's forehead seemed to deepen as he shook his head. "Well, the die is cast. There's no turning back now.''

Dunny peeked around the edge of the drapery again to see the stableyard, a smirk on his thin lips.

"No, indeed, my friend. No turning back.''

Chapter 8

"May I assist you in mounting, Miss Morgan?" Jamie offered, cupping his hands to create a stepping place for her. "I'm determined to be an employee worthy of your generous compensation."

Mariah frowned, not only at his mocking tone, but also at the roan mare she'd be riding. She wasn't about to admit she hadn't ridden since she was ten years old. Swallowing hard, she watched the horse shake its head and sidestep away from them. Dimetrius Cobb grabbed the harness to steady the animal.

"A less spirited horse, as well as a sidesaddle, would have been more to my liking, Mr. Lancaster," she informed him, placing her boot in his hands. In a smooth motion, he lifted her to the height of the saddle, steadying her until she settled astride it. His mocking smile widened when she hastily adjusted her long full skirt around her legs.

"But less reliable on our journey. Lilac Wind is a stout-hearted lady, your father's favorite. She'll be surefooted on the rough terrain we'll be encountering. As to the saddle, I assure you, you'll find it more comfortable in the long run."

"Very well. For now, I'll defer to your judgment

and wait to see whether or not it's correct in the end. Is Mr. Cobb accompanying us for the entire trip?''

''No, just part of the way.''

She saw him exchange glances with the small man, and she pondered the strange system of communication they seemed to employ. She remembered they hadn't spoken to each other at all during the coach robbery, yet they'd managed to foil the thieves quite handily. She could only wonder about the meaning behind the looks they cast between them now.

She felt uncomfortable in their company. After all, she barely knew either of these men. Just because her father seemed to trust both of them didn't mean she should do the same. She took some consolation in knowing she could defend herself if the need arose. She'd taken care to bring a small, two-shot pistol with her when she'd left Boston. It was now nestled in the deep side pocket of her riding skirt. Her Uncle Obediah had taught her to use it with a measure of expertise.

At that moment, Lilac Wind snorted and pranced, startling Mariah. She clutched the leather reins more firmly.

''Your horse appears eager to begin the venture,'' Jamie noted as he mounted his fine bay stallion. Dimetrius climbed upon a much smaller pony, outfitted with diminutive stirrups and saddle.

''As am I, Mr. Lancaster,'' Mariah stated, keeping her tone cool and distant. ''Worcester lies some twenty-five miles to the west, if I'm not mistaken? Shall we proceed?''

"By all means. If all goes well, we'll be there by this evening. Follow me."

Jamie put on his black tricorn and touched heels to his mount, trotting the stallion out of the stable-yard. Mariah was too unsure of her horse and un-used riding skills to do anything but grit her teeth and let Jamie lead the way through the iron gate. Dimetrius Cobb brought up the rear.

Had Mariah been on a casual outing, she might have enjoyed the journey more and taken better notice of the temperate July morning, the darting flights of color-flecked birds and the rolling summer-green landscape. But this was no pleasure trip. She was being forced to accompany two men who seemed determined to communicate only with each other, all but ignoring her existence.

It didn't take her long, however, to discover that Lilac Wind, while spirited, was well trained. The mare responded to the lightest touch on the reins. Mariah's lessons as a child quickly came back to her, but she still had to use all of her concentration to negotiate the roads, watching carefully for deep ruts and hidden holes that might test the mare's footing.

Jamie remained in the lead, except when he and Cobb rode abreast where the width of the roadway allowed it. Late in the morning, he reined in his bay and waited for Mariah to catch up. Cobb rode on ahead.

"Are you faring well, Miss Morgan? Or do you require a rest?"

His patronizing tone left no doubt that he ex-pected the latter. She was beginning to feel the muscle-stiffening effect of riding for several hours and would have welcomed a break, but she'd never admit that to him.

"I'm quite all right, Mr. Lancaster." She gave him a sweet smile. "But if you and Mr. Cobb are fatigued and need a respite, I suppose a delay wouldn't be too inconvenient."

She saw one of his dark brows cock slightly, but otherwise his expression gave no outward indication of his reaction to her barb.

"You're too kind. But I think Dimetrius and I might manage to press on for a while longer."

"Good. I'm glad to hear you have a little stamina. Do try to keep up, won't you?"

She didn't even try to keep a smirk from turning up her mouth as she touched her heels to Lilac Wind's sides. They swiftly passed Jamie on his bay. He frowned, pulling up his horse's reins to steady the animal before following her.

By midday the sun shone bright in the cloudless sky and the heat caused perspiration to trickle down the inside of her navy-blue cotton jacket. She was grateful when they left the main road and stopped by a brook. The water looked inviting. She wished she could throw propriety to the wind and plop down in the refreshing water, clothes and all. At the very least, she longed to pull off her boots and soak her feet.

When Jamie helped her dismount, the muscles in the lower half of her body stiffened agonizingly. Sharp jabs of pain streaked through her legs when she tried to stand on them. Without thinking, she grabbed hold of his arm to keep from falling.

"Steady there, Miss Morgan." His hands stayed

around her waist to support her. An amused smile
flickered at one corner of his mouth. "You'll get
your land legs in a minute. Feeling a bit tight in
the muscles?"

She twisted out of his hold and stepped away
from him.

"My muscles and all other parts of my anatomy
are none of your business, Mr. Lancaster. How
long will we remain at this stop?" She looked away
from him, and began to summarily pull off her riding gloves.

Jamie let his lips spread into a smirk as he noted
the haughty upturn of her dainty nose, a nose
smudged with the dust of travel. Strands of her
auburn hair strayed about her face. He almost
reached out to brush one away from her cheek, but
stopped himself just in time. She was a feisty one,
all right, and he was glad of it. He had no desire
to be escort to a whiny female who expected to be
pampered at every turn. But he was a little surprised that she hadn't complained about the ambi-
tious pace he'd set.

"How long will we be stopping here, sir?"
Mariah repeated, glancing up at him. A sudden
awkwardness surged through her when she found
him watching her intently.

"We'll eat and give the horses a rest. That
should take about an hour. See to setting out the
food." He tossed Mariah's saddlebags on the
ground as he passed her to lead the horses to
the water.

It was an order, not a request. She glowered at
him, but he didn't see because he'd turned to toss
his hat and vest on the grass. Then he rolled up

his sleeves to the elbows and opened his shirt at the collar, unfastening several buttons down the front to reveal a deep vee of bare, lightly-haired chest. Mariah was reminded of when she'd seen the whole of his powerful upper body exposed at the hospital in Boston.

She forced herself to turn away. Ignoring the saddlebags, she strolled to the grassy bank of the stream and slipped off her jacket, leaving only her beige high-necked blouse. Then she stooped down to dip her handkerchief in the cool water. The sharp pain that jolted through her thighs and buttocks when she did made her cry out softly before she could stop herself. She heard Jamie chuckle over her discomfiture. Scowling, she shot him a scathing look.

Squeezing the excess water out of the white linen, she gratefully bathed her face with it, then decided she was hungry enough to follow Jamie's orders about setting out the food. But when she turned from the stream, she saw Dimetrius Cobb already carrying out the task. Thick slices of roasted chicken and chunks of yellow cheese lay spread out on the brown paper in which Wilhemina had packed them. The little man used a poniard to carve wide slices of dark bread from a round loaf.

Mariah thought the dagger looked vaguely familiar. When he finished and tossed it to Jamie, who caught it deftly by the pearl handle and tucked it completely out of sight in his dust-covered black riding boot, she remembered where she'd seen the knife before. It was the one Jamie had used to foil the highwaymen. Now, at least, she knew how he'd conjured it up out of thin air that day.

They ate in silence, washing down the food with tin cups filled with the crisply cool stream water. Mariah leaned against the thick trunk of an old maple tree, resting her head as she scanned the peaceful glade. It stretched in a wide circle around them, edged by forest. Sounds of buzzing insects among the wildflowers and the chirping of birds mingled with the gurgle of the stream rushing over submerged rocks. The gentle noises began to have a hypnotic effect on her. Filled with the delicious food, she breathed deeply, relishing the shade cast by the leaf-thick branches overhead. She let herself relax and give in to the heaviness tugging at her eyelids. They closed of their own volition.

Jamie sat across from Mariah, his back against a large boulder. From his saddlebags, he took out a sheaf of papers, a quill, and a small bottle of ink. Intending to sketch only the picturesque clearing, he soon included Mariah in the drawing. Studying her lovely features with an artist's inner eye, he purposely noticed details about her that he hadn't had a chance to see before. Her thick auburn lashes rested on the pale skin of her upper cheeks. Short wisps of hair, curled by perspiration, framed her thin face. Her dark brows arched delicately.

Though he couldn't see it, he knew the vivid turquoise shade of her large eyes beneath the closed lids. He remembered how they could glisten with fear, as they had when the coach had been attacked by the outlaws. And he recalled how they could light with anger when her temper flared.

He wished he had paints and brush with him so he could add color to the sketch. The shade of her skin would be a challenge to capture. This morning when they'd set out on their journey, she'd been pale, the result, no doubt, of her labors indoors at the hospital. But now, exposure to the July sunshine had tinged her cheeks a becoming blush-pink. She'd likely be upset to learn that fact, for a pale countenance was considered fashionable among ladies—so much so that they sometimes wore masks when outside to shield their complexions. He found a less bland coloring much more appealing. The touch of sun on Mariah's cheeks was most attractive. The pink matched the hue of her full, sensuous lips.

He studied her mouth, concentrating on the gentle ripple in the top lip, the almost imperceptible protrusion of the lower. Soft, delicate. His pen ceased moving as he stared. He flicked his tongue over his own lips to wet them, unable to think of anything except what her lips might feel like, taste like on his. He felt a stirring curl inside him. What would she do if he kissed her now? Those lips were made to be kissed.

She'd be outraged. She'd likely try to slap his face. He'd parry her hand and kiss her again—into submission this time. Then her lips would be soft and yielding, releasing a small moan of surrender.

The breeze suddenly ruffled the edges of his sketch, drawing him back from his contemplation. He felt reluctant to give up the thoughts. They were pleasant, arousing.

The ink had dried on the quill point, requiring him to dip the pen in the bottle again before he could capture her mouth on the paper. When he did sketch in the lips, he made them slightly pursed in readiness and anticipation. He barely glanced at the white paper while he finished the drawing, for the shadows and contours of her face and body flowed easily through his eyes to his hand and quill. The affect on him was double-edged—soothing, but also puzzling. He found pleasure in drawing her unawares, watching her relaxed in a nap. Dimetrius, the horses, the rest of the glade slipped from his consciousness as he transformed the blank sheet.

He stared at the drawing for a long time after finishing it. It was then that he noticed he'd put little of the clearing, the grass, the stream in the sketch. Mariah dominated it completely. He reached for the pen again to add those details, then stopped, his hand in midair. For some reason he didn't want anything else cluttering the drawing.

Setting the papers aside, he used a fist-sized rock to secure them against the breeze. While he was returning the quill and ink bottle to his saddlebags, Dimetrius came over to him.

"When're you goin' to tell her about the detour to the cabin?" he asked, his voice low.

"Right now. Get the horses ready."

"Aye, I'd much rather be doin' that than breakin' the news to her." Dimetrius nodded toward Mariah and grinned before he moved away toward the mounts.

Jamie reached over and prodded Mariah's boot tip. "Miss Morgan." Her eyes flew open.

"Oh, Mr. Lancaster, I—I must have dozed off. I'm sorry," she stammered, flustered to be caught so off guard.

"You probably needed the rest. I hope you're

refreshed, because we're about to resume our journey. Prepare to mount.''

Mariah noticed he made no gentlemanly gesture to help her, but instead turned to gather some papers from the grass. When he removed the small rock weighing them down, a wisp of breeze caught the top sheet. He made a lunging attempt to catch it, but the air tossed it just beyond his fingertips, bringing it to rest at Mariah's feet. She stooped to pick it up before he could retrieve it.

''What's this?'' She stared in surprise at her own countenance depicted in perfect detail on the white paper.

''That's obvious, isn't it?'' Jamie retorted, snatching the sketch out of her hand and adding it to the sheaf.

''You did this drawing?'' Her tone sounded incredulous, then quickly turned reprimanding. ''I didn't give you permission to do it.''

''Let's have this clearly understood, Miss Morgan. I'm not in the habit of asking *anyone's* permission to do *anything!* I felt like sketching you, therefore I did. Doing so amused me. Whether you like it or not makes no difference to me. Now, if you can possibly manage it, prepare yourself to leave. We have quite a distance to go this afternoon.''

Frowning, he stuffed the papers into his saddlebag, then stalked to his horse. Dimetrius was closer to Mariah, so he held out his cupped hands to assist her in mounting. She brought up the rear as Jamie led the way back to the main road.

''You didn't tell her about the detour,'' Dimetrius reminded him, pulling his pony abreast with Jamie's bay.

"Don't nag, Dimetrius." He shot a sideways glance to the smaller man, one dark eyebrow slanting down at a fierce angle. "Let her find out about it in due time."

He didn't appreciate the dwarf's amused smile, but he said nothing more as he slammed his black tricorn down more firmly on his head and touched heels to his horse to take the lead out of the glade.

Chapter 9

Mariah let her eyes blaze into the broad expanse of James Lancaster's back. The pace he'd established was grueling, but she had no intention of complaining. If he and Dimetrius Cobb could endure it, so could she!

During the many hours of monotonous riding, she had time to question her impulsive decision to get involved in her father's ludicrous treasure scheme. It probably really was some cruel joke he was playing on her, though she couldn't reason out why he'd inflict such a punishment on her. Did he hate her? Wasn't being deserted when she was ten years old penalty enough for being born his child?

She found herself wondering about her escort, as well. Supposedly, he was her father's friend. Would Dunny lead him on a fruitless chase, too?

For some reason she didn't think Jamie Lancaster was a man who would be easily duped. There was a tense energy about him, an ever-so-subtle force rippling just below the surface. That he'd survived often on his instinct alone, she had no doubt. His command of himself showed even in the way he handled the bay stallion—firmly, yet gently. Despite herself, she realized she was watching him again, admiring his expert horsemanship.

It was then that it struck her—they were no longer traveling west. She sat up straighter in her saddle. The descending afternoon sun was positioned far to her left. They were heading north, where thick clouds were gathering overhead. Their billowy pewter-grayness appeared laden with the promise of rain, further troubling her. This trip was unpleasant enough without adding a summer thunderstorm to it.

"Mr. Lancaster! I want to talk to you!" She pressed her heels into Lilac Wind's flanks and urged the mare forward. The two men reined in their mounts to wait for her.

"What is it, Miss Morgan? Do you wish to rest again?"

"No, sir, I demand an explanation!" She drew Lilac Wind next to Jamie's horse. "Worcester lies due west. Why are we traveling north?"

"You noticed that, did you?" He exchanged glances with Dimetrius Cobb, who rolled his eyes heavenward.

"Yes. Explain yourself. Are you lost?"

"Hardly, Miss Morgan. I know the route well. We're taking a short detour."

"A detour? Why? You'll recall we both want to complete this journey as quickly as possible." She met his cool gaze levelly.

"I have personal business to attend to, a matter in which I was involved before making the agreement with your father. It won't take long to accomplish. The delay will be minimal."

"No! There will be no delays, no detours! As leader of this expedition, I demand that we turn west and continue toward Worcester."

Jamie smiled, but there was no warmth in it.

"Really, Miss Morgan, by now it should be obvious to you that you certainly aren't leading anything. But I'm not an unreasonable man. I always allow for choices. Your possibilities are these. You can go back to Framingham, or you can try to find your way to Worcester on your own. Of course, Mr. Flannery has been instructed not to give you the directions for finding the next piece of the puzzle unless I'm there. So your best option would seem to be to go along with us on this detour."

"You lied to my father and you lied to me! I won't associate with anyone so contemptible! I'll find my own way back to Boston, where I should have stayed in the first place!"

Mariah snapped up Lilac Wind's reins, but Jamie reached out and grabbed the horse's bridle, halting the animal.

"Your judgment has no basis in fact. I gave you and your father my word that I'd see his wishes accomplished, and so I shall—but *my* way. Whether you believe my oath or not doesn't matter. More to the point is how quickly you've forgotten about the outlaw bands who prowl these roads. What do you think they'd do to a lone woman they'd happen to find? Besides, wouldn't you rather return to Boston with your arms laden with Spanish doubloons, Miss Morgan? Think of the look of welcome that sight would bring to your good Dr. Hastings' face."

Mariah glared at him, for his tone sounded

heavy with sarcasm. Did he suspect her true feelings for Samuel? He made good points, she hated to admit, though she allowed no sign of agreement to show on her face. She hated him for being so right!

For a long moment, she said nothing, making herself think of Samuel and the work they could accomplish with the gold—if it were found. Finally, and with great effort, she swallowed her stubborn pride.

"Very well, Mr. Lancaster, you have the advantage for now. Against my better judgment, I'll follow the route you choose, as long as it ultimately achieves our goal. And I hope it involves finding shelter soon, for the weather seems to be taking a turn for the worse." A rumble of thunder vibrated in the distance, underscoring her words.

"It does, but we'll have to quicken our pace. Try to keep up." He wheeled his stallion around and urged the big animal to a canter.

"I'll keep up all right, James Lancaster, or die trying!" Mariah murmured angrily under her breath, digging her heels into Lilac Wind's sides. The roan mare snorted and plunged forward down the road.

The sky looked as full of wrath as Mariah felt. No patches of summer blue showed among the thick layers of churning gray clouds overhead. The breeze had turned fierce now, bringing with it the smell of impending rain.

Mariah began to wonder if they'd reach shelter before the clouds broke open and deluged them with rain. She was about to hail Jamie again to ask him how much farther they had to go, when a cabin loomed into view, amid a grove of pine trees.

Jamie pulled his horse up short and quickly dismounted, grabbing Lilac Wind's bridle as soon as Mariah came close.

"Dismount and keep your mare quiet!" he ordered in a low voice, gesturing to Dimetrius Cobb to come up beside him and do the same. Then he pulled his horse behind some tall bushes, motioning for Mariah and Dimetrius to follow.

"Reckon they're here?" the dwarf asked in the same hushed tone, glancing toward the cabin.

"I can't tell from this distance, but I don't want to take a chance on their seeing us first. I'm counting on the element of surprise."

"Right. Want me to circle 'round to the tunnel?"

"As usual, you read my mind. Have your pistol ready. I'll come in the side door."

"Aye." The small man nodded and hurried away, skirting to the left of the dense bushes.

"Mr. Lancaster, I demand—"

Jamie's hand came up swiftly to cover her mouth. His voice was commanding, close at her ear. "Don't talk at all, Miss Morgan, just listen to my orders. Trust me when I say it's very important that you do exactly as I tell you. Stay here with the horses. Don't make a sound, and keep the horses quiet, as well. Hold the reins securely and stroke their muzzles. If all goes well, we'll soon have that cabin to shelter us against the rain." He glanced skyward at the low-hanging clouds, then back to her. "Do you understand?"

She frowned and mumbled something against his

hand as she tried to pull it away from her mouth, but he only pressed his fingers harder against her lips and grabbed her wrist to pin it down to her side.

"Do you understand? Just nod your head."

After a pause, she moved her head up and down.

"Good. Remember, stay here."

She opened her mouth to lash out at him, but he was gone in a flash, ducking down and stealing away behind the bushes in the opposite direction from Cobb.

Putting her hands on her hips, she strained to see where he'd disappeared to, but the gathering darkness and the thick undergrowth kept her from doing so. Cobb's pony tossed his head then, almost wrenching the reins out of her hand. She gripped all the leather straps harder, murmuring soothingly to the horses, sensing they were nervous about the coming storm.

The cabin looked deserted, she noted, peering through an opening in the pine tree branches nearest to her. Made of log, it appeared to butt up against the high grassy hill behind it. A lean-to opened off the left side, but she couldn't tell if any animals were inside.

She sensed danger, yet couldn't say why or where it lay. Perhaps it had been Jamie's severe tone, the intense look in his eyes that had alerted her. Who could be in that cabin, here in the middle of nowhere?

Only normal forest sounds surrounded her—insects buzzing, birds singing, the increasing rustle of leaves moved by the rising wind.

"One thing's certain," she mumbled under her breath to the horses, "if the storm breaks, we're not waiting out here to be drenched or struck by lightning!"

Chapter 10

Jamie had visited Toby Jones and Lem Hollister's cabin little more than a month ago, when he'd brought in his furs. Now the cabin looked even more dilapidated than it had then. Of course, Jones and Hollister weren't the type to appreciate fine lodgings, and most likely considered it the perfect, deserted lair. They wouldn't be bothered by the fact that the roof over the front porch was collapsed on one end, and the porch itself was strewn with several broken chairs and logs for the cookstove. The front yard was overgrown with weeds and high grass and was the final resting place for a number of barrels and an unpainted freight wagon, minus its wheels.

He stood upright, pressing his back against the wide trunk of an oak tree he was using for cover. He knew he had to be extremely cautious. Hollister and Jones were not adversaries to be taken lightly. His last confrontation with them had nearly cost him his life.

Pulling his pistol from his waist holster, he checked the priming. Then he scanned the woods behind him, making certain no one was trailing him. A few more seconds, and Dimetrius would

be in position for the ambush. He was sure that
someone occupied the cabin. From this close
range, he could see the shape of at least one horse
in the lean-to. Was it Lem's powerful stallion, Sultan?

Squatting down and staying low, Jamie eased
himself away from the tree and headed for the far
side of the cabin where he knew a door was located.
When a stick cracked under his foot, he
froze and dropped to his belly, every muscle in his
body tense. His eyes and ears strained to catch the
slightest sound.

After a few seconds, he got to his feet and loped
to the side of the cabin. Huge raindrops pelted him
as he slammed his back against the rough-hewn log
wall next to the closed door. As he did, a bolt of
lightning suddenly streaked through the air, followed
instantly by an earsplitting crash of thunder.
He jumped at the loud sound, gripping his pistol
tighter and cursing the storm's poor timing.

The cabin was completely silent. Perhaps no one
was here after all.

There was only one way to find out. Raising his
pistol and cocking back the hammer, he stepped in
front of the plank door and smashed it in with a
swift kick. It crashed loudly against the inside wall
as he dashed inside, diving for the floor and rolling.

A man jumped to his feet and snatched at a pistol
lying within easy reach on the table. Jamie
raised himself up and fired.

"Ow!" the man yelled, grabbing for his right
hand, where the bullet had grazed him. Losing his

balance, he fell over backward, hitting the floor hard.

Jamie immediately jumped to his feet and stood over his adversary with his knife pointing at the man's chest. He held his smoking pistol in his other hand.

"God Almighty, Jamie, what're you doin'?" his victim demanded, wincing in pain. "You mighta killed me!"

"Just my way of saying hello, Toby, old boy. I wanted you to know this isn't exactly a social call. If I'd wanted you dead, you know you wouldn't be talking now. Where's Lem?"

"He ain't here. I ain't seen him in a while." Jones didn't meet his eyes.

"You never were a very good liar, Toby. You two are never far apart." He kept his gaze fastened on the short, burly man with Indian-braided black hair, knowing he could be as quick as a striking rattlesnake and just as deadly. He bent over and yanked Jones up by the shirtfront, pushing him at a straight-backed wooden chair next to the table. Jones landed hard on the rickety seat, making it teeter precariously.

"Take it easy, will you? My hand's killin' me!" he complained, clutching at his injury.

Jamie glanced around the single open room comprising the inside of the run-down cabin. Another chair, the wooden table, and a dilapidated bed in the far corner were the only other pieces of furniture. Faded red curtains hung over a nearby window. Reaching out, he ripped one off its rod and threw the ragged material toward Jones, who wrapped it gingerly around his bleeding palm.

"Now, I'm only going to ask you this one more time, Toby. Where's Lem?" He fingered the poniard's blade. "The way I see it, you still owe me for those pelts, plus a hell of a lot of aggravation."

"I don't know where he is, Jamie, I swear," Jones answered, swallowing hard as he stared at the deadly-looking knife.

"Ah, Toby, you disappoint me." He brought the poniard down with a swift slash, jamming the tip of it into the tabletop only a hairsbreath away from Jones' injured hand.

"Lord, don't!" Jones begged, snatching his hand away. Perspiration beaded his forehead.

Without warning, Mariah suddenly burst through the front door. "If you think I'm—"

Jamie's gaze flashed to her and Jones took the opportunity to smash out with his good fist. He caught Jamie squarely on the chin, sending him reeling backward to fall over the other chair and crash to the floor. Jones dove for his pistol on the table. As he raised it to fire at Jamie, a wooden trapdoor in the floor by the fireplace whipped open and banged against the wall. Dimetrius Cobb jumped out of the hole and fired his pistol at Jones, just as the other man's weapon exploded at Jamie.

Mariah screamed, covering her ears with her hands. Jones howled and grabbed for his right leg, falling to the floor. Outside, the storm erupted with another deafening peal of thunder and pounding hailstones.

Cobb was the first to move. He swiftly crossed the floor, yanked Jamie's knife out of the table, and held it threateningly over Jones. When he'd ascertained that the moaning man presented no threat, he quickly moved to Jamie, who was struggling to get to his feet, blood showing at his head. Mariah rushed forward to assist the dwarf in getting him to the chair.

"You could have gotten us all killed! Why the bloody hell didn't you stay with the horses?" Jamie demanded, shrugging her off and grabbing her by both wrists. Then he grimaced as his head began to spin, causing him to lose his balance and fall back hard into the chair.

Shaken, Mariah stared at him wide-eyed, stammering to defend herself. "I—I'm sorry. The storm broke. The lightning was so violent. I didn't want to be out in the open. I put the horses in the lean-to for protection."

"At least you did one thing right!" Jamie's frown was malevolent as he used the back of his hand to brush at the blood oozing down the side of his face.

"Somebody help me, I'm bleedin' to death!" Jones hollered, still holding his leg as he writhed on the floor by the door.

"I'll need some water and bandaging," Mariah informed Dimetrius, who nodded and moved to a cupboard near the cookstove.

While the small man searched the battered, paint-chipped storage cabinet, Mariah touched her handkerchief to Jamie's head where it was bleeding.

"The pistol ball only grazed you," she assessed. "You'll have to wait. Hold this in place." After he'd done so, she turned away, hurrying over to the side door to close it against the high wind and hail. Then she went to Toby Jones' side, stooping down next to the injured man.

"Stop moving and let me look at the wound," she ordered sharply. With nimble fingers, she carefully examined his leg.

"You can't do nothin'! Ow! That hurts! Get me to a doctor!"

Though the man ranted mightily, Mariah detected fear in his voice.

"I'm as close to a physician as you're going to find around here, so stop bellowing!" She tore open the man's trouser leg and peered at the wound. "It looks like the ball passed through the fleshy part of your thigh, but I can't be certain. Probably didn't hit a bone, judging by the movement you still have in your leg." She gestured toward the dwarf. "Bring those things here, please. This man needs attention first. His injury is worse than Mr. Lancaster's."

"You should let him bleed to death," Jamie stated, watching Dimetrius carry a wooden bucket half-filled with water and two dingy gray dish towels over to her.

"He probably wishes the same fate on you," Mariah snapped back. "These towels are too filthy to use for bandages. Mr. Cobb, could you please retrieve my valise from my saddle so I'll have more medical supplies with which to work?"

"I'll fetch it fer you, ma'am. I'll go by the tunnel. It comes out in the lean-to. Keep yer eye on this one, though." He waved a finger at Jones and handed Mariah Jamie's poniard. Then he disappeared through the trapdoor.

"What is this altercation all about, Mr. Lancaster? I demand an explanation.'' Mariah looked toward Jamie as she kicked the injured man's pistol out of reach. Then she quickly turned away from the men to lift her skirt and cut off a piece of her petticoat with the knife.

"Who in bloody blazes is this wench, Jamie?" Jones demanded through gritted teeth when she bent to swab his leg wound once again.

"More trouble than you'd care to have, Toby," came Jamie's sarcastic answer. "But she does know something about doctoring—maybe just enough to finish you off for me."

Mariah shot Jamie a scathing look, then fumbled at her patient's belt buckle.

"Hey! What're you doin'?" He tried to pull away, but couldn't.

"Toby—is that your name? I need your belt to try to stanch the flow of blood." Gently, she freed the leather strip and quickly wrapped it around the upper part of his thigh. Then, pulling as hard as she could, she cinched it up tightly. Working fast, she slashed the section of white petticoat into two pieces and folded them into thick wads. "Hold these over the wound," she directed. When he had them in place, she hurried to the only other window in the cabin and snatched down the two remaining ragged red curtain pieces. She tied these over the wads made from her undergarment, then turned her attention to his wounded hand.

Jamie watched her closely. The treatment she gave Toby exhibited calm efficiency and experience. Her ability was admirable—and surprising. While she'd done a good job wrapping his ribs back in Boston, more skill was necessary for treating gunshot wounds.

"You haven't told me what this is all about, Mr. Lancaster," she reminded, glancing toward him as she used the water in the bucket to wash Toby's hand.

"Jones here and his no-good partner, Lem Hollister, took something that didn't belong to them—beaver pelts. They were mine. I spent six months trapping for them up north. You see, Toby and Lem are a bit on the lazy side, light-fingered, and as ruthless as they come. They wait until someone else has done all the work, then they lay an ambush with a few bloodthirsty brigands like themselves, try to commit murder, then walk off with all the profits."

"Murder?" Mariah stopped to look from Jamie to the man he'd called Toby. The burly fellow averted his eyes.

"Disappointed you, didn't I, Tob?" Jamie's voice was heavy with sarcasm. "You and Lem should have checked the river after you and your boys throttled me and dumped me over that cliff. I managed to swim to shore with the cracked head you so generously bestowed on me, then make my way to Framingham. And speaking of heads, I could use a little attention here." He removed Mariah's handkerchief and looked at the bloodstain on it.

"You mean you'd lower yourself to let me tend you again?" She couldn't resist the gibe as she wrapped another petticoat piece around Toby's hand.

"Well, as you said before, you're as much of a doctor as we can get out here."

Mariah frowned, but carried the water bucket over to the table anyway. Dimetrius returned then and brought her faded tapestry valise to her. She rummaged around in it, drawing out a roll of white bandaging and several square wads of cotton. Wetting some of the cotton she dabbed at Jamie's head wound to clean it.

"You could use a lighter touch," he protested, wincing away from her ministrations.

"I would if I thought you deserved it. The bullet creased the skin, but not deeply enough to require suturing. Here. Hold this in place." She thrust one of the squares of cotton into his hand, then guided his fingers to his forehead. Taking the roll of bandaging, she cut off a long strip of it with the knife and wrapped it around his head to hold the pad in place over the wound.

She tended his injury as speedily as possible, very much aware of being so near to him. When her fingers brushed his damp black hair as she was applying the bandage, her stomach rippled, and small details about him jumped out at her. She saw the dark beginnings of whiskers shadowing the lower half of his face, making his ruggedly handsome features stand out even more. Beads of sweat dotted his forehead, and tiny untanned creases edged his eyes—those vibrant, mesmerizing pale-blue eyes.

She blinked, surprised by the turn her thoughts had taken. Then for an instant, she thought how her impulsive run into the cabin to escape the storm might have gotten Jamie killed. Just a little more to the right, and the bullet would have ripped through his brain and ended his life. She couldn't bear to be responsible for his death—for *anyone's* death, she added quickly to herself.

But then anger flashed through her. None of this would have happened if he hadn't detoured from the original route.

"Lem ain't around, but Sultan's in the lean-to," Dimetrius stated, breaking into her turbulent thoughts.

"I thought so," Jamie replied, turning toward Toby Jones. "I assumed you two bootlegged my pelts for any price you could get. No doubt you spent the money as fast as you got it."

Jones grinned. "And a right high old time we had, too, last month! Whiskey and women for over two weeks. We almost felt guilty that you couldn't enjoy yourself with us."

"Almost," Jamie repeated coolly. "Well, there's restitution to be made. Sultan should just about square the score."

"You must be daft!" Jones leaned forward, then grimaced from the quick movement. "You can't take him. You know how Lem feels about that black."

Jamie's smile was diabolical. "Precisely. He'd rather get shot than lose Sultan, which is exactly why I'll be taking the stallion. He's a grand animal, with much too fine a bloodline for the likes of Hollister."

"There'll be hell to pay for this." Jones shook his head.

"Any time Lem is ready."

Mariah, watching intently, shuddered at the

coldness she heard in Jamie's voice. She decided she didn't want to be in the same place when he and this Lem Hollister finally met again.

She busied herself changing Toby's makeshift curtain bandage, suturing the two bullet holes, and applying a more secure covering. Toby clenched his teeth while she cleaned and stitched the shredded skin, but he didn't prevent her from doing the grisly task.

"We're going to be your houseguests for the night, Toby, old man," Jamie informed him after he'd walked to the front door to check the weather. "Looks like we're in for a long, steady rain."

Mariah saw him look down and shake his head. His left arm was pressed close against his side.

"It's not unusual to experience dizziness with a head wound like that. And your bruised ribs weren't helped in the fall you took. You should get off your feet." She started forward to help him.

He raised his hand to stop her. "I can manage. See to finding some food here. This place isn't elegant, but it's where we're staying tonight."

Mariah wanted to argue as she gazed around the dirty cabin. Her skin crawled at the thought of spending the night in such a place—and with an accused murderer, no less. But what alternative did she have?

She suddenly felt too tired to face an argument with Jamie. Though it galled her to admit it, she realized she'd lose anyway. She already knew that much about defying him. As much as she mightily resented the fact, he did hold the upper hand here. And he knew it.

Chapter 11

"By all means, you take the bed, Miss Morgan," Jamie offered, his voice mockingly gallant.

"All right. Thank you," she replied, looking at him warily.

"Think nothing of it. The floor's more comfortable than that bed anyway. I'll be on guard in case Toby tries anything or Lem Hollister makes an appearance."

"Well, I'll sleep much easier knowing *that!*" she snapped as she watched him shake open his blanket and spread it out on the floor. He positioned his saddle at the head of the makeshift bed for a pillow. While he was bent over, his hand shot out to grab one of the posts of the bed. He closed his eyes and stood still for several moments.

"You shouldn't move about so much," she warned. Instinctively she stepped forward to help him, but then stopped, reluctant to touch him again. She felt more comfortable keeping her distance.

His eyes opened again. "I'm no stranger to such injuries." His words were curt. "I know the symptoms."

"In my medical experience, I don't recall testiness being one of them."

"That occurs when the malady was caused by a careless female!"

"I'm not going to get into that debate with you again!"

She turned her back to him, focusing her anger on the so-called bed. The rickety cots at Samuel Hastings' hospital looked more inviting—and stable. But she felt too weary to care. Her body ached in every muscle and her limbs felt as heavy as boulders.

She smoothed the ragged cover on top of the lumpy mattress, then spread her traveling blanket over that. When she punched up the nearly flat feather pillow, she noticed how dirty and stained it was. Reluctant to put her head directly on it, she rummaged in her valise for a clean blouse, which she wrapped around the pillow.

Before lying down, she glanced about the cabin. Dimetrius Cobb's bedroll was arranged on the floor by the unlighted fireplace. Jones hadn't moved from the spot where he'd fallen by the side door. His eyes met hers in a look that could only be read as lecherous. Frowning, she lifted her chin and moved her gaze to Jamie, who'd settled himself on his blanket. He lay directly in line with the front door, which had been left open to allow the coolness from the now abating storm to penetrate the stifling room.

"Turn down the lamp, Miss Morgan," he advised. "Your silhouette makes a fine target. Someone might be tempted to shoot at it."

She glared at him angrily, but decided it would be prudent to do as he said.

For the next few hours she tossed and turned on the lumpy mattress. Though she was exhausted, sleep would not come. She winced as the prickly straw jutting through the blanket stuck her in several places.

The storm had ended, and quiet prevailed. So what could be the reason for her restlessness? Perhaps it was caused by the fact that she was in a dirty, pest-infested cabin with a wounded thief, a dwarf who was more than a little handy with a pistol, and Jamie Lancaster, who defied description, but who was more disturbing to her than the other two men put together.

A mosquito whined near her ear. She batted at it, hating its annoying sound and potential sting, feeling hot, itchy, and miserable. She shuddered, remembering the huge cockroach she'd spotted darting out of the bed earlier.

Jagged rays of bright moonlight streamed through the few clean places on the two filthy windows and through the open doorways. Mariah's glance strayed over Toby Jones. He appeared to be sleeping soundly, despite his wounds. She let her gaze meander to where Jamie lay, and wondered how much of a headache he had. Then she reminded herself that he deserved it and more for dragging them into this mess!

He turned over on his back just then, and Mariah could see his face profiled in the moonlight. A quivering began in her stomach again as she studied his strikingly handsome features. They were in shadow mostly, but her mind's eye filled in the lines of his straight nose and strong, square jaw. The strip of bandaging around his head gave him a rakish look, almost like an eye-patched pirate.

A sigh escaped her lips before she could stop it. What was this attraction she felt toward him? It stirred her body, troubled her mind. How could she feel so drawn to him? She didn't like him at all—he was overbearing and deceitful. So why did her senses react so crazily whenever she looked at him? Even now, when he was asleep, she felt her pulse quicken at the sight of him. Samuel Hastings never made her feel this way, and she was in love with him!

She turned over, disgusted with herself for acting so foolishly. She suddenly couldn't stand it in the humid cabin. Swinging her legs off the bed, she stood up and tiptoed around Jamie, careful not to let her skirt brush him as she passed.

As soon as she stepped through the doorway, she froze at the sound of a pistol hammer being cocked.

"You should take care and go back inside to sleep, ma'am," came a voice in the dark. "That way you won't get shot."

Mariah saw Dimetrius step out of the darkness behind two wooden barrels stacked together on the front porch. He uncocked his pistol and stuck it into the waistband of his black breeches.

"I couldn't sleep. I only wanted to come out here for a few minutes where it's cooler."

He nodded and leaned back against a vertical post supporting the porch. Mariah sat down on the stone front steps. After a few minutes, she couldn't resist questioning him.

"The furs that Mr. Lancaster claims were stolen by Mr. Jones—did they belong to you, too?"

"Naw, Jamie trapped all of them. I met up with him in Boston after Lem an' his boys tried to do him in."

"Then why did you come along today?"

"I wanted to help Jamie get back at them. I owe him." The small man shifted around toward Mariah. He was hardly taller than one of the barrels he'd been hiding behind.

"Jamie saved my life more'n once since I've known him," he continued in a low voice. "An' I lost count of all the times he stood up fer me agin' folks who figure it's right to poke fun at a man's size." He shook his head and snorted a laugh. "We bin in some powerful good brawls together."

Mariah noted the respect in his voice when he spoke of his friend. But why these two men found such enjoyment in fighting escaped her. At the same time, she liked hearing how Jamie had befriended Dimetrius and gained the small man's loyalty. So there was a measure of compassion in her escort. That fact surprised her. She wouldn't mind seeing more of that side of him. As it was, she knew only his violent, arrogant, and overbearing side.

"How long have you known each other?" she asked, sensing Dimetrius' willingness to talk.

"Oh, Jamie an' me go way back, to when he first left his family an' went to sea. His folks is real well-to-do an' important. His pa's in bankin' in New York City. Wanted his sons to do the same. Jamie's two brothers—they're older'n him—did what their pa wanted. Jamie was goin' to, too. He

told me he was plannin' on weddin' up with a
pretty little thing—a preacher's daughter, name of
Evangelene. But she got killed with her pa in a
Indian raid. So Jamie decided he'd do what he always wanted, that bein' to see the world. He signed
up on the same ship as me. That was ten years
ago. He's bin followin' his dreams ever since. Far's
I know, his family'd jus' as soon fergit he's one of
them.''

"Somehow that doesn't surprise me," Mariah
agreed.

"Yer mighty interested in Jamie."

"N-no, not really," she stammered, caught off
guard. "I was only making conversation."

"Most folks are curious about *me*, wantin' to
know if'n there're any more like me at home an'
such.''

"That's too impolite to ask," Mariah replied
quickly.

"Well, there ain't," Dimetrius continued, as
though she hadn't spoken. "My ma died birthin'
me. My pa always said it was a blessin' she did,
'cause seein' how I turned out would've killed her
anyway. We didn't get on together too well, me an'
my pa. I ran away to sea as soon as I could.''

Hearing the bitterness in his voice, Mariah's
heart went out to him. Life must be so hard for
him. God knew, it was difficult enough for men
and women of normal size to try to live decently
and carve a country out of the North American
wilderness.

"Reckon I'll be checkin' on the horses," he
said, descending the steps and disappearing into
the shadows at the side of the cabin.

Mariah stood up and strolled out into the yard. The night was sultry but fresh-smelling from the rain. The wet grass felt good under her bare feet. Coming to an old fallen oak tree, she sat down on the trunk and gazed up at the stars, breathing deeply of the warm summer air.

"You shouldn't be out here alone."

She started and almost fell off the log at the sound of the deep voice close behind her. Spinning halfway around, she glimpsed Jamie. She hadn't heard him approach at all. He walked around the tree to stand in front of her.

"I couldn't sleep," she explained, hastily coming to her feet.

"Neither could I. My head's pounding like a herd of horses is galloping around inside it. Don't worry, I don't expect any sympathy." He rubbed the back of his neck with his hand.

"And you'll get none. The pain will likely last for a day at least." She knew she was talking too fast, but he could unnerve her so easily. The vibrations from his deep-timbred voice seemed to find her spine and run swiftly down it, shocking her senses to alertness.

"You really *do* know what you're doing, don't you?"

His question surprised her. "What do you mean?" she asked warily.

"I'm talking about your medical knowledge. I watched you in the cabin. You acted quickly and expertly."

"W-why, thank you." She felt uncertain of how to react to his praise.

"I'll admit I've never known a woman to have

a talent for doctoring. Most of the women I know would've either shot Toby to put him out of his misery or fainted dead away at the sight of his wound.''

"I'm not like the women you know, Mr. Lancaster. Don't compare me to them." She started to move past him to return to the cabin, but he grabbed her arm and swung her around, forcing her to face him.

"Now you've made me regret my compliment. You are by far the most exasperating, stubborn, judgmental woman I've ever had the misfortune to meet. I thought your father and I were friends. But somewhere along the line I must have done something to make him hate me—seeing as how he's saddled me with *you.*"

Mariah wrenched her arm out of his rough grasp. "It's amazing that you should say that, because I've been thinking the same thing! But at least we understand each other, Mr. Lancaster. I know exactly what to expect from you, and now you know what to expect from me—"

"So you know what to expect, do you?" His wrath exploded. Clutching her by the upper arms, he yanked her forward against him. Then he lowered his head and planted a hard kiss on her mouth.

Mariah's protests were smothered against his lips. His body was like rock against hers; she could feel every part of it where it was molded against her. Her mind screamed resistance, but she was helpless to express it. Her flesh ignited with sweet sensations as he overpowered her and held her prisoner in his arms. Then, just as abruptly as he'd grabbed her, he let her go, setting her away from him. Seething with fury, she swung her hand up, but he easily parried her intended slap, gripping her wrist so tightly she winced from the pain.

"Now that was most predictable, Miss Morgan," he said coolly, masking the excitement he felt surging through him. "But you'll learn that I never do the expected. I live by my own rules, holding myself accountable to no one, only to my own conscience. You'd do well to remember that fact." He released her wrist but kept his eyes locked on hers. The moonlight illuminated her face, revealing her outraged expression. The thought of the sweet taste of her lips and the heat of her body coursed through him, arousing him and setting his blood afire. By great effort, he resisted the urge to kiss her again.

"We need to have one more point understood," he made himself continue. "*I* am in charge of this expedition. When I give you an order, you're to obey it to the letter. You might have gotten yourself killed today by acting on your own and bursting into the cabin. How would I have explained your death to Dunny?"

"Ha! I'd be dead and all you'd worry about would be how you'd explain my demise to my father! I'm certain you'd never blame yourself or admit to any negligence."

"Negligence? You're the one who disobeyed my orders. I won't allow—"

"*You* won't allow!" she cut in fiercely. "*You* were the cause of our being thrust into such a dangerous situation in the first place! Yet you blame *me* for nearly getting myself and everyone else shot. Incredible! You didn't bother to explain anything to me before you went to the cabin. You ordered me to stay with the horses, but I could barely hold them when they became skittish in the storm. You left me exposed to the pouring rain, winds, and dangerous lightning. And you wonder why I burst into the cabin seeking shelter?'' So angry was she that she had to pause for a moment to suck in a large gulp of air before being able to go on. ''Well, I've had just about all I'm going to take of your arrogance and bullying condescension. I consider you a contemptible barbarian! There's no reasoning with you. Stay away from me, James Lancaster. Don't give me orders, and don't ever touch me again!''

Whirling around on her heel, she hiked up her skirt and stomped through the tall grass back toward the cabin.

Jamie watched her departure, allowing a smirk to curl his lip. He wasn't sure what had possessed him to suddenly kiss her. It had been just an impulse, nothing more. But he enjoyed sparking her anger and seeing it burst forth in her blue-green eyes, animating her lovely features. No shrinking flower, this Miss Mariah Morgan! She wouldn't be cowed. While that trait about her exasperated him mightily, he couldn't help but admire her for standing up to him.

An owl hooted in a nearby tree. Jamie turned his head toward the sound, but heard it absently. His thoughts remained on Mariah. He felt surprised by the effect she had on him. His heart had raced when he'd held her close and kissed her. Only now had it begun to slacken. He could still feel the softness of her body pressed against his. He'd felt the tense power of her resistance, and it only served to intrigue him, not discourage him.

"I'm thinkin' that one's more wildcat to handle than most of the wenches yer used to." Dimetrius stepped out of the shadows to stand next to Jamie.

"Perhaps. But you know I've never been one to pass by a challenge. She could use some taming."

"And you reckon yer man enough to do it." The dwarf spoke the words more as a statement than a question.

"Have you ever met the woman I couldn't master?"

Dimetrius chuckled. "Nay, I don't think I have—until maybe now! I'm goin' to check the back of the cabin. All's quiet out here. No sign of Lem."

"Good. I'll spell you in two hours."

He watched the small man walk away, still thinking about Mariah. Had she ever allowed her body to be consumed by the passion he'd sensed in her? Would loving her completely be as sweet as the taste of the brief kiss he'd just stolen from her? She'd warned him not to touch her again. What would she do if he not only touched her, but demanded her ultimate surrender?

Chapter 12

Dimetrius helped Mariah mount Lilac Wind the next morning.

"The weather's cleared," Jamie observed, glancing at the cloudless azure sky. "We should reach Worcester by mid-afternoon. Dimetrius, old friend," he said, clasping the small man's hand, "thanks for your help in there yesterday." He tilted his head toward the cabin, then swung up onto Sultan, the magnificent black stallion he had appropriated from Lem Hollister.

"You'd have done the same fer me, Jamie. Good luck to you on the rest of yer journey." Dimetrius looked over at Mariah, then back to his friend, adding in a voice too low for her to hear, "You're goin' to need it!"

"I know," Jamie agreed, blowing out his breath in a heavy sigh that suggested resignation to a terrible fate. "Sell my horse when you get back to Framingham and use the money any way you wish. See that a doctor is sent out here for Toby. I wouldn't want him to die before he tells Lem about our visit. Lem kept a woman on a farm just south of Framingham. I suspect he's there with her, so take care you don't stay around the town too long after he finds out I've taken Sultan. If all goes well, I'll soon have the money for my ship, and you can come with me to all the far ports we've talked about for so long. I'll see you in Boston as soon as the treasure hunt is through.''

Dimetrius grinned and nodded as he mounted his pony.

''You're really going to steal that horse, aren't you?'' Mariah accused Jamie.

He swung around to look at her, his eyes narrowed. '' 'Steal' is a harsh word, Miss Morgan, and inappropriately used in this instance. I view my actions in an entirely different light. Sultan is merely collateral against the debt Lem Hollister owes me for my furs.''

''Won't this Hollister come after us to regain his horse?''

''Most assuredly. That's what I want him to do.''

''Then you risk not only your life—which is of no consequence to me—but also mine. I resent being put in that position.''

Jamie spurred Sultan up beside her. ''Resent all you wish, woman, but this is the way it's going to be. You can take heart in hoping that Lem doesn't catch up to us until we've attained all the remaining pieces of your father's puzzle. Then if he kills me, the map will be entirely yours. That should delight you. Of course, Lem might try to kill you, too. I'll try to prevent that occurrence, *if* you don't antagonize me to the point where I'm tempted to strangle you myself!''

With that, he kicked his heels into the big black's sides and plunged into the woods, leaving Mariah to follow after him the best she could.

She pushed Lilac Wind to keep pace with the stallion, riding a little behind Jamie so conversation with him wouldn't be possible. He aggravated her so much! How different he was from Samuel Hastings. Heaven help her, but for five years she'd longed for Samuel to do what Jamie had done so spontaneously last night—grab her and kiss her. But Samuel would never do such a thing. He was a totally self-sacrificing man, a complete gentleman, who wouldn't dream of taking such liberties with her. And, of course, as a properly bred woman, she shouldn't wish him to do so. But she loved him so much, and even though he was much older than she—almost her father's age—she longed to be more to him than just a valued assistant. Would Samuel ever see her as filling more than that capacity? Would he ever love her? Would Jamie Lancaster ever kiss her again?

Her eyes widened in shock at the sudden change of direction her thoughts had taken. Of course, she didn't want that self-important, ill-mannered bully to kiss her again! How could she even think about the taste of his lips on hers, the feel of his body molded against hers, how handsome and self-possessed he now looked astride the big black stallion? She hated him, hated the way he'd snatched her breath away in a grassy, moonlit yard and left her tossing and turning all night, assailed by troubling dreams of him!

She forced her thoughts back to the hospital and how happy Samuel would be to not only see her again, but to receive the money she'd be bringing him. Every mile she traveled with Jamie Lancaster brought her closer to that most-desired goal, she reminded herself, gritting her teeth and plodding on.

Late in the afternoon, they came upon four riders whose scruffy appearances reminded Mariah of the gang of thieves who'd attacked the Framingham coach. Their faces sported shaggy beards and their clothes looked dirty and well worn, likely accounting for the offensive odor that reached her as they neared. They stopped their horses, blocking the road.

"Well now, good day to you, mistress," the tallest of them said, doffing his hat in her direction. "Lovely day, ain't it?"

The other three men grinned in agreement. The leader was thin and wide-shouldered, perhaps in his late thirties. It was difficult to tell his age because of the grime and whiskers covering his face. He snatched off the tricorn of the man next to him and batted him with it.

"Ain't you got no manners, Hock? This here's a proper lady. Git them hats off, lads." The other two followed his orders.

Mariah gave a little nod of acknowledgment, but said nothing. She didn't want to encourage their attentions.

"These be mighty fine pieces of horseflesh an' womanflesh you got here, stranger," the leader continued, turning toward Jamie.

The man's tone was friendly enough, but Mariah noticed his squinty dark eyes darted about, apparently taking in everything.

"You've a good eye for quality, mate, as have

I. Now, I'll thank you and your friends to allow us to continue on with our journey.''

Jamie's voice sounded casual, his manner seemingly at ease. Yet Mariah saw he kept his right hand poised on the handle of a pistol held in a holster built onto his saddle. The leader's eyes fixed on the same point.

"Sure enough, stranger. You an' yer lady pass right on by. We got to be gittin' on to our business, too. Move over, lads."

"Come along, Miss Morgan." Jamie beckoned, giving his head a sharp tilt toward the direction in which the road lay.

She quickly urged Lilac Wind forward. As she passed the four men, she felt the leader's eyes on her. The others called raucous farewells, elbowing each other.

Jamie pulled up Sultan after they'd rounded a bend and lost sight of the men.

"I didn't like the look of that bunch," he said. "The next stretch of road is fairly secluded. No farms that I know of in the vicinity."

"Do you think they mean to harm us?" She suddenly felt more frightened.

"Perhaps not. They may have been just passing by. To be on the safe side, we'll leave the main road here and follow this side fork." He pointed to his right, then wheeled Sultan in that direction.

Mariah didn't argue with him. He seemed much more sure of himself in the wilderness than she ever could be.

They followed a winding course, turning off the narrow side road often, then returning to it. Finally, Jamie signaled for her to stop by a small stream and dismounted.

"We'll water the horses here," he said, coming to help her down from Lilac Wind.

His hands didn't linger on her waist after he steadied her on the ground, but she felt the imprint of them on her sides as if he were still holding her. The sensation added to her uneasiness.

She could tell by the way he glanced around that he was distracted. All was quiet, except for the trickle of the water in the stream. She welcomed the chance to walk around and stretch her legs.

"Don't wander off," he warned when she made her way over the narrow stream along a number of stones.

She stopped just before she reached a patch of tall, pink-tinged white wildflowers. "I was only going to look at the blossoms. Do you think those men are following us?" She watched him lead the horses to the edge of the stream.

"I don't know. It's just a feeling . . . His eyes darted to the trees and thick undergrowth around them.

Was she feeling the same thing, or was it just her imagination? She negotiated the rocks to go back across the stream, hating to admit inside that she felt safer close to Jamie.

"I'm going to double back through these trees to see if we are being stalked. I won't be gone long. You stay here and—"

"No!" she interrupted, then realized how defiant she sounded. "I mean, I'll do what you say, but I'd prefer to go with you."

His eyes held hers. "You'll do as I say?" he repeated, looking surprised.

"I just wish you'd ask instead of order. I'm still angry with you over all that happened back at the cabin, but we could be in grave danger here. We both sense it. I think it's wise to set aside our differences for the meanwhile."

"I fully agree." He still looked skeptical about her cooperation as he came around to help her mount. This time his hands did stay around her waist a little longer than necessary. "At times, you do show good sense."

"Well, you needn't sound so amazed by that."

A short distance from the brook, they tethered the horses and crept to a small clearing. Lying on their stomachs on the ground and pushing aside some of the tall weeds, they could see the leader of the men who had stopped them talking to the one he'd called Hock. They stood by a campfire where a tripod made of sturdy tree branches held a steaming iron kettle suspended over the flames.

"What do you mean, you can't find no trail for 'em?" the leader demanded. "They couldn't jus' disappear! You saw that big black stallion an' heard the fancy way he talked. They was rich folks, likely carryin' plenty of money. Can't you three do nothin' right?"

"Well, you couldn't find 'em neither," Hock said defensively. "Otherwise, you wouldn't be back here to camp."

"Aah, quit yer blabberin'. I was jus' goin' to check the west trail. You git Borden an' Teems an' meet me by the dead oak. We'll find 'em b'fore dark. I got me a real itch to have that woman."

Mariah gasped but the sound didn't carry to the camp. Jamie shot her a fierce glare of warning, then looked back toward the men. Without hesitation, they strode to their horses, mounted, and rode away.

Jamie rolled over onto his back and expelled his breath through his teeth. "I told you before we departed on this journey that it wouldn't be like a stroll through the Boston Common. Don't worry, they haven't found us yet. But they're a bad bunch, all right. They likely know this area much better than I do, and four against one isn't to my taste."

"But you can't let them find us. You took on six bandits who attacked the coach and captured them."

"Dimetrius was with me then."

"But I can help."

He sent her a disparaging look. "As I said, four against one." He turned onto his stomach again to continue his survey of the clearing.

She frowned at his dismissal, but held in her terse retort, because she really couldn't think of any way to assist him. What did she know about capturing cutthroats? The very thought sent a terrible fear pulsing through her. She still had her small pistol hidden away in her pocket, but she'd only shot it at an old tree for target practice years ago under her uncle's supervision. She'd never aimed at a man. She couldn't think of shooting a person. Yet what if the men looking for them captured her? She shuddered at the thought of what they'd do to her. Could she use her pistol to defend herself then?

"What are you going to do?" she asked somberly.

"I don't know. Keep quiet so I can devise a plan."

He sounded annoyed. She knew it wasn't directed at her, but was caused by their dangerous situation. She turned her attention to the campsite. Her eyes flicked over the fire, the cook kettle. Suddenly, a thought flashed through her mind. She sat up quickly.

"What is it?" he said, raising himself to his knees and turning toward her.

"I have an idea!"

He seemed to relax a bit, but his voice held a note of skepticism when he spoke. "Of course, you have an idea. All right, I'll entertain any suggestion at this point."

"What if we could take some action to prevent them from following us? That would be better than confronting all of them, wouldn't it?" She grew more excited as the scheme filled out in her mind.

"Of course. But what, pray tell, could stop them, short of pistols at close range?" Impatience showed in his creased brow.

"We could use *Veronicastrum virginicum* on them." She jumped to her feet. "We must go back to the stream!"

"Stop!" He stood and grabbed her arm. "What in the name of heaven are you talking about, woman?"

"*Veronicastrum virginicum*—Culver's Root." Now she was growing impatient with him. "It's a tall perennial herb with pinkish-white flower clusters. Its roots can be used as a powerful physic.

Fresh Culver's Root has a strong cleansing effect on the intestines. Indians have used it in many ways, including during ceremonial purifications. Dr. Hastings has made a brilliant detailed study of native American plants and their medicinal uses. Believe me, I've seen Culver's Root work. I think I saw some of the flowers back at the stream. If I can get the root and add it to their simmering stewpot over there . . ."

Jamie smiled. "I follow your line of thinking. If this substance works as you say it does, after our would-be ambushers eat their suppers, they—"

"Won't be able to stand up, let alone sit their horses to search for us," she finished for him. "By the time they recover, we'll be far away. Come, we must work quickly."

Hiking up her skirt, she hurried past him toward the place where they'd concealed their mounts. Jamie followed her, marveling that she might have conjured up an ingenious solution to a dangerous dilemma.

A quarter of an hour later, they cautiously returned to their spying place.

"You remain here while I go into the camp. Can you shoot a pistol?" Jamie asked, checking the priming of his weapon.

"Yes, though I don't guarantee my accuracy. I have my own weapon." She fished the hidden pistol out of her skirt pocket.

His eyes widened. "Where did that come from?"

She looked directly at him. "I brought it with

me as a defense against you, if need be. Unfortunately, I didn't have it with me last night.''

His dark brow cocked. ''And if you'd had it?''

''I likely would have shot you and wouldn't be in this predicament now!''

His brow furrowed slightly. ''That's a point I'll argue with you another time. Right now we have other problems to attend to.'' He glanced again at her pistol. ''Shooting accuracy won't matter at this long range—you couldn't hit anything anyway. But the noise would cause a diversion if I needed it.'' He jammed his pistol in the waistband of his breeches, then took her handkerchief with the Culver's Root wrapped inside. ''Now, I'm just to add these pieces to the pot of food?''

''Yes. It will mix with whatever hot liquid is steaming in the kettle to release the potent ingredient.''

He nodded, then caught her eyes with his. ''If they return to camp and I should run into trouble, you escape from here as swiftly as you can, understand?''

''But—''

''No argument! Just do as I say.'' His look was fierce. ''Just ride the main road as fast as you can to Worcester.''

He turned away before she could say anything more and scurried over the rocks through the thick grass and weeds to the camp.

She hardly dared to breathe. Her heart pounded with fear that the miscreants would return and discover Jamie. Nervously clutching the pistol, she scanned the clearing.

Jamie made quick work of tossing the physic root

into the cook pot and stirring it with his knife blade.

Suddenly, she heard a shout. With a small cry of alarm, she swung around in the direction of a grove of dense pines to her right, from where the call had come. The evil men must be coming back! An answering shout a little closer by met her ears, sending panic through her.

"Oh, hurry, Jamie!" she urged under her breath, afraid to call the words to him. He must have heard the same shouts as she, for his head turned in that direction. Without another moment's hesitation, he sprinted toward her, jumping over the boulders and bushes she was using for cover. He ducked down beside her out of sight just as the four men rode into camp. For a few tense seconds, they waited to see if the men had seen anything amiss.

Finally, three of them dismounted, acting as if nothing were wrong. She glanced at Jamie, who was breathing hard from the exertion of his mad dash. His eyes met hers in unspoken communication—he'd succeeded, but just barely. Another few seconds and . . .

She didn't want to think about that horrible possibility. He was safe beside her. For the moment, they were both unharmed.

"I ain't goin' out lookin' agin till I git some victuals in me. I ain't had nothin' to eat all day," one of the men announced, taking a wooden bowl out of his saddlebag. All of them but the leader followed suit.

"Always thinkin' of yer bellies!" he snapped, shaking a fist at them. "Bah! Eat quick then, you fools. I'm goin' to the east road. Meet me there.

They must've give us the slip an' headed that way."
He wheeled his horse around, then twisted in the
saddle to look back at his men. "Save me some of
that rabbit stew, you hear? I'm jus' as hungry as
you pack of wolves, but I'm seein' to business
first!"

He spurred his horse away, leaving the others to
attack the steaming kettle. They pushed and shoved
each other, vying for the first ladlefuls of the stew.

"Was there time enough for the root to mix?"
Jamie whispered.

"I think so. You put in a large enough quantity
of it to make up for the lack of steeping time. That
will be a rabbit stew they won't soon forget!"

Despite the danger they were in, she couldn't
keep a slight smile from touching her lips. Jamie
smiled back at her.

"Come on," he said, "we can't afford to stay
around to enjoy the results of your medicinal root.
Stay low."

On hands and knees, they stole silently away
from the clearing.

Chapter 13

They met no other adversaries on the road. Jamie spent the rest of the trip pondering his companion's unexpected resourcefulness. He knew that women often used native plants for medicinal purposes, but he doubted that they used them for self-defense. The very thought of it made him chuckle.

Their arrival in the thriving town of Worcester that afternoon went virtually unnoticed by the townspeople, whose attention appeared to be consumed by a traveling gypsy troupe entertaining from three wagons set up in front of the blacksmith's shop. Mariah thought they were going to pass the crowd gathered to watch the colorfully dressed entertainers who were juggling and performing acrobatics, but Jamie reined in Sultan by the third wagon, where a beautiful, black-haired woman danced barefoot on a makeshift stage to the lively music of a mandolin. A large group of men enthusiastically encouraged her gyrations, which sent her full red skirt whirling out to reveal her long, naked legs. Her low-cut bright pink blouse left little to the imagination concerning the voluptuous mounds that lay underneath. When she ended her dance by collapsing to the stage in a graceful pose that left her skirt to float down about her, uproarious applause erupted from the audience. The dancer was quickly on her feet to gather up the coins being tossed by the men.

"Antonya Natouri, divine dancer!"

Mariah was shocked to hear Jamie call the greeting. The woman's head jerked up, and she let out a shriek of joy when she spotted him. Bounding down the steps, she reached him just as he dismounted, and threw her arms around his neck, covering his face with kisses.

"Oh, Jamie, my love, my heart, is it really you?"

He laughed and pulled her against him with one hand. With the other, he captured her chin and held her face still while he gave her the longest, deepest kiss Mariah had ever seen. When he finally pulled away, the woman called Antonya was breathing heavily and leaning back limply in his arms.

"My life is complete again," she gasped. "No man's kisses turn my blood to liquid fire like yours do, my passion!"

"You're as beautiful as ever, vixen!" he proclaimed, entwining his hand in her long hair and guiding her mouth to his again. Her arms clung to him as she pressed her body against his and moved one leg between his two to get as close to him as possible.

Shocked at their wanton behavior, Mariah stared at them dumbfounded. Then her anger flared. Apparently, James Lancaster was quite prone to accosting women and kissing them!

The crowd of admiring men cheered the two of them, but Mariah felt outraged. Those kisses were the most blatant display of sensuality she'd ever witnessed. She knew she shouldn't watch such a disgraceful scene, but she was powerless to turn away from it. Finally, the rest of the gypsy troupe moved in to surround Jamie and Antonya, breaking their embrace and pounding him on the back and pumping his hand in greeting.

Her face flushed with heat, Mariah yanked on Lilac Wind's reins. At the edge of the crowd she stopped an old man crossing the street, leaning down to speak to him.

"I'm looking for Flannery's dry-goods store. Can you direct me to it?"

"Turn left at the next street. It's five buildin's down on the right," he answered, showing a tooth-less grin as he pointed the way.

"Thank you." Putting her heels into Lilac Wind's sides, she cantered the horse up the dirt street to the front of the store and quickly dismounted, tying the reins around the hitching rail.

Brushing at the travel dust on her dark-blue jacket, she paused for a moment just inside the doorway to let her eyes adjust to the dimmer light.

"Can I be helpin' you, young woman?" came a hearty voice from a man standing behind a long counter.

"Uh, yes, I'm trying to locate Ezra Flannery."

"Well, I'm him, so look no further."

The store was deserted, so Mariah stepped further inside, dodging around tables laden with shoes, boots, pots and pans, and bolts of colorful material before she stopped at the counter. The man who'd spoken was well into his fifties, his head bald on top but covered with unruly long gray strands along the sides and back. He wore a tan cotton shirt that strained over his large paunch of a stomach. Bushy gray sideburns jutted out from the sides of his face, almost obliterating his cheeks. Happily, there was a gentleness in his deeply-lined brown eyes.

"I'm Mariah Morgan. I believe you know my father, Dunsley Morgan. He sent me to obtain a letter from you."

The man eyed her for a long moment. "Mama, come out here," he suddenly called over his shoulder. A heavyset woman wearing a plain green dress and a long white apron emerged from behind a curtained doorway. Her graying chestnut hair was pulled back in a tight bun much like Mariah's.

"What is it, Ezra?" she asked, casting a glance toward Mariah.

"This be Dunny's girl," Ezra told her. And to Mariah he said, "This be my wife Molly."

"How do you do, Mrs. Flannery?"

"Oh, child, I'm so pleased to meet you." The older woman smiled warmly, taking one of Mariah's hands in both of hers.

"You be Mariah, all right," Ezra continued with a decisive nod of his head. "You've your pa's coloring."

"Dunny always used to say she looked like her ma," Molly Flannery observed.

"Aye, and he claimed his Faith was the most comely woman in the world. He took it real hard when yer ma died—real hard. But that ain't neither here nor there. You come fer the letter. I'll fetch it.''

Limping heavily, he walked to the opposite end of the long counter and bent down. Standing again, he carried a small square metal box back to the place where he'd been talking to Mariah and set it down in front of her, making no move to open it.

''When Dunny come by a few months back, I thought him askin' us to hold onto this here letter fer you were a little strange. But he coulda asked me to grow two heads an' I woulda tried to do it. Me an' Molly here owe a powerful lot to Dunny.'' He paused to look affectionately at his wife and put an arm around her shoulders.

''Aye, that we do,'' Molly verified. ''But fer Dunny Morgan, we wouldn't be ahavin' this here store nor the fine house we be alivin' in with our five sons. He give us the means, he did.''

''You're saying my father loaned you the money to buy this business and a house?'' Mariah asked in surprise.

''Yer father *give* us the money. No owin' notes was set forth,'' Ezra explained. ''I lost me a leg in a sea battle with some pirates nigh onto ten years past.'' He slapped his left thigh. ''Got me a wood one now. Couldn't keep sailin' an' didn't have no money saved up what with Molly an' all my boys to feed an' clothe. We was in a right royal mess till Dunny stepped in. Him an' me was shipmates when I took the cannon hit.''

''We owe yer father everythin', child.'' Molly smiled and patted Mariah's hand. ''He be a fine an' generous man. We was glad to hold this letter fer you.'' She turned to her husband then. ''Fetch it out now, Ezra.''

The big man reached for the metal box, but stopped with his huge hand on the lid. ''You'll be pardonin' me, Miss Mariah, but Dunny's orders was to give this letter to you an' one other, together.''

''Yes, James Lancaster. He's with me, but he's been detained.'' Mariah tried not to let the anger she felt at Jamie tell in her tone. She hoped she wouldn't have to relate the cause for his lateness.

''But I am here, Miss Morgan,'' Jamie's deep voice sounded from behind her. She whirled around to see him standing in the doorway, and was surprised to see he had no one else with him.

''You must be Flannery.'' Jamie crossed the room in easy strides and shook hands with the older man, doffing his hat to Molly.

''Aye, Lancaster. That were the name of the man Dunny said would be helpin' his daughter come here.'' Ezra nodded and eyed Jamie closely before he seemed satisfied enough to open the metal box. ''You have something to show me?''

''I think he means the puzzle pieces,'' Jamie informed Mariah when she looked uncertain. He readily produced his from inside his dusty white shirt, where he'd attached it to a thong of rawhide. Slipping the cord over his head, he laid the wooden puzzle piece on the counter.

Mariah quickly found hers in the side pocket of her riding skirt. Handing it to Ezra Flannery, she watched with growing excitement as the older man fit the two pieces together on the counter surface.

''An' here be another part,'' he said, reaching

into the box and bringing forth a large brown envelope. Opening it, he let the third puzzle piece spill out. With agile fingers, he fit it into place at the bottom edge of Jamie and Mariah's pieces. More of the map was revealed, but still too little to show the treasure's location.

Mariah's excitement waned a little, but she hid her disappointment and took heart in knowing they were one piece closer to completing the map.

"You must know there's more to be got," Flannery went on. "Instructions are in here." He held out the envelope to Jamie, but Mariah grabbed it away just before his fingers closed over it.

"I believe my father meant for *me* to read the instructions," she snapped, plunging her hands into the envelope. A single sheet of folded parchment met her grasp. Pulling it out, she quickly opened it and scanned the few lines. "We're to proceed to Northampton to find a Mrs. Anna Wilkes," she read from the paper. "She holds the fourth piece."

"Northampton. That's a three-day journey," Jamie observed, showing little enthusiasm. "Dunny seems intent on leading us all over the countryside."

"That could be," Molly chimed in. "So you best be plannin' on astayin' the night with us so's you kin rest up fer that part of yer travelin'. It be too late in the day to be ridin' more anyways. We got plenty of room since our two oldest boys is married an' gone now."

"Oh, we couldn't impose," Mariah protested. She wanted to continue on with their trip.

Molly Flannery held up her hand to stop her and

started to untie her apron. "Nonsense, we'll hear no other plan. It'll be fine havin' visitors. Please, child, let me an' Ezra open our home to you. We want to do it."

"That be right, Miss Mariah, Mr. Lancaster," her husband agreed. "We'd be honored."

Mariah could see the older couple wouldn't take no for an answer. And the thought of a clean bed and some privacy was appealing at the moment. She'd just have to hold her anticipation in check.

She looked at Jamie, but decided it was her right to make the decision. She turned to the Flannerys.

"Very well, we'll be staying. Thank you for the invitation."

"Oh, I'm so glad!" Molly smiled widely. "Come, follow me. I'll show you the way to the house. Don't be late fer supper, Ezra."

Mariah saw Jamie frown slightly, but he said nothing. She brushed past him to follow the determined woman out the front door.

Jamie retrieved the horses from the hitching rail and drew them along with him up the street behind Mariah and Molly Flannery. When they walked out onto the main street, he glanced to the opposite end where music still sounded from the gypsy wagons.

What a stroke of luck it was running into Antonya like this, he thought with a sly smile. He'd seen Mariah's angry look when she'd ridden away from him and Antonya earlier. She'd no doubt give him a tongue-lashing about his encounter with the lovely gypsy, just as she had after the incident with Toby Jones. But he was used to going his own way and doing as he pleased, and he didn't like being berated for it. He'd liked kissing the fiery Antonya—and seeing the shocked disapproval on Mariah's face had made the embrace even more enjoyable. Antonya would be balm for the grueling punishment of playing nursemaid to Mariah Morgan! Tonight he would—

Suddenly his wandering thoughts jolted to a halt as he spotted a figure dressed all in black near the farthest wagon. As if the man sensed Jamie's scrutiny, he turned and looked in his direction. A twinge of dread shot up Jamie's spine and his grip on the horses' reins tightened. He'd easily recognized the thick-bodied, barrel-chested man who stepped out of the crowd around the wagon to stand alone in the street for a moment before slipping quickly away down a narrow alley.

It was Doyle Iverson. And Iverson had seen him, too.

Jamie cursed his bad luck in running into the man. Iverson was obsessed with hatred for Jamie, all because of a tragic occurrence involving Iverson's wife. To this very day, he held Jamie responsible for her death, even though the law had found otherwise. He'd vowed to avenge her by going after Jamie, and there was simply no reasoning with the man.

Thus far, Jamie had managed to avoid Doyle Iverson, who ran a sawmill outside Worcester. But when Dunny had sent them Worcester-way, he'd known he could do little more than hope to steer clear of the madman, and get in and out of town fast.

"Unfortunately, not fast enough," Jamie mumbled under his breath, scowling as he turned up the

street again. He almost crashed into Mariah, who'd
stopped to wait for him. He saw her look from him
to the solitary figure down the street. She looked
puzzled and started to speak, but Jamie wasn't in
the mood to talk. Striding briskly past her, he
yanked on the horses' reins and followed on after
Molly Flannery.

Chapter 14

"I'm so pleased to be havin' you fer guests," Molly Flannery declared as she, Mariah, and Jamie approached a rambling single-story house. The middle section was made of logs, but two additions, one on either side, were constructed of white clapboard and in need of painting in some places.

"I hope we won't be a burden to you," Mariah replied, stepping carefully along a tree-shaded gravel path leading to the front door. She glanced at the Flannerys' home again, noting that the dwelling, while far from elegant, did have a welcoming, lived-in feeling about it.

"Oh, no burden at all, dear. We love havin' company. Jus' tie the horses there at the post, Mr. Lancaster. I'll have one of my boys fetch them to the barn fer the night."

"I won't be staying," Jamie informed her. "I just wanted to see you and Miss Morgan to your home." He turned to Mariah. "Something's occurred which necessitates my leaving. I'll come for you at seven o'clock tomorrow morning, and we can continue our journey to Northampton. Can you be ready to travel that early?"

"Of course. This 'occurrence' requiring your attention happened rather suddenly, didn't it?'' Mariah eyed him closely. The unaccountable anger she suddenly felt crept into her voice. ''Was it caused by that wanton gypsy woman or the sinister-looking man in the street I saw when we left the store just now?''

Jamie was surprised by her attention to those details and annoyed by her haughty tone. He'd be damned if he'd tell her she'd be safer with the Flannerys if he weren't there. Keeping his voice casual, he answered her.

''Your observations seem to go beyond what it's your business to know, Miss Morgan. Besides, I should think you'd be glad to be rid of my company, since you've made it so obvious you find it to your disliking.'' His eyes held hers unflinchingly.

''You're correct in that last statement, sir. As long as I have the two pieces of the puzzle in my possession, you're welcome to sleep wherever you like. Just don't misplace your section of the puzzle.''

''Fortunately, there are some women who do value my company.'' A cool smile played about his lips as he gracefully swung up into Sultan's saddle. ''Until tomorrow morning, Miss Morgan. Good day, Mrs. Flannery.''

He nodded to the two women in turn, then urged his mount forward into the street, turning in the direction leading toward the gypsy wagons, Mariah noted with disdain. She clenched her teeth together to hide her scorn from Molly Flannery.

''Lordy, there be no love lost betwixt the two of

you, it seems," Molly commented, raising an eyebrow.

"Love?" Mariah's short laugh was touched with disgust. "Hardly, Mrs. Flannery. James Lancaster is the most ill-mannered, infuriating man alive! I don't know what my father sees in him."

"Well, I don't know either, dear, but I do recollect Dunny were a good judge of character. You sure you're areadin' Mr. Lancaster rightly?"

"Quite sure," Mariah answered emphatically. "Each day, each *hour* we travel together only reinforces my low opinion of him!"

"More's the pity. He's surely a fine form of a man. Reminds me of my Ezra when he were younger—all handsome an' proud. Turned many a lass' head, he did." She grinned and brushed at a stray strand of graying hair at the side of her face. "But I were the lass what got him, an' I ain't never regretted it. Come inside now, child. I'll be showin' you to yer room."

"Jamie, my soul, you came back!" Antonya threw back the wagon door and lunged into his arms.

"I couldn't resist your charms, Tonya," Jamie replied, hugging her hard against him.

She made no resistance when he brought his mouth down on hers possessively. Her black eyes sparkled with exciting promise as they parted for breath. Kicking the door shut behind him, Jamie swept her up in his arms and strode the few steps through the cramped quarters to the bed.

"How can you live in this clutter?" he teased, letting his gaze travel around the wood wagon that was like a small house on wheels. Clothes were strewn everywhere. Unwashed pots and pans balanced in precariously tilted piles on the small cookstove in the far corner. He tossed her onto the narrow, rumpled bed. "Can you ever find anything?"

"I can find this place to make love." She smiled provocatively, patting the mattress beside her. "What else matters?"

"A good point, my lovely." He placed one knee on the bed and yanked at the white ribbons holding together the low-cut bodice of her pink blouse. The loosened material fell away from her shoulders, exposing her ample breasts.

Antonya laughed and threw her arms around his neck, pulling him down on top of her. He buried his face in the curve of her neck and let himself be consumed by the feel of her soft skin. Her breath came in gasps when his hand began to move over her breast.

"I have hot dreams of you every night, my Jamie," she murmured hoarsely, "of being with you like this, of pressing my body to yours and feeling you inside me. It's been too long—almost a year, no?—since we came together last. Hurry and undress. I am so hungry for you." She pushed him off of her onto his back, then sat up and all but ripped the buttons from his shirt in her eagerness to remove his clothes. His breeches and boots quickly followed, along with her flowing red skirt.

Jamie whispered her name as he pulled her to him, entangling his hand in her thick black hair. They'd met five years ago, and spent a rapturous fortnight together. But Jamie had business obligations that had forced him to move on. After all, he couldn't live the life of a gypsy. Still, Tonya never changed. She always wanted him whenever their paths happened to cross.

"I am your slave," she murmured breathlessly against his mouth, covering it with kisses. "Command me, my master. I shall do anything you wish."

Antonya. Jamie basked in the familiarity of her knowing touch. He remembered the nights they'd spent consumed by fiery passion. She never seemed to have enough of him. Always she coaxed and tormented, until she'd aroused him again. Then she'd bite and scratch and writhe like a wild creature, taking all he gave her and giving all of herself in return. The physical attraction between them was strong, compelling, even obsessive to Antonya. But he could always detach himself when he'd had enough of her, when his need for her was filled. He didn't love her. He had loved only one woman in his life—Evangelene. The terrible pain of losing her had ended his youth. Never again would he give his heart to a woman and risk that awful hurt.

He closed his eyes and let her move her hands over him with a touch perfected by long experience. Quickly, she found just the right places to tantalize and arouse him. But the fire that usually ignited in his loins only smoldered now.

Focusing his senses, he concentrated harder on the woman, feeling the long tresses of her hair sliding like silk through his fingers. He remembered the fragile fragrance of lavender that drifted over him when he held her close. Somewhere in the back of his mind he didn't smell it now. In his memory, her eyes widened in surprise and then anger at his boldness—eyes blue-green and tempest-filled like the glistening Caribbean Sea. Now he needed only to taste her nectar-sweet mouth and hear his name murmured on her soft lips to excite his body to the ultimate climax.

"Jamie . . ." She spoke his name just before he consumed her lips with his. But the voice confused him. And the taste of her mouth was wrong.

In her mounting passion, the woman beneath him dug her fingernails into his shoulders and bit his lower lip hard. The sharp nips brought him back to consciousness. His eyes flew open, revealing Antonya Natouri, and dispelling the misty vision of the woman haunting his mind—Mariah.

The effect was like having a tub of cold water wash over him. His quick-rising excitement instantly crashed down from the brink. A shiver of disappointment shot through him, nearly causing him to push Antonya away. She sensed the change in him immediately.

"Jamie, my heart, what is it? Why have you stopped? Take me now. I am so ready for you!"

She clung to him, pulling him by the hair to force his head back down to where her mouth could possess his. But he twisted his head away and rolled off of her. Immediately, she draped herself over his chest, pressing her naked breasts against his hot flesh and covering his face and neck with kisses.

"Don't torture me like this, my soul. Take me, please!"

He grasped her arms and lifted her upper body, holding her away from him. Her black eyes widened in surprise.

"No, Tonya. Not this time. I must leave." He set her away from him and swung off the bed, quickly pulling on his breeches.

"Jamie, why are you going? I do not understand. What have I done?"

The anguish in her voice made him pause to look at her. She knelt at the edge of the bed, begging him with her voice and her voluptuous naked body. Her full breasts glistened with perspiration, their nipples hard and ready for the touch of his hands and mouth. He would be crazy to leave her now. Yet he knew that was exactly what he must do. His desire to make love to her had been overpowered by the tormenting apparition of another woman—a woman who enraged him! In confusion, he rubbed a hand across his forehead.

"You've done nothing except to be as beautiful and desirable as always, Antonya. The fault is mine. There'll be another time for us, but not tonight.

"No, my passion, please don't go!" she cried, reaching out for him as he swept by. He was gone from the wagon before she could utter another word, leaving her to stare after him openmouthed.

Chapter 15

Jamie winced at the pain that shot through his back when he dismounted from Sultan to wait for Mariah to say good-bye to the Flannerys. He felt stiff and sore after spending a restless night tossing and turning in the stale-smelling straw of the loft above the stifling hot livery stable. He glanced at Mariah, who appeared well rested and ready for the day's journey. Every auburn hair was tucked neatly into the usual tight bun at the back of her head. He noticed how her clean, crisp white blouse and green riding skirt clung to her gentle curves. Hiding a scowl of apprehension over spending yet another day with her, he approached the front door of the Flannery house where the others stood. In no way did he want Mariah to know about the disquieting time she'd given him in the stable. During the long, dark night, he'd used reason, anger, logic, *anything* to try to banish her from his churning thoughts, yet she'd remained to haunt him. He'd turned from Antonya because of Mariah. Voluptuous, passionate Antonya! Was he going mad?

"Good morning," he greeted them with forced cheerfulness, sending a nod toward the Flannerys and Mariah as he halted on the stone walkway and removed his tricorn.

"Good morning, Mr. Lancaster," Molly Flannery returned, giving him a wide smile. " 'Tis a fine day. Have you had breakfast, sir?"

"Yes," he lied, not wishing to delay their departure any longer than necessary. The delicious aroma of frying bacon reached his nostrils through the open doorway and made his stomach growl; but he wouldn't let himself give in to hunger. "We should be on our way, Miss Morgan."

"Yes, I'm aware of that, Mr. Lancaster, but are you fit for traveling? You look rather fatigued. Did you have a . . . strenuous night?" With a cocked brow, she gazed directly at him, noting the dark circles under his eyes.

She was surprised that the anger she'd felt at him the night before for going to that strumpet of a gypsy wench still lingered this morning. She was furious with herself for having let the thought of the two of them together keep her awake so long in the big feather bed.

"I'm quite fit," Jamie snapped. "But thank you for your concern."

Mariah bristled at the sarcasm, but decided not to dignify his last remark with a parry. Instead, she turned to Molly Flannery.

"Thank you so much for your hospitality. I'll remember you to my father."

"Oh, yes, please do, dear," the older woman replied, taking Mariah into a hug. " 'Twas an honor havin' you stay with us. We was so glad to do what Dunny asked in holdin' the puzzle piece fer you. Tell him he's bin in my prayers all these years fer what he done fer us. I'll be sayin' extra ones fer him now, hopin' the good Lord will heal his afflictions."

"Yes, thank you, Mrs. Flannery," Mariah stammered, disturbed by the genuine concern for her father that she saw in the older woman's lined face.

"You keep Dunny's girl safe, you hear, lad?" Ezra Flannery grabbed Jamie's hand in a hard clasp.

Jamie only nodded his agreement as he took Mariah's valise from the big man and tied it on Lilac Wind. Then he helped Mariah mount. With a last wave to the Flannerys, they headed on their way.

"You seemed surprised to learn of your father's generosity," Jamie commented, riding next to Mariah as they made their way toward the main road out of Worcester.

"Mr. and Mrs. Flannery seem to regard him as some sort of saint." She shook her head.

"And you don't, of course."

"Absolutely not! Never has my father shown such generosity to me."

"Until now."

"What do you mean?" Her turquoise eyes flashed at him.

"I'd say he's being most generous toward you now—regarding the gold. He could have spent it all on himself. Or he could have given it to someone else—someone who'd be grateful to him, like the Flannerys."

Mariah's glare intensified. "Grateful? I should be grateful for all the years of neglect, the dashed hopes and dreams?" She pulled up on Lilac Wind's reins, halting the mare. All the things the Flannerys had said about Dunny still rang in her ears. But she didn't want to hear glowing accounts of him. To survive the heartache he'd caused her over the years, she'd closed off her emotions regarding her parent, thinking of him as dead. She didn't want him nobly resurrected. And no one was going to change her mind about him. "As far as the Flannerys are concerned, I'm certain my father's charity toward them was an aberration. Perhaps he was drunk at the time and didn't realize the magnitude of his gesture. He did like his rum, didn't he? Most sailors do."

Jamie didn't miss the disparaging way she said the word "sailors." He knew she was including him. His tone was cold when he answered her.

"You have everything reasoned out, don't you? You assess people and stubbornly hold to your nearsighted opinions even in the face of evidence to the contrary. I won't deny that Dunny enjoyed his spirits well enough, but he never let them cloud his judgment. When he gave the Flannerys money, I'm certain he knew exactly what he was about. I know your father much better than you do. He's a man who's not afraid of hard work, or of helping his fellows when there's a need. He's gone his own way, making no excuses. And I, for one, envy him."

"That's no wonder. You're just like him," Mariah replied disdainfully. "The Dunny Morgan you just described, the one the Flannerys praise so highly, is not the man I knew. After my mother died, he got rid of me as quickly as he could, sent me to live with two people who were extremely narrow-minded and strict to the point of cruelty. It was like living in a prison, with work so hard and rules so harsh as to destroy all feeling and spirit. I was forced to fear the Lord's wrath, and my aunt and uncle's as well. But I didn't let them break my will. Many were the times I was beaten for rebelliousness. They tried to purge me of the devil, as they so righteously called it. But I came to learn that the devil was in them, not me.'' She paused for a moment, as if lost in wretched memories. ''That life was what Dunny Morgan condemned me to when he deserted me, and I hate him for it. I'll always hate him.'' Jamming her heels into Lilac Wind's sides, she hurried off down the road, leaving Jamie to follow in a cloud of dust.

Jamie was glad to leave Worcester behind. He'd managed to avoid further contact with Doyle Iverson and that was just the way he wanted it. The more miles between them, the better. Iverson would cut his heart out if he ever got the chance, because of the tragedy of Eleanora.

But that morning, as he led the way down a secluded, narrow trail, thoughts of his past involving the Iversons haunted him. Eventually, his hand fell lax on Sultan's rein as events he wished he could forget rose up in his mind.

He and Doyle Iverson had formed a partnership three years ago. He'd just come home from sea and had a bit of spare change, so he'd financed the purchase of a sawmill in Worcester. Iverson's share involved operating the business, while Jamie remained in the background. But Iverson's hot-blooded young wife, Eleanora, saw more than a silent partner in him. Almost from the moment he'd entered the business, she'd set her sights on seducing him, along with a number of other men. She was beautiful and clever, and easily fooled her love-blinded husband into believing her visits away from home were for the purposes of tending sick friends and performing other works of charity.

Jamie frowned, remembering how she blatantly offered her body to him. He'd been repelled by her adulterous conduct, though. Many women had known his arms and his bed over the years, but none of them had been wedded. He regarded the vows of marriage as sacred. He would not bed another man's wife. And he respected Doyle Iverson, who was an honest, hardworking man.

Though he'd rebuffed Eleanora, she'd persisted in hounding him until . . . His tormented thoughts held him captive as the road wound on.

The sun was high in the sky and Mariah was day dreaming about a cool bath when suddenly, she felt her senses sharpen in warning. In the space of a second, she saw Sultan rear and Jamie fighting to keep his seat on the big stallion. Lilac Wind tossed her head and pranced sideways. Mariah whirled her head around, searching for what was spooking the horses. In that instant, a huge shadow shot forward from the rim of a rock overhead. As the dark bulk lunged at her, a powerful, clawed paw swung across Lilac Wind's croup just behind the saddle. The mare reared and twisted, neighing in fright and pain. Mariah lost her hold and fell backward, hitting the ground with violent force. Gasping painfully for the breath that had been knocked out of her, she could only stare in horror as the large black bear came toward her.

Only a few feet separated her from the charging beast when Jamie forced Sultan between them. Dagger in hand, he dove off his mount toward the four-hundred-pound beast, shoulders first. The snarling animal was thrown off balance by the blow. With four paws clawing at the air, it tumbled into a thicket. Swiftly regaining its footing, it attacked again, dashing at Jamie with a dexterity that belied its weight. Jamie rolled away just as the bear pounced. Then it reared up on its two hind legs, looming to strike again. The loose gravel hindered Jamie's efforts to scramble out of the bear's path. He slipped and fell onto his back, just as the beast swept its huge paw down. The blow flattened Jamie, sending sharp claws ripping into his belly. He clutched at the wound, trying to dodge when the enraged animal lunged. When it still bore down on him, he instinctively tried to defend himself by grabbing it by the thick loose folds of furred skin under its neck and holding fast, wrestling the animal to prevent the long-fanged jaws from closing over his face.

Panicked, Mariah spun around, searching for a weapon, anything to use to help Jamie. A dead tree branch lay close by on the ground, partially covered by a boulder. With a strength she didn't know she had, she yanked the limb free and, grasping it with both hands, ran to where Jamie struggled against the bear. With all the force she could muster, she raised the thick branch and hit the beast squarely on the back. The wood splintered and broke as the bear growled and swung around in her direction. But it still kept Jamie pinned to the ground.

Digging her fingers into the short piece of limb still in her hands, Maria rushed at the animal again, plunging the pointed end of the branch into the bear's side. Roaring with pain, the beast twisted around. For the longest second Mariah had ever known, she stared into its black eyes, paralyzed with fright. Then she screamed as it leaped off of Jamie and came toward her. Turning too quickly, she became entangled in her skirt and fell backward to the ground. Instinctively, she raised her arms to protect herself as the bear charged her on all fours.

But when the beast was only two strides away from her, Jamie leaped onto its back and swung his arm down to bury the blade of his knife deep into the animal's neck. He let it sink to the hilt before he yanked it out and thrust it back into another spot. The bear dropped instantly, and Jamie jumped free just in time to avoid being crushed when it rolled over on its side in death. Its huge black head came to rest on Mariah's leg.

Shaking and weaping, she jerked her leg away from the sharp teeth of the beast's open jaw. Jamie crawled to her on his hands and knees, gasping for breath as he took her into his arms.

"Are you hurt, Mariah?"

"N-no, I think I'm all right," she stammered through her sobs. She clung to him tightly, so glad for his strong arms around her.

Suddenly, she felt his hold on her loosen. Before she could catch him, he sank down to the ground next to her.

"Jamie!" She scrambled to her knees and eased him over from his side to his back. He was conscious, his scratched and dirty face contorted in a grimace of pain. Blood-soaked shreds of his tan shirt lay across his torso. "Dear God, the beast ripped you open. You're bleeding badly. I must get it stopped. The horses—where are they? I need my medical supplies!"

She was babbling, her heart still beating wildly, her mind whirling in confusion. She was no longer frightened about the bear, but for Jamie. How badly was he hurt?

Jumping to her feet, she raced down the trail, first in one direction and then another, until she finally spotted Lilac Wind near a tall pine tree. The mare shied at her approach, but Mariah spoke to her and patted her neck. Blood oozed from the deep gashes on the horse's rump. She'd need to be tended, too, but that could wait until later.

Fumbling at the rawhide ties holding her valise and water canister, Mariah finally managed to unloosen them. Clutching them both, she ran back to Jamie. He hadn't moved. Trying to ignore the great hulking corpse of the bear so close by, she sank to her knees next to Jamie again and dumped out the contents of the bag. Gently lifting his head, she placed the luggage piece under him for a pillow.

"Sultan—where is he?" Jamie's voice sounded tight through his gritted teeth.

"I didn't see him, but he's probably not too far away. Lilac Wind is hurt. The bear clawed her, too." As she talked, she pushed aside what remained of his shirt so she could get at the wound. Wetting a clean cloth, she wiped it gently over the claw marks on his midsection. Relief flooded over her when she saw the extent of his injury more clearly. Though the eight-inch-long gashes were deep, they appeared to be only flesh wounds. No vital organs were exposed. Still, the slashes bled profusely.

"Are you feeling light-headed? You've lost a great deal of blood."

"I'll be all right. Just put something over the cuts so we can get—" He started to rise up, but Mariah put firm hands on his shoulders to stop him.

"Don't even think of moving. I must suture these gashes or you'll soon lose so much blood that you'll be unconscious. Now, lie still. This will pinch some."

Finding the suture needle in her medical supplies, she quickly threaded it with thin gut string and began sewing up the damage the bear had done.

"Don't you have a needle with a *sharp* point?" Jamie complained, wincing at the first prick to his belly.

"This one has a good point. Dr. Hastings gave it to me himself. I'll stitch as quickly as I can."

"Your aunt didn't teach you the art of *delicate* sewing, did she?" he muttered through clenched teeth, twitching as the needle repeatedly pierced his injured skin.

"Now is not the time to insult me, lest I pull this thread a little too tightly. I can hardly see what I'm doing, there's so much blood." She wiped her dirty white sleeve across her perspiring brow, then continued the precise, even stitching to close his ragged flesh. Her hands were covered with his blood. She had to get the flow to ebb. She didn't want Jamie to . . .

She stopped her thoughts, shocked to realize that she really didn't want him to die. But, of course, it was only professional medical concern that made her think about him like that.

"As much as I am *not* enjoying this treatment of yours, keep stitching, Madam Doctor," Jamie prodded.

Mariah hadn't realized she'd paused with the suture needle in midair. At his remark, she swiftly resumed the sewing.

"Why did the bear attack us? Was it perhaps a female protecting some cubs nearby?" As if looking for the answer to her question, she glanced up to the rock rim from where the beast had first emerged.

"It was a male—a boar—and an old one, by the look of the white on its muzzle. Probably became temperamental in advancing age. Its den must have been in the rocks up there. Maybe we startled it coming around the bend like we did."

A silence fell between them. Mariah kept stitching. And thinking.

"I couldn't have held it off much longer," Jamie said. "It was a powerful animal, despite its age. Thanks for wielding that branch the way you did. As much as I hate to admit this, you probably saved my life. I hope that thought doesn't disturb you overmuch."

"Of course not. I still need you to help me acquire the remaining puzzle pieces so we can find the gold." She kept her voice light as she knotted off the gut thread, snipped it with a small pair of scissors, and began sewing on the next gash in his belly. "Stop tightening your stomach muscles. You're making it harder to stitch."

"Well, I'm damned sorry about that, madam, but the stabbing you call suturing bloody well hurts! By the heavens, woman, you can exasperate a man out of his mind! Do you think it was easy for me to *thank* you for saving my life?" He raised himself up on his elbows, then sank back again when pain washed over him.

Mariah stopped her work to look at him.

"Not any easier than it is for me to thank you for saving my life, Jamie. So now that we've gotten all that gratitude over with, I can get this task finished. Oh dear, I can't hold onto the needle with all this blood on my hands." She was babbling again, she knew, and she couldn't look into those light-blue eyes of his any longer. They did something to her insides, unnerved her. She busied herself, wiping her hands with the wet cloth and rinsing water over it again.

"You called me Jamie."

"What?" She looked at him.

"You called me Jamie—finally."

"And you called me Mariah, not 'Miss Morgan' in that condescending way you have."

"*I* have a condescending way? You could write the text on haughtiness." He had to stop talking to catch his breath.

Mariah opened her mouth to argue, then stopped. He looked so battered. The realization of the terrible danger they'd been in suddenly overwhelmed her. They could both be lying mangled and dead now. A shudder of horror swept over her as she stared at Jamie.

The silence grew between them again as their eyes held. The wet cloth lay in her lap. She gathered it up and leaned forward to wipe it across his brow. When she started to move her hand away, his fingers closed around her wrist to stop her, and he pulled her slowly down to his side.

Curling tresses of her auburn hair, loosened during the fracas, wisped about her face. He gently wound one thick coil around his hand and drew her to him until her lips met his. He touched her mouth lightly at first. Then he pressed little kisses on and around it.

Mariah closed her eyes, afraid to move. Confusion blocked her reason. She shouldn't let him kiss her, but his lips were so tender. Why was he doing this to her?

Her own lips moved slightly to protest, but no sound came forth. Instead, her head turned as if of its own volition, so her mouth could meet his. Tentatively . . . once . . . twice they touched his.

His hand twisted tighter in her hair and pressed her face closer. Then the asking gentleness was gone. His mouth consumed hers. His lips demanded and she answered, timidly at first, holding her breath, drowning in the feel of him. Her breasts, pressed against his bare chest, felt the tension in his muscles. Her hand touched the thin covering of dark hair there. The roughness of his starting beard rubbed into her chin. The taste of his mouth was exquisite, his lips warm, possessive.

Her heart raced frantically. When her lungs felt at the point of bursting, she pulled her lips a little away and rested her forehead against his chin, breathing hard. After a long moment, she sat up. She couldn't look at him.

"I must finish the stitches, then apply medication. And Lilac Wind has to be tended. We must make camp and—"

"Mariah." Jamie caught her hand. Her eyes darted to him. For a long moment he just looked at her. When he spoke, his voice sounded strained with weakness. "You're quite a woman, Mariah Marie Morgan. Quite a woman, indeed."

Then his eyes drifted closed as he lapsed into unconsciousness.

Mariah sat back on her heels, stunned. The kiss meant nothing, of course, she mumbled to herself. You'd be the *last* man in the world I'd wish to kiss!

She frowned at him, knowing he couldn't hear what she was saying. She bathed his face again with the water and cloth, still shaken. If he were Samuel Hastings, it would be another matter altogether.

She studied Jamie, comparing him to the man she knew she loved. They were as different as night and day. James Lancaster was at least fifteen years younger than Samuel, she judged, and dark, while the doctor was blond. Jamie was taller, too, and much more virile-looking. Samuel was a humble man, unselfish and hardworking to the point of jeopardizing his health.

"I doubt that the word 'humility' is even in your vocabulary," she chided Jamie's still form. "And you're probably the most handsome man I've ever seen, as I'm sure many other woman have noted," she reluctantly admitted as she brushed a stray strand of his thick black hair from his forehead.

After finishing her suturing she changed the dressing on his head wound. That injury was beginning to mend. He'd had a battering couple of days lately. Was his life always so fraught? Well, hers usually wasn't, and she was glad of it. The routine of her life with Samuel Hastings at the hospital was steady, dependable, ordinary . . . dull. In Boston, she never felt the rush of fear she'd experienced in the last few days, nor known the pulsing energy of excitement. She and Jamie had teetered on the precipice of death, and they'd survived! That was an exhilarating new feeling for her.

A week ago, she hadn't even heard of James Lancaster. She still knew very little about him, only that he was infuriating! Yet, in risking his own life, he'd saved her from the bear. He had kissed her against her will. But with those caresses, he had changed her dramatically, opened up a wellspring of feelings inside her that she didn't know existed.

She sighed, touching his brow to check for fever. It was cool, yet she let her fingers linger against his skin. Her stomach did a curious little flip-flop, a sensation Samuel Hastings had never caused in her.

"Nor will you again, James Lancaster, for I'll not allow it!" She rose quickly to her feet. "I've spent too much of my life trying to forget my father. I'll have nothing to do with any man who is just like him!"

Brushing aside a hot tear that suddenly overflowed her eye, she concentrated on building a fire and cooking a meal in a small iron skillet. Then she went to tend to the horses.

After sunset, the July night promised a cooling respite from the day's heat. Crickets filled the night with their steady rhythmic chirp. The white glow of the gently rising moon was just beginning to light the ebony evening sky when Jamie awoke.

"Are the horses all right?"

Mariah jumped at the sound of his voice. "Yes, I've seen to Lilac Wind's wound. The horse you stole wasn't injured. They're both tied and grazing close by." She kept her tone curt to hide her relief that he'd finally awakened.

"Why are you so angry? I didn't steal Sultan from Hollister. Lem owed me."

Mariah glared at him as she reached over to check his forehead again. "He stole from you. You stole from him. You're both thieves."

Jamie grabbed her wrist in an iron grip. "Nothing is ever that simple. You and I will never see anything eye to eye, will we? Are you so angry because I kissed you, or because I didn't bleed to death?"

"No! I mean, don't be ridiculous. That kiss was just a foolish mistake, a ridiculous impulse brought on by our alarming circumstances." She felt confused again, thrown off balance by his touch. She tried to twist out of his grasp, but he held her fast. "Let go of me, Mr. Lancaster," she demanded.

He released her. "So we're back to formal titles. Well, I won't wrestle another bear just to get you to call me Jamie. Damn!" He touched his wound. "Am I still bleeding?"

"No, that isn't blood. It's St. John's Wort, a balm made from the wildflower of that name and mixed with olive oil for a dressing for wounds. I had a small jar of it in my medical supplies."

Jamie watched her in the firelight. She was a spirited one, all right. Like her father. But he'd better not tell her that fact! Or perhaps he would, just to see her blue-green eyes flash. Her hair was down. It fell well below her shoulders, its auburn highlights reflecting the red-gold glow of the fire. His head was clear now. He remembered the feel of those thick tresses, the touch and taste of her lips on his. A ridiculous impulse, she'd called their kiss. He agreed. They'd both almost been mauled by the crazed animal. For some wild reason, he'd wanted to kiss her. Needed to kiss her, to know she wasn't hurt. It had seemed like the right thing to do at the time. He regretted it now, of course.

Mariah was like no other women he'd ever known. She'd helped him fight off the bear, and tended his wound as expertly as he'd ever seen done. She'd fixed up an injured horse, made camp, and was now preparing some kind of food that smelled absolutely heavenly.

"What's cooking?" he asked, feeling his mouth water at the delicious aroma.

Mariah looked at him over her shoulder.

"Bear steak."

Chapter 16

Early the next morning Mariah awoke to a dreary, cloud-covered sky. A feeling of dread inched through her. If a storm broke, where would they find shelter?

"You had no right to go through my possessions."

Mariah turned from where she sat on a log by the banked fire and looked at Jamie, who lay on the ground behind her. His angry expression made her cringe. Her first impulse was to deny his accusation, but she realized that would be futile, for his drawings were spread out around her. She'd only intended to glance through them, but she'd become enthralled by their power and precise detail.

Forcing herself to remain calm, she carefully gathered the sheets into a neat pile on her lap, then lowered her eyes to keep from looking at him directly.

"I found these accidentally when I was searching in your saddlebags for the cooking utensils last night. I apologize for looking at them without your permission. My curiosity got the best of me." She made herself meet his cool gaze. "You're a gifted artist. The people you've drawn here seem alive, filled with emotion and vitality. This one—'' She leafed through the papers to find the one she wanted. ''The old Oriental. He's magnificent. The deep lines in his face show such character!''

Jamie watched her intently. He was wary of her praise, but hearing it pleased him nonetheless. ''I met him in Italy many years ago.'' His voice was quiet, no longer angry, as he reached for the drawing. ''I stayed with him for three months, until he died. He taught me many things. Chang Shenyang was his name. As long as I live, I'll never forget him.''

''Is he the reason you wish to sail to the Orient? And on this ship?'' She found the detailed sketch of the sleek, three-masted merchantman and held it out to him.

Jamie took it from her, smiling slightly. ''You didn't miss anything, did you? Yes, he's the main reason. Chang was Chinese, a priest in his homeland. He'd lost favor with the Emperor and had to flee.''

Mariah studied the lines of the ship. ''I haven't ventured very far from home, never even out of the Massachusetts Colony. But I know it's a long, dangerous trip to China. Yet you wish to go there. Why?''

''During my travels, I'd heard stories from other seamen about the wonders of the Far East, but I'd never met anyone like Chang. With him I felt like the great Venetian explorer, Marco Polo, when he first traveled to China in the thirteenth century—overwhelmed, eager to learn more.'' He started to sit up, but a stab of pain made him think better of it.

Mariah hurriedly knelt down beside him, frowning. "Don't try to move. You'll open the stitches and start to bleed again." She lifted the edge of the wide bandage. "Miraculously, they seem to be holding."

"Good, then we can get on with our journey." He rolled onto his side and gingerly used his hand to push himself up to a sitting position, gritting his teeth against the throbbing pain.

"Don't be ridiculous." She scrambled around in front of him to stop him if he tried to stand. "You can't ride yet, not for a day or two at least. I insist you lie down again. We will not be leaving!" She planted her feet firmly and crossed her arms, presenting a picture of determination.

"Very well, I defer to your doctoring skills." He was in enough pain already. Riding would only increase it. "Tomorrow will be soon enough to continue." He eased himself back against her valise.

"A wise decision," she agreed with a curt nod, though she watched him suspiciously. "I'm surprised to hear you admit I have some medical abilities, after the way you complained about my suturing yesterday! Of course, Samuel Hastings has taught me well. He's a brilliant physician."

She saw Jamie scowl, looking as if he regretted his compliment. She stifled any further comment and set about preparing breakfast. When she'd served them both tea and the last of Molly Flannery's buttermilk biscuits, the sheaf of papers caught her eye again.

''Your style is unique,'' she finally said quietly. ''It shows your boldness and vitality.''

She put her cup down on the ground beside her and picked up one of the drawings which had caught her attention before.

''Who is this young woman? You've made her eyes so expressive.'' She tried to keep her tone casual, to give the impression she was only noticing the details. In truth, she was curious to know his relationship with her.

''That's my only sister, Felicia, ten years younger than I. We haven't seen each other in over four years.''

Mariah saw his face change, heard the softening in his tone. He stared past her into the distance.

''Never was there a woman so full of joy and sweetness. Her heart is pure generosity, devoid of any malice.''

''You miss her.'' She spoke the statement softly, surprised by the tenderness in his voice.

His eyes flicked to her. ''At times.''

''Estrangement from one's family can be difficult.'' She felt empathy for him, stemming from her own lack of any real parents.

''I've had a good deal of time to become accustomed to the separation. It was my choice.''

Cool detachment returned to his voice. But for a few moments, she'd glimpsed a vulnerability in him that touched her deeply.

He changed his position against her valise. She saw him wince, then close his eyes and take a slow, deep breath. He must be hurting considerably, she thought. But he didn't complain. She had to admire his stoicism.

"I must change your bandage," she informed him, setting the drawings aside. She popped the last remaining piece of her biscuit into her mouth and took a sip of tea before locating a clean roll of bandaging and the small jar of St. John's Wort salve. "Now lie still while I tend to this task." She knelt down beside him and gingerly moved aside the tattered pieces of his shirt to lift the wad of cloth she'd applied to his wound the night before.

She tried hard to work as quickly as possible, knowing the dangers of being so near him. But his breath disturbed her hair as she leaned over him. She could feel his eyes on her. His skin was warm beneath her fingertips, and inflamed red in color at the edges of the cuts. She felt her face grow just as heated.

She applied a fresh coating of the dark-crimson salve, and then covered the wound with a clean bandage. She saw his stomach muscles tighten, but he made no sound to indicate she might be hurting him. Wrapping a strip of cloth around his midsection to hold the bandage in place proved to be awkward, because she had to reach around and underneath him, almost as if she were hugging him. Her eyes lifted to his face, and she saw him smile slightly. Her heart missed a beat.

"Will I live, Madam Doctor?" he quipped.

"Yes, if you follow my orders." She sat back, wiping the salve from her fingers. "I'll get you a more suitable shirt. That one is beyond repair, I'd say." She stood up.

"Perhaps it could be sewn. You could practice your stitching technique on it so as to have a gentler hand the next time you do flesh."

She scowled at him. "For your information, those sutures were expertly applied. Dr. Hastings takes great care with such procedures, and has taught me well. He wouldn't have sewn you up any differently."

"Then remind me never to go to him for doctoring!" His jest was delivered more sharply than he'd intended, but he felt irritated by the way she kept bringing up the Boston physician.

"You'd do well to have him tend you," she said defensively. "He's highly knowledgeable and compassionate and—"

"And obviously a candidate for sainthood," he finished with a sardonic air. "You sing his praises so much, he must have a halo over his head!"

"What? W-well no, of course he doesn't." The snappishness of his tone startled her. "It's just that I admire him so very much."

"You've made that abundantly clear. Anyway, let's speak no more of him." He averted his eyes from her, and only then went on. "If we're going to stay in this area today, we should move the camp away from the bear corpse. In this heat, it'll start smelling soon." He sat up, gritting his teeth, then attempted to get to his feet.

His sudden change of subject amazed her. For a second, she wondered why he sounded so annoyed.

"Let me help you," she offered, stepping to him.

"I can manage!" Frowning, he waved her away. "Start moving our belongings over to those maple trees." He nodded his head in the direction he meant.

Confused by his behavior, she determined it best to do as he said. But as she started to drag her saddle away, she watched him out of the corner of her eye. Slowly and with difficulty, he got to his feet. What stubborn pride, she thought with exasperation.

While she moved her saddle, and then his, to the new location, she puzzled over his attitude toward Dr. Hastings. Suddenly she stopped, midstride. He was jealous—that was it! But why? Did he see the great merit of Samuel's life and work, and none in his own?

Jamie slept in the early afternoon. Mariah went for a walk, but was careful to take her pistol along and not wander too far away.

When he awoke, she was again looking at his sketches. How she wished she could draw as well as he.

"How are you feeling?" she asked, coming over to feel his forehead.

"Like I wrestled a bear and the bear won. You seem very interested in my artwork. Would you like me to show you one or two drawing techniques to pass the time?"

"Y-yes, I'd like that very much," she stammered, surprised that he seemed able to read her mind.

He sat up carefully and leaned back against his saddle. Then from his leather saddlebag he drew out a quill, the small bottle of ink, and a clean sheet of paper.

"All right, come over here." He motioned for her to sit down on the ground beside him.

"An artist sees people, objects, places with an inner eye, going beyond the obvious surface features. I try to depict the less easily seen qualities in my sketches." He took her chin in his hand and cocked his head to the side. "For example, in you I see not only the delicate arch of your brows, the high cheekbones, but a certain willfulness."

One of her eyebrows raised at his observation. She studied his face to see if he was baiting her, but his expression remained serious. His touch was gentle, but it greatly unnerved her, as did being so close to him.

"Then for the eyes, I try to see in them something I know. Yours have always reminded me of the vibrant turquoise waters of the Caribbean. One moment they reflect serene calm, and in the next, they burst with tempestuousness when the explosive winds of your temper stir them. A man could drown in eyes like yours."

She suppressed a sigh, trying to hide the disturbing effect his silken words had on her. She wished he would start drawing and stop touching her and speaking in that mesmerizing voice. She was having a good deal of difficulty remembering this was supposed to be an art lesson.

"Then there are the lips—full, sensual, their softly rounded shape hinting at a kiss." His voice dropped to a lower timbre. "These lips can sting with sharp words or sway with passionate murmurings."

Too well, he recalled the sweet taste of her lips on his. He stared at them now, with his own parted slightly. He wouldn't mind sampling them again now, sliding his fingers along the smooth, creamy skin of her cheek and tangling them in the thick tresses of her hair.

She cleared her throat and moved her chin out of his grasp. ''You have a knack for turning a phrase—well practiced, I'm certain, on many other women. But how do you convey these traits on paper?''

He smiled. ''Let me show you eye and brow expressions first.''

He began to draw, transforming the empty white paper with every confident stroke of the pen. Amazed, Mariah saw details about eyes she'd never noticed before he pointed them out to her—how lashes start from the inner edge of the lid and fan out to the opposite side, and the way a few lines of the quill under the eye and at the outer edge added age and weariness.

The hours of the afternoon slipped by unnoticed as Mariah became absorbed in the magic created by Jamie's expert hand.

''Now it's time for you to try drawing something.''

''Oh, no, I couldn't,'' she protested. ''I have no gift such as yours.''

''Thank you for that praise. But come, give the quill a try.''

''You won't ridicule my efforts?'' Though she was eager to make an attempt, she regarded him warily.

''No.'' He smiled slightly, and she could tell by his tone of voice that he was sincere. She felt a strange warmth curl inside her. He was sharing his talent, his knowledge with her. She liked that very much.

"No, that's not right!" she declared, laughing at the lopsided result of her initial attempt to draw his mouth. To make matters worse, a large drop of ink fell right in the middle of the upper lip she'd drawn. "Look, a moustache! Have you ever had one?"

"What, a moustache? Yes, several years ago. I was trapping beaver during a cold winter, and decided to keep my face warm by letting my beard grow. It came in black and thick, quite frightening to behold, I discovered, when I attempted to make friends with an Iroquois squaw. She called me the Iroquois equivalent of a devil-man and ran for the woods as fast as she could. Of course, the fact that I hadn't had a bath in several months might have contributed to her reluctance to become acquainted."

They both laughed. She enjoyed the easy mood spinning out between them, and his sense of humor. Chuckling again, she stared at him, trying to picture him with a faceful of black hair.

"When I returned to civilization that spring, I shaved off the beard. It itched terribly. I think a number of insects had taken up residence in it. I kept the moustache, though. The ladies seemed to think it dashing."

"I'm certain ladies must find you appealing even without a moustache." She lowered her eyes and busied herself sketching again, stunned that her thoughts had slipped out in words.

Silence fell between them. She inked the quill again, taking care to dab the point on the edge of the bottle to rid it of excess ink.

"Perhaps I should try something else. Is a tree easier to draw?" She looked at him questioningly.

"Do you?"

"Do I what?"

"Do you find me appealing?"

"No." She stated the word simply, giving a nervous little laugh and keeping her eyes on the paper.

"I didn't think so. Most women do, but you're not like most women."

A rumble of thunder turned their attention to the western sky. The low-hanging cloud cover of the morning had deepened, and clearly a storm was in the making.

"We can't stay here," Jamie said, gathering up the sketches. "Judging by those clouds, I'd say it's going to pour any minute. There's no shelter in this clearing."

Mariah's mind worked fast as she recapped the ink bottle and wiped the quill clean. "What about the bear's den? You said there might be one up in those rocks. Perhaps there's a cave or something we could use. Stay here while I go and look."

"Mariah—" he started to protest, but she was already on her feet, running toward the hill. "Come back here!" he shouted, but she continued around the bend and disappeared from view. "Damn, woman, why don't you listen?"

Pressing his left forearm against the wad of bandaging over his wound to hold it secure, he struggled first to his knees and then to a standing position. For a moment, he stood still, waiting for the pain in his midsection to subside. Then he carefully reached down to his saddle and drew his pistol out of the holster.

"It'd serve her right if she found another bear in some cave up there and it ate her!" he complained aloud, gingerly following Mariah.

"There's an overhang up here," she called from above just as he reached the base of the hill. She was standing on the jutting ledge of rock from which the bear had hurled itself yesterday. "Wait and I'll show you the way. There's a narrow path on this side." She pointed to her left, around the bend. It was starting to sprinkle when she reached him.

"Do you think you can make it?" she asked. "It's not too steep. Move slowly."

"My drawings. Get them and the saddlebags."

She didn't argue. She knew what the sketches meant to him. Nodding, she ran back to the log. Gathering up the sheets of paper, she placed them into one side of his saddlebags, being careful not to crumple any of them. Then she closed the protective flap of the bag and hurried back to him.

"I don't suppose you could bring up the saddles and blankets, too," he quipped.

She shot him a look of disbelief. The two saddles were very heavy.

Thunder rumbled in the distance. Larger raindrops began to fall, pelting Mariah and Jamie hard as they slowly rounded the bend to the path. They only made it a few feet up the slope when the clouds opened and the deluge began.

"So much for getting to shelter!" he shouted as he sank to a sitting position and pressed his back against a boulder. Glad to rest, he turned his face toward the sky and closed his eyes, letting the warm rain beat over him.

Mariah thought about making a dash for the shallow cave without him, but then realized the foolishness of such an action. The path was quickly turning to mud and she was already drenched to the skin.

Seeing the futility of the situation, she started to laugh. As she began to ease herself down next to Jamie, she slipped on the mud and landed near his lap.

"Oh, I'm sorry! Did I hurt you?"

He shook his head, sending more water at her from his hair. "No, I'm all right."

Laughing again, she leaned back against the arm he'd used to catch her and turned her face skyward, as he was doing.

"Have you ever sat in the mud in a downpour before, Mariah Marie Morgan?" He grinned as he brushed water out of her eyes. Then he opened his mouth to catch the rain.

"No, James Lancaster, never! I think I like it!" She grinned too and closed her eyes, putting her hands under her hair to raise it to the deluge.

Jamie couldn't remember when he'd seen a woman look more beautiful and appealing. Her long, dark eyelashes lay spiked apart against the tops of her cheeks. Water slid off the end of her slightly up-turned nose. Her lips were parted in a smile of delight. Her wet white cotton blouse appeared nearly transparent, revealing a lacy undergarment clinging to the lovely curves of her breasts.

Pain shot through Jamie's midsection when he moved his arm to draw her near, but he paid no attention to it. Leaning, he covered her mouth with his.

Her eyes opened in surprise, then closed again as the feel and taste of his lips made her senses explode. She raised her arms to encircle his neck. The downpour continued its steady drumming against them, but they hardly noticed. The parched earth bathed in the nurturing kiss of the rain, and the awaiting woman basked in the awakening kiss of the man who held her in his arms.

The embrace ended when Jamie pulled away a little. Mariah's eyes opened slowly to look at him. For a moment she couldn't react. She felt as if she'd been struck by a blow which sent her reeling, and yet she experienced no pain, only stunned amazement.

She saw his smile. He seemed amused! She squirmed out of his arms and jumped to her feet, nearly falling again on the slippery path.

"This must stop!" she declared, angrily brushing at a strand of wet hair in her face.

Jamie rested his head back against the boulder and looked up at her. "Are you referring to the rain or the kissing, Miss Morgan?"

"Both!" she shouted with exasperation. "Why do you keep kissing me?"

"Don't you mean, why do *we* keep kissing? You participated as well, I believe."

Mariah started to protest, then closed her mouth and eased herself down to sit in the mud next to him.

"Well, I didn't *want* to kiss you!" She crossed her arms over her chest for emphasis.

"Nor was it my intention to kiss you."

They both looked straight ahead out over the clearing, falling silent while the rain beat down.

She wanted to be outraged at him for taking such liberties, but the more she thought about the situation, the funnier it seemed. And the more disturbing. Here she was sitting in the mud in the middle of the wilderness, looking out over a campsite containing a dead bear, with a man she didn't think she even liked, but whose kisses sent an excitement racing through her veins that she'd never before known.

Gradually the rain slowed. She closed her eyes, wanting to think of Samuel. Surely if he had ever kissed her, he'd cause the same sensations to pulse through her, wouldn't he? She tried to focus on his face, picturing his warm light-blue eyes. No, Samuel had *brown* eyes!

She fought back the tears of frustration and confusion welling in her eyes. What did she feel for Samuel now? She'd been so sure she loved him. Until now. Until Jamie Lancaster burst into her life and set her levelheadedness, her reason spinning out of control.

Chapter 17

"Lift your end—*now!*"

"And you call *me* stubborn!" Mariah declared with exasperation the next morning. She heaved up the back side of the saddle while Jamie lifted the front end onto Sultan's back. "You're weak from loss of blood. Why do you insist on doing this?"

"Because I have a job to do, and I want to get on with it. I rested enough yesterday. Hand me that cinch strap." He had to pause until the pain in his midsection subsided.

Shaking her head, she followed his orders, helping him saddle both horses and tie on their gear.

"You'd better let me put a clean dressing on your wound before we start," she told him, unrolling another wad of bandaging. She didn't like the ashen color of his face.

Reluctantly, he let her tend him. Though he could find no complaint with her handling, he felt impatient with himself for the way his body reacted to her nearness. She'd brushed her hair, and now it tumbled about her head in deep russet waves. The rain yesterday had washed away the dust and grit from her face, leaving it flushed with color. He didn't wish to be drawn to her like this. Inside, he fought against it mightily. But somehow she was inching her way into the place deep within his heart that he'd kept carefully guarded. He must prevent her from reaching any further.

"These stitches are holding, no thanks to you," she informed him, removing the bandage covering his gouged flesh. "Still, I advise against riding."

"Your recommendation has been noted and rejected. We're leaving here."

Frowning, she secured the clean cotton wad in place. When she finished the task, she stood before him, fidgeting nervously with a fold in her skirt, but determined to say what was bothering her before they continued their journey.

"There must be no repetition of what occurred on the slope," she blurted out too quickly, forcing herself to look at him. "You gave me your word of honor back at my father's house that you would conduct yourself in a gent—"

"I agree," he cut in. "I did give you my oath, and I'll do exactly that, as long as you don't throw yourself at me."

"Throw myself—" Thrusting her hands on her hips, she opened her mouth in disbelief. "I slipped in the mud and accidentally fell. I certainly did *not* throw myself at you, I assure you!"

"Well, however it happened, we both seem to want to forget those kisses," he went on, keeping his manner aloof. "We have a business relationship. I'll do my best to see that it remains exactly that."

"Fine!" She marched to Sultan's side. "Do you need assistance mounting your horse?"

"No, madam, I do not." He snatched the reins out of her hands. "Do you?"

"No!"

"Then let's proceed."

It took more effort than he thought it would to climb onto Sultan's back. Pressing his arm close against his side, he moved very slowly, raising himself in the stirrup. Sultan pranced and seemed anxious to break into a run, but he held the horse in at tight rein, forcing the powerful animal to a walk.

Mariah quickly mounted Lilac Wind and followed Jamie. She knew he had to be hurting from his wound, but if he stubbornly refused to admit that fact, then she'd show no sympathy for him.

During the rest of the three days required to travel to Northampton, Mariah and Jamie spoke to each other very little. Other than dressing his wound, she stayed as far away from him as possible. When they rode, she tried to concentrate on the passing forest landscape and furrow-patterned farm fields. Negotiating the treacherous routes they traveled, near bogs and swampland, required her complete attention.

Jamie seemed of the same mind. His exchanges with her were polite and succinct, limited to such subjects as the weather and the roadways.

At night, they stopped at inns located along the main road, always obtaining separate chambers. After they ate supper in the dining room, Jamie stayed to talk with the local men who frequented the establishments to discuss all manner of business and politics. Mariah would retire. Though she'd become accustomed to the long hours of riding, she was always bone-weary by nightfall, and glad for the comfort of a bed. Sleep came easily, but her dreams were often disturbed by visions of Jamie.

Last night, she'd awakened during the hot night, not knowing what time it was. Wondering if Jamie had returned to his room next to hers, she'd listened for sounds of movement. None came. Was he asleep? Or was he, perhaps, lying awake, thinking about her?

Her thoughts had given her no rest. Did he consider her anything except a trial to him? She certainly held no attraction for him. Of course, she'd said the same thing to him, knowing all the time that it wasn't true. If only he weren't so handsome and virile. Then she wouldn't waste precious time thinking about him!

She'd taken out her disgust on the feather pillow, punching it with far more vigor than was necessary to plump it up. Then she'd turned over, putting her back toward the common wall between their rooms.

Now, as she rode beside Jamie, she wished she'd been able to get more sleep during the night. The July day was very warm; the scenery, monotonous. Her chin nodded against her chest more than once, before the small town of Northampton finally came into view.

"A friend of mine owns the only inn here," Jamie explained. "He knows everyone in Northampton and should be able to tell us how to find Anna Wilkes. The inn isn't fancy, but it's respectable and clean enough." He rubbed his hand along his throat. "I could use a tankard of ale right about now to wash away some of this dust. You needn't fear entering the place. Mack won't allow any of his customers to abuse a lady.'' He gave her a quirk of a smile that left her wondering about his seriousness.

She'd had enough of the hot sun. Any place that might offer a respite would be welcome.

Jamie reined in Sultan at the hitching rail of the first building they came to on the edge of the well-populated settlement. Made of rough-hewn logs, the one-storied dwelling had a square, hand-chiseled sign over the wood-plank door that said, ''The Boar's Ear.''

Mariah groaned. A respectable inn, Jamie had called it. She doubted that.

''Saints preserve me! Jamie Lancaster, as I lives an' breathes!'' came the robust shout the moment they entered the alehouse.

Mariah blinked to adjust her eyes to the dimmer light inside and managed to jump aside just in time to let a three-hundred-pound giant lunge by her and capture Jamie in a crushing hug.

''Easy, Mack,'' Jamie cautioned the older man, laughing but wincing with pain as he was lifted off his feet. ''I had a run-in with a black bear a few days ago that left me with some claw decorations on my belly.''

The man set him on his feet again. ''An' how did you leave the bear, lad?''

''Dead, just the way you taught me.''

''Aye, you was always a fast learner!'' The huge man slapped Jamie hard on the shoulder, then threw back his head and roared with laughter, revealing a set of yellowed teeth, with one missing in front.

Mariah could only stare at him. She'd never seen anyone so big. He had to be nearly seven feet tall, she judged. About sixty years old, he wore his gray hair parted down the middle and twisted in two long, thick braids, Indian-fashion.

"An' who's this here pretty little thing with you, Jamie? Yer wife?"

The big man turned his grinning countenance to her. His dark eyes swept over her from head to toe, making her step a little closer to Jamie for protection.

"You know me better than that, Mack. This is Miss Mariah Morgan, my . . . employer." He said the last word as though it tasted bitter on his tongue. "Mariah, this is Mackintosh Phelps."

"Pleased to meet you, ma'am." Phelps gave her a nod, then turned back to Jamie. "Ha! I won't be askin' what services she might be hirin' you fer!" He winked and laughed again.

Jamie grinned at the joke, realizing how wrong his friend was. He could tell by Mariah's scowl that she was not amused.

"We're here to find a Mrs. Anna Wilkes. Do you know where she lives?" he asked.

"Widow Wilkes, with all them nine kids? Aye, she's got a farm jus' outside of town. Can't miss it. Follow the main road north. Goes right by her place. But you ain't leavin' yet, Jamie. Not till you an' yer lady has had a pint of me best ale."

Phelps guided them to a small square table and held out the wooden chair for Mariah. She didn't want any ale, but good manners—and prudence—

told her it wouldn't be wise to disappoint the giant innkeeper. She sat down on the straight-backed chair.

There was only one other person in the ale-house—a man of slight build who was slumped over a table by the stone hearth, snoring loudly. Phelps maneuvered his bulk over to the man and hauled him up by the collar.

"Time to go home, Joseph. Yer woman'll be awaitin'."

Phelps guided him to the door. The man only nodded as he departed.

"Tell me all about what you bin doin' these past three years since I seen you, Jamie," Phelps insisted when he returned with three tall tankards of ale and settled down on the chair across from Jamie. The wooden seat creaked loudly under his weight, but held. "Made it to China yet, lad?"

"I've been at sea mostly and done a bit of trapping. But the Orient has eluded me so far. However, that may change in the near future." He glanced toward Mariah and smiled slightly. The look she returned clearly indicated her distaste for the tavern. "How have these years been for you, Mack?"

"Good, good. Me daughter, Mercy—you remember her. She up and wed a year ago. Give me a grandson already. I tried to keep her fer you, Jamie, but you was never in one place long enough fer her to catch you!" He laughed heartily again and tipped the metal tankard high overhead, draining its contents.

"Now that news saddens me, my friend. Good, sturdy women like your Mercy are hard to come

by. Too many of them are skinny, like this one.''
He waved a hand toward Mariah, who gave him a
black look. ''Nothing to get hold of, if you know
what I mean. You tell Mercy she's broken my
heart.''

''Ha! That I will, that I will. I jus' got back
home myself three days ago. Had me some family
business to take care of up New York way. I heard
about the Albany Congress while I was there. You
know about it, don't you?''

''I heard the Five Nations Indian tribes were unhappy with us and a meeting was going to be held
to try to reconcile grievances. Those tribes are important allies in our fight against the French. The
meeting's taken place, then?''

''Aye. Them savages got their ruffled feathers
smoothed out agin. But the news that everybody
was abuzzin' about was what Benjamin Franklin
done after that. Yer acquainted with Franklin, ain't
you?''

''We've met several times, yes,'' Jamie answered. ''I like his ideas about making the colonies
a stronger political force.''

''He's got ideas, all right. Give 'em to the rep-
resentatives at the Congress, too. Right out said
we need to unite so's we can have better control
over ourselves, especially about Indian affairs an'
settlements farther west. He give a plan fer raisin'
a tax to pay troops and build forts to protect the
frontiers. Said we needed a colonial congress to
oversee it all. You should of heard the uproar 'round
the city. Some called his ideas treason, sayin' good
King George the Second and the Parliament in England would see to them things, jus' like they al-

ways has. Others said we should look after ourselves.''

"I follow that second view, and Franklin's,'' Jamie stated. "We're capable of seeing to Indian matters, new settlements, defenses. And much more.''

Mariah couldn't keep silent any longer. "The King is our sovereign. The English colonies here in North America were founded in his name and remain under his rule and protection. We must abide by the laws of our monarch and Parliament.''

"We do abide," Jamie retorted, "when the laws are just. When they are not, we must speak out.''

Mariah sat forward in her chair, a deep frown creasing her forehead. "You'd question King George's policies? Such views do smack of treason!''

"I consider myself an American as well as an Englishman. I'm loyal to my king, but give blind allegiance to no man. Whatever policies promote the greatest good—those are the ones I endorse.''

Mariah rose to her feet. "You mean the policies that line your pockets with cold, hard cash.''

"One could say the same about you, Miss Morgan.''

She glared at him, too angry to find words to reply. Lifting her head high, she turned away from him to address their host.

"Excuse me, please, Mr. Phelps, but I must be on my way. You've been a most gracious host, but I've business to tend to. Good day, sir.''

Before either Phelps or Jamie could stand, she stood quickly and left.

Phelps gazed toward the doorway. "Saints be praised, but that one's quite a woman, lad."

Jamie took up his tankard and swallowed a large draught of mellow ale. "She's a bloody test of my patience, my friend, and a constant trial."

Chapter 18

"I'm looking for the Wilkes farm," Mariah called to an older woman sitting in a rocking chair on the front porch of a rambling clapboard house. Her hair was completely gray, wound into a thick coil on top of her head. Lines creased her forehead and the edges of her twinkling blue eyes, and her figure was well rounded. Two young blonde girls, who looked to be identical twins of about fifteen years in age, sat on stools on either side of her, peeling potatoes over a large wooden bowl, just as the woman was doing.

"You've found the place," the woman replied, getting up and handing the bowl to the girl on her right. "I'm Anna Wilkes." She walked to the edge of the porch, wiping her hands on her long white apron.

"My name is Mariah Morgan. My father is Dunsley Morgan. I believe you have something for me."

"Dunny's daughter . . ." The woman looked stunned as she murmured the words. Then she seemed to recover. "At last you've come, child." She hurried down the front steps of the porch to hold Lilac Wind's bridle. "Bradley, come help this lady down from her horse,'' she hailed a young man on a ladder who was wielding a paintbrush over the rough board siding of the big, single-story house.

"No, please don't interrupt your work. I can manage,'' Mariah protested, swinging down from the saddle. She was surprised when the older woman suddenly hugged her tightly.

"Forgive me, my dear,'' she apologized, releasing her a moment later. "It's just that I'm so happy to meet you. Welcome to my home. Please, come in out of the hot sun.'' She started to lead the way up to the porch, then stopped, turning back to Mariah behind her. "You are alone, Miss Morgan? No one else is with you?''

Mariah had to work to keep a frown from wrinkling her brow. "A man named James Lancaster has accompanied me as my guide. At my father's request,'' she added quickly. "I expect he'll be along shortly. I left him visiting a friend of his, the proprietor of the Boar's Ear.'' She didn't add that she wished she could leave Jamie there once and for all!

"Ah, good. Yes, he must be here, too. Those were Dunny's terms. Mr. Lancaster will be welcome when he arrives.'' She gestured toward the two girls on the porch. "These are my daughters, Lydia and Lucinda.''

The girls shyly bobbed curtsies to Mariah, who nodded in return. Then she followed Anna Wilkes into the house.

"Let's sit in the parlor,'' her hostess invited, leading the way through the first door they came to in the hallway.

They entered a bright, cheery room. The walls were painted a soft lavender shade. White woodwork lined the borders of the room and the wide hearth. Cream and gold brocade fabric covered the two wingbacked chairs and the sofa. A large, oval mirror framed in gilded wood hung on one wall, reflecting two glass, double-globed lamps and a round, marble-topped table.

"What a lovely room, Mrs. Wilkes," Mariah complimented her sincerely, thinking about the vast difference between this parlor and the Boar's Ear.

"Oh, call me Anna, dear. Sit down here on the sofa with me. I'm so glad you like my little parlor. This may be an out-of-the-way farm, but there's no reason why we can't enjoy the pleasures of civilized living. Thanks to your father, I can afford many of them, even if some must be freighted all the way from Boston."

"Please call me Mariah. My father helped you?"

She stared at the woman across from her, wondering what story she would hear about her father this time.

"Yes, Dunny is responsible for all of this—my farm, my house. We make a good living from the land. My seven sons are nearly all grown men now. They work the fields. My daughters help me here. We are a large and happy family. But that hasn't always been true.

"Eight years ago, Charles, my husband, died suddenly. His heart failed him, the doctors said. We lived in Boston then, in a house too small for us all. We had both come from good families, but I fear Charles had very little business sense. Your father saved us from overwhelming debts when he went into partnership with my husband in an importing company. He provided the necessary capital and developed sound procedures for running the business, which my husband followed to the letter. Then Dunny shipped off to sea on one of his adventures, leaving Charles in charge of the enterprise.

"When my husband died, I had no desire to continue the company. Dunny sold it. But he would take nothing for himself; instead, he gave all the profits to me. It amounted to a great deal of money, enough to pay our debts and invest in this farm, as well. I wanted to come here to Northampton, as this was my home before I married. All my people live here.

"Your father helped me move everything from Boston. It took three wagons to transport all ten of us. He had his hands full during the nearly four weeks it took us to travel here." She stopped to laugh softly, a faraway look in her eyes. "Yet he saw us here, helped me purchase the land, even stayed a month longer to make repairs to this house."

Anna was silent a few moments, then she looked directly at Mariah.

"How is your father? I hope he's well."

Mariah couldn't hold her steady gaze. The emotion she saw in the older woman's face implied much more involvement than her casual words.

"I—I regret to tell you that his health is very poor," she managed to answer, fidgeting with her cuff to hid her surprise at hearing further testimony to her father's generosity.

"Oh. I'm very sorry to hear that."

Mariah heard the life go out of Anna Wilkes' voice and saw her clench her hands together in her lap. She couldn't think of anything to say to the woman, who was so clearly devastated to hear of Dunny's illness.

She herself didn't want to hear stories about her father's kindness and noble nature. They warred with the image she'd held of him for so many years. She wanted to think of him as selfish, irresponsible, neglectful. Seeing him in that light made it easier to hate him. She was deeply hurt to learn that he'd been so giving to others, while withholding himself from her.

"I must tell you something, Mariah." Anna took hold of her hand and smiled. "Something I've never told to anyone else." She sighed deeply before she continued.

"I was a good wife to my husband. We had nine wonderful children together. I loved him very much and I always will. His memory is very dear to me. But so is the memory of your father." She paused, staring off across the room. "Dunny Morgan is like no other man I have ever known. When he burst into our lives, it was as though a hurricane had blown in." Anna paused.

"How Dunny would talk about his many dreams and adventures. We all knew he'd gotten involved in the importing company for business reasons only. He couldn't remain land-bound for long.

"I know I probably shouldn't admit this, but I must. It really doesn't matter now anyway." Anna looked at Mariah, holding her gaze steadily. "I think I fell in love with your father the first moment

I met him. I was in a terrible quandary, for I loved
Charles and my children, too. I likely would have
made a terrible mess of all our lives if Dunny had
let me. But he was strong, stronger than I. He loved
me a little, I think, but most of all, he loved your
mother's memory. His grief for her was very great.
I wanted so much to help him bear it. Yet even
after Charles died and I was free, Dunny wouldn't
be more than a dear friend to me. He told me he
could never love again. We parted, and he went to
sea once more. He visited me here on the farm two
years ago, but only stayed for a short while. Has
he by chance married since?''

"No," Mariah murmured, shaken by Anna's
words. Although she was his daughter, she was
beginning to see that she knew very little about
Dunsley Morgan.

"Nor did I ever take another husband," Anna
added softly.

"Mother?" The girl, Lydia, stood at the open
parlor door. "Your pardon, but Mr. Lancaster is
here."

"Ah, finally." Anna rose to her feet. "Show
him in, dear."

Lydia stepped aside to let Jamie enter the room,
then departed down the hallway.

"James Lancaster, madam," he introduced
himself, darting a glance at Mariah before taking
the older woman's outstretched hand.

"And I am Anna Wilkes. Welcome to my home,
sir. I trust you found Mackintosh Phelps in his
usual robust spirits."

"Yes, madam, he nearly crushed the life out of
me."

"Ha, yes, that's Mackintosh all right. Come, sit down. Mariah and I have been having a nice chat. But now that you're here, I shall fetch the items Dunny sent me to hold for you both."

She walked to the marble-topped table and pulled out the small drawer at the front of it. Mariah followed her movements attentively. She felt anxious to see the fourth puzzle piece.

The drawer yielded a long black leather wallet, which Anna Wilkes handed to Mariah.

"Dunny sent me this some months ago. His letter said only that the contents of this wallet were part of an inheritance you were to receive, Mariah. I was to give it to you only if Mr. Lancaster was accompanying you." She paused, looking thoughtful. "James Lancaster. I'm certain we've never met, sir, yet your name is familiar to me for some reason. Well, perhaps I'll recall why later. Meanwhile, I'm glad to do this small favor for your father, Mariah, for, as I told you, I owe him much. You may open the wallet now."

Carefully folding back the two halves of the leather case, Mariah laid it open in her lap and reached into first one side and then the other to withdraw a wooden puzzle piece and a sheet of folded parchment. Excitement caused her hand to tremble a little. Her eyes darted to Jamie, then back to the paper, which she unfolded.

"It says we're to go back to Boston from here to the home of an Addington Braythwaite," she read, frowning. "He has us running in circles, it would seem."

Anna shook her head and smiled. "Dunny and his schemes. How he delighted in them. He told me in his letter that the wooden piece was part of a puzzle that would be very important to both of your futures. Am I to assume those futures will be together?''

Mariah felt her face flush. She jumped to her feet. ''I assure you, *no,* Mrs. Wilkes!'' She frowned at Jamie, whose smirk revealed his amusement at the older woman's words. ''Once we've solved the riddle of my father's absurd scheme, Mr. Lancaster and I intend to go our separate ways—to opposite ends of the earth, don't you agree, sir?''

''Most adamantly, Miss Morgan. As far apart as possible.''

''Oh, I see.'' Anna cleared her throat, but didn't seem too upset by her faux pas. ''Well, I assume you are both fatigued from your journey. I'll have my daughters make up quarters for you both. Come, we'll take tea in the dining room while your rooms are made ready.''

Chapter 19

After breakfast the next morning, Mariah and Jamie stood with Anna Wilkes in her parlor studying the four wooden puzzle pieces.

"This map is very crude," Mariah exclaimed, using her fingers to push the pieces closer together. Excitement coursed through her at seeing the puzzle nearly complete, but she held the emotion in check, fearing her enthusiasm might be premature. This scheme could still turn out to be a fiasco.

"Yes, it's crude, but it definitely shows the city of Boston." Jamie stroked his clean-shaven chin, gazing at the pieces on the marble-topped table. "See, these lines indicate the Charles River to the north." He waved his finger in the air over the place he meant. "And here is the narrow neck of land that connects the city to the mainland. And here, I'd guess, must be Beacon Hill and Boston Common. But Boston is a city of well over fifteen thousand people. We need the fifth and final piece to fit here in the center to show us the exact location of the gold."

"This is all so like Dunny," Anna declared with a smile. "A map to a treasure of gold for your inheritance." Her expression seemed to sadden suddenly. "What a loving father he is. I wish . . . But never mind. It doesn't matter now."

"We should be starting on our way. It's no short journey back to Boston. It could take as long as five days," Jamie noted, picking up his piece of the puzzle and slipping the long rawhide cord on which he'd strung it over his head and inside his white shirt. "I'll see to the horses. Your pardon, ladies."

After he'd left the parlor, Mariah slowly gathered up the remaining puzzle pieces and tucked them in the leather wallet. Anna Wilkes' kind words about her father still bothered her greatly. Had he sent her on this extraordinary journey only for the purpose of finding the gold? Or did he have some ulterior reasons?

"Please be certain to take care while you're traveling, Mariah," Anna admonished, putting a tall, elegant crystal vase back in its place in the center of the round table. "We've heard rumors of late about renegade Indians, allies of the French, raiding settlements to the north of us. You're fortunate to have James escorting you. He appears to be a most capable man. I enjoyed hearing about his plans to travel to the Orient over supper last night. Why is there such great animosity between the two of you?"

"We have very different opinions." Mariah didn't meet the older woman's gaze, but instead busied herself packing the wallet away in her faded valise.

"You know, when I first met Charles, my husband, I didn't like him in the least. He was very handsome, much like James, but I thought he was

arrogant and far too friendly with other ladies.''
She smiled, remembering. ''But there was something about him that drew me to him.'' She gave a
little laugh, placing her hand over her stomach. ''A
young woman's foolishness a long time ago, but I
still recall it vividly. I don't suppose James causes
you to feel anything like that, does he, dear?''

''No, certainly not!'' Mariah frowned, unwill-
ing to admit the truth. ''I'll be very glad when we
can part company forever!''

At that moment, Lucinda Wilkes came to the
parlor door, a worried expression on her face. ''I'm
sorry to interrupt, Mother, but there is a gentleman
here asking for Mr. Lancaster. He's very—''

Before she could finish the sentence, a stocky
man dressed all in black pushed her aside and
strode into the parlor.

''What is the meaning of this, sir?'' Anna demanded.

''I'm looking for James Lancaster. I was told by
the tavernkeeper that he was here, with you.'' He
pointed at Mariah. ''His latest whore!'' He
frowned menacingly, his thick dark eyebrows
nearly meeting at the bridge of his nose. ''Where
is he?''

Mariah's eyes were wide with shock.

''Lucinda, fetch your brothers here at once,''
Anna instructed, coming to her feet. ''Who are
you, sir, and by what right do you barge into my
house like this?''

''Stop where you are,'' the intruder ordered
sternly, drawing a pistol from under his thigh-
length coat and pointing it at Anna's daughter. The

girl shrank back in fear, hurrying to her mother's side.

"I'm Doyle Iverson and I'm here to see justice done. Lancaster is a murderer. He's been sentenced to death, and I intend to see that sentence delivered before another day is out. Where is he?"

"He went down to the barn for their horses!" Lucinda blurted out, clinging to her mother's arm.

"Hush, child, don't say another word!" Anna warned. "Explain yourself, Mr. Iverson. What murder are you referring to? Surely, you're mistaken. James—"

"He murdered my wife two years ago!" Iverson cut in, taking a threatening step toward her.

Mariah was too stunned to speak. She stared at Doyle Iverson, recognizing him as the sinister-looking man she'd seen in Worcester.

She watched Iverson intently, realizing she and the other women were in great danger. His dark eyes stared unblinking, and his hand clenched and unclenched around the wooden stock of the pistol he pointed at them.

Reaching into the breast pocket of his coat, he yanked out a folded sheet of paper and threw it on the marble-topped table next to Mariah.

"Read it!" he commanded, waving the gun.

Fearing to do anything but obey, Mariah slowly picked up the paper and opened it, revealing a printed poster. Turning it so Anna Wilkes could see the contents, she stared at the words.

"Read it out loud!" Iverson demanded.

" 'Wanted for the heinous crime of murder— James Lancaster of Boston. Ten thousand pounds offered for information leading to the capture of this ruthless killer. Description—six feet, two inches tall, two hundred pounds, black hair, blue eyes. Known to be a seaman. Good with a knife. Murderer of Eleanora Iverson. Contact Doyle Iverson, Worcester, Massachusetts.' ''

"The punishment for murder is death!" he ground out through gritted teeth. "And Lancaster deserves a slow one for what he did to my sainted wife. I've worn black for these two years to honor her memory. Killing Lancaster won't be punishment enough, but I'll have to settle for it. I've waited a long time. Now, sit down, all of you. Don't make a sound and maybe you won't get hurt. We'll just wait here till Lancaster returns. He's the one I want.''

The three women crowded together on the small sofa. No one spoke. Mariah knew Iverson was deadly serious. But she couldn't believe his terrible accusation, or the shocking words she'd read on the poster.

True, she hated Jamie's arrogance, but she couldn't believe he was a murderer. If he were a ruthless killer, then surely she'd know. Some sixth sense would have told her so. Yet not once had she felt a threat to her life from him. Just the opposite— he'd risked his own life to save hers.

"Dear God . . ." Anna's whispered exclamation reached Mariah at the same time she heard Jamie enter the outer hall, talking to Bradley Wilkes. She tensed. Her eyes darted to Iverson, who moved swiftly to hide behind the open door. In the next second, Bradley entered the parlor, followed by Jamie.

"Raise your hands, Lancaster!" Iverson kicked

the door shut and jammed his pistol into Jamie's back. "Move farther into the room and turn around. I want you to see your executioner!"

"Mr. Iverson, please!" Anna cried, leaning forward on the edge of the sofa.

"Be quiet and don't move!" Iverson ordered, his expression fierce. The deadly pistol swung in her direction.

Jamie started to swing around, but Iverson quickly drew a matched firing piece from a waist holster inside his coat. "Stand, Lancaster! I'll kill you soon enough." He brandished the gun at Bradley Wilkes. "You, get over by the fireplace where I can see you."

While Anna's son backed slowly across the room, Mariah tried hard to think through her fear. Her eyes darted around looking for a means of summoning help, a weapon, anything, for she had no doubt that Doyle Iverson fully intended to carry out his terrible death threat against Jamie. She could see the cold-blooded intent in his black eyes. He might even kill all of them, to leave no witnesses.

Was Jamie guilty of the murder of Eleanora Iverson? She had no time to even wonder; she had to go with her instincts, and they were telling her he wasn't a killer. Her eyes flicked to him. His hands were raised at shoulder height. She saw a small muscle in his square jaw twitch and knew he was tensed to spring. Yet his voice was calm when he spoke.

"Don't hurt these people, Iverson. They're not involved in this. This is between us."

"You don't want your new bitch to die like my

Eleanora did, do you?'' Iverson's hate-filled gaze swept to Mariah.

Her heart seemed to stop beating when he smiled malevolently and cocked back the hammer of the pistol he'd been pointing at Anna, but now aimed directly at her.

Jamie's teeth clenched. God, he'd kill Mariah! The terrible thought twisted in his gut. ''Eleanora's death was an accident, Iverson! You know that!'' He sought desperately to divert the man's attention back to himself.

''You murdered her!'' Iverson waved the other pistol closer to Jamie's chest, glaring back at him. ''She spurned your evil advances, and you pushed her down the staircase!''

''No, Iverson, you know that isn't the truth.'' Jamie said the words slowly, quietly, trying to calm the man. ''You were there in the hall. You heard what was said. It was Eleanora who offered herself to me. When I refused, she became hysterical. She flew at me in a rage, wielding the letter opener. We struggled when I defended myself. She fell backward down the stairs. I tried to catch her. She died of a broken neck, not by my hand. Examine your conscience, man! You know how Eleanora acted. She had many men.''

''That's a filthy lie. There were no others. She loved me, only *me!*

His face twisted in an ugly grimace of demented wrath as he leveled both pistols at Jamie. In the same instant, Mariah kicked over the marble-topped table, sending it and the tall crystal vase crashing to the floor right next to Iverson. In the split second that the burly man's attention was caught by the noise, Jamie sprang at him, tackling him around the waist. One of the pistols discharged as it flew out of Iverson's hand. Lucinda screamed as the bullet whizzed by, mere inches from her head.

"Mother, get behind the sofa!" Bradley cried as he moved in to help Jamie. But the two men struggling on the floor rolled away before he could lend a hand.

Mariah should have joined Anna and Lucinda behind the sofa, but she was too riveted to the fight. She watched, horrified, as Jamie teetered atop the stocky Iverson, struggling to hold down the hand that still gripped a pistol. Iverson clutched at Jamie's throat with his other hand. Again they rolled until Jamie was astride Iverson once more. Grabbing the other man's wrist, Jamie repeatedly banged his hand on the floor until Iverson lost his grip on the pistol. Then Jamie raised up on his knees and swung his right fist down with a force so powerful that it whipped Iverson's head to the side, dazing him. Lifting him by the coatfront, Jamie punched him again. Iverson hit the floor with a resounding thud, unconscious.

Jamie staggered to his feet, breathing hard and clutching his midsection. Mariah rushed to him.

"Jamie, are you all right? Your wounds!" She quickly let her eyes slip over him to his stomach, where a small patch of red was soaking through his white shirt. Leading him to the sofa, she spoke urgently to Anna Wilkes.

"Please, I'll need some clean cloth for bandaging him."

"Yes, of course. Hurry, Lucinda, run to my

sewing cabinet and fetch the cotton backing cloth I use for my quilting. Bradley, get some rope to tie this man before he regains consciousness.''

''Yes, Mother,'' the young man replied, moving swiftly from the room. Lucinda followed him.

''Dear me, how did this happen?'' Anna bent down to watch as Mariah unbuttoned Jamie's shirt and started to remove the bloodied bandage.

''We were attacked by a bear several days ago. Jamie was clawed before he was able to kill the animal.''

''My, those are nasty marks. But someone stitched you together well, I'd say. The sewing held even in that awful fight. Only a little blood has seeped through.''

''Mariah did the work,'' Jamie replied. ''She's a very capable physician.''

His eyes caught Mariah's for a moment, but she was too surprised by his compliment to do anything but stare.

''What? A physician? Why, that's extraordinary!'' Anna sat down near Jamie's feet on the edge of the brocade sofa. ''This has certainly been an astounding day. You know, now I recall why your name sounded so familiar to me when I heard it yesterday, James. Dunny spoke about the unfortunate death of Mrs. Iverson when he was here two years ago. He told me your name and that you were a friend who'd gotten involved in a terrible accident. The authorities cleared you of all blame, but the woman's grief-stricken husband still sought revenge. He had those posters printed and distributed. Dunny was trying to track down and destroy as many of them as possible.'' She shook her head

and brushed back a strand of gray hair that had
fallen loose.

Bradley returned and immediately knelt down
beside Iverson's limp form and tied his hands and
feet securely.

"The poor man," Anna went on. "His grief
drove him to madness. He would have killed you,
James, I'm certain. Thank our merciful Lord you
were able to subdue him."

Lucinda brought the cloth then, and Mariah took
a wide piece of it and began tearing it into long
strips that she could wrap around Jamie's torso.
Anna's words echoed in her mind. For a moment,
she paused and looked directly at Jamie. She hadn't
wanted him to die. And like Anna Wilkes, she silently thanked God that Jamie still breathed beneath her touch.

Chapter 20

Late that same night, unable to sleep, Mariah sought the haven of the sprawling grassy meadow behind the Wilkes' barn to escape the oppressive heat of the house and gather her wayward thoughts. Leaving the quiet, dark farmhouse behind, she meandered slowly through the tall grass, relishing the warm breeze which caressed her face. The chalk-white moon was partially obscured by wisps of clouds, but she still had enough light to find her way.

Rolling up the long sleeves of her cream-colored cotton nightgown, she strolled to a tall, stately maple tree, then leaned back against the wide trunk, and loosened several ribbons at the top of her gown.

The sounds of crickets and locusts filled the air. Mariah judged the time to be just past midnight. She knew she should be sleeping. She and Jamie would likely continue their journey tomorrow, and she would be so tired.

She closed her eyes, hoping to coax her over-worked mind into calmness, if not sleep, but thoughts of Jamie tormented her. She wondered if he'd returned yet from taking Doyle Iverson to the county sheriff. Because of the aggravation to his claw wounds, she'd protested Jamie's leaving. But he and Bradley had gone, nonetheless. When he'd regained consciousness, Iverson had continued to threaten and curse Jamie, and no amount of reasoning could still him.

Again she speculated on how close Jamie had come to death, and how that had shaken her. She knew that sooner or later, she must come to grips with her feelings about James Lancaster. When they'd first started this journey, she'd loathed him. But what did she feel for Jamie now? Or for her father, for that matter. The image she'd held of him all these years was slowly being destroyed as she met and spoke to people he'd helped over the years, people who loved him and were grateful to him.

"I couldn't sleep either."

Mariah whirled around to see a familiar tall figure standing behind her. Jamie.

"Oh, y-you startled me."

"I'm sorry. I was standing at the window in my room and saw you leave the house. I wanted to talk to you."

"When did you return?" She tried to make idle conversation as she leaned against the tree again, her hands behind her back. She was suddenly awkwardly aware of the way she was dressed. She shouldn't be out here in her nightgown. Or alone with Jamie. Yet she couldn't have made her legs take her back to the house if she'd wanted to. They wouldn't obey her. They felt too weak at the moment.

"Bradley and I returned about an hour ago."

"What will happen to Iverson?"

"The authorities will investigate. Then there'll be a trial." He ran a hand through his hair, then shook his head. Weariness told in his voice. "I didn't want it to come to this. For two years, I've avoided Iverson. It wasn't that difficult because I was away most of the time. I knew he was insane. Even now, he says no prison will hold him, that he'll see me dead yet. But his vengefulness isn't just directed against me. There are warrants out on him in connection with the deaths of two other men who were rumored to have associated with Eleanora. She was an evil, heartless woman. She knew her husband was irrationally jealous, yet she enjoyed goading him by having affairs with other men. I was never one of them."

He moved in front of Mariah, just as the gauzy cloud cover fell away from the moon, allowing her to see his handsome features outlined in the silvery light. He was looking at her steadily. Clearing her throat, she lowered her eyes, feeling more uncomfortable.

"Y-your wounds," she said quickly, "are they all right?"

"Fine, Mariah. You've seen to them expertly." He stepped closer.

"We really should be getting back to the house." She started to turn away, but he caught her by the arm, stopping her.

"Not yet. There's something I must know." He moved her around by the shoulders so she was in front of him. For a long moment, he let his eyes drift over her face, studying it, searching it. He felt her tense. The heat of her body radiated through the thin cloth of her nightgown and seemed to burn his hands where he touched her shoulders—but he couldn't release her. She looked so beautiful, bathed in the glow of moonlight. He noticed the ribbons at the top of her gown were untied, exposing her long, tapered neck and the beginning of the cleavage between her full breasts.

"What is it you wish to know?" she asked timidly. She wanted to run away from him, for she felt his virile presence overwhelming her. But the touch of his hands paralyzed her. He was standing so close, surely he could hear the loud pounding of her heart.

"You must tell me this. When Iverson showed you that poster, what did you think? Did you believe him? Did you believe I was capable of killing his wife?"

His grip on her shoulders tightened. Mariah bit the edge of her lower lip.

"I believe you are capable of killing." She spoke barely above a whisper. "I've seen the way you use your knife. You've admitted to being a seaman, a hunter and frontiersman, a soldier of fortune. I'm certain you've been in circumstances that required you to take a life."

He let go of her and turned to the side. "I've done what was necessary to defend my own life. I won't deny that fact."

"But you did not kill Eleanora Iverson." She said the words simply and with conviction. "I knew that, even before Anna told about having heard the story of her death from my father. Iverson was very convincing in his accusation, and the poster clearly described you. But I couldn't believe . . ." Her voice dropped off as she gathered the courage to go on. ''In my heart I knew you could not commit such a horrible crime.''

Jamie turned toward her again and gently took hold of her arms. He spoke softly. ''How did you know, Mariah? How could your heart take measure of me so well?''

''I—I don't know, Jamie . . .'' Confused, she put her hands on his shirtfront to hold him at bay, lowering her head to keep from looking at him. She trusted him, was strongly drawn to him. Yet she hung back, fearful of the feelings he stirred in her. When she touched him like this, she felt an exhilarating energy sweep over her. It made her want to be near him, as close in body and spirit as a man and woman could ever be.

He tipped her chin up with his fingers. ''You do strange things to me, Mariah Marie Morgan.'' His voice was hushed. ''At times, you exasperate me to the point where I'd like to turn you over my knee and beat you. You're stubborn and opinionated, beautiful and courageous. We think so differently, yet you, too, have stood against strong opposition to pursue the path you've chosen for yourself. And you're fiercely loyal to your convictions, whether they concern a charity hospital or the King of England.

''I've wished you out of my life almost since the first moment you entered it. Yet when Iverson pointed his pistol at you, I couldn't bear it.''

Jamie knew he should stop talking, for with every word he could feel the carefully built barrier deep inside him cracking, weakening. He must not lose his control, must not let Mariah reach him. She wasn't even trying to force her way in. Rather,

her hands pushed against his chest, keeping him at a distance. She, too, seemed to be resisting the compelling force churning around them. If he walked away now, he'd be safe. All he had to do was let go of Mariah, move back one step, two steps, then go to the house.

Do it, he ordered himself. Do it before her lips whisper your name again.

He started to take the first step back.

"Jamie . . ." She murmured his name with an anguish that tore into his heart. Her fingers pressed into the loose material of his shirt. Her eyes beseeched him. "Help me, please. I don't understand what's happening between us. It's all strange and new to me. I'm confused. When you kissed me before—"

He kissed her now, suddenly, roughly. His arms came around and pulled her hard against him. His hand entwined in her long hair, holding her so she couldn't pull back.

But she wouldn't have resisted even if she could. His mouth tasted too good on hers. His lips demanded, yet asked. Her pulse racing, she molded her body to his, clinging to him, meeting him kiss for kiss. When she had to gasp for breath, she felt his lips move down her throat, then return to claim her mouth again. A deep need smoldering within her suddenly burst into flame, igniting her senses.

He felt her trembling. "Don't be afraid, Mariah," he whispered against her soft mouth. Then he forced himself to take a small step away from her. With the gentlest of touches, he ran his finger along the side of her face, over her lips, and down the length of her slim neck. He kept his eyes locked on hers. He heard the breath catch in her throat and knew he must go slowly. She was young and untried—certainly a virgin. He could sense how fragile she was at this moment, how vulnerable. He must take time and great care.

Holding her face between his hands, he kissed her tenderly. Still making himself stand a little away from her, he moved his hands down her neck and then to the ribbons of her nightgown. The thin velvet laces yielded to his gentle tug. Ever so slowly, he slid the cotton gown from her shoulders. It fell noiselessly to the ground. It took great control not to look at her naked body, but he would not do it yet. Instead, he kept gazing into her eyes. The glow of moonlight was reflected in their depth. It floated over her face, lighting it just enough to show its pale smoothness. He raised his hand to touch her cheek and feel the softness of her skin. With growing excitement, he knew the rest of her body would have the same velvet texture beneath his fingertips.

He reached for the buttons of his own white shirt. Moving slowly, he unfastened them. Then the shirt and his breeches joined her gown on the grass.

Only inches separated him from Mariah, but he resisted the urgent need he felt to take her into his arms. In a hushed voice, he spoke. "You must want this between us, Mariah. I made a vow to you, and I will not break it. You must release me from it. Listen to your heart. Hear what it's saying to you. I want you. My desire speaks to yours. What is your answer?"

She stood looking into his eyes. Without even touching her, he was overpowering her body, her will. Her hands trembled at her sides. Her legs felt weak. Anticipation mounted in her, making her heart pound wildly. Dear God, how he frightened her. Not because he might harm her. She didn't fear that. These feelings he caused frightened her. But not enough to make her turn away. Her body answered, and her heart echoed its choice.

She lifted her hands to his shoulders. Following the cords of muscle running along them, she let her fingers slip slowly down over his bare, powerful chest. She felt him tense under her light touch. He closed his eyes. His chest rose and fell with his quickened breathing.

"Kiss me, Jamie, and you shall have your answer . . ." She pressed her naked body against his length and drew his head down to find her waiting lips.

At first there was gentle searching in their kiss. But the closeness of their bodies quickly demanded more. His hands caressed the flesh of her back.

"Mariah . . ." he breathed against her mouth, crushing her to him.

She clung to him. Even when he lifted her in his arms and eased her down to the soft, cushioning grass, she kept her arms entwined tightly around his neck, afraid to let him go. Perhaps this was all a dream—the sweet taste of his mouth on hers, the feel of his magnificent, hard-muscled body.

He drew her arms away, placing them gently at her sides. "Lie still, Mariah," he said, his voice hushed. "Let me learn of you . . ."

He began kissing her then. Small, exploring caresses like wisps of breeze touching her, over her forehead, her eyes, passing lightly over her cheeks, her mouth, down her neck. When his lips found the mound of her breast, she gasped, shocked and paralyzed by the pleasure of that kiss. She waited unmoving, with a rising expectation that made her heart pound wildly. When his lips brushed over the tip of her breast and pulled away, she had to bring his head back to it. The feel of his tongue as it circled the hardening nipple again and again tortured her, but it was the sweetest of torments. Her pleasure grew, and with it came a mounting tide of desire.

His lips sought her other breast, exploring around and over it, repeating the torrent of passionate caresses until the fiery excitement surging through her veins made her writhe beneath him, murmuring his name.

His hands followed his seeking lips over every curve and hollow of her body. She had no will, no consciousness of anything except Jamie touching her. An aching urgency surged to tempest force inside her. She couldn't endure his bold journey over her any longer, and yet she knew she must bear it, for it was the greatest of ecstasies. Her body and soul desired more, needed more of him.

Crying out softly, she twisted her head, clinging to him, feeling the blazing heat of his body spread to her. And just when she thought she could know no greater rapture than she already felt, he gently parted her legs and touched her most intimate places with his fingertips, driving her mad with pleasure. She was doomed. Suddenly, her exquisite climax burst upon her in violent pulsing waves, shattering her body to the depths. He moved over her then, sliding inside her to penetrate her throbbing womanhood. For a moment a wave of pain overcame her, but soon it felt more like pleasure. She arched her hips to welcome him, draw him deeper. He pulled back and plunged again and again, until the culmination of his own arousal burst forth within her.

Time hung suspended as they held fast to each other. His weight crushed her into the thick grass, but she felt so much a part of him that she wanted only to keep him very close.

Breath and pulse finally began to slow to normal pace. Holding Mariah in his arms, Jamie began kissing her slowly, softly—her hair, her face, her neck. His hand gently caressed her breasts, easing her back to reality from the pinnacle of magnificent excitement she'd reached. He marveled that his own desire had been ignited so tumultuously. He'd sensed her chasteness, her virginity, and had sought only to expose her to the wonder of passion that could exist between a man and a woman. He hadn't reckoned that his own rapture would be so great. Her innocent fire had spread to him like a spark to dry tinder, creating a blaze within him like no other he'd ever known with a woman. The flame had seared his soul, forcing an unwanted, deeper need to surface. He knew he must crush it while he still could. When Evangelene died, he'd promised himself never to allow anyone to reach his vulnerable inner self. Mariah could do that, if he let her. But he wouldn't. He'd share the pleasures of the body with her, as he had with other women, but no more. He made that vow in his mind.

He kissed her eyes and tasted the saltiness of tears. "Did I hurt you?" he whispered, touching her cheek.

"No, I weep from joy. But what about your wound? Was there much pain?"

He smiled down at her. "If there was, I didn't notice it. I was occupied with other things."

"I never realized . . ."

"I know, Mariah. The first time is truly an awakening."

"I—I know so little, Jamie." Her words came haltingly, for she feared to learn his reaction. But she must know. "Was your pleasure as great as mine?"

He smiled again. "Yes, silly one. I enjoyed our lovemaking as much as you."

He rolled onto his back then, but still cushioned her head with his arm, holding her close against his side.

She raised up on her elbow to look at him. She wasn't so naive as to think this had been the first time for him. His handling of her was too expert, too knowing. She stroked her fingers over the dark hair on his chest.

"Teach me, Jamie. Show me how to pleasure you. You create such excitement in me. I want to give the same feeling back to you."

He caught hold of her hand just as it moved around his bandaged wound and down over the tight muscles of his belly. "You know enough already, milady. I think you've had enough lessons for one night. It's late. We should go back to the house."

"I know," she agreed, but she made no move to leave his side. Instead, she leaned down, pressing her breasts against his chest. She kissed his cheek, rough from new whiskers. She trailed her

lips down to his neck, then back up the side of his
face to his ear, where she nibbled at the lobe, as
he'd done to hers. He flinched.

"Mariah," he warned, seeking to stop her before she rekindled his desire, making him vulnerable once again.

"Jamie," was all she murmured before she
found his mouth. First she kissed his top lip, then
the lower one.

Unable to resist, he moaned and twisted his hand
into her hair, forcing her head down so he could
consume her mouth. Then he pulled her over so
she was completely on top of him.

Lifting her head for breath, she pulled away from
his mouth and slid downward so she could kiss his
chest. She rubbed one hand roughly over his
breasts. When she followed with her lips, she felt
his heart racing, heard his jagged breathing. She
pushed herself up and threw her head back, gasping when his hands found her breasts.

His fingers stroked her hardened nipples, then
he drew her closer so his lips could follow the same
searing path.

His sensual torment excited her body to a frenzy.
She twisted, rubbing against him at every place
possible. When he aligned her hips with his and
plunged into her, she gasped again, welcoming him
with all her being. They moved back and forth in
one fluid rhythm, until the splendid climax burst
between them once more, passing from one to the
other and back again.

Panting for breath, Mariah collapsed across Jamie's chest. His arms encircled her and his hand
stroked her hair. She didn't want to think, wouldn't

let herself reason. Her body, her instincts told her this joining with him was right. Her spirit soared to the same heights of joy that her senses had reached. He was magnificent, all manly power and will. Yet she knew he gave as much as he claimed. His kisses could be tender, his touch gentle.

She kissed him. She never wanted this night to end. At last her confused feelings about him were sorted out. She realized she was falling in love with him. It would likely bring a new and different turmoil to her life, but she didn't want to worry about that now. She would only think of Jamie holding her, caressing her. Tomorrow was soon enough to face the future.

Chapter 21

The next morning, Mariah and Jamie pretended nothing had happened between them in the meadow the night before. They had crept quietly back to the house, where Mariah had spent a blissful night, alternately dozing, then dreaming of Jamie. She was too tired to say very much at breakfast, even if she'd wanted to, which she didn't. There was too much to think about. Too many questions plagued her mind.

"Are you up to continuing your journey, dear?" Anna inquired, passing the fresh cinnamon muffins to Mariah. "Yesterday was very distressing for all of us."

In more ways than one, Mariah added in her thoughts, suppressing a groan. Her eyes darted to Jamie sitting across the table from her. He returned her gaze, his expression inscrutable.

"I'll be all right, Mrs. Wilkes. Please don't worry. I just didn't get very much sleep last night."

Realizing the ridiculous understatement in her words, she rolled her eyes toward the ceiling and forced herself to eat another spoonful of hot porridge.

After breakfast, Bradley brought the horses around for them.

"I wish you good fortune on your quest, dear," Anna exclaimed, hugging Mariah. "I hope you find the treasure, and I pray your father's health has improved by the time you return to him. Give him my best regards. Tell him I miss him and that he has a very special place in my heart."

"I shall. Thank you."

Jamie helped her mount Lilac Wind, then joined her on Sultan.

"Take care, both of you," Anna cautioned. "There are many perils in such a journey."

The weather grew quickly warmer as the day progressed. Riding east once more, mostly across open countryside, there was no shade to deflect the sun's hot rays. Not a single cloud punctuated the azure sky. Flies buzzed close to the sweating horses. Mariah batted at them, annoyed by their stings. She grew impatient with the slow pace Jamie had set, even though she knew he walked the horses to keep them from overheating.

She and Jamie spoke little to each other as they traveled. She didn't know what to say to him. And he seemed just as reluctant to converse with her. In the light of day, the wondrous magic they had woven between them in the moonlit meadow seemed to have faded, replaced by stark reality. She argued with herself about their differences, the impossibilities of a serious relationship between them. He'd made it clear all along that he wanted no ties in his life, that he was a loner who drifted wherever the wind took him. They didn't agree about anything, be it a woman's place or the future of colonial rule in America. He hardly knew the meaning of the word commitment. But she did. She'd made serious commitments in her life, to medicine, to the patients at the hospital in Boston, to . . .

Samuel Hastings. She'd been trying to close all thought of him out, but couldn't any longer. In her heart, she believed she loved him, wanted to share his life, his work. At least those had been her feeling until last night. Now she could barely conjure up his features in her mind's eye. Jamie's kept surging to the fore.

Unwittingly, she glanced to where he rode just ahead of her. He wore a full-sleeved beige shirt today and buff breeches. She saw how the material stretched across his broad shoulders. His sleeves were rolled up, revealing his powerful arms. How well she now knew the strength in those arms that had held her so possessively most of the night, demanding her surrender, yet giving her a glorious pleasure unmatched by anything she'd ever known. She felt safe wrapped in them.

But they weren't holding her now. Instead, his strong back was turned away from her, and she sensed his feelings were turned from her as well. They had to talk, but she was afraid to broach any subject, fearing it would lead to the one she most dreaded—what they felt for each other. What would he say? What did he feel? Last night as they searched and discovered each other's needs and desires, everything had seemed so clear. They were the only two people in the whole world, and that world was a shining and splendid place.

But in the daylight, Mariah knew life was not always so wonderful. She'd seen its harsh realities too many times before.

At noon, Mariah and Jamie crested a hill and halted. A wide, pristine pond spread before them in a tree-lined valley below. In open places, where the shade from the trees didn't reach, hundreds of white and purple wildflowers carpeted the ground.

"How beautiful," Mariah murmured, drinking in the sight.

"We'll stop there to eat and rest the horses," Jamie announced. "This heat is taxing our mounts."

"Not to mention us," she added under her breath as she gave Lilac Wind her head and pointed her toward the pond.

Soon she was setting out the meal of cheese, roasted chicken, and fruit that Anna Wilkes had sent with them, while Jamie led the horses to the pond for water, then to a shady grove of dense pines to unsaddle them. With growing alarm, she saw him take off his shirt and sit down on a rock to pull off his tall black boots. Then, to her surprise, he slipped off his tan breeches and took a running dive naked into the clear blue-green water of the pond.

She was shocked by the quick glimpse of him that she'd caught before the water closed over him. Her mouth dropped open and she froze, holding an apple nearly to her mouth. In the seconds that he'd taken to undress, her eyes had swept over his deeply tanned chest and back and then to the very white portion of the lower half of his body. She swallowed hard, stunned because of her own feelings of embarrassed modesty. Yet she felt wantonly drawn to watch him and follow his movements in the water. He swam with powerful, smooth strokes, then floated with an abandoned leisure.

She longed to do the same. Suddenly she envied Jamie's free spirit, his lack of restraint. The water looked so cool and refreshing. Her deeply ingrained sense of propriety warred with her body's natural yearning to be rid of the hot, sweaty, confining clothes. She sighed. Well, at least she could take off her riding boots and let her poor feet delve into the pond.

Walking to the grassy bank closest to her, she avoided looking at where Jamie swam, and sat down to unceremoniously yank off each boot. She turned her back to him to lift her skirt and roll down her stockings, removing them. Then, still holding her skirt above her knees, she walked into the pebble-bottomed pond, sighing with pleasure as the cold water inched up her calves. Stopping, she bunched the material of her skirt into one hand and used her other to splash water over her face. Running her wet hand down the side of her neck, she closed her eyes and smiled with pleasure.

"You should shed those clothes and really enjoy this pond," Jamie piped up close at hand.

Her eyes flew open and darted to where he stood in waist-deep water not ten feet away from her.

"This is fine, thank you," she informed him aloofly, turning to the side to try to ignore him.

"You must be as hot as I was in those clothes. Come, no one will see you."

She spun around, frowning at him. "*You* will see me! I have no intention of—"

"I've already seen you without clothing, Mariah."

She saw a slight smile turn up one corner of his mouth.

"Don't remind me of last night and my disgraceful weakness!"

A hot flush washed over her as she whirled and started to stomp out of the water. But Jamie's hand caught her ankle, tripping her so she fell into the shallows. He immediately knelt beside her. Rolling her over on her back, he roughly gripped her wrists and pulled her up to a sitting position directly in front of him. His angry frown held her unmoving in his grasp.

"It did happen, Mariah. I don't deny it, and I won't let you deny it either. We made love in the meadow and there was nothing disgraceful about it. It was beautiful. That was last night. This is now. Damn, I just suggested you come into the water to cool off. That's all. I've no desire to ravish you, nor do I wish to be burdened with a woman afflicted with heatstroke. But if you won't swim without clothes, that's your choice."

He was flaming mad at her, but he wasn't sure why. Lurching to his feet, he yanked her up after him, dragging her toward deeper water.

"No, Jamie, stop!"

She tried to shrink back and pull out of his grip. When they were nearly chest-deep, he turned, grabbed her around the waist with his hands, and tossed her forward into deeper water, causing her to submerge completely. She came up sputtering and scrambling to get a footing on the rocky bottom.

"How dare you!" she railed at him, fuming with anger as she hit the surface with the flat of her hand to send a broad arc of water splashing at him. It hit him full in the face.

After slowly wiping the wetness away, he put his hands on his hips, scowling at her.

"I dare whatever I wish, madam. You needed cooling off, and I don't think you've yet reached the right temperature to douse that temper of yours!"

"Yes, I have! Don't you come near me again!" She held out her hand to fend him off, backing away.

Jamie dove underwater and in the next instant, Mariah felt her legs being pulled out from under her. The water closing above her drowned out her cry of protest. She shot to the surface again, coughing and tossing her head to get her wet hair out of her eyes.

"Oh! You beast!" She hit the water with her fists, but Jamie didn't see her. He'd turned to wade in toward the shallows. Letting her temper get the best of her, she forged through the water, hampered by the drag of her soaked skirt, but determined to take her revenge. She caught him just as he was about to step up the bank. Grabbing his forearm, she yanked him back so hard that she lost her balance and stumbled backward into the knee-deep water. Caught off guard, Jamie fell too, almost landing on top of her.

Satisfied with sinking him, she started to rise up out of the water to go toward the bank. But a strong arm came around her waist, forcing her over onto her back. The lower half of her body was still in the water. Jamie threw his leg over her wet skirt to halt her thrashing.

"Let go of me!" she demanded, swinging her fist up to hit him. He easily caught her wrist with his hand and pinned it down to her side.

"Damn, but you're a spitfire. You don't like to be bested, do you, Mariah?"

"You will never best me! You can overpower me, but never best me!"

He smiled. "Is that so? Now you've set the challenge, milady, and I never was one to resist a call to contest. We'll just have to see whose will is stronger."

He leaned over and tried to kiss her, but she twisted her head away so his mouth fell on the side of her cheek. Grabbing her chin, he forced her face back so he could meet her lips.

Her anger gave her complete control of her body. She set her mind not to react in any way to his caress. She stopped struggling, instead making herself go limp beneath him. He could even rape her and she wouldn't fight him. She'd kill him with his own knife after, yes. But now she wouldn't resist or take part.

Jamie saw her ploy and would have none of it. All of his sense were aroused by her nearness. The cold water had caused her nipples to harden. He saw that clearly as her breasts strained at the wet cotton fabric of her blouse. Her face glistened in the sunlight. Drops of water lay on her long dark lashes. The vivid memory of their night of passion in the meadow set his heart racing. His fingers tingled to unfasten the buttons of her blouse and peel away the material to claim her again. But he made himself wait, knowing the delay would excite him more. He was determined not to force her surrender. The challenge lay in making her realize her own need, so she gave in to him of her own free will.

He saw her lips pressed tightly together. Her eyes, too, were tightly closed. He smiled and ran a fingertip ever so lightly over her mouth, first the lower lip, then the upper. He traced every contour of her face—the small rises over her cheekbones, the lines of her finely arched dark brows, the indentation above her small chin. She remained still, but he saw a tiny muscle in her delicate jawline twitch and knew she was having trouble continuing to resist him.

His fingertips explored down the side of her slim neck and along her collarbone. When he rested the palm of his hand on her breast, he felt her tense, heard her suck in her breath. Slowly, he unfastened the buttons down her wet blouse and the thin satin ribbons holding her chemise together underneath.

His own breath caught as he gazed at the beautiful creamy mounds revealed to him. For a few moments, he touched each of her breasts in turn with his fingertips, caressing the taut nipples. Then he followed with his lips and tongue, nibbling at first, as if sampling a banquet. His gentle kisses quickly became more consuming as his appetite for her deepened. His mouth captured one peak; his hand, the other. Though he knew she tried to suppress it, he heard a small moan sound in her throat.

"Surrender, Mariah," he murmured. "Let me

give you pleasure. I want you . . ." The words "I need you" almost spilled from his lips, but he stopped them from coming. He didn't need her. He only wanted to share his body with her, as he had with other women. Nothing more.

Mariah felt helpless. His tenderness defeated her more surely than forced ravishment ever could have. She tried not to respond, but her body wouldn't obey her. When his lips found her mouth, her own lips moved to meet them. Her hands stroked up his powerful, naked back to his head, where they entwined in his thick hair.

She would not think or reason. How easy it was to shut off her mind, much easier than trying to resist Jamie. Every fiber of her body seemed to be drawn to him, reaching for him. She must get close to him. She needed to feel his strength, know his desire, become part of him, even if only for a brief time.

She couldn't voice her surrender; instead, she showed him—by gazing into his pale-blue eyes, then slowly drawing his head close so her lips could find his again.

He lifted her in his arms and carried her from the shallows to the grassy bank, hastily removing her clothes. Lying together in the secluded clearing, the world seemed so far away.

There was only Jamie and his hands and lips causing a frenzied upheaval of her senses. His deliberate slowness in arousing her was pure torture and delight at the same time. In her veins danced the fire he ignited within her. His mouth and fingers roamed over every inch of her, only to return again to her breasts and then her lips.

She wanted to touch him in return. She was timid at first, then grew bolder when the sharp intakes of his breath told her she was pleasuring him. She urged him to lie still while she used her hands and lips to caress the bulging muscles of his arms and chest. Her fingers stroked over his hard belly, carefully avoiding his healing wound.

He could bear no more delay. Rolling with her, he rose up over her. Her name spilled imploringly from his lips. He leaned down, feeling her legs part to receive him. As he plunged deeply into her, the warm, moist feel of her closing around him made his senses explode. His mind and body knew nothing but Mariah, her softness, her sweet taste, her cry of rapturous pleasure as he moved forward and back inside her with powerful thrusts. Their climactic joining raged thunderously between them, forcing them to cling to each other as the glorious pulsations surged through their bodies.

The sun beat down relentlessly, but its heat couldn't compare to the burning passion arcing between Jamie and Mariah. It transcended their rivalry, their anger, their differences, melding them into one entity for an all-consuming, suspended fragment of time.

Chapter 22

"Will you think of me when you're sailing to the Orient, Jamie?"

"What?"

Mariah lay in his arms in the soft grass. For a long time she'd stayed still at his side, basking in the contented afterglow of their lovemaking. But now, suddenly, she felt uncertain. She sat up and turned her back to him.

"I'm sorry. That was an unfair question. I know you won't remember me at all."

"You know nothing of the sort," Jamie replied.

"What does the future hold for us?" She lowered her head to study her hands.

"I don't know, Mariah. I'm not a seer. Don't sound so bloody morose." He sat up, too, and put out his hand, but withdrew it just before it touched her.

"I've always wanted commitment—certainly something more than an occasional tryst with a man."

"You've made it clear all along that you want a man like your Dr. Samuel Hastings, a man determined to live as a beggar and save all the wretches of the world."

Her head whirled around. "Don't speak of him in that condescending tone! You have no idea what kind of man Samuel is!"

Jamie grabbed her by the arms and pulled her roughly back against his chest, speaking huskily close to her ear. "And you cannot fathom the kind of man *I* am! You're just angry because in the short time we've been together, I've taught you about love, while apparently your Samuel Hastings taught you only about medicine in all the five years you've been with him. Has he touched you, Mariah?" He ran his finger along the length of her arm and felt her tremble beneath his touch. "Kissed you?" He leaned down and pressed his lips to her shoulder.

She shuddered and twisted out of his grasp, moving a little away from him.

"You've taught me how to *make* love, Jamie, but not about loving. The two are not the same."

"Loving means chains, and I'll have none on me. You've known that from the beginning. I must be free to follow my own course, wherever it takes me. I can't be caged to a hospital or a bank or a barrister's bench. I've fought for causes I've believed in, offered my life for crown, country, and my fellow man, just as wholeheartedly as your Samuel has. And I'll do so again when I see that the risk counts for something. Otherwise, a stout ship beneath my feet and a destination of my own choosing are all that I seek."

"And I am the means to those goals."

"That wasn't the reason I made love to you."

She turned halfway around to look at him then, her blue-green eyes glistening like the crystal pond at the edge of the bank.

"Why did you make love to me, Jamie?"

She hardly dared to breathe, waiting for his answer. He stared off toward the water. His reply was several long moments in coming.

"Because you fire my blood, torment me. Every waking moment, you're in my thoughts. And even when I sleep, visions of you haunt me. But nothing lasts, Mariah. It's better not to pretend that anything does." He put his hands on her shoulders, speaking gently. "Just enjoy the pleasure we have together for the time being, and don't examine it too closely or ask for everlasting promises. They can crumble before your eyes. Life is fragile, precious. Live for the moment, enjoy it to the fullest, and let the future fall where it may."

Mariah felt her heart breaking into tiny, sharp shards of pain. With great sadness, she realized how much this man had awakened in her. He'd introduced her to adventure, danger, fear, courage, even laughter. She remembered getting drenched in the rain with him and feeling more happy and carefree than she ever had in her life.

His hands on her shoulders branded her with their heat. She longed to lean back in his embrace, have his arms come around her and shield her from the evil and harshness of the world. But she resisted that yearning, rising to her feet instead.

"I want more than just the moment." She kept her back to him so his compelling eyes couldn't draw her to him. "And I won't be one of your fleeting, meaningless romps. When I choose, I'll give myself completely, and with total commitment. You live for the moment. I'll plan for a lifetime with someone."

She walked to where her valise lay on the ground next to Lilac Wind's saddle and sought out dry clothing.

Jamie watched her for a few moments, deep in thought, then he strode to the pile of his clothes and dressed.

He'd just pulled on his boots and tucked his knife inside when a bloodcurdling scream shattered the tranquility of the clearing. His gaze shot to Mariah, who looked back at him with the same stunned surprise.

"The other side of the hill!" He waved toward the rise as he dashed for his pistol in the saddle holster. "Stay here with the horses," he instructed, checking the priming on the weapon.

"No! That was a woman's scream. I'm coming with you!"

He frowned, but didn't argue with her. "Keep down when we get to the top."

The view from the narrow trail running along the top of the hill revealed nothing. Crouching low, Jamie ran across the dirt path, with Mariah following. Pushing aside a branch, he squinted to see down into the deep ravine. A curse issued from his lips at the scene which met his eyes.

"Oh, dear God!" Mariah exclaimed, looking over his shoulder.

His hand clamped over her mouth. "Silence!" he whispered fiercely. "Voices carry."

He looked back through the bush to where a war-painted Indian wearing only a loincloth slid off his horse and grabbed for a white woman slung across the animal's withers. He dragged her kicking and screaming toward a tree, and when he reached it, struck her hard across the face. She lay dazed while he tied her hands and feet with a length of rope, then threw the rope over a high branch jutting out from the tree. Pulling on the slack, he hauled her up so she hung helplessly by her wrists, her bound feet dangling inches off the ground.

"We must help her!" Mariah cried in a hoarse whisper, clutching Jamie's arm. Without thinking, she started to get up, but he yanked her back down.

"Stay down! Do you want to end up with her?"

"W-what are those things hanging at his waist?" she asked, staring at the fierce-looking red man. His long black hair hung separated into two braids on each side of his face. His features were nearly indiscernible because of the streaks of bright color painted over his forehead, cheeks, and jaw. His naked chest and back bore the same wild marks. Red dripped down one leg from the objects hanging from the cord of his loincloth.

"Trophies from a raid," Jamie answered grimly. "Scalps."

Mariah's hand flew to her mouth and she gasped, horrified.

Jamie gazed through the bush again, then sat back, leaning an elbow on his bent knee, shaking his head. "I don't recognize his tribe from the war paint. He could be a renegade, perhaps paid by the French to raid English settlements in the area."

"Anna Wilkes warned me that she'd heard rumors about renegade savages to the north."

"He may be raiding alone, but that possibility seems slim. More likely, he's separated from the rest of the band to keep from having to fight his fellow braves over the woman. At any rate, we have little time. Her life isn't worth much at the moment."

"What will he do to her?" Horror stories she'd read in Boston newspapers about brutal rapes, scalpings, and mutilations by Indians sprang into her mind.

Jamie looked at her. "Let's just say she'll beg for a quick death, but won't receive it."

"Oh, Jamie, what can we do?"

"All right, listen closely. We must create a ruckus to distract his attention. You stay here where you'll be well hidden. I'll circle around the trail to the right." He pointed toward five oak trees close together. "When I'm in position, I'll raise my hand. You call for help as loudly as you can. I'll attack him when his attention is drawn to you. But whatever you do, don't show yourself, Mariah. If anything happens to me, get to the horses and escape. Try to make it back to Mrs. Wilkes'."

"But, Jamie—" she started to protest.

"There's no time for argument." He turned to crawl away.

"Wait!" She pulled on his foot to draw him back. "Too late!" She pointed through the bush to where five more braves had just ridden into view.

Her heart filled with pity for the poor young blonde captive. How terrified she must be. What horrible fate awaited her?

"Our only chance to help her is to wait until after dark," Jamie whispered.

"No, by then they could—"

"I know what they could do to her, but we have no choice! Can you count? There are six of them to one."

"Two," she corrected.

"All right, two then." He gritted his teeth and wiped the back of his hand across his sweaty brow, angry at their helplessness. "Let's get back to the pond. We'll saddle the horses and conceal them. The savages might seek the water for their own mounts. We must conceal our presence there."

When they returned to their spying place a half hour later, they saw the Indians chanting and dancing around a blazing fire. A brave sitting on the ground beat out an irregular rhythm on a small drum in his lap. Jamie pointed to the tall brave who held a crockery jug on his shoulder, tipped toward his mouth.

"Whiskey. They must have gotten it in the raid. They're getting drunk. Perhaps luck is with us. We may not have to wait until nightfall. The young woman doesn't seem to have been harmed yet."

The captive still hung in the tree, her head lying limp against her chest. Was she still alive? Mariah could see no visible wounds on her. The Indians seemed to be ignoring her as they laughed and danced in exaggerated circles, making whooping sounds and passing the jug around.

But Mariah's hope that the young woman wouldn't be hurt quickly vanished when she saw one of the braves trip toward her. He grabbed her around the waist to keep from falling. She screamed and tried to twist away from him. Regaining his balance, he swayed drunkenly on his feet, but kept an arm around her waist. His hand whipped up to clutch at the scooped neckline of her soiled green dress and yank it downward. She screamed again as her breasts were exposed to him and he leaned forward to bury his face against them.

"No . . ." Mariah murmured, sick with foreboding. "Jamie." Her eyes beseeched him.

"Stand fast, Mariah." He put a restraining hand on her shoulder. "We won't help her by being captured ourselves. We must wait a little while longer."

A loud outburst in some language she didn't understand drew her to look back at the gruesome scene. The Indian who'd arrived first had shouted the words just before he grabbed the brave molesting the hostage by the braids and jerked him away from her. Then he swung his fist down and dealt his companion a powerful blow that knocked him unconscious.

"That's one less," Jamie noted, though he'd winced at the sound of the fallen Indian's cracking jaw. "And look, that one by the tree just slumped over—passed out from the liquor. The odds are improving."

The Indian who'd disabled his fellow now yanked the white woman's head back by her blonde hair and bent down to kiss her roughly. When she tried to kick him with her tied feet, he laughed and pushed her away, so she swung back and forth on the rope. Then he staggered to another one of the renegades and grabbed the crockery jug from him, tipping it to his mouth again.

"That's right, you big heathen bastard, keep drinking," Jamie urged through clenched teeth. His finger twitched on the trigger of his pistol as his eyes scanned the other braves.

"That one with the drum looks intoxicated,

too," Mariah noted, pointing to him. "If I had a branch or something, I could hit him from behind."

"No, I don't want you in the camp. There're too many of them."

"Well, you can't rescue her alone. I'm not helpless."

"I know you aren't." His eyes held hers for a moment. "Well, we won't get a better chance than now to aid that woman. Stay hidden here, as we planned before. I'll circle around. Don't do anything unless I get into more than I can handle. If I do, use my pistol." He handed her his weapon, then drew his long-bladed knife out of his boot.

As he started to turn away, she quickly leaned over and planted a kiss on his cheek. "For luck!" she whispered with a feeble smile.

Jamie kept his head low as he circled around to the oak trees on the opposite side of the camp. He hoped the liquor in the jug would help even the four-to-one odds. Having Mariah involved worried him as well. He'd probably need her help, but no matter what, he couldn't let her fall into the hands of these savages. He wasn't keen on the idea of meeting that fate himself.

He stopped moving when he was just ten feet from the closest Indian. The red man's back was to him as he danced in place and beat on the small drum. Dropping to his belly behind a bush, Jamie startled a rabbit. It bounded away, running right through the Indian's legs. Swaying precariously, the savage whirled around in surprise. Jamie rose up and hurled his knife, catching the man squarely in the chest. His mouth opened as he clutched at the hilt of the blade, but not a sound emerged from his mouth as he fell backward in death.

Jamie swiftly jumped forward, yanked the knife free, and lunged into a second Indian, catching him with his shoulder and tumbling to the ground with him. This opponent hadn't been taken by surprise. Nor was he as drunk as the other. He quickly reacted by rolling just out of Jamie's reach and drawing his own knife from a leather sheath tied around his chest. Jamie darted sideways just as the Indian's slashing swing whizzed by him, making no connection. But then powerful arms seized him around the chest from behind, lifting him off his feet. The leader had a crushing hold on him. The Indian with the knife plunged toward him from the front. Though Jamie could barely breathe, he used all the strength he could muster and pushed against the Indian holding him to kick his legs up. His boot tips caught his attacker squarely under the chin. There was a loud cracking sound from his neck as his head whipped back and he fell to the ground. He didn't rise again.

The momentum from the kick caused the Indian at Jamie's back to lose his balance. When he hit the ground, he lost his hold on Jamie, who rapidly regained his footing. At that instant Jamie whirled around to see an Indian approach Mariah's hiding place, brandishing the whiskey jug over his head, as if to throw it in her direction. Suddenly a shot rang out.

Mariah stood up. From the clearing, Jamie could see the stricken look on her face. In her hand, his pistol smoked, but she could only stare at the bleeding body of the brave she'd just shot.

At the moment, Jamie was still too busy to go to her. The last remaining Indian was coming at him now, his huge fist descending on him, but he couldn't lurch away in time to avoid the blow. The force of it flattened him. He heard a deep, ferocious growl over him—a primal animal-like sound—then felt a malicious kick to his claw-injured side that made him double over into a fetal position.

Dazed by both blows, Jamie clutched his rib cage and blinked hard, trying to focus his blurry vision on his attacker, who was moving away from him toward Mariah. From Jamie's angle on the ground, he had a clear view of the three bloody scalps dangling at the warrior's waist. In that split second, an image of Evangelene flashed through his mind. The cruel memory of the way she'd died overwhelmed him. He couldn't let Mariah be killed in the same way.

He swung around, swaying with dizziness as he searched for his knife which had been jarred from his hand when he'd been hit. He couldn't see clearly enough to catch sight of it in the dirt. But he did see the campfire. Stumbling to it, he pulled out a stout branch, burning red-hot on the end, and ran toward the Indian.

The red man lunged at Mariah, catching her around the waist. She screamed and fought with kicking legs and flailing fists. Suddenly he yelped loudly with pain as the burning limb seared his back. He dropped Mariah and turned around, falling upon Jamie like an avalanche. With what seemed like little effort, the Indian lifted him over his head, spun around once and then tossed him hard to the ground.

The breath flew out of Jamie's lungs, but with death stalking him so closely, his body rallied. As the Indian pounded toward him, he thrust his leg upward, catching his vicious adversary squarely in the stomach. Using the momentum of the savage's weight, he lifted him and sent him pitching forward, to land face-first in the dirt.

"Your knife!" the captive woman screamed. "By his foot!"

Puffing hard and shaking his head to try to clear it, Jamie realized he had only a moment to act. He didn't have the strength to fight off another assault by the powerful renegade. Pushing his battered body to the final limit, he spotted his knife, lurched forward to retrieve it from the ground, and fell across the Indian's back, just as he was rising to his knees. The effort forced the red man to fall again. Jamie's hand shot out and clutched a fistful of the savage's black hair to yank his head back. A deep slash with his knife across the Indian's throat, and the fight came to a swift finish.

Chapter 23

"Jamie!" Mariah forced her eyes away from the carnage around her as she ran to his side. "Are you all right?"

He was on his knees next to the renegade's body and could only nod in answer as he waited for some of the pain pervading his body to subside. Wiping the bloody blade of his knife on the grass, he handed it to Mariah.

"Cut her down." He had to stop for breath and put his arm out to steady himself. "We'll use that rope to tie up the other two before they regain consciousness."

Mariah felt alarmed by his pale countenance, even though she knew her own face must be ash-white, too. Taking the knife from him, she hurried over to the woman, who fell into her arms, sobbing hysterically when freed.

"God bless you! God bless you both!" she cried, kissing Mariah's hand. Then she stumbled to Jamie and did the same to him. "You killed them! Bless you! They deserved to die. The filthy, vicious, evil savages!"

She buried her dirty, bruised face in her hands, crying harder. Mariah put an arm around her shoulders and led her away from the bodies to the edge of the makeshift camp. They sat down in the grass together, and she held the young woman, who appeared to be only a little younger than she was. She smoothed her tangled hair away from her face, cooing gentle words to comfort her. But Mariah kept her eyes on Jamie all the while.

How could he even stand after the blows he'd taken? Yet he'd struggled to his feet, retrieved the rope used on the captive, and in only a few minutes had both unconscious Indians bound securely. Judging from the way he kept his forearm pressed against his stomach, she knew his wound must be paining him.

She was relieved to see that some of the color had returned to his features when he joined them on the grass.

"Can you tell us your name, Miss, and what happened to you?" he asked when the kidnapped woman finally calmed down some.

"I'm Prudence Collins," she explained, trying to hold her torn dress together to cover herself while she clung to Mariah. "My parents and three other families live in a small settlement north of here. When the savages struck us by surprise just after dawn today, they herded everyone together." She stopped speaking, overcome by sobs again. When she could continue, her voice sounded raspy with anguish. "It was so terrible! They made me watch while they raped my mother and the other women. Then they butchered everyone, even the children. I was the only one left." She covered her face again and wept.

Mariah hugged her shoulders, glancing at Jamie.

She felt too numb to take in all she was hearing, all she'd just seen and done. She didn't want any of it to be true. Biting her lip to hold back her own sobs of sorrow, she tried to block out the picture of rape and children being massacred. Yet she knew she herself had shot a man only moments ago. As long as she lived, she'd never forget the shocked look on his face when the bullet hit him between the eyes.

"Were there any more Indians besides these?" Jamie asked. It was a few minutes before Prudence could answer.

"Y-yes," she stammered. "Six or seven others. They went a different way—west, I think."

"You're certain no one was left alive at the settlement?" he persisted.

"You saw the scalps, didn't you!" She pressed the back of her hand against her mouth, squeezing her eyes shut.

Jamie rose to his feet. The tone of his voice matched his grim expression. "We shouldn't stay here any longer than necessary. The others might come looking for this band. I'll get the horses. We'll take Miss Collins and the two Indians still alive back to Northampton."

They reached Northampton with their prisoners in tow that evening, without encountering the rest of the ruthless renegades. The local citizenry was quickly up in arms, ready to defend the town against any other attack. A group of men volunteered to bury the dead at the raided settlement.

"You don't have to go with them, Jamie," Mariah argued, trying to dissuade him from joining the townspeople. They stood together in the stableyard behind Anna Wilkes' house, where they'd returned with Prudence Collins. "You're in no condition to engage in more fighting if they encounter the rest of those Indians. You might be killed." She put her hand on his arm. "Please stay here."

Jamie was touched by her plea. He turned from cinching up Sultan's saddle to face her.

"These men are farmers and shopkeepers. They're brave enough, and certainly outraged, but they need someone to lead them. Otherwise, there could be more deaths. I've commanded men. I can help them."

She saw the determined set of his jaw and, though she hated to have him go, she admired his willingness to see the grisly task through.

"Let me come with you," she beseeched. "Perhaps some of the people are still alive. I could give them medical—"

"No, you're staying here." He cut her off, his voice firm. "I'll have enough to occupy me, without having to worry about you."

"So you'll leave me here to agonize over whether you're dead or alive!" Her grip tightened on his arm. "You were almost killed in the fight with those savages."

Her hand seemed to burn through his shirt-sleeve, leaving a scorched imprint on his skin and his heart. He softened his voice and smiled. "I'll return, Mariah. We have a treasure to find together, remember?"

"The gold isn't why I want you safe."

"I know."

Their eyes held, though they said nothing more.

Jamie knew he'd come close to losing her to the Indian butchers. If her life had been taken . . .

He shut off his thoughts, concentrating, instead, on memorizing the lovely features of her face. He raised her chin with his fingertip and touched his lips to hers, basking in the warmth and softness of them.

She stepped closer to him, wrapping her arms around his waist. She closed her eyes and let her lips speak a farewell she knew words could never convey. There was so much she wanted to say to him, but his kiss swept it all away. She held him, wanting to keep him near, but after a few moments, he stepped back, gently pushing her arms away.

"I'll be back, Mariah." He smiled again and turned to mount Sultan. Then without saying anything more, he rode out of the stableyard.

She waved when he glanced back over his shoulder, then pressed her fingers against her lips, which still tingled from his soft parting kiss.

"Two days," Mariah murmured. It seemed more like two years since she'd last seen Jamie. She was standing in the meadow just behind the Wilkes' barn. The townsmen had been expected back that night, but it was already past midnight, with no sign of them. She could think of nothing else except having Jamie return safely. A chill ran down her spine every time she remembered the rest of the vicious Indians Prudence had reported seeing, the ones who'd gone a different way after their murderous spree. What if they'd returned with more of their bloodthirsty kind to the doomed settlement while Jamie and the others were performing the awful task of burying the dead?

She closed her eyes and hugged her arms around her. She'd barely slept at all either night since Jamie had been away. They'd been through so much together. Was that the only reason she couldn't get him out of her mind, why even now his handsome features filled her mind, tormenting her?

Opening her eyes again, she peered anxiously down the dark, empty road that led from Northampton, then glanced up at the cloudless sky. Deep inside, she was beginning to accept the fact that she'd come to care deeply for Jamie. No, if she truly listened to her heart, she had to admit she'd fallen in love with him.

"Heaven help me," she whispered, shaking her head as she walked to the tall maple tree where they had made love for the first time. She wanted to command herself not to feel this way. Loving him made everything so complicated. He didn't love her in return. He wouldn't let down the guard around that heart of his. And loving him was hopeless, too. They could have no future together. Their lives were too different. If they found the gold, he would disappear from her life forever, sail off to the other side of the world. And she'd return to Samuel and the hospital, which had always been her dream.

The whinny of a horse made her turn toward the barn. Her heartbeat quickened as she hurried toward it. Something had disturbed the horses inside. Had she somehow missed Jamie's return?

All was quiet again when she reached the open double doors. The smell of freshly mown hay stored in the loft filled her nostrils when she entered. A lantern had been left burning with the wick turned low. She turned it up, causing the glow of light to spread to the stalls surrounding her. A plowhorse close by snorted and tossed its head, but nothing else stirred. For a moment, she felt a twinge of warning. Tensing and standing very still, she strained to see into the dark corners of the barn, but nothing seemed amiss. Sighing, she decided that fatigue had made her jumpy.

She was standing at the barn door with the lantern in hand when Jamie rode into the yard only a few minutes later. She hurried to take hold of Sultan's bridle, feeling relief overwhelm her.

"You're up late," he said, swinging down from the horse. "You should be asleep. We must start for Boston early tomorrow to locate Addington Braythwaite, as your father instructed."

"I was waiting for you. Are you all right? Your injuries . . ."

"They're mending."

She sensed his distance, saw the clenched set to his jaw. Saying nothing more, she watched him lead the stallion to the first empty stall. She carried the light in behind him, hooking it on a nail on a wooden post.

"Was the settlement as Prudence described it?" she asked quietly.

"Yes." A tightness touched his voice. "Everyone was dead. We found all twenty-one bodies and buried them. There was no sign of the other renegades."

She saw the deep lines of exhaustion around his eyes and mouth. His clothes were dirty from traveling. His movements in tending to Sultan were slow, deliberate, marked by weariness. She put her hand on his shoulder.

"It must have been terrible."

He paused in removing the saddle. His eyes took on a hard glint. "Life is often ugly, Mariah. You must know that from your work at the hospital. You have to close your mind to it or it can consume you."

"Won't you let anything touch you, Jamie—or anyone?" She barely whispered the words. How she longed to caress away his tiredness, his pain.

"I did once." His voice was hushed and he wouldn't meet her gaze as he began to wipe down the sweating horse. "A long time ago."

"But you still know the hurt. The horrible events of these past two days have opened the wound again, haven't they? Is it Evangelene who haunts you?"

He frowned as he turned his head to look at her. "How do you know about her?"

"While we were at Toby Jones' cabin, I asked Dimetrius about you. He told me you once loved a young woman named Evangelene and she was murdered by Indians."

"Dimetrius' tongue wags like an old woman's."

"Are you still in love with Evangelene?" Thinking about her father's consuming love for her mother, even after her death, she had to ask the question.

He scooped a portion of oats into the feeding bin for Sultan before replying.

"No, Mariah. She's only a memory from my

youth. What else did that old gossip Dimetrius have to say?''

She was glad he'd changed the subject. She wanted to believe no other woman held his heart. The ghost of a past love would torment them both.

''He mentioned your family in New York and how you chose to follow your own path rather than your father's. Dimetrius is devoted to you, you know. I could hear great admiration in his voice when he spoke of you.''

''He's been a good friend.'' He turned back to Sultan to finish the wiping down.

''Like my father?''

''Yes, like Dunny.''

Mariah sighed and walked to the barn door, leaning back against it to peer out at the night.

''I thought I had everything neatly reasoned out,'' she began, feeling awkward. But she had to say these things to him. She wanted him to know her feelings. ''I hated my father. I didn't want to know him. But now that I've learned more about him through the eyes of others, I find my anger, my loathing of him is waning. He's an old man now, broken and in ill health. It seems foolish, even childish, to fight against someone like that.

''So much has happened in the little time we've been together, Jamie. I never imagined I could ever take another human life, yet I did just that only two days ago.''

''You had to, Mariah. That Indian would have killed you.''

''I know. I just didn't think I was capable of such an act. I thought I had you all figured out, too. I thought I'd be glad to have this journey with you come to an end as soon as possible.''

He came to stand before her, resting his hands on her shoulders. ''And now?''

She bit her lip as she looked up at him, knowing she risked much if she revealed her heart. The light from the lantern cast flickering shadows over his handsome face. She knew his features so well now. His deep voice caressed her with only those two words. She felt his warmth spreading through her.

''I—I'm glad it isn't over yet.'' She looked down at the ground.

''And why is that, Mariah?''

When he said her name in that soft and tender voice, her heart sighed with pleasure. But she realized he wasn't going to make this easy for her. He said nothing more, obviously waiting for her to answer, making her say the words. At last she found the courage to speak.

''You frighten me because of what you make me feel. Yet I trust you with my life. I don't know where these feelings came from. They took me by surprise. I'm not sure what they mean.'' She looked up at him. ''I think I've fallen in love with you. I didn't want to. Dear heaven, you must know that, what with all the ranting and raving we've done at each other. I shouldn't let my heart rule my head, but right now I just want to be with you.'' She stepped nearer to him, slipping her arms around his narrow waist. ''Hold me. Please.''

His arms encircled her. She closed her eyes and melted into them, reveling in his closeness.

''Mariah . . .'' He whispered her name, molding his body against hers. She looked so beautiful, even in the dim light. He was surprised by her sudden confession. And pleased. "I was hoping you'd be waiting when I returned. I longed to see you alive and safe. What I've witnessed and had to do in the last two days has made me feel like a stone inside. But somehow you wash away the brutality, the ugliness."

She rested the side of her head against his chest. "Don't close me out, Jamie. Share your pain with me, your weariness. Come to my room. We can hold each other all the night through."

"What you ask . . . I can't love you as you need in return."

"Stop . . ." She touched her finger to his lips. "No more words. I'm asking only to be near you, nothing more. I've heard what you've told me about your need to be free. I require no promises."

He stared down at her for a long time. Then he gently cupped her face in his hands and kissed her softly on the lips. Arm in arm, they walked to the back door of the darkened farmhouse.

As they left the barn a man emerged from the shadows in the hayloft. He was smiling. He crawled to the ladder at the side of the loft and climbed down, stopping by the first stall.

"Ah, Jamie, you bloody bastard, you do know how to pick them pretty doxies," he murmured in the darkness. "But she'll be yer downfall this time. Bein' with her's made you careless. You left a trail even a young'n could follow. I got me a real hungerin' fer a milk-skinned female like her. Think she'll be puttin' up much of a fight when I git hold of her, Sultan?" He chuckled, patting the stallion's neck. "Well, that'll be jus' fine. I hope she does.

Me havin' Jamie Lancaster's woman—an' him tied up an' watchin'. Now that be a mighty sweet thought. As fer you, Sultan, you an' me'll be ridin' t'gether again real soon. But first I got to make a little visit to the local jailhouse fer a friend—Doyle Iverson. I heard in town how him an' Jamie had a run-in. Ol' Doyle don't fergit easy. An' I don't neither. Shouldn't take much to break him out of jail. So we'll be meetin' agin in Boston, Sultan, old boy.''

Lem Hollister turned away from the horse and stroked the bristly stubble on his chin as he gazed toward the closed back door of the farmhouse. ''Mariah he called her. Yessir, that wench is a mighty sweet thought . . .''

Chapter 24

Six days later, Mariah and Jamie rode into Boston. It was a bright summer afternoon and as they rounded the Common, Mariah caught sight of a squad of volunteer Minutemen drilling on an open field. Other townsfolk strolled the Common's patterned pathways while children ran and laughed among its shrubs and trees. From a church across the road a bell began to peal. A smaller, tinkling chime sounded as a customer opened the door to a tailor's shop nearby.

Mariah listened to the music of Boston's bells and breathed deeply. They were approaching the harbor; its pungent salt smell delighted her and made her feel that she'd at last come home.

She knew this commercial part of the city well, along with the dock area, which was where Samuel Hastings' charity hospital was located. From the vantage point of the hilltop street they were traveling, she caught her first glimpse of the water, dotted with merchant ships from all over the world. How often she'd passed crowds of seamen working at the docks and heard them talking in their strange, wonderful languages. Their voices summoned images of all the exotic places from which they'd come.

Would she ever see those places? Or would Boston be all she'd experience of the wide world?

With a sudden jolt, the realization struck her that she'd never felt such longings until her father had come back into her life, bringing Jamie. It was Jamie who'd awakened her curiosity. And if the gold they'd come to Boston to claim really existed, she'd be a woman of means, free to go wherever she chose . . .

Quickly, though, she stopped herself from following that line of thought. It was too dangerous. They didn't have the gold yet. And even if they did ultimately find it, she must not forget her commitment to help Samuel, to continue in the struggle to make a place for herself in the medical profession.

Suddenly she felt anxious to see Dr. Hastings again, to assure herself that the life she'd known before Jamie Lancaster really did still exist. But she decided to put off seeing Dr. Hastings, as well as her aunt and uncle, until she'd finally solved the puzzle of the gold. For a moment, though, she let herself imagine Samuel's joy when she offered him the means to save the hospital, how together they'd go forward, sharing their passion for healing the sick and helping others. But she'd shared an even greater passion with Jamie. How different this emotion was from the one she felt for Samuel. Jamie fired her heart and her spirit with his touch, his compelling glances, his overpowering presence. In the six days it had taken to travel from Northampton to Boston, they'd come to know each other so well. At inns, or lying under the twinkling stars in each other's arms, they'd made love long into the nights, closed out reason and the harsh realities of the world, and experienced only each other. Their bodies had sung with the harmony of mutually given caresses. For those half-dozen blissful days, she'd never been happier. Jamie filled her every thought, her every waking moment. He touched her very soul with his courage, his dreams, the zest he had for living, and his hunger for her. They had lived each moment to the fullest, not allowing thoughts of the future to color the present. But in her heart, she knew she couldn't have Jamie . . .

"You there!" She heard Jamie hail the driver of a coach who sat waiting for his next fare to come along. She halted Lilac Wind next to Sultan.

"Aye, what you wantin'?" the whiskered man replied, turning toward them.

Jamie produced a silver coin, flashing it toward the driver. "Would you know the route to the Addington Braythwaite estate?"

The man gave a curt nod and held out his hand. Jamie flipped the coin toward him and he adroitly caught it. "North end. Turn left on Hanover, go to the end of the street," he directed, pointing over his shoulder with his thumb. "You can't be missin' it. A big red-brick place, gray slate roof, with a half-circle drive in front."

"My thanks, mate," Jamie said, touching two fingers to the brim of his black tricorned hat. He swung Sultan in the direction the man had indicated and motioned with his head for Mariah to follow.

He knew their journey was coming to an end. Soon he'd know if the gold really existed, and if it did, he'd have his ship and his voyage to the Orient. But by gaining his dream, would he lose Mariah? When they located the doubloons, she'd be a wealthy woman. She'd help Hastings save his damn hospital, and likely marry him too. Hastings was stable and dedicated, just what she professed to want in a man. And surely Hastings wouldn't jump at the chance to take her for his wife, for she was beautiful, desirable, and she'd share his life's work, guaranteeing that it would continue without financial worry.

He hated the thought of her in another man's arms, hated knowing she'd stand at Hastings' side, building a future with him.

Would she give up all that if he asked her to sail with him to distant lands? Could he tie his life to hers, take on the responsibility and commitment of a woman, a wife?

He couldn't answer that question. It was better to concentrate on finding the gold, and leave perplexing dilemmas to settle themselves.

There could be no doubt that the Braythwaites lived in one of the finest sections of the city, which was perhaps why Mariah hadn't known of them. Even though the main house was situated somewhat apart from the other elegant dwellings lining affluent Hanover Street, it would have been difficult to miss. The sprawling, two-storied Georgian mansion was surrounded by a three-foot-high wall made of the same red English brick as the house. Six long, many-paned windows fronted the ground level of the dwelling, three on each side of the door.

Mariah stared in wide-eyed wonder as she rode with Jamie onto the gravel driveway. She'd had few opportunities to visit such a grand estate, and when she had, she'd always been accompanying Samuel Hastings when he solicited money from wealthy society folk to aid the hospital. She felt a pang of regret, wondering if her family home of Windhaven had ever been this stately and imposing. What would her life have been like if she could have grown up in such a home? The Morgans had been members of affluent Boston society at one time, until her father, the last heir in the line, had squandered away the family fortune with his irresponsible adventuring. At least that was the story she'd often heard from her embittered aunt and uncle.

"Do you suppose my father somehow helped the Braythwaites as he did the Flannerys and Anna Wilkes?" she asked Jamie. "Look at this house. It's so elegant. The Braythwaites must be wealthy. How could my father have helped them?"

"We'll soon find out," he answered, as two grooms in maroon livery stepped forward to hold the horses and help them dismount. He waved them aside and helped Mariah down himself, setting her gently on the ground. Then he brushed at the dust on his white shirt and black breeches, and held out his elbow for her to slip her hand through. "Shall we?"

"Do you think we're presentable?" she asked worriedly, shaking her long brown skirt.

"You never looked lovelier, Mariah," he told

her softly, tipping her chin up to kiss her lightly on the lips. "They're just people, remember. Money doesn't change that."

She smiled up at him, warmed by his affectionate look. With Jamie at her side, she felt confident she could meet the Braythwaites proudly.

The sober-looking butler who answered the door caused her to have some doubts though.

"Yes?" he asked, eyeing them up and down. His serious expression soured as he assessed their travel-worn appearances.

"I'm James Lancaster and this is Miss Mariah Morgan. We're here to see Mr. Addington Braythwaite."

"Is he expecting you, sir?"

At that moment, a dark-haired boy of about four pushed his way through the man's legs, nearly knocking him over. He had to grasp for the doorframe to keep his balance.

"Hello, I'm Timothy!" the lad introduced himself, thrusting his small hand out to Jamie.

The butler grabbed the boy by the ear. "Timothy, come inside at once!" He pulled the boy around with a firm hand and gave him a slap on the backside, then hoisted him through the door.

His expression remained somber as he turned back to Jamie and Mariah. "I regret to inform you that without an appointment, you cannot possibly see Mr. Braythwaite. He's very busy today."

The sound of squealing and giggling children emanated from behind him. One dark eyebrow dipped in a frown, but he kept his gaze on Jamie and Mariah.

"The matter we must discuss with Mr. Braythwaite is most important," Jamie persisted. "He's expecting us, but didn't know the date of our arrival. Report our names to him, and I'm certain he'll want to see us."

Jamie's tone made his words more a command than a courteous request. For a moment, the butler hesitated. Then he gave a curt nod and stepped aside, gesturing for them to enter.

Mariah blinked to adjust her eyes from the bright sunlight outside to the dimness of the wide, wood-paneled hallway just beyond the door. Her riding boots clicked loudly on the white marble floor. A muffled giggle made her look up to see Timothy in the company of five other children, ranging in ages from about three to twelve. They all hung over the wrought-iron bannister of the long, curving staircase, laughing and pointing through the openings in the scalloped railing.

"Richard, Herbert, Janet, Ned, Marilyn, and Timothy, upstairs at once!" the butler ordered, clapping his hands sharply. The children quickly jumped to their feet and scurried up the stairway, pushing and laughing all the way. When the butler turned back to Jamie and Mariah, his face still hadn't lost its stern expression. "Wait here in the parlor, please," he instructed, opening an ornately carved oak door to his right.

Mariah hardly had time to glance around the spacious, richly decorated room, when a middle-aged man of medium height hurriedly joined them.

"I'm Addington Braythwaite. You're Mariah Morgan, Dunny's daughter?" he asked, bustling to her and grabbing her hand.

She pulled back a little from the bald man in surprise. "Yes, sir, I am."

"Well, I'm certainly pleased to meet you, young woman." He gave her hand a brisk shake, then released it to turn toward Jamie. "And you're Lancaster." He thrust it out again.

"Yes, sir," Jamie replied, shaking hands with him.

"This is fine, just fine. I'm delighted to have you both here in my home. My wife, Rowena, is away at the moment, seeing to some last-minute details for a summer gathering we're having this evening." He paused, appearing to be struck by a sudden thought. "This is grand! You both can attend. There will be music and food enough to feed twice the number of guests who'll be attending. You'll have a splendid time! But enough of that for now. Come, sit down. You must be fatigued from your journey."

He led them to an ochre camelbacked sofa appliqued in flowered crewelwork, then sat himself in a gold wingback chair.

"You've come for the puzzle piece, of course."

"Yes, Mr. Braythwaite," Mariah answered, her excitement growing as she fished in the side pocket of her skirt for the leather wallet. "Mr. Lancaster and I have the other pieces to show you as proof of our identities."

She drew out her three parts of the puzzle, and Jamie produced his. Braythwaite assembled them on the top of a cherry tea table next to him. He stoked his neatly trimmed gray beard, studying the wooden map.

"Yes, and I have the fifth and final piece for

you, which goes in the middle. Then you'll have the location of the gold.''

"You know about the treasure?" Mariah asked.

"Of course. Dunny told me of it when he gave me the puzzle piece months ago. How is the old sea salt?"

Mariah glanced at Jamie, who answered for her.

"Dunny wasn't well when we last saw him. He was bedridden, with a doctor in almost constant attendance."

Braythwaite's countenance sobered. "I feared that might be the case when Crothers told me of your arrival. I'm very sorry to hear that news. Dunny is a special friend. I owe him much. Years ago he gave me a great deal of money, which enabled me to reverse several bad business transactions I'd made. Today, I have a highly successful shipbuilding company. Your father wouldn't let me return any of the money he gave me. He said only that I should help someone else the way he'd helped me. And I've fulfilled his wish always with the same stipulation your father made me. Your father is a fine man, Miss Morgan. I'm proud to say I've had his friendship and trust."

The sound of giggling suddenly reached them from the hall door which had been left ajar.

Braythwaite smiled. "Come in, children, and meet our guests."

Immediately, three little girls of identical appearance bounded into the parlor and ran to surround Braythwaite.

"Miss Morgan, Mr. Lancaster, these beautiful young ladies are my daughters, Barbara, Nan, and Jane."

The dark-featured triplets giggled behind their hands and bobbed quick curtsies.

"My wife and I have twenty-one children," Braythwaite explained, smiling proudly. "They're all orphans whom we've adopted, but they're as precious to us as any natural children could be. Has your mother returned yet, girls?"

"No, Papa," they chimed together.

"Well, run along now and tell Rob, Joan, Rebecca, and William it's time for your lessons with Mr. Hathaway."

The girls' faces registered disappointment, but they obeyed their father.

Mariah watched them leave the room. She envied Addington Braythwaite his family. Little Timothy had won her heart with his first smile at her. Someday she wanted children. Did Jamie? She scoffed inwardly at the ridiculousness of the notion. How could he be a good parent when he was always sailing off to sea? He'd be no better than her own father had been!

"If you'll excuse me now for a moment," Addington Braythwaite was saying, "I'll retrieve the last puzzle piece from my study."

Mariah nodded and sat forward in her chair, feeling excitement swell in her. She glanced at Jamie. He gave her a quirk of a smile, and she knew by it that he felt the same anticipation. They were so close to gaining the gold!

When Braythwaite returned, he carried a small lacquered box, which he placed on the table and opened. From it he drew the last wooden piece and a folded sheet of parchment. She added her pieces to it, as did Jamie. The puzzle was now a completed rectangular-shaped map.

"That black square must mark the place where the doubloons are hidden," Braythwaite observed, pointing to the center.

"I know that section of the city," Jamie noted. He picked up the folded paper and read the words written on it. "This is just like Dunny. The gold is hidden in the Palmer mansion." He handed the paper to Mariah, who rapidly scanned the sheet.

"But that old house has been abandoned for over fifty years," she said.

"Many say it's haunted by evil spirits," Braythwaite added. "Of course, I don't give much credence to such stories, though many people do."

Mariah was amazed. As if they hadn't faced perils enough, now they must hunt through an old house, abandoned and reputedly haunted. And, according to the instructions on the parchment, they must solve a confusing riddle besides, which read:

A walk left through the upper hall is all you will
  need;
To dwell among flowers is restful indeed.
Beneath the right angles, the left side panel
  slides;
Down the dark passage is where wealth abides.

Puzzle pieces, riddles. Mariah sighed, folding the paper. How had she ever let her father persuade her to take part in this escapade? Probably there were no doubloons at all.

"Well, we'll take a look around the Palmer place anyway," Jamie replied, reaching over to pick up the puzzle pieces. He handed Mariah her four parts. "We've come too far to abandon this venture now, wouldn't you say, Mariah?"

"Yes, we'll see it through to the end," she consented, trying to bolster her enthusiasm.

"Our thanks, Braythwaite, for finishing the map for us." He extended his hand.

"It was the least I could do for Dunny. I wish you both well in your search. I can send several men with you, if you wish. Perhaps they can aid you in solving the riddle, as well."

"I'm afraid we can't accept. You see, all along, Dunny's instructions have been that we accomplish this alone. But your offer is appreciated."

"As you wish. But it's growing late in the day to begin such an adventure. If you can put off thoughts of doubloons until the morrow, you just might have a grand time at the gathering tonight. I shall be glad to introduce you both to all of our friends." Braythwaite smiled as he rose from his seat and came around to stand in front of Mariah. "The young men in attendance tonight will be stumbling over each other to claim you in conversation."

Mariah felt a pang of apprehension at the thought of meeting so many well-to-do people. Whatever would she talk to them about all evening? But Addington Braythwaite had been so kind. She felt they really couldn't refuse. She'd manage somehow. After all, she'd survived attacks by a wild bear and renegade Indians. Surely, members of Boston society's upper class couldn't be any worse!

"We'd be happy to attend," she said. A glance toward Jamie told her he agreed.

"Superb!" Braythwaite exclaimed. "The only addition I'd make would be to somehow have Dunny join us. How he could enliven a gathering! The ladies were always eager to catch his eye. Ah, yes, your father and I had some splendid times together. That we did."

"Richard and Herbert, stop that at once!" Rowena Braythwaite ordered, rushing out of the sewing room to snatch a large silver tray out of the taller boy's hands just as he was about to smash it down on his brother's head. "If you must settle your differences with violence, at least don't use weapons. A tray is meant for serving tea, not bashing heads! Now, shake hands and be friends again."

The nine- and ten-year-olds hung their heads, looking contrite.

"Your hands, gentlemen," Rowena insisted.

Slowly, their palms joined.

"That's much better. Now, run along and play."

Rowena was smiling as she rejoined Mariah in the sewing room, where they'd been trying on gowns for the ball that night.

Mariah studied her hostess. Pale-featured, with golden-blonde hair, Rowena Braythwaite was a beautiful thirty-one-year-old woman, overflowing with humor. Mariah had met her only an hour ago, when she'd returned from her shopping expedition, yet she already felt as if they were friends.

"Excuse the interruption, my dear," Rowena apologized, "but boys will be boys. We can't have any dented skulls today, not with the ball only hours away." She laid the silver tray on a wooden bench near the door. "My, but that dress is just perfect on you."

Mariah had never worn anything so elegant in her entire life. As she twirled before a gilt-framed, full-length mirror, she saw how the wide skirt of the sapphire-blue gown flared out, shaped by the wide oval hoop beneath it. The silk bodice clung to the curve of her breasts in a most alluring manner. The low-cut square neckline was edged with a scalloping of ivory lace, which matched the long ruffles extending from the tight, three-quarter-length sleeves. The long, fitted bodice had a stomacher embellished with tiny ruffles of the cream lace.

"But I can't possibly wear your dress, Mrs. Braythwaite," Mariah lamented, running her fingers over the soft fabric.

"Nonsense, of course you can. I have this gown I'm trying on and three other new ones from which to choose. You're helping me with my decision by taking this blue one. It's just fortunate we're the same size." She turned toward a young maid who had been assisting Mariah. "Iris, I can't see where you'll need to alter Miss Morgan's dress at all. I want you to arrange her hair later. Powdering won't be necessary. Your auburn hair is so lovely, Mariah. Iris will coil it for you in the most becoming fashion. Now, I must be off to see to the children. My goodness, where does time go? Our guests will be arriving shortly and there is so much yet to do! Come, Iris, I'll need your help with the girls." She hurried toward the door, followed by the maid. Pausing, she glanced back over her shoulder and gave a little laugh. "I do adore giving parties. We'll all have a fabulous time, you'll see, Mariah."

The sewing room was suddenly very quiet after the bubbling Rowena Braythwaite had disappeared. Mariah shook her head in amazement. She wondered how the much older Addington Braythwaite kept up with his energetic young wife.

She whirled again, delighting in the way the elegant skirt billowed out. Here was a gown fit for a princess. What would Jamie think of her in it? The question flashed through her mind, surprising her. Would he find her beautiful, alluring? Many other women would be present at the dinner party tonight. How would she compare to them?

She sighed with dismay, suddenly fearing the coming night. She was a laundress and midwife, an unofficial medical apprentice raised since the age of ten by strict Puritans, who frowned on gatherings for anything other than religious purposes. How could she dare to mingle with these society folk? She'd feel more at ease in the kitchen or serving the food and drink. She was sure to blunder. Likely, she'd spill her wine or trip over a chair—something horrendously mortifying. And Jamie would no doubt witness it all!

Chapter 25

Mariah took a deep breath, which wasn't easy to do in her tight-bodiced gown. Butterflies raced around in her stomach as she stepped through the wide archway into the crowded reception room. Hundreds of candles glowed brightly from silver candelabras, giving the high-ceilinged room an air of festivity.

Her mouth fell open a little in surprise. She had never seen such a beautiful room. The symmetry of the white walls was attractively broken by wide panels of carved molding, painted blue-gray in tone, which outlined the ceiling, the French double doors, and windows. Long, dark-blue damask draperies pulled back by gold cords adorned the four windows along the one outer wall. The floor was a gray-and-white checker pattern of marble.

People chatted and laughed in small gatherings. Mariah saw several of the Braythwaite children—all dressed in elegant finery—chasing about among the guests. She scanned the reception room for Jamie. She'd seen him briefly late that afternoon, and arranged to meet at the archway at eight o'clock, but Iris had needed longer than had been anticipated to arrange her hair. It was already half-past eight.

She spied Jamie talking to Rowena Braythwaite near the white marble fireplace. What a picture the two of them made. Outfitted by Addington Braythwaite's personal tailor, Jamie looked rakishly handsome in a formal suit with a flared coat of purple satin, wide turned-back cuffs, and thigh-hugging, matching breeches. His long-length waistcoat was of pale purple taffeta, decorated with elaborately embroidered trim. His powdered white wig gave him a distinguished air. She saw many of the other women present noticing him also. Using their dainty lace fans to cover their interest, they cast coy glances in his direction.

Rowena Braythwaite was resplendent in a scarlet silk gown with a skirt flared by three tiers of gathered flouncing. The graceful curve of her bosom was emphasized by the low-cut, snug-fitting bodice. She smiled brightly, appearing to be enthralled by whatever Jamie was saying to her.

Mariah felt a pang of jealousy. Did Jamie find Rowena attractive? Mariah knew he had an eye for beautiful women, like that fiery young gypsy back in Worcester. Rowena looked stunning. There was a glowing aura of confidence and sophistication about her that Mariah realized she didn't begin to have. A virile, handsome man like Jamie could easily be drawn to such a woman.

The members of the string quartet began tuning their instruments. Mariah suddenly felt very warm in the crowded room. Her feelings tumbled about in confusion, centering on Jamie. How she wished she were more sure of what she felt for him. She had no right to be jealous of his attention to Rowena Braythwaite. He was free to choose any woman he wished, just as she could pick from the many men present. They'd made no commitment. She knew that well enough. And tomorrow, their quest would be over. They would either find the gold or not. Either way, she and Jamie would part.

The thought sent a sudden wave of sadness over her. She longed to find the doubloons, and yet again, she didn't. She must think. But the many people and the noise in the room distracted her too much. She turned on her heel and moved through the crowd toward the open double doors leading to the garden.

Outside, she breathed easier. The gentle breeze brushed against her face and arms as she walked the grass path. The fragrance of roses reached her. She glanced around the lovely garden lighted by glass-globed lamps hanging at intervals from wooden poles. The neatly sculpted shrubberies and privet hedges appeared perfectly balanced with the vividly colorful planting of geraniums, snapdragons, French marigolds, sweet violets, and many other flowers Mariah didn't recognize.

A few guests roamed the paths with her, mostly couples presumably seeking privacy. The gentle strains of the instruments carried to where Mariah now stood alone. She closed her eyes and hugged her arms around her, letting her body sway to the music.

Jamie stood behind an arched wooden trellis nearby. The lush covering of English ivy enveloping the trellis hid him from Mariah's view. He watched her moving her body so gracefully to the melodic music, and thought that a woman of her beauty was meant to wear such finery as the gem-colored silk gown she held in her fingertips. The lovely, sensuous contours of her face and body were softly visible in the golden glow of lamplight. His fingers tingled to sketch her, longed even more to touch her, hold her. Deep inside, he felt an aching need to be close to her. His body reacted as it did every time his eyes caught sight of her—liquid fire seeped into his veins. The boredom he usually felt after being with a woman for a while hadn't struck yet with her. It seemed as if the more he had of her, the more she captivated him. His need for her mounted in intensity, instead of subsiding. He was falling in love with her, he knew. He'd tried summoning his will to prevent his heart from being drawn to her, opening to her, but his efforts had proved to be in vain. Her smile melted him like spring sunshine on snow-covered earth. The lyrical ring of her laughter was sweeter music to him than that composed by the masters. And her compelling turquoise eyes penetrated to the heart of his being with only a glance.

Mariah. He smiled when he saw her make a curtsy to a tall bush.

"Wouldn't you rather have a real partner?" he asked, finally stepping into view.

She whirled around. Her hand flew to her throat.

"J-Jamie, you startled me. How long have you been watching me?"

"I spied you sneaking away from the reception room and followed you. But I see why you've sought the coolness of the garden. The heat inside is stifling. If you'll excuse me, I'll remove this for a few moments." He slipped off his purple coat and folded it on a stone bench nearby. "Your apparel is more suitable to this warm temperature than is this suit and long-sleeved shirt." He stepped to her, softening his voice. "It also reveals how breathtakingly lovely you are, Mariah." He put his hands on her tiny waist. "I saw you leave the party because I sensed your radiance from across the room. Whether sitting in the mud, laughing in a downpour, or dressed in fine silk and lace as you are now, you're the most beautiful woman I've ever seen."

If his striking handsomeness hadn't already stirred her blood and made her powerless to resist him, his whispered words would have rendered her helpless. She moved closer until their bodies touched, and encircled his neck with her arms, drawing his head down so their lips met.

Gently at first, they kissed. Then he pulled away a little and stepped into the rhythm of the music, drawing her with him to dance on the garden path.

The soft grass made no sound beneath their feet. Mariah was barely aware of touching the ground. Without realizing it, she moved in perfect step with Jamie. Being in his arms was pure heaven. He overwhelmed her senses, making her conscious of only him, his hands holding her, his eyes seeing into her very soul.

The music went on, but Jamie stopped, gathering her close. He kissed her then, ardently, possessively.

"Oh, Jamie, I love you so much," she murmured against his lips when they parted for breath.

"And I love you," he whispered huskily. "Tonight, later, we must be together. I'll come to you in your room.''

Suddenly, a young couple rounded the corner of the path.

''We should go back inside,'' Jamie noted when the man and woman had passed them. ''The Braythwaites will be wondering where we are.''

''Must we?'' She hung back as he retrieved his coat and turned toward the house.

He smiled. ''Yes, but we'll be together later, I promise.''

''All right, but stay by my side,'' she entreated.

''Then everyone will see the passion in my eyes.'' His expression hinted at mischief.

''They'll see the same in mine!'' She laughed and tucked her hand in the crook of his elbow, enjoying his teasing.

''Just be careful of flashing that beguiling smile, my lovely temptress, or I'll be forced to spend the entire evening trying to keep all the other men in the room away from you.''

''You mean you'll have time for that when every lady present will be trying to attract the attention of the handsomest man present?'' she teased.

''Handsomest?'' He grinned, pulling her close again.

She placed her hands on his chest, coquettishly pretending to hold him at bay. ''Yes, without a doubt. But don't become puffed up by the compliment, sir.''

''Vixen . . .'' His eyes twinkled with amusement as they held hers for a moment before he leaned down to brush a kiss across her lips.

Chapter 26

When Mariah and Jamie rejoined the party, she was quickly overwhelmed by attention showered on her by the many other male guests.

Jamie couldn't help observing her popularity. He tried to stay close at her side, as she'd requested, but the press of her male admirers soon separated them. Though he never found himself wanting for a lovely and willing conversational partner, he gave only passing attention to each one. His eyes were continually drawn to Mariah. He could hear her delicate laughter above all other sounds in the hall. He became angry with himself for feeling jealousy toward the men around her. He worried that Mariah, in her innocence and inexperience, might have her head turned by another man, more sophisticated in the art of flattery than he. He didn't like the feeling of insecurity that prospect evoked. It wasn't an emotion he'd ever before felt concerning a woman. It prompted him to seek her out when he saw her unattended for a moment.

"Oh, Jamie, you were right in persuading me to come back inside," she bubbled, as he steered her to an unoccupied gold sofa located along one wall. "I'm having a wonderful time!"

285

"So I've noticed," he replied, trying to make his tone light. Inwardly, he cursed her radiance, the glistening in her blue-green eyes and the pink flush to her cheeks that made her look so beautiful. The deep sapphire hue of her gown only accentuated the pale loveliness of her skin. The gentle mounds of her breasts rose and fell alluringly, barely concealed by the ivory lace trim, yet he knew she was unaware of their enticement. He realized the heat in his veins was caused by more than just the sultry temperature and the closeness in the crowded reception room. It was all he could do to control himself from sweeping her up in his arms in front of this whole gathering and carrying her to his room.

At last the announcement came that the buffet dinner was being served. Slowly the crowd of guests began to merge toward the arched entrance to the adjoining dining room.

Mariah and Jamie started to join them, when she stopped so suddenly that Jamie, who was slightly behind her, had to grind to a halt to keep from crashing into her.

"Oh!" he heard her gasp.

"What is it?" He noticed how her lovely features visibly paled, and he took hold of her elbow. "Mariah?"

Her expression was inscrutable when she finally turned to look at him, but she waved her fan in short, quick motions, as if nervous or agitated.

"Please excuse me, Jamie. I see someone I must speak to without delay."

She started to move away from him, but he caught her arm.

"Who? You look shaken. I'll come with you."

"No! You must not!" Her eyes beseeched him. "Samuel Hastings is standing over there. I must talk to him."

Before Jamie could say anything more, she twisted out of his grasp and hurried away across the marble floor.

Her heart was pounding loudly when she came to a halt beside Samuel.

He turned to her immediately. "Mariah! What in heaven's name are you doing here? When did you arrive back in Boston? My God, you look ravishing."

"Thank you," she replied absently. "I returned only today. I meant to contact you, but the business for my father, about which I wrote you, is still not yet completed." She vigorously waved her fan, trying to regain her composure so she could think clearly enough to make explanations to him without revealing anything about Jamie. "It was necessary for me to visit the Braythwaites, and they generously invited me to attend this party. It's quite nice, don't you think?"

An inane question, she knew, but it gave her a moment to gather her thoughts. How weary he looked, as always. His compassionate brown eyes were darkened with rings of fatigue, his face deeply creased. His burdened air made him appear much older than his forty-five years. He wore the frayed dark-blue formal suit she'd seen him in so many times when he'd set out to attend an affair frequented by the affluent members of society. Soliciting funds from them was no doubt the reason he was here tonight. But she'd been so caught up in

Jamie, and the excitement of gaining the final piece
to the treasure map puzzle, that she hadn't thought
at all about the possibility that Samuel might be
here.

Now that they were together again, her heart
went out to him as it always did. Everything for
which he stood—the practice and advancement of
medicine, unselfish dedication and sacrifice, compassion toward unfortunates—flooded over her. All
the old feelings of deep respect, admiration, tenderness, worry, and even frustration, came too.

"I've had some good luck here tonight—the
promise of financial support for the hospital,"
Samuel replied. "But I fear it won't be enough. I
have the operating funds for perhaps two months
longer, no more. But enough of that sad subject for
the moment. What of your father's health? Has it
improved?"

"I—I don't know," she answered truthfully.
"He wasn't well at all when I left him to pursue
the business venture he wanted settled. I hope to
find him still alive when I return to Framingham
the day after tomorrow."

"Then your stay here in Boston will be brief?"
She nodded.

Samuel drew her aside to an unoccupied corner
of the room. "I must confess I was hoping you'd
returned here to rejoin me at the hospital, Mariah.
We've greatly missed your help there." His gaze
met hers. "This is most difficult for me to say, but
I must. I've missed you at the hospital. I didn't
realize just how important you were to me and my
work until you were gone. I've taken you for
granted, and, for that, I apologize. Your absence

left such a terrible void in my life. There's so much to be done. I'll find a way for the hospital to continue operating somehow, I know. But I want you to help me, Mariah. You have great ability. I haven't allowed you to make use of it as I might have. That will change, I promise. You will return to me eventually, won't you? My life would be empty without you."

"Oh, Dr. Hast—Samuel," she said quietly, "if you only knew how long I've waited to hear you say those words."

Now it was she who couldn't hold his gaze. Jamie crashed into her mind, and she realized, with great dismay, that she would have to make the choice she'd been dreading. She forced herself to look back at him.

"I've admired you as a man and a physician for a long time. I want to continue our work, but I confess I feel unsure of my heart and my feelings about many things right now. Will you please be patient and allow me time to sort things out?"

"I understand. Of course, my dear. Your father's grave condition is your main concern now. You cannot make critical decisions. When you're ready to decide, though, seek me out. I know this isn't the time or the place to tell you this, but I feel the need to do so. Listen to me very carefully, Mariah. I see a wonderful future for us. And perhaps even more than just a working relationship, if you'll allow it. I'm not much of a catch, as you well know. I work too much. I don't take care of myself. But I need you. I realize there's a great difference in our ages, and I don't have very much to offer you except myself and the pursuit of a worthwhile work that we both love.''

"Dear Samuel," she whispered, reaching for his hand and closing her eyes for a moment. Her heart ached, not with joy at hearing about his feelings for her at last, but with a great sadness she couldn't explain. Too late, he'd revealed his feelings. She was in love with Jamie.

"I know this confession seems to come rather suddenly," Samuel explained, squeezing her hand slightly. "But it's been seriously on my mind for these three weeks you've been away. Take whatever time you need in deciding. I'm anxious to know your answer, but have no desire to add to your difficulties. Will you allow me to escort you into the dining room to partake of the buffet?"

He looked so vulnerable. She couldn't bear to tell him she was in love with another man. Not yet, when the realization was still so new even to her.

"Of course. Please, let's go in." She placed her hand through his arm and walked with him into the crowd.

Jamie watched Mariah and Samuel Hastings until they disappeared from view among the many guests. Though the reception room was uncomfortably hot, he felt a chill. Mariah and Hastings together again. That was what she wanted. She certainly deserved a man who would commit his life to her. Did Hastings know about the treasure? Had she confessed her feelings to him at last? He'd seen the earnest expression on her beautiful face while they'd been talking so intently in the corner just now. How he wished he could know what they'd said to each other.

"Damn you, Mariah!" he cursed under his breath. Why did she have to be so lovely, so innocent, and yet so full of the fires of passion? She was an irresistible challenge.

A silver tray holding four filled champagne glasses had been left on a table near the musicians' platform. He downed two in quick succession, while he vowed silently to himself that he'd learn about Mariah's conversation with Hastings before the night was through.

Later, Jamie stood brooding alone at the side of the reception room. He'd been waiting for Mariah to rejoin him, but she still remained with Hastings.

"Quite a gathering, wouldn't you say, Lancaster?" Addington Braythwaite exclaimed from behind his back.

He turned to face his host. "Yes, very enjoyable."

"I wish we could have some dancing though, but the Puritan influence is strong in this city." Braythwaite gave a snort of laughter. "Leads to sinfulness, they say. Of course, so does just about everything else enjoyable. But I remember the balls during my youth in England." He elbowed Jamie in the side. "Perhaps it would lead to sin with a lady like Mariah for a partner. She's certainly worthy of being the center of attention tonight. I saw her on Samuel Hastings' arm a while ago. He's one lucky devil. The rest of the women here will be gossiping about her for weeks to come, and the men will be picking up the shattered pieces of their broken hearts for just as long. No wonder Dunny sent you along as her protector.''

Jamie eyed the older man, but decided that Braythwaite suspected nothing about the depth of his relationship with Mariah.

"What are your politics, Lancaster?'' Braythwaite continued. ''You've heard about the latest setback we've suffered at the hands of the bloody French, haven't you?''

"I'm sorry to admit that the pursuit of Dunny's map has kept me out of touch with current developments.''

"Well, Robert Dinwiddie, the governor of Virginia Colony, sent a force into the Ohio Valley a few weeks ago to chastise the Frenchies and their Indian allies for trespassing in the King's dominions. They've been trapping, building fortresses, and establishing settlements illegally for years in that part of the country. Dinwiddie's man, a young militia colonel named George Washington, engaged his troups against the enemy from a makeshift stockade he called Fort Necessity. As I heard it, it was raining torrents when the battle occurred. The fort turned to a muddy bog, guns were rendered useless. Washington was outnumbered. The clash was quickly over. A damned disgraceful rout, it was. Washington will have no further career in the military, I'm certain of that. If he's smart, he'll go back to his Virginia plantation to stay.''

"I know Washington,'' Jamie said. ''He's only in his early twenties. He lacks experience in battle, perhaps, but he's courageous and fiercely loyal to causes he deems just. I'm sorry to hear about the defeat.''

"Because of him, the bloody French now control the Ohio Valley, and we British have no influence west of the Alleghenies!'' Braythwaite halted his tirade to wipe his perspiring brow with a white handkerchief. "That battle could well lead to yet another war with the French. But at least some successes were scored recently at the Albany Congress.''

"Yes, I've heard that Benjamin Franklin made brilliant strides with the Five Nations tribes and toward bringing our colonies together to discuss joint ventures. What's your opinion that such plans will be ratified?''

"I, for one, am for unity,'' Braythwaite answered. "But many will be against it, feeling it a usurpation of King George's authority.''

"If you'll pardon me, sir,'' the stoic-faced butler suddenly interrupted, stepping up to them and bowing slightly.

"Yes, what is it, Crothers?'' Braythwaite asked.

"There has been some difficulty down at the stables, sir. The head groom reports that a man was caught sneaking about the horses.'' He glanced toward Jamie. "More specifically, around Mr. Lancaster's stallion. When ordered to halt and explain his actions, the man put up a dreadful fight and made good his escape.''

Jamie frowned, leaning toward the butler. "What description do you have of the man?''

"The incident occurred so quickly that there wasn't time to observe details. He was taller than average, strong, and swarthy.''

"Well, we can't have miscreants invading the premises and endangering our guests and their property!'' Braythwaite declared. ''I shall speak to the grooms myself about this matter. Excuse me, Lancaster.''

Left alone near the arched entrance to the reception room, Jamie no longer heard the conversations around him or saw the guests. The tightening in his belly told him more than his host would be able to learn from his servants about the identity of the intruder.

His hand clenched into a fist. With his attention drawn to Mariah and all they'd been through together lately, he'd nearly forgotten about Lem Hollister.

Chapter 27

"I won't need you any longer, Iris," she told the maid, sighing as she watched her fold the elegant sapphire dress over her arm. "Tell Mrs. Braythwaite I very much appreciated the loan of the gown."

Mariah relished being free of the confinement of the tight bodice, but she hated to part with the garment.

"Yes, Miss Morgan, I'll tell her so. You surely was the talk of the party, from what I heard tell. All the ladies was jealous, an' the menfolk about busted their eyeballs tryin' to get looks at you. I could tell that when I was helpin' to set the food about."

Mariah smiled. "Thank you, Iris. It was a most interesting evening." And very disturbing, she added wearily in her thoughts. A yawn escaped her lips, but she knew she felt too tense to be able to sleep. Her nerves were raw from smiling and acting attentive during the long evening. She wished she could have gotten away from the crowded reception room sooner, to be alone to think.

"Well, then, if you don't need me to help you

get ready for bed, I'll be goin'. Sweet dreams, Miss Morgan.''

"Good night, Iris."

Just as Mariah slipped on her white cotton nightgown, a pounding came at the door.

"Did you forget something, Ir—" She stopped dead still with the door half-open.

"It seems *you* forgot something, Miss Morgan. *Me!*" Jamie kicked the door open all the way and strode past her into the room.

"What are you doing here?" she demanded, darting out to peer into the hall to see if anyone had heard the commotion. The corridor was empty. Quickly, she ducked back into the bedroom and closed the door.

"How soon you forget. Down in the garden, we planned this little tryst. You and I are going to have a talk, woman." He swung around to face her.

She smelled the liquor on his breath and frowned at him, hands on hips. "I think you're intoxicated!"

"Not nearly as intoxicated as I'm going to be *after* we have this talk. I've sworn off women, not spirits. You can depend on liquor."

"I suggest you leave at once."

She stepped to him and tried to guide him by the arm toward the door, but he jerked away from her, glaring furiously, and grabbed her arms instead.

"Damn you, Mariah, what happened between you and Hastings tonight?" he thundered. "I demand an explanation!"

Mariah's nerves were much too frayed to contain her anger. It exploded at his command. "I'll ex-

plain nothing to a fool who's had too much to
drink! You have no claim on me. Let go of me at
once!''

''I'm far from being drunk, and I've *never* been
a fool!''

His fierce ice-blue stare burned into her. His
hands felt like hot irons as they slowly moved up
her arms and across her shoulders.

''No, Jamie, don't touch me.''

''Why not, Mariah? What are you afraid of?
Damn you for being so flaming beautiful . . .''

His mouth covered hers roughly before she could
protest again. His arm encircled her waist and
pulled her hard against him. His possessive kiss
robbed her of breath and will. When finally he
ended it, his words at her mouth tormented her.

''I won't touch you if you tell me to stop, if you
say you can't tolerate my touch because you love
Hastings, and you have no desire to feel my body
against you, within you. Say these words to me,
Mariah, and I'll leave you now.''

The rational part of her mind began to form the
syllables to halt him, but her heart and her now-
awakened body stopped them from reaching her
lips. Even searching for an image of Samuel's face
didn't work. Her consciousness filled to overflowing with only Jamie, his strength, his powerful will
rendering her helpless to resist.

He ravaged her mouth again and knew by the
soft moan he heard in her throat that he'd won. But
the smug feeling of triumph lasted only a moment,
for he sensed by his own body's urgent insistence
that he was far from being the conqueror. His compelling need for her made him powerless to main-

tain control of his own will. Her tempting breasts, straining through the thin cotton material of her nightgown, pressed into his chest. The soft yielding of her body against his, the sweet taste of her mouth, the tantalizing fragrance of her perfumed hair entangled in his fingers fired him with desire.

He tore the fragile nightgown from her and whisked her up in his arms to carry her to the canopied four-poster bed.

"Undress me, Mariah. Now . . ."

She couldn't refuse. With trembling fingers, she reached for him and began the disrobing. And all the while, his hands never ceased touching her, stroking over her naked breasts, her flat stomach, her neck, face. Then they moved lower, where his knowing touch could evoke the most rapturous pleasure.

When finally he lay beside her as naked as she, he pulled her against him and bent to kiss her breast. Mariah's breath caught in her throat from the shock of sensation his embrace sent through her. She willingly let him claim her. His lips found her mouth and consumed it, while his hand caressed the tightening tips of her breasts. He tortured her, and she longed for that sweet torment. The racing of her heart brought the rest of her body to an even higher degree of sensuous arousal. She must touch him, taste him, drink him in with her eyes, her lips.

She clung to him desperately, never wanting to let him go. In his arms, she felt safe, protected, loved. Nothing else mattered, except how long he would hold her, love her, make love to her.

"You are so beautiful," he murmured. "You en-

slave me with your fire. My God, I've never wanted
anyone as much as I want you. I love you, Mariah. Surrender to me. I must have all of you.''

''Yes, oh yes, my love.''

His hands explored her with growing fervor. Her
breathing became ragged. She moved beneath him,
stroking the flesh of his broad back and taut, naked
buttocks. He parted her legs and searched her most
intimate womanhood, creating an even more urgent, throbbing ache within her. She cried out his
name and dug her fingers into his shoulders when
she thought she could not endure his tender, yet
demanding, handling of her body any longer. He
entered her with a slow deliberateness. She moved
her hips to meet his powerful thrusts. Surrendering
all to him, she captured all from him. They moved
together in perfect rhythm, clinging frantically to
each other as the rapturous climax pulsed hard between them.

How long she held onto him, she didn't know.
Even after the waves of fierce pleasure had ebbed,
she didn't want him to leave her. When he gently
kissed her and caressed her straining breasts, she
couldn't keep from weeping with joy.

Their desperate hunger for each other raged all
that night, bringing them together again and again.

The early-morning songs of birds drifting
through the open window of the bedchamber
aroused Mariah from sleep. She opened her eyes
in the dim dawn light and sighed with happiness
as her glance fell across Jamie still asleep at her
side. She longed to stroke her hand over the soft,
dark hair on his naked chest, but resisted doing so

for fear of waking him. She wanted to bask in these quiet moments of sunrise, lying next to the man she loved with all her heart.

How handsome he looked relaxed in sleep, with his black hair tousled over his forehead and the dark outline of a new beard encroaching along his square jawline. Her flesh still tingled from the intensity of their repeated lovemaking. She felt completely spent, but contented beyond measure. Her heart was so full of love, she thought it would burst and overflow. Never had she known such joy. How she would cherish being able to awaken beside him like this each morning for the rest of her life.

That thought brought a troubled uncertainty to her heart. She and Jamie whispered words of love to each other, but said nothing more. They'd been together for only a few short weeks, yet they'd endured so much that she felt she'd known him for a lifetime. But never would he speak of marriage. And loving him without being wed troubled her greatly. Although she'd rebelled against her aunt and uncle's strict Puritanical teachings, they'd had their effect. Now a dark shadow of guilt clouded the bright glow of love she felt for him.

She'd never thought about wedding anyone except Samuel Hastings. Her long-held dream of practicing medicine was tightly bound to him. If Jamie were to choose her as his wife, would she have to sacrifice her professional goal? How could she pursue it with him when his ambition was to sail the world? The wife of a seafaring man stayed behind at the home port to keep the house and raise the children. Was that the kind of life she wanted?

Last night, Samuel had willingly offered her exactly what she'd thought she wanted. Before Jamie exploded onto the scene, she would have accepted what Samuel offered in a moment. But now the thought of spending the rest of her life with him didn't have the tremendous appeal it once had. Life had been so simple a few weeks ago, centered around learning, work, devotion, sacrifice. Each day had been fulfilling, yet always the same.

But Jamie had complicated her life beyond belief. There were no easy choices where he was concerned. She admired his courage, and his strength of will, even when it went counter to her own. His zest for life and need for adventure created a longing for the same in her. How exciting it would be to explore far-flung places.

Samuel and Jamie. The two men who loomed in her life represented two starkly different choices—with Samuel lay security, certainty; with Jamie, adventure and the unknown.

"Why the frown?" he asked softly, propping himself up on his elbow and gazing down at her. "That's no way to welcome the day when you're about to become a wealthy woman."

She smiled, then grew serious. "I was thinking about us, and how much I love you." She raised her hand to touch the side of his face. "Let's forget about my father's doubloons. Please. We don't need them. Finding them will end our journey and part us. I don't think I could bear that."

"Don't be silly, love. Gold won't part us. It'll just enable me to have my own ship so I can carry you off like some villainous pirate and ravish you any time I wish!"

He bent to nuzzle her shoulder, making her squirm and giggle. But her laughter quickly died.

"Stop, please, Jamie. We must talk."

"I believe that was why I came in here last night." His pale-blue eyes twinkled, but then he remembered the subject that had brought him to her room in the first place. The thought of Samuel Hastings sobered him quickly enough.

"You were going to tell me about your meeting with Hastings . . ."

"Jamie—he asked me to share his life and his work."

Jamie made no reply. He turned away from her and climbed out of bed. Going to the disheveled pile of clothing on the floor, hc found his purple breeches and white shirt and put them on.

Mariah held her breath, fearful of what he would say when he finally did speak.

"You're planning to return to him, of course. You've always made that clear." There was a cold edge to his voice as he buttoned his shirt and didn't look at her. "Then all that remains is for us to find the gold so the two of you can get on with it."

"How can you be so unfeeling? I haven't decided anything yet. This is no simple choice. Do I mean nothing to you?" She swallowed hard and forced herself to ask the questions tormenting her. "With or without the gold, do you love me enough to wed me, Jamie, and make a life together?"

He kept his back to her. The silence in the bed-chamber grew heavy as he delayed answering.

"We shared great passion, Mariah, but wedlock isn't a step I'm prepared to take. I've told you that.

Our time together has been brief. We found ourselves in extraordinary circumstances, and so, our emotions ran high. But I won't be caught in a web of obligation because of physical desires we didn't control. Neither will I shackle the future to promises that may be too difficult for either one of us to keep. I can't give you what your Samuel offers—security, work you love and have a tremendous talent for. I won't stay in one place. There's too much I need to see, explore, experience. Such a life is not for a woman.''

''And what if a child has been conceived from our joinings? Will you cast us both aside for your precious freedom?'' She threw the words at him, shaken by the coldness in his voice. ''I know what it's like to be abandoned and not know my father. Would you inflict that awful hurt on an innocent child—our child?'' She tried to search his face, but he stood by the open window, looking out. With sinking heart, she saw his jaw tighten, and feared he'd closed his heart to her.

The pain in her voice ripped into him, forcing him to face her accusations. He'd seen her anger and bitterness toward Dunny. He didn't want to cause such hurt to anyone. It made him question the high regard he'd always had for the Irishman.

A child . . . Caught up in the throes of desire, he hadn't thought beyond Mariah and himself and the blazing passion between them. How could he punish a babe conceived from their love by just sailing away? Had he become obsessed with his need to be free and unhindered by obligations? But that was the way he'd chosen to live—*must* live! He'd made that decision years ago. But honor dictated that he not turn his back on Mariah and their child, if one had been conceived. His thoughts whirled, but he knew Mariah waited for an answer. With difficulty, he made himself look at her.

"I accept responsibility for my actions. If you are with child, I'll marry you to give the babe my name, then send you to my parents in New York. They'd like nothing better than to have a son or daughter of mine to raise—it would make up for the disappointment I was to them. You'd both be well cared for."

"But you wouldn't be part of our lives?"

He turned from the window to look directly at her. "No, Mariah, I would not."

Had he taken his knife and plunged it into her heart, she couldn't have felt any more pain. She sat up in the bed, keeping the fine linen sheet tucked around her. Looking at him levelly, she took a deep breath to steady her voice, determined to keep emotion out of her words.

"I wouldn't force you to make the supreme sacrifice of marriage. Neither would I burden your family. I, too, take responsibility for my actions. You've made your feelings clear from the start. So now hear mine. Whether we find the gold or not, today our liaison is finished. If I am pregnant, you will never know about it, nor will I hold you accountable to the child. I don't need you. Have your cherished independence. Grow old alone with it! I want you out of my life. Everything is over between us, except the business we must yet transact. Leave me now. I'll be ready to go to the Palmer mansion whenever you wish." She turned her shoulder to him, indicating with her body as well as her words that the discussion was ended.

Jamie frowned, torn between his new longing for her and his much-longer-held need to be a free man. Separating was the best solution for both of them. The heavy sadness he felt in his heart would pass, he was certain. Mariah would dim from his mind. In time . . .

"I must leave the house for a while this morning, but I'll return before noon," he said flatly. "We'll go to the mansion then."

"As you wish." She matched her emotionless tone to his. Still turned toward the wall, she heard him walk to the door. The strength of will she'd forced herself to muster suddenly melted away.

"Jamie . . ." she whispered, twisting around. She couldn't see very clearly because of the hot tears blurring her eyes, but she knew he was no longer in the room.

Chapter 28

Mariah and Jamie arrived at the old Palmer mansion just after noon. They'd spoken little since leaving the Braythwaite house. Though the day marked the beginning of the month of August and continued the hottest period of summer, the atmosphere surrounding Mariah and Jamie reflected a January freeze. Their conversation was formal and succinct, with neither one of them again mentioning the difficult topics they'd discussed at dawn.

Mariah tried to concentrate on their goal of locating the gold, but the excitement she'd experienced before had vanished. Jamie filled her mind, haunting her—after today, they would part forever.

"But the sooner, the better!" she mumbled vehemently under her breath when he rode ahead of her down a narrow alley. Once he was gone, her life would return to normal.

She should have taken comfort in that fact, but she didn't. Instead, she was tormented by the thought that this might be their last ride together.

She studied the unwelcoming six-foot-high stone fence surrounding the Palmer property. Through the wide bars of the wrought-iron front gate, she glimpsed the imposing two-story house. It had been left to fall into ruin long ago. She was certain that, at one time, it must have dominated the hill on which it stood. But now the once-regal building was faded and weathered. Sections of the slate roof gaped open, exposing rafters; it made her think of the bleached skeleton of a decaying beast. Tall weeds and overgrown shrubbery nearly obscured the front of the house.

" 'Tis a shame such a fine residence fell into disuse," Jamie noted, reining in Sultan. "The story goes that the first Palmer from England to set foot in this colony was a cobbler's apprentice, an industrious fellow who worked hard to acquire this piece of land. But his family didn't like living here in the New World, so he sold the parcel to a mysterious man named Wenchill, who built the mansion. He'd accumulated a great deal of wealth and spent it freely. For a time he was the toast of Boston, until it was discovered that his vast fortune was built on piracy against the Crown. It's said he hanged himself here in the house rather than face capture and prosecution, and that his ghost haunts the mansion seeking revenge against those who betrayed him."

"It *is* a rather forbidding place," she replied. "But I don't believe in ghosts. Do you really think my father's treasure trove is here? What if this whole journey has been a hoax all along? Perhaps my father paid everyone—the Braythwaites and the others—to fabricate their stories about his generosity toward them."

Jamie shook his head. "Dunny Morgan is no

liar. And neither are the Braythwaites or any of the others.''

His tone carried more than a hint of chastisement in it, causing Mariah to bristle. Her words were curt when she spoke.

''By all means then, let's proceed inside and put an end to all this speculation once and for all.''

He nodded and leaned forward on Sultan to push open the old gate. He could hardly budge it. Finally he forced it open enough for them to steer their horses through one at a time.

Mariah followed him on Lilac Wind along the weed-choked driveway to the front entrance, noticing that he took in more than just the house with his sweeping gaze. He seemed intent on the high, untrimmed hedges and draping willow trees in the overgrown front lawn. When he climbed down from Sultan and came around to help her dismount, she saw that he'd stuck his pistol in the waistband of his tight-fitting black breeches. The fullness of his cotton shirt nearly concealed it from view, but not quite.

''Are you planning to shoot the ghost if we encounter it?'' she asked sarcastically.

Apparently, he didn't wish to dignify her quip with an answer, for he only cocked a dark eyebrow, then turned to ascend the stone front steps and enter. When the front door wouldn't open he walked around to the back of the house, with Mariah following in his wake.

The pressure of his shoulder easily opened a plank door in the rear. Mariah fully expected the hinges to creak loudly on the wood frame, but they didn't. Instead, the door swung open noiselessly.

Their entrance stirred a thin cloud of dust in the small anteroom. She coughed and covered her mouth and nose with her gloved hand until the dirt settled. She saw Jamie glance out the door before he closed it behind them.

"What are you looking for out there? The ghost is supposed to be in here."

"Just taking precautions," he answered off-handedly. "We're trespassing, after all, even though I don't think anyone really knows who owns this old place now. Do you have the riddle?"

"Yes." She was certain he'd deliberately changed the subject, but she let the matter drop and fished out the folded sheet of parchment from the side pocket of her blue riding outfit. "The first line of the poem mentions a hallway and a left turn." She looked up from the paper and meandered from the anteroom through a low archway to emerge into a wide, wood-paneled corridor.

"This could well be the area, though there's likely a similar hall on the second floor as well. Does the riddle give any hint as to which one it is?" Jamie tried to read the parchment sheet over her shoulder.

"Yes. It says the upper hall." She pointed toward a rickety-looking staircase about ten feet away to their left. "There's the way up."

"You'd better let me go first to test my weight on those steps." He moved around her, batting at low-hanging cobwebs as he approached the stairs.

She stayed two to three steps behind him, pausing anxiously as he tried each one. The old oak planks creaked and even sank in spots under his boots, but held well enough for her to follow him.

When they reached the second floor, she held the parchment sheet toward the light streaming through the broken glass of the nearest window.

"We're to turn to the left here in this hallway and look for flowers somewhere—'To dwell among flowers is restful indeed,' " she quoted. "But how can there be flowers in this old place? Wouldn't a garden be a better place to look?" She frowned, trying to decipher her father's puzzle.

"This is a riddle, remember," Jamie noted. "The words shouldn't be taken literally. Let's try looking through the rooms at this end of the corridor."

The first door they came to opened at a touch to reveal a small bedchamber, much like a child's room. Mariah followed Jamie inside, and while trying to step up beside him, plunged face-first into a huge cobweb hanging from a lamp. Sputtering and swatting at it, she tried to wipe away the sticky threads, with only minimal success.

Jamie grinned. "Beware of the present inhabitants, too."

She screwed up her face in displeasure, then sneezed because of the thick layer of dust that had settled over the room.

No carpets remained. The only furnishing was a broken, child-sized rocker upended in one corner with one armrest and a curved runner missing. The plastered walls, once painted a light green, were cracked and spotted with grime. Only a pair of ragged white lace curtains hung from one of the long, narrow windows.

She couldn't keep from wondering about the children who must have occupied this nursery. A heavy sadness fell over her at seeing the emptiness, the lack of life in the bedchamber. Thinking of children resurrected the worry that she might be pregnant by Jamie.

"While you look around here, I'll investigate the next room," he said, turning to go out in the corridor.

Forcing down her troubled thoughts, she examined the nursery more closely, but could find nothing which even hinted of flowers.

"Mariah, come here," she heard Jamie call from down the hall.

There were even more cobwebs in the larger bedchamber she entered, but this time she avoided them. Jamie waved to her to join him across the room.

Three of the plastered walls had been whitewashed and patterned with delicate, hand-painted pink roses at one time, but now they were faded and yellow with age. The fourth wall, surrounding the gray marble fireplace, was covered in oak paneling. There were no rugs or furnishings in the room. The only evidence of habitation appeared to be a small, murky oil painting of a forest landscape set in an ornately carved gilt frame hanging slightly askew on the wall over the mantel.

"See what you think of this deduction," Jamie suggested. "The riddle uses the words 'restful' and 'flowers.' A bedchamber is used for rest and the painted roses here are flowers."

"Yes, you're right." She let her gaze sweep around the room, feeling a sudden excitement flutter through her. Were they close to the gold?

"Look here." He squatted down, resting his elbows on his knees. She saw him wince from the movement and knew the injuries he'd received during their journey still pained him.

Bright streaks of sunlight beamed through the broken panes of two widely spaced windows, illuminating the dust particles floating in the air and covering the floor. Jamie pointed at several nearly imperceptible footprints, which she'd certainly have overlooked.

"Boot prints, a man's, judging by the size of them. Made some time ago." He followed them with his eyes. "They cross the room and go to the hearth."

He stood up and walked to the fireplace, with Mariah following.

"Do you think my father made them?" She met Jamie's gaze.

He shrugged. "If this room proves to be the one referred to in the riddle, then he must have walked here months ago when he contrived this scheme. Read the verse aloud." He put his palms on the marble mantel, scanning the paneled wall from ceiling to floor with his eyes.

Suppressing her mounting excitement, Mariah spoke up clearly, quoting from the parchment sheet.

     " 'A walk left through the upper hall is all you
         will need;
     To dwell among flowers is restful indeed.
     Beneath the right angles, the left side panel
         slides;
     Down the dark passage is where wealth
         abides.' "

Jamie smiled and shook his head. "Ah, Dunny, you old salt. It would've been much easier if you'd just told us plainly where you hid the doubloons. Always one for the games, you are."

He ran his hand along the wood panel framing the left side of the marble hearth, but found no trip lever.

" 'Beneath the right angles . . .' " he repeated aloud, studying the whole wall again.

"Could this landscape painting form the angles?" Mariah stood on her tiptoes to straighten the frame on its hook over the mantel. "Maybe there's something behind the painting."

"Perhaps . . ." he replied, but he sounded doubtful as he reached up and removed the painting.

Mariah was disappointed to see only the same oak paneling beneath, no hidden openings or levers in the wall. She watched while he turned the work of art over this way and that, examining it. She'd almost given up hope, when Jamie shook the picture hard. Something fell out and hit the floor with a thunk. A key. She stooped down to retrieve it. The metal was tarnished black with age and was cold to the touch. After looking at it closely, she handed it to him.

"Do you think it might fit here somewhere?" Her pulse quickening, she ran her hand along the left side of the marble fireplace, as he'd done moments before.

"There must be a keyhole," he agreed. "Keep looking."

They both carefully stroked their hands over the oak panels and seams of the wall and the cool, smooth marble of the hearth.

"Here!" Jamie exclaimed, kneeling down to peer at the underside of the gray marble mantel. "There's a hole here. I'll try the key."

Mariah held her breath. She had only a few moments to wait as he fumbled to insert the long metal key and give it a twist. With a loud scraping sound, the oak wall panel next to her swung back, revealing a hidden passageway. The smell of stale air reached her nostrils, making her screw up her face and wave her hand to try to disperse it.

" 'Down the dark passage,' " she repeated, barely able to contain her excitement. "Oh, Jamie, this must be the place! The gold is surely here!"

"We'll soon find out." Excitement sounded in his voice, too, as he came up beside her. "Since you're to inherit the treasure, it's only fitting that you cross this threshold first. But take care with your footing once inside. This old house *seems* sturdy enough, but let's be cautious."

Eagerly, she stepped into the passageway, with Jamie following. The sunlight from the bedchamber penetrated the darkness only enough for her to see a little way. The windowless room around her was tiny, with space for perhaps four people, at most. She noticed Jamie's head brushed the ceiling of it when he stood at his full height. Looking around, she glimpsed two wooden crates and an old sea trunk stacked in a pile just inside the door.

"Here's a candle," Jamie announced, picking up a tipped-over pewter holder from atop one of the crates. He struck the flint of the attached tinderbox, and lit the wick of the short, yellowed candle. "Here," he said, handing the holder to her.

While she held the candle overhead, he carefully

checked the crates and trunk, even pounding on the bottom and sides of the sea chest with the hilt of his knife.

"Nothing here. These probably held weapons or supplies at one time. Old houses like this often had secret rooms. People used to hide here during Indian raids. Move the lamp over there." He pointed toward a narrow space running behind the bedchamber fireplace.

Nodding, she raised the candle again and carefully felt her way along the studs of the wall frame. The space appeared to be only wide enough for one person to pass through at a time. Without warning, Mariah sneezed loudly, nearly extinguishing the candle. Coughing, she rubbed at her nose to try to ease the tickling the dusty air caused.

Jamie coughed, too, as he held out his hand to take the candleholder while she caught her breath. "I'll go on," he said, trying to squeeze by her. For a moment, their bodies pressed close together, front to front. Their eyes caught and held, but Mariah quickly lowered hers and stepped aside to give him room to pass. The floorboards creaked under her weight, giving her a start, but they seemed firm.

Just beyond the brick back side of the bedchamber hearth, the passageway made a sharp right turn. Jamie followed it slowly for six feet or so, until it ended at a wall. He raised the candle to examine the cramped space when Mariah joined him.

"It stops here," he explained, glancing around at the rough-hewn boards of the inner walls. "There doesn't appear to be any other exit or entrance besides the sliding panel we used in the bedchamber." He fell silent and again used his knife hilt to tap the walls around them. They each echoed a solid sound, giving no indication of another hidden room.

Mariah felt her excitement evaporate. A terrible disappointment surged through her. "Then there is no treasure after all. My father is a cruel and heartless liar, just as I always thought . . ." Her voice trailed off, constricted by the lump that rose in her throat. She leaned back against the wall for support and closed her eyes to try to prevent the hot tears from spilling out.

"Perhaps there's another passage we haven't yet found," Jamie offered, but with little conviction in his tone.

"No, you know as well as I do this is the right one. And no one arrived here before us and stole the gold either. The dust-coating on the floor here and in the bedchamber clearly shows that." She slowly shook her head. "Now you know as well as I do that my father is a merciless, evil man who enjoys manipulating people, toying with them as if they were mindless puppets. I hate him!" She buried her face in her hands, letting deep sobs wrack her body.

"Mariah . . ." He came to her and gently pulled her to him.

Now, for the first time in all the years he'd known Dunny Morgan, he felt anger for the man. The anguish in Mariah's voice ripped through him more painfully than his own disappointment over losing his dream of a ship. A fierce protectiveness toward her welled up within him, triggering his fury. He despised being duped himself. But Mariah's involvement made the cruel trick even more infuriating to him.

Suddenly a sound beneath them made him tense.

Mariah had heard it, too. Trying hard to quiet her weeping, she looked questioningly at him.

"A door closed," he stated in a low voice.

"By the wind?" she whispered.

"Perhaps, but I want to investigate."

Leading her by the hand, he slowly retraced their steps, halting a few seconds to listen when his boot hit the creaky floorboard Mariah's had earlier. When they reached the secret opening, he drew his pistol.

"Stay in here. Close the panel and remain hidden inside until I return."

She shook her head and kept a firm hold on his arm. "No, Jamie, I'm coming with you."

He frowned but didn't want to take the time to argue. Besides, he wasn't certain about the safety of the passageway. There could be an opening from another place in the house that someone else might know about and use.

Crossing the bedchamber, he used the door as a shield and carefully scanned the outer corridor in both directions. Seeing nothing amiss, he stepped out into the hall. With Mariah right behind him, he kept his back turned to the wall and slowly started toward the main staircase. No other sounds emanated from the house, save the muffled click of their boots on the wood floor as they tiptoed over it.

Mariah's nerves were taut with apprehension. What was Jamie expecting? Whatever it was, she was glad to have him near and with a loaded pistol.

As they came abreast of the nursery room, he started across the hall. Suddenly the slightly ajar nursery door burst open, and before Mariah knew what was happening, a powerful arm wrenched around her neck, imprisoning her. The barrel of a pistol pressed hard against her temple. Jamie whipped around.

"Drop your weapon, Lancaster," her assailant commanded fiercely, "or I swear I'll kill her."

Jamie halted stock-still, knowing the big man strangling Mariah meant every word he spoke. He saw any chance at resistance swiftly dissolve when a second adversary stepped into view from behind the same door.

"You'd best do what my friend here says, Jamie," the other man remarked with a snide grin as he toyed with the pointed end of a sword.

With no other choice at hand, Jamie slowly lowered his pistol, letting it drop to the floor. His eyes narrowed as he fought to control his smoldering fury over the fact that his arch enemies—Doyle Iverson and Lem Hollister—now held the upper hand.

Chapter 29

"Get in here!" Iverson ordered, dragging Mariah with him as he stepped back to clear the doorway into the bedchamber. Jamie had to obey. Hollister kicked the door shut behind him.

"Git yer back up against the wall over there, Jamie," Hollister directed, pointing with his sword. "I'll be takin' that boot knife yer so handy with next."

Slowly Jamie bent down and drew out the weapon.

"Put it right there on the floor. See, Iverson, I told you it'd pay to keep watch on them Braythwaites' house. We got you both as easy as huntin' hens in a chicken coop. You musta let this pretty little thing addle yer brain, Jamie. 'Twas a time I never could've ambushed you so easy-like." He sidled over to where Iverson still held Mariah around the neck.

"Hello, pretty lady. We ain't bin introduced proper-like. I'm Jamie's close friend, Lem Hollister." He turned toward Jamie again. "That's right, ain't it? We share everythin', don't we? Why, we've shared furs, horses, ships, even bullet wounds. You won't have no objections to me an' Iverson sportin' with this here fine wench of yers, now will you, Jamie, me boy? You shore do know how to pick the beauties.''

He kept grinning, showing empty spaces along the top row of his yellowed teeth. His lecherous gaze swept over Mariah as he ran a callused hand along the side of her face, then over her breast straining against the blue linen of her dress.

He was filthy and reeked of sweat, horses, and cheap tobacco. She gasped and tried to cringe away from his loathsome handling, but couldn't move because of Iverson's iron grip. She could barely breathe from the pressure around her neck.

''Don't touch her, Lem.'' Jamie didn't raise his voice, but the deadly threat in his words was unmistakable.

A deep laugh cackled from Hollister's throat. ''Jus' stand fast an' keep yer hands in sight. Don't fergit Iverson's a right nervous sort. That pistol of his could go off real easy-like. Be a shame to shoot yer pretty little woman b'fore we had a chance to become friends—real close friends.''

''I want no part of her!'' Iverson countered fiercely. ''But I'll see you have her, with him watching. Then I'll kill them both.''

''Kill?'' Hollister frowned. ''You didn't say nothin' about killin'. When we made the deal fer me to git you outta jail an' pay me the ten thousand pounds fer helpin' you find Jamie, you said you was jus' gonna haul him in to the authorities an' have him locked up fer a long dry spell.''

Iverson's smile was cold. His closely set brown eyes glinted with hatred, casting a look as black as the clothes he wore. ''I lied. I've meant to destroy

Lancaster since the day he murdered my wife. But I don't just want to shoot him. That would be too easy. Have your filthy play with his whore. Watching that should torture him worse than the final bullet will.''

He let go of Mariah and shoved her hard toward Hollister, who threw both arms around her to catch her. Then he swung his gun toward Jamie and swiftly withdrew a second pistol from inside his black coat, which he leveled at Hollister.

''Now get at her, you bastard, before I put a bullet in you!'' He clicked back the hammers of both weapons.

''Bloody hell, Iverson, watch yourself,'' Hollister tried to coax. ''You don't have to threaten to shoot me jus' to git me to rape a wench.''

''Then do it *now,* on the floor!''

With narrowed eyes and muscles tensed until they ached from the strain, Jamie gauged the distance between himself and Iverson, judging whether or not he could reach the madman before he could get off a shot. He'd have only one chance.

For several long moments, he was forced to bide his time, watching as Lem Hollister threw Mariah to her back on the dirty wooden floor near the broken rocking chair. She struggled bravely, but was no match for Lem. Jamie's consuming rage exploded in his veins when Hollister held her wrists imprisoned in the grasp of one big hand, while he used the knife in his other to cut away the ribbon ties gathering the scooped neck of her dress and camisole underneath. Her milk-white breasts were immediately exposed to the rough pawing of his hands. She screamed Jamie's name and twisted from side to side. Hollister only laughed, then moved to push her skirt up around her hips.

Suddenly the door burst open, the force swinging it back so hard that it hit the wall with a loud crash. All eyes darted to the empty entryway. Iverson fired one of his pistols, but the bullet sailed through the air, burrowing into the wall on the other side of the corridor. In the next instant, Hollister lurched sideways, grabbed the broken chair, and hurled it at Iverson, knocking both pistols from his hands. At the same time, Jamie lunged forward with the ferocious power of an enraged tiger, catching Iverson squarely in the chest with his shoulder. They hit the floor with a mighty thud that elicited loud grunts from both men.

Mariah didn't know what was happening. She stared dumbfounded at Jamie and Iverson thrashing wildly on the floor. A flash of color whizzed by the corner of her eye as Hollister suddenly came under attack from a new adversary—Dimetrius Cobb. The dwarf kicked the kneeling man in the rear end, flattening him to the floor, stomach-down. Then he pounced feet-first into the middle of his back, knocking the wind out of him.

Jamie's knife lay close to Mariah's grasp. Fumbling to hold her dress together, she reached for the blade, whisked it up, and tossed it handle-first to Dimetrius, who caught it deftly and pressed it threateningly to Hollister's neck.

Suddenly a powerful blow from his opponent sent Jamie careening into the wall. Free for a moment, Iverson leaped for his loaded pistol where it had fallen to the floor near the window. But Jamie dived for him, catching his wrist to keep him from leveling the weapon at him.

The intense strain of holding each other at bay bulged veins in each man's neck. Mariah watched in frozen horror as their powerful arms shook with the effort to gain the upper hand. At last Jamie smashed Iverson's arm against the wooden frame of the window with such force that he lost his grip on the pistol, and it crashed to the floor again, discharging harmlessly into the wall.

But Iverson was far from defeated. When Jamie punched him in the belly, he reeled, but returned a vicious right cross to the jaw that instantly bloodied Jamie's mouth and knocked him backward to the floor.

The child's rocker had shattered into pieces after hitting Iverson. With pure demonic malice twisting his features, the demented man snatched up a pointed piece of the splintered armrest and lunged.

"Jamie!" Mariah screamed in warning from across the room. Her hand flew to her mouth, fearing he might be too stunned to protect himself.

But he did see the weapon coming at him. As Iverson lurched toward him, he suddenly kicked up his leg. Jamming his boot into Iverson's midsection, he used the man's own forward momentum to hurl him up and over his head. Too late, he realized the close proximity of the window. With a bloodcurdling yell, Doyle Iverson plunged headfirst through the jagged broken glass of the window. His echoing scream trailed behind him, but then stopped when his body hit the ground.

Gasping for breath, Jamie glanced over to where Dimetrius still held Hollister at knife-point. He nodded at the dwarf, then, clutching his arm to his midsection, scrambled to the window to look down. Iverson's body lay sprawled face-up on the stone steps below, the mouth and eyes wide open in a last gaping grotesque expression.

Mariah ran to the window and knelt down beside Jamie, touching his shoulder. "Dear God, are you all right?"

"Yes," came his answer in a low voice. "But Iverson's finished."

She leaned over the sill, then quickly pulled back to avoid the shocking sight.

" 'Tis a damned ugly way to die," Jamie continued, leaning against the wall and using the back of his hand to wipe at the blood oozing from the corner of his mouth, "but at least now his torment is ended. He never could accept what Eleanora was."

She nodded. "He was insane."

"Are you hurt, Mariah?" His eyes met and held hers.

She still clutched at the front of her dress to hold the fabric together over her breasts. "No, I'm all right. But I thank God for Dimetrius' timely arrival."

"Speaking of timely . . ." Jamie struggled to his feet with her help, and they crossed the room together to join Hollister and Dimetrius. "You took your sweet time getting up here to help," he chided the dwarf, holding out his hand.

The small man tossed the knife to him. "When you found me at Rose's place this mornin', you saw I had to sober up some," he said, squinting and rubbing the side of his temple. "My head's still poundin'. Yer lucky I found my way here at all. This place is mighty big to go sneakin' 'round in when yer my size, you know. Climbin' that main staircase 'bout did me in.''

Jamie gave a little laugh. "My thanks anyway for your help. You likely saved our lives." He gestured with the knife for Hollister to get up. His expression hardened. "And as for you, Lem . . ."

"Now take it easy, Jamie." Hollister looked worried as he took a step backward, holding up his hand and keeping his beady eyes fastened on the knife. "I wasn't gonna harm yer woman. I was jus' waitin' fer a chance to git at Iverson without him shootin' me. Threw that chair at him an' knocked them pistols outta his hands, didn't I? He would've shot you an' her.''

"And you, too," Jamie added coldly.

"Maybe. But you know I wouldn't have let him kill you," Lem countered. "Why, things would be too bloody dull if you an' me wasn't at each other's throats from time to time. We go back a long ways, Jamie.''

"Too long, Lem. What you did to Mariah—" He scowled fiercely and started toward Hollister, but Mariah caught his arm to stop him.

"No, Jamie, there's been enough killing. What he did to me doesn't matter. He helped by disarming Iverson. Turn him over to the authorities and let them judge his actions as Iverson's accomplice.''

Jamie glanced at her, then back to Hollister. "You're fortunate the lady has a heart, Lem, and that I choose to oblige her.''

"I reckon this means I won't be gittin' Sultan

back?'' The man looked more regretful about that than he had at hearing he'd be going to jail.

"I'll take good care of him." Jamie gave him a cold smile.

Chapter 30

In the late afternoon, Jamie strolled the tranquil formal garden of the Braythwaite estate, glad to be alone, for he had much on his mind. His disturbing thoughts no longer involved Doyle Iverson and Lem Hollister. He'd reported Iverson's death to the authorities, with Mariah and Dimetrius' corroboration. Lem had been arrested as an accomplice to attempted murder, and Iverson's body put into the care of an undertaker. What remained to trouble his mind was Mariah.

He paused by the tall shrub she'd pretended to dance with last night during the party. He vividly remembered how lovely she'd looked in Rowena Braythwaite's blue gown. She should wear nothing but elegant satins and silks. He smiled. But for more intimate times, she should wear nothing at all . . .

"Damn your clinging memories!" he muttered, suddenly angered by the way thoughts of her were so hard to banish. He knew parting from her was the logical thing to do. Then he'd be free. It sounded so simple. The only problem was his heart rebelled. Of course, he'd been fighting his heart's demands almost since the moment he first met

Mariah. Against his will, she'd gotten inside him and taken a firm hold on his being. Just how strong that hold was had been brought home sharply to him at the Palmer mansion, when Iverson and Hollister had threatened her so brutally. He'd thought of nothing but saving her, just as when the bear attacked, and the renegade Indian had turned on her. Not for a moment had he considered his own well-being. And that unselfishness wasn't like him. His usual practice—learned from years as a lone adventurer—was to think of himself first.

"Am I disturbing you?"

He'd been so deep in thought that he hadn't heard Mariah's approach behind him on the grass path.

"No," he replied, turning around to face her. He felt his heart turn over. Appreciatively, he let his eyes drift over her, taking in every line and curve of her loveliness. Her thick, auburn hair framed her delicately rounded face and tumbled in soft curls around her shoulders. She'd changed her torn clothes from the Palmer mansion attack and now wore a simply cut cotton dress of a deep mauve. The short sleeves revealed the creamy smoothness of her arms, which were crossed in front of her.

"How are you feeling?" she asked, forcing herself to make conversation. It was difficult to speak at all when he looked at her that way, as if he were searching her soul.

"I have a few new bruises to add to all my collection."

"You suspected we'd be in danger at the mansion, didn't you? That's why you arranged for Dimetrius to meet us there, and why you carried your pistol. But how did you know Iverson and Hollister would be there?''

''I didn't. But from an incident Crothers related to me last evening during the party, I had reason to believe Lem was stalking me here. I didn't know he'd helped Iverson escape from jail to join him, as well. But I wanted Dimetrius around as a precaution.''

''You should have warned me.''

''I didn't want to distress you further. You were already upset by our conversation at dawn.'' He stepped closer to her and touched her arm. ''Were you able to rest at all this afternoon?''

She pulled away, taking two steps back. ''Y-yes, a little.''

''I'm sorry, Mariah. I didn't think. You must find a man's touch repulsive after what happened with Hollister earlier today.''

''No, that's not why I want a distance between us.'' Her eyes held his. She swallowed hard, feeling her pride slip away. But she must tell him the truth. ''I don't want you to touch me. I—I can't bear it. Even being this close to you is a torment, for I want to be in your arms.''

''Mariah.'' He started to come to her, but she held up her hand to stop him.

''No, Jamie, please. I don't think a relationship between us could ever work. I love you. We're strongly drawn to each other now. But I know that, in time, you'd feel trapped and burdened by my presence, cheated of your freedom. We must part. I've only come out here to say good-bye. I've decided I'm not going with you to see my father again, or even his grave, if he's dead now. I want to try to forget that he and his cruel scheme ever existed. And I shall try to forget you, too, Jamie, though I know that won't be easy. Tomorrow, I'm returning to the hospital. Samuel needs me.''

''And I don't.'' His hushed words were a statement, not a question.

''You've made that fact clear.''

Jamie came to a decision at that moment, one which his heart demanded. He couldn't lose her.

''I was wrong, Mariah.'' He reached out and touched her face with his hand, a feeling of rightness surging through him. ''Before you came up just now, I was going over all that we've been through together in these few short weeks, how more than once, we came dangerously close to death. If we part now, I know it would be forever, just as if one of us had died and the other continued the journey alone. I always thought I could survive happily without anyone. Even after you came into my life, I planned to keep my memories of you tucked away in a neat little compartment where I could pull out them only when I wanted to. But I know that won't work. I want something more than memories.'' He gently drew her into his arms. ''I need you. I couldn't bear it if you were gone from my life. Marry me, Mariah. Right now, I don't have much to offer you besides my love. But I'll have more soon. You can continue your medical work. I'll go to my father and persuade him to help me go into business, perhaps even banking. Then you and I can make a good life together.''

''Oh, Jamie.'' She clung to him, resting the side of her head against his chest. Her eyes filled with tears. "What are we to do? I love you so much. But I couldn't ask you to make such a sacrifice. You know you couldn't endure being a banker, tied to a desk and a daily routine. You'd soon grow to hate me for forcing you into such torment. You must sail the oceans as you've dreamed. I'll give you sons to carry on your name. I'll be a devoted wife and make a fine home for you to return to after your voyages."

He pulled back from her to look into her blue-green eyes. "You'd give up Samuel Hastings, the hospital, medicine?"

"Yes. I thought I loved Samuel, but I realize now that I mistook admiration and respect for love. He never touched my heart, my soul as you have. My life would be empty and without meaning if I couldn't share it with you."

"My love," he murmured, stroking her hair. Then he bent to kiss her with a tenderness that spoke more than mere words. His arms encircled her, pressing her against his length. The joy he felt in holding her filled his heart and all of his being. That she would make such sacrifices overwhelmed him.

Mariah slid her arms around his neck and filled her kiss with all the love consuming her. She felt more alive with joy and excitement than ever before. His strong arms protected her, made her one with him. He loved her. He'd offered to give up his dreams for her. She wanted nothing more than to spend her life making him happy.

"It would seem your father gave us a great treasure after all," he murmured when they separated to catch their breaths. "One far more precious and rare than gold. He gave us each other."

"Yes, I am grateful for that. But his cruel joke about the doubloons is hard to forgive."

Jamie was silent for several moments. "Perhaps it wasn't a joke."

"What do you mean?"

"Perhaps we just didn't find the treasure yet. We really didn't have a chance to search the whole house before Lem and Iverson burst in on us."

"But we found the passageway and it was empty."

"At first appearance. We didn't examine it closely. And perhaps there's another passageway."

"Oh, Jamie, I don't want to get my hopes up, only to be disappointed again. We have each other, that's all that matters."

"But if we had the gold, I could buy my own ship—*our* ship, Mariah. Then you could travel the world with me." His eyes glistened with a hint of excitement. "I know Dunny. I can't believe he'd hurt you or me in this way. I thought perhaps his illness might have affected his mind. But when we spoke in his room that day, he was lucid. And this elaborate plan he devised, sending us to find the puzzle pieces and meet with his friends whom he'd contacted months ago, was not devised by a mind distorted by sickness. He said the treasure existed. I believed him then, and I trust him now. He gave me his word that the doubloons were real. A man's word is his honor. I'm returning to the Palmer mansion—now, while there's still light."

His growing excitement spread to her. She felt

almost certain another search would be futile, but if there were yet a chance, even a small one . . .

"I'm coming with you."

"Don't think about what happened in there, Mariah," Jamie entreated, as they approached the nursery in the Palmer mansion. He held her hand and urged her down the hallway to the bedchamber with the hand-painted flowers on the walls.

"We'll check in here first, then search the rest of the house, if this passageway yields nothing. We won't give up." He flashed her a smile of encouragement, and she tried to return it, despite her sense of doubt and apprehension.

The panel scraped along the floor, smoothly sliding open again when Jamie turned the key in the secret lock under the mantel. The short candle in the pewter holder that they'd used before still remained where he'd left it atop the wooden crate. He struck the flint of the tinderbox and lit it, hoping enough remained of the wax and wick to enable them to make a more thorough search this time.

Mariah held the candle high so its light spread in a wide arch to enable him to search the wooden crates and the old sea trunk again.

Finally he stood up. His hair brushed the ceiling of the cramped room. "Nothing here." He cocked a dark eyebrow and stared into space, as if deep in thought. "A half-million pounds in Spanish doubloons would take up considerable space. There must be a hidden opening somewhere in here."

He used his knuckles to tap the walls again. Moving along the short, narrow corridor, he passed over the creaky floorboard. He started to move on, then stopped.

"What is it?" Mariah asked behind him.

Jamie turned around in the narrow space and knelt on one knee before her. "Strange that only this board creaks out of all the old ones making up the floor of this passageway. I wonder . . ."

He didn't finish his thought, but instead used his knife blade to pry at the edges of the six-inch-wide board. The nails holding it in place gave way with a squeal when he was able to get a firm grip on the end of the piece of wood and pull. Mariah knelt beside him.

"Hold the candle closer," he told her, leaning forward to see into the small opening beneath the floor. A glint of yellow flashed in the darkness. He sat back on his heels.

Mariah saw the grin on his face. Excitement made her pulse jump. "What is it, Jamie? What did you see?"

"Dunny, you old rascal." He shook his head and reached into the shallow hole, drawing out a gold coin. The candlelight reflected off the shiny metal. "Doubloons, but not all of them. Only a few carefully laid in a pattern to form an arrow pointing here."

He leaned down again to retrieve the other pieces, handing them to Mariah. Her hand shook with the excitement of feeling the cold, smooth metal in her palm. She nearly dropped the candleholder.

Jamie turned to his left where the red bricks of the hearth adjoined the passageway. "The rest must be hidden here somewhere.'' He ran his fingers over the rough bricks.

''Look! Here there's no mortar between them!''

Jamie used his knife again to pry into the tight crack between a pair of bricks two feet above floor level, edging one of them out far enough so he could get a grip on it. Crumbles of dirt and tiny pieces of baked clay hit the floor as he pulled the brick free. Seven more quickly followed, before he found no more loose ones. The remainder were held firmly by mortar. But the bricks he had removed created an opening large enough to see into.

''What's there?'' Mariah asked anxiously, stretching to glimpse over his shoulder.

''It's too dark to tell.'' He reached inside. ''There is something. A box or keg. It's cold to the touch, so it must be metal. I can feel a handgrip here on the side.'' He gave a pull. Nothing happened. ''It's heavy,'' he said, gritting his teeth and yanking again.

Crumbling mortar and dirt accompanied the keg-like container's removal from the opening. Jamie carefully eased it to the floor.

''It's too dark to see the contents here. I'll carry it out to the bedchamber. Light the way.''

Mariah turned quickly and had to restrain herself from hurrying out of the passageway. Jamie's slow pace testified to the fact that the object he carried on his shoulder was heavy. Her heart was pounding wildly. At last, perhaps this held the treasure!

Dusk tinged the sun rays streaming through the bedroom window a pale crimson, but enough light remained to enable them to examine the black metal container. With an effort, Jamie set it on end

in the middle of the floor, and leaned over to examine it.

"Appears to be made of iron. It doesn't look
like a pirate's treasure chest," he observed, using
his hands to wipe away some of the dust and cobwebs covering the two-foot-high, hexagonal-shaped
coffer. The flat lid had no hooks or hinges to hold
it in place. Only a rounded handle on top suggested
that it could be pulled off.

Mariah stood next to him and placed her hand
over his on the handle. Exchanging glances with
him, she took a deep breath to try to control her
excitement and knew by the smile creeping over
his lips that he felt the same expectation as she.
Together they gave a hard tug on the metal lid.

"Again," Jamie urged when it didn't yield. He
squeezed his other hand under the handle for a better grip. "On the count of three. One, two, *three!*"

The lid gave way this time. Jamie tossed it to
the floor, where it landed with a dull clunking
sound on his knife, laid aside a few moments before. But he paid no attention to his weapon now.
He heard Mariah gasp. His own heart seemed to
stop when he followed her gaze to the inside of the
thick-walled chest. No shiny Spanish gold doubloons glistened up at them in the twilight rays
lengthening in the bedchamber. The narrow cavity
in the chest was completely and undeniably empty.

Chapter 31

"If Dunsley Morgan isn't already dead when I return to Framingham, I'll personally put an end to his worthless life!" Jamie felt furious at Dunny for duping them, and he was just as angry at himself for beginning to imagine the tall masts and billowing sails of his own ship, and Mariah standing at his side on the gleaming deck. Venting his wrath, he shot a swift kick at the empty chest, then winced when the action did more damage to his foot than to the metal container. It teetered from the boot blow, but remained upright.

Mariah eased her wobbly legs by sinking down to sit on the floor. She sighed heavily with dismay, swallowing back the lump rising in her throat from her deep disappointment. All the wonderful possibilities the gold might have afforded them vanished into thin air like a foggy mist after sunrise.

"Getting rich this way was just too easy," she mused aloud. "Anything of true value can only be gained by diligence and hard work."

"That's your self-righteous Puritan aunt talking, and pitifully, too, I might add," Jamie countered, frowning with annoyance. Running his hand through his black hair, he paced in front of her.

"I've done enough in my life to know that sometimes hard work gains you nothing. Sometimes, everything depends on luck. But there wasn't anything easy about this treasure hunt. It nearly killed us. Damn, but I was so certain the gold would be here! Dunny's stubborn and cantankerous and full of tricks, but I've never known him to be deceitful and deliberately cruel."

"Until now." Mariah sighed again and studied the wrinkled folds of the skirt of her mauve dress, her spirit as shadowed as the darkening room. She didn't see Jamie lower his hand to help her to her feet.

"Full of tricks . . ." he repeated.

She glanced up to see him open his right hand fully to study his palm, as if he'd just noticed something about it. A thin black line ran across his fingers, too dark in color to be just a smudge of dirt. He rubbed his thumb over the substance. Leaning down, he picked up the lid, and turning it toward the receding light, ran his fingers over it.

Mariah got to her feet and stepped up next to him. "What is it? Have you found something?"

"I'm not certain. It's almost too dark to see anything clearly." He turned the lid over. A gouge marred the black metal where the lid had hit his knife before. He rubbed his thumb over it. Slowly, a smile spread across his lips. "Always the trickster, your father. He wasn't going to make finding the gold too easy . . ."

"The gold? What do you mean? Where is it—here?" She touched the indentation, almost fearing to give in to the hope that sprang in her heart.

Jamie quickly bent down to retrieve his knife

from the floor. "If the light had been better in the passageway and in here, I'd have seen it sooner. Whoever created this chest for Dunny was a good artist." He paused to scrape the blade of his knife around the gouge. Black peels of paint flaked off. "He painted the chest to look like iron when, in truth, it was cast of a far more precious metal."

He worked the blade some more, while Mariah stared in astonishment.

"The doubloons?" she murmured, gently touching the now-bright yellow spot on the lid.

"No longer coins." He handed the top to her and knelt down on one knee next to the chest. Carefully applying the blade, he scraped a thin line down the side. The golden color burst out from beneath the thick black paint. "Dunny had the doubloons melted down and recast into this chest, no doubt to test our persistence. It also protected the gold from being discovered by someone else."

"It was you who persevered, Jamie," Mariah murmured, overwhelmed by their discovery. "You had faith in my father . . ."

He stood and drew her into his arms. "Don't despair, my love." He held her against his chest. "I've had more of a chance to know him than you have. I think in his heart he wished to make amends for being absent as your father. Giving you this was the only way he knew."

"*Us*, Jamie—he gave the gold to us." She hugged him tightly, feeling her heart surge with love. "Now you can have your ship and your journeys to the Far East, just as you've always dreamed."

He tipped her chin up with his fingertips. His

pale-blue eyes held hers. "I have no dreams without you, Mariah." Tenderness touched his voice. "Marry me and sail the seas at my side. Every merchant vessel of distinction, venturing to the far corners of the world carries a ship's physician to see to the health of the captain and crew."

"Especially the captain?" She smiled and pressed closer to him, feeling his loving look warm her to the depth of her being. Suddenly she saw her own hopes and dreams falling within her grasp.

"Yes, especially the captain. And if the last few weeks are any indication of what my life will be like with you in it, I'll have plenty of need for a good doctor to patch up all my injuries!"

"You blame me for bear attacks and renegade Indians and confrontations with enemies you've had since long before I met you?" She tried to look affronted, but didn't succeed.

"Yes, I blame you for everything, especially stealing my heart when I was unaware." He bent his head to kiss her lightly, holding her close. "I must have you with me. There's so much I want to show you of the world. What great adventures we'll have together. And you won't have to give up your work in medicine. People wherever we go will have need of your skills. And you can learn from their physicians as well."

"Oh, Jamie, all of it sounds too good to be true! Yes, I'll wed you and love you for the rest of my life!"

"Then, my Mariah, my darling, before this day is through, we'll pay a visit to a friend of mine here in the city—Father Jacob Dunn. Tonight, when we hold each other before we sleep, we'll be husband and wife.''

Her glowing smile touched him to the soul, bringing him a deep joy he'd never before known. They kissed then, filling their caress with all the tremendous love and passion they'd known only together.

When they parted for breath, laughter and happiness shone in Mariah's blue-green eyes. Jamie hated to say anything that would mar her bliss, but he knew one difficult task yet remained to be done.

''Tomorrow, we journey back to Framingham, my love. We must learn your father's fate.''

She expelled a long sigh, resting her forehead against his chin. ''I know. Now I pray he still lives. There's so much I must say to him.'' She raised her eyes to meet Jamie's. ''Do you think I'll have the chance to mend the past?''

''I don't know, love. That question must be answered by the will of God and Dunny Morgan.''

Chapter 32

Mariah and Jamie were married that very night in a mission chapel at the end of a narrow alley near Dock Square. The bride wore no fancy blue silk gown as she had at the dinner party. Instead she chose to say her marriage vows before God adorned in a simply tailored crimson dress given to her by Rowena Braythwaite. Jamie, too, wore the plain clothing he'd preferred during their travels—black boots, buff-colored breeches, and a long brown leather vest over a white shirt. His profile was partially obscured in the dim church, but she thought she'd never seen him look handsomer.

The wedding guests were few—Addington and Rowena Braythwaite and Dimetrius Cobb. Father Dunn officiated calmly. As the service was drawing to a close, he spoke directly to Mariah and Jamie.

"Before I make the final pronouncement, do you wish to make any special pledges to each other?"

Jamie turned to her. He looked deeply into her eyes, hardly blinking as he began to speak.

"Mariah, my love, you light my life like the sun. We have dreams and challenges before us, but our great love will meet any test, rise above all storms. Our hearts, our lives are one from this day forth. I love you.''

Mariah's eyes brimmed with tears, making his handsome features blur before her. But she blinked back the wetness. She knew the tightness in her throat would hamper her own words, but still she must speak what was in her heart. Holding tightly to his hand, she looked into his eyes.

''You honor me with your pledge of love. I cherish you more than life itself. We cannot know what the morrow may bring, but whatever comes, we'll face together. Our strengths are made greater when joined. Our love will grow as we meet life side by side. I will walk with you through sunlight and shadow, share your triumphs and sorrows. I offer you my trust and my everlasting devotion. I give you no less than all that I am. I love you, Jamie, now and forever.''

No mere kiss passed between them. When their lips met, a bond already created by their hearts sealed their promises. Jamie and Mariah became husband and wife.

Two days later, Mariah stood at the farthest end of the weed-strewn path which led to her father's house.

She pulled her knitted shawl around her shoulders more tightly. An early-morning rain had washed the August day clean, leaving the trees and grass and brilliantly colored flowers glistening with wetness. The sun shone brightly, but now at mid-morning, the coolness brought by the showers still lingered.

Jamie accompanied her. James Lancaster, the man who had become her husband.

She cast him a tremulous smile, grateful for the support of his arm under her elbow. The tenderness in his look warmed her. Their love had blossomed amid strife and danger, and grown faster and more deeply than she ever could have imagined possible. She faced a bright future with him, one filled with love, passion, and adventure. But she still lacked one thing—a reconciliation with her father. She said a silent prayer that time and his severe illness hadn't worked against her to prevent it from taking place now.

"Have courage, my love," Jamie coaxed, giving her arm a gentle squeeze as he walked up the stone path with her. "Whatever happens, we face it together. I'm always at your side."

Wilhelmina Hooper answered his knock at the door.

"Lord be praised! You've returned at last, the both of you!" A full smile filled the plump housekeeper's lined face as she quickly stepped aside to allow them room to enter the house.

Mariah took her hand as soon as they were inside. "Wilhelmina, please, you must tell us. Is my father still alive?"

"Er, your father?" the older woman stalled, casting down her eyes and clearing her throat.

"What's wrong, Minnie?" Jamie persisted. "Where's Dunny?"

Mariah held her breath, waiting for the servant woman to answer.

"You'd both best be seeing for yourselves."

Mariah turned and started to hurry down the hall toward her father's bedchamber.

"No, not there, Miss," Wilhelmina called to her. At Mariah's questioning glance, she added, "He's in the dining room."

Mariah and Jamie exchanged perplexed glances. They would have questioned the housekeeper further, but Wilhelmina was already leading the way down to the other end of the hall.

At the sliding doors leading to the dining room, Wilhelmina stopped and turned toward them. "I hope his present state won't be too much of a shock to you. You'd best prepare yourselves."

Mariah felt her stomach tense with apprehension as Wilhelmina touched the tarnished brass door pulls. She bit her lower lip and reached for Jamie's hand to fortify herself. She felt certain they'd arrived too late. They were about to see a black-shrouded coffin bearing the last remains of her father, laid out in the dining room in preparation for burial. A tightness rose in her throat as she squeezed Jamie's hand, realizing she would never have the chance to say all the things she'd hoped to her father.

At Wilhelmina's yank, the two oak doors slid wide. She entered the dining room, and Mariah and Jamie stepped over the threshold after her.

Mariah froze stock-still at the sight that met her eyes. She felt the color drain from her face as her jaw dropped open and her eyes widened in surprise. For there at the formal dining table sat her father, Dunny Morgan—not only alive, but looking positively robust as he enthusiastically devoured a huge plate of sliced ham and baked eggs with cheese cream sauce!

"It's about time the two of you showed up!" he declared, reaching for a steaming bowl of boiled potatoes and spooning a goodly portion of the vegetables onto his plate. "Well, don't stand here gawking! Sit down and have some food!"

"We've already eaten," Mariah answered lamely, too shocked to think. Then realization suddenly hit her. *"Father!"* she cried, running to his chair. "You aren't dead! You look wonderful!" She stopped, just as she reached out to hug him. "But how have you recovered so well? When we left you a few weeks ago, you were—"

"Looking like death's next victim, I know," he finished for her, grinning. "Marvelous performance, wasn't it?"

"Performance?" Jamie spoke for the first time. A deep frown creased his forehead. "Explain yourself, Dunny."

"All in due time. Did you find the gold?"

"Yes, but, Father, are you ill? Were you ill three weeks ago?"

"You aren't much of a doctor, are you, daughter?" Dunny chided with a smug gleam in his brown eyes. "If you hadn't been so full of stubbornness, you would've been able to see past my ruse and realize my jaundiced color from my 'fatal liver disease' was actually expertly applied ashes and sulfur powder. I starved myself for weeks in order to achieve that very convincing emaciated look I had when you first laid eyes on me. Good Dr. Osborn played along with my trick to make it more credible to you. He suggested the death-rattle coughing, which I thought I executed most convincingly. I counted on your emotional prejudices against me to cloud your medical judgment, and that ploy worked. You both played right into my hands, just as I planned.''

Jamie shook his head, angry with his friend, but compelled by curiosity and amazement to know more about the elaborate scheme. ''Why, Dunny? Why all the deception and playacting?''

The older man smiled again, but now the look of snide self-satisfaction disappeared from his features.

''Come, sit down, both of you, and I'll explain,'' he urged, his irascible tone mellowed to a much gentler one. He waited until they were seated in the ladderbacked chairs next to him. Then he began.

'' 'Tis a story going back much longer than three weeks—over fifteen years now, to be exact. I loved your mother more than any other woman on earth, Mariah. I still love her. No one has ever taken her place in my heart. She was my life, as were you, our daughter.'' His brown eyes shifted from Mariah to the window and took on a faraway look. ''When her illness destroyed her, I felt as if I'd died with her. I had to go to sea to try to escape the memories of the happiness we'd had. I couldn't take you with me. Seafaring was no life for a child. And you looked so much like your mother. You still do. Every time I saw you, the anguish of losing her was renewed. I couldn't bear it. So I sent you to your aunt and uncle to be raised. From time to time I visited you, thinking the years between might have dulled the pain, but that was never the case. It was always difficult to leave you, but it would have been harder to stay. I don't know if you can possibly understand how much I loved your mother.''

"Yes . . ." she whispered, looking at Jamie. "I can understand.'' She glanced down at her hands in her lap. "But I needed you, Father. I was so lonely. Aunt Josephine and Uncle Obediah gave me a roof over my head, but they were so cold and strict. How I'd long for you to return, hoping each time that you'd take me with you when you left. But you never did. Finally, those nine years ago, I'd had enough of the heartbreaking disappointments, and I decided never seeing you again couldn't hurt any more than seeing you did. I pretended I had no father, that you were dead. And I went on with my life. I'd begun to believe you were truly dead.''

"And I'd intended to stay out of your life, for your sake, as well as my own. Unbeknownst to you, I've kept careful track of you, though. But I didn't interfere. I didn't want to hurt you, daughter. Yet it seemed that was all I *did* give you—deep and lasting pain.

"Nearly a year ago, the ship I was sailing on became involved in a nasty sea battle with a pirate vessel off the coast of Jamaica. I was manning a cannon when we took a broadside that nearly sank us. I was knocked senseless and thrown overboard by the impact. If a mate of mine hadn't jumped in after me with a rope, I'd have the sea as my burying place right now. I'd never come that close to dying before, and I was shaken by the experience. For years after your mother's passing, I'd wanted to die, too, but when I came so close to actually dying, I realized how much I wanted to live. I needed to reconcile the bitterness between us, Mariah. I knew you hated me, but when Bartholomew Post all but laid his treasure in my lap when he died, I thought perhaps I could find a way to regain your affections, and also provide for your future. I felt certain you wouldn't believe my explanations, so I devised the puzzle scheme to let my friends convince you.''

''Why did you involve me, Dunny?'' Jamie asked. ''Anyone could have guided Mariah on the journey.''

The devilish grin returned to the older man's face. ''No, not just anyone, lad. I needed a man I could trust, one I knew possessed honor and integrity, who wouldn't steal the treasure from Mariah once it was found. You met the requirements beyond a shadow of a doubt. During our adventures together through the years, I've come to know and love you like a son, Jamie. Indeed, I couldn't choose a better man for a son than you. But since there is no blood between us, I decided that I'd at least have you as son-in-law. I knew you were the man for my daughter. She'd realize that fact, too, if she just had a chance to be thrown in with you for a time. And my plan worked, didn't it?'' Smug satisfaction sparkled in his alert brown eyes again. ''I can tell you've found each other. I see it in the way your eyes meet and your hands touch.''

''The truth is Mariah and I were married two days ago,'' Jamie admitted, shaking his head at Dunny's incredible success in directing their lives.

''Ha! I knew my ploy would work!'' Dunny

slapped his knee, then jumped to his feet and thrust his hand out to grasp Jamie's in a vigorous handshake. "The gamble is won! Welcome to the family, lad. You haven't the slightest idea what you've gotten yourself into, but you'll have a lifetime with my daughter to find out!"

His expression softened as he turned to Mariah. "I know gold can't buy your pardon, Mariah Marie, but can you somehow find it in your heart to forgive me for the hurt I caused you?"

"Oh, Father!" She sprang to her feet and threw herself into his arms, hugging him with all her might. Here was the father she remembered and had longed for all these fifteen years. Tears welled up in her eyes and spilled down her cheeks as she felt his arms strong around her. She reached out her hand to Jamie, who took it into his own in a firm hold.

"Now I have everything," she murmured, overwhelmed with gladness. "All my heart has ever desired and more, you have given me. I love you, Father . . ."

slipped his hand. Then hinged to his feet and thrust
his hand out to grasp Jamie's in a vigorous handshake. "The pride is won! Welcome to the fam-

Chapter 33

"You're a very fortunate man, Lancaster."
Samuel Hastings' tone sounded envious as he thrust
his hand out.

"I'm well aware of that fact, Doctor," Jamie
replied, taking his hand and casting a sideways
glance toward Mariah at his side.

The three of them stood on Long Dock, one of
the many wharfs serving the incoming and out-
bound vessels using busy Boston Harbor as port.
They'd gathered at the foot of the gangplank leading to the trim merchantman *Free Spirit*. The newly
built ship's sleek hull, decks, and three tall masts
gleamed in the early dawn light. The pier bustled
with activity, as men carried load after load of
freight to and from the anchored ships, and ped-
dlers hawked their many wares to the workers. The
Free Spirit's cargo hold had been filled the day before.

"Looks as if you'll have a clear sailing," Hastings continued, gazing at the cloudless sky,
streaked crimson by the rising sun.

"Yes, the winds are with us," Jamie replied. "I
ask your pardon now, for I must see to the final
preparations. Hastings." He gave the doctor a

quick nod, then turned to Mariah. "There isn't much time."

"Yes, I know. I'll come quickly." She watched her husband ascend the gangplank, then faced Samuel Hastings.

"So this is good-bye, Mariah." He took her hand and looked at her steadily, giving the tired smile she knew so well. "The hospital won't be the same without you. I'll miss you very much, and not just because of the work we did together. You are very dear to me. I regret I didn't tell you that long ago. Now it's too late."

The sadness in his brown eyes made Mariah's heart ache. "Dear Samuel, your most important needs always have been your work, your hospital, your patients. You are totally dedicated. There's no room in your life for anyone else. I don't say this truth harshly to you, but you know I'm right. I admire you with all my heart, but we must go our separate ways. Have no regrets, for I have none. Think only of the great work you can accomplish now that the financial future of the hospital is secure. You'll help so many people. And so shall I. You've given me so much, Samuel. You'll always have a place in my heart."

She hugged him then, and he held onto her tightly.

"Thank you, dear Mariah," he whispered against her hair, "for saving the hospital, for your unselfish generosity, and your unwavering faith in me. You've been a great blessing in my life. I wish you every happiness."

She pulled away from him and smiled. "And I hope the same for you. Good-bye, Samuel." She leaned forward to kiss his cheek, then turned and hurried up the gangplank.

"First Officer Morgan!" Jamie shouted, bringing Dunny hurrying to him on the quarterdeck with a speed and agility that belied his fifty-eight years.

"Aye, Captain!"

"Pass the order for all hands on deck. Weigh the gangplank and let go all securing lines!"

"Aye, aye, sir!" Dunny grinned, throwing him a cocky salute. "And about time it is that we're getting underway. Much longer and we'd be missing the tide! 'Twas a stroke of good luck that Braythwaite lost the customer for whom he'd built and fitted this ship, and we were able to buy her so quick-like. China's a far spell away, you know. I'd like to get there before I'm too old to enjoy those pretty slant-eyed ladies I've heard about for so long!"

He whirled and shouted the orders in a robust voice, bringing the crew scurrying over the deck. Jamie smiled and shook his head, calculating that there'd be no dull moments on this voyage with Dunny Morgan along, or Mariah either, for that matter. His smile broadened when he saw her running up the deck toward him.

"Jamie, wait!" she cried. "We can't sail yet. Dimetrius isn't aboard!"

"What? He was due back two hours ago." He scowled, glancing toward the wharf.

Two crewmen were just making ready to haul in the gangplank when the dwarf suddenly appeared on the dock. Running with short, quick steps, he managed to spring onto the narrow wooden bridge just as it left the quay.

"When you dock agin, I'll be awaitin', Demi, me pet!" a young woman dressed in a gaudy red robe called loudly, waving and leaning far out of a window on the second floor of a building across the street from the dock.

The dwarf paused on deck and vigorously waved in return. "I'll be true to no other, Rose, my fairest of flowers!" Then he turned and hastened to the quarterdeck, amid the good-natured gibes of his crewmates.

"Breaking that poor wench's heart, bo's'n?" Jamie chided when he skidded to a halt just in front of him.

"Can I help it if the doxies can't resist me?" His sly grin showed through his bushy brown beard.

Jamie chuckled. "No, 'tis a curse we both must live with, Dimetrius." He winced and laughed when Mariah jabbed him in the ribs with her elbow. "To your post, bo's'n."

"Aye, aye, Cap'n." Flicking his hand to his forehead in a salute, he left the quarterdeck.

"Anchor aweigh, Mr. Morgan!" Jamie shouted.

"Anchor aweigh!" Dunny repeated the command in a booming voice.

The *Free Spirit* slowly eased away from the dock, just as the fiery red sun cleared the horizon and streaked the choppy water of the harbor with traces of scarlet. Mariah stood at the bow rail, happily listening to her husband's crisp orders to his crew. She sensed the men's enthusiasm for the voyage as they called to one another and worked to raise the sails to catch the stiff wind. Each unfurled white canvas rigged along the tall black masts billowed full to life, straining at lines and pulleys to hold the wind captive.

She inhaled a deep breath of sea air, feeling her own excitement filling her body. The steady breeze tossed her auburn tresses about when she turned her head to watch Jamie. He stood tall and rakishly handsome in black breeches and full-sleeved white shirt as he expertly directed his men to their tasks. His legs, in thigh-high black jackboots, were wide apart, braced against the roll of the ship. The look of pride and unabashed happiness on his face filled her heart with joy and exhilarating anticipation. When they cleared the harbor and reached open water, he joined her at the rail.

''Is the captain's lady still game for this adventure?'' he asked, encircling her waist with his arm and pulling her possessively to his side. He smiled down at her, his pale-blue gaze sweeping over her face.

''The captain's lady is indeed game.'' She sighed and rested her head against his shoulder. ''She will follow you to the ends of the earth and back again, if you ask it.''

He chuckled. ''Well, we'll just start with putting into New York first. I'm glad you talked me into seeing my family before we sail east. It's time to reconcile differences. I realize I've missed them, especially Felicia. I'm anxious for you to meet my little sister.''

''Do you think your family will like me?'' she asked, worry touching her voice.

''Don't be silly. They'll love you just as I do. I'm certain you'll win their affection even more quickly than I was able to win over your aunt and uncle.''

Now it was her turn to laugh. ''We gave them quite a shock, didn't we? I'll never forget the look on Aunt Josephine's face when we told her about my father's scheme to bring us together and find the gold.''

''I'm not sure they're entirely happy about having me for a nephew-in-law. Your aunt hinted they would've preferred seeing you wed to that burly butcher fellow down the street from them. Perhaps you would be happier with him.'' His eyes twinkled with mischief.

''Perhaps,'' she replied loftily. ''But I suppose I'll never know now. I'm bound to you and cannot escape.''

He turned her to face him, wrapping his arms tightly around her. ''I see no chain holding you to this deck, milady.''

''The bond is in my heart, my husband, and is called love. It is much stronger than the thickest chain.''

''Ah, Mariah, my love, you know my heart.''

He bent to kiss her softly. Wisps of sea spray splashed over them. The great Atlantic stretched all around them.

''Have I told you this morning how much I love you?'' he murmured when they separated a little.

''You showed me most convincingly in our cabin all last night. But I would happily hear the words any time you wish to speak them.'' She held him tightly around the waist, pressing her body close.

He read the depth of her feelings in her blue-green eyes. The words came easily to his lips, for he felt them with all of his being.

"I love you, Mariah Marie Morgan Lancaster, my wife, my life's joy. Our future together is as limitless in possibilities as the far-reaching horizon before us. For me, there can be no other love but you."

"My heart speaks the same, Jamie. My love is only for you."

Words ceased. A kiss began. The bright promise of the morrow cast its glowing rays over them, erasing all shadows and lighting the triumph of their everlasting love.

NANCY MOULTON

"Love is the brilliant sunlight of Life,
Bask in it again and again and enjoy!"

So says undauntable romantic NANCY MOULTON. An avid reader of love stories, she credits a severe winter blizzard in her home state of Ohio for starting her in the direction of writing her own romantic novels. When a case of cabin fever struck, she retaliated by clutching pen in hand and attacking a stack of virgin paper with adventurous ideas culled from years of sigh-punctuated daydreaming about swashbuckling heroes. An avid interest in American history, acquired while earning a degree in education at the University of Toledo, inspired her to set her first novel during America's tumultuous beginning years. That novel sold to Avon Books on first attempt. DEFIANT HEART is her fifth novel for Avon Books. She has an inexhaustible supply of ideas for love stories, which she pledges will always have happy endings!

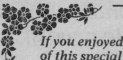
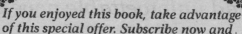

*If you enjoyed this book, take advantage
of this special offer. Subscribe now and . . .*

GET A *FREE*
HISTORICAL ROMANCE
——— NO OBLIGATION (a $3.95 value) ———

Each month the editors of True Value will select the four best historical
romance novels from America's leading publishers. Preview them in
your home Free for 10 days. And we'll send you a FREE book as our
introductory gift. No obligation. If for any reason you decide not to keep
them, just return them and owe nothing. But if you like them you'll pay
just $3.50 each and save at least $.45 each off the cover price. (Your
savings are a minimum of $1.80 a month.) There is no shipping and
handling or other hidden charges. There are no minimum number of
books to buy and you may cancel at any time.

send in the coupon below